Secrets & Curses of Cerithia

Shay Taylor

WESTWIND PUBLISHING LLC

Contents

For those who have felt the fire of rage and transformed it
into strength

Please be advised that this story contains heavy themes
that may be triggering for some readers, including but not
limited to:
Violence, physical and mental abuse, torture, killing, gore,
death, kidnapping, drugging, blood, manipulation, betrayal, mental health issues (trauma, anxiety, depression),
fighting, and explicit sexual content.

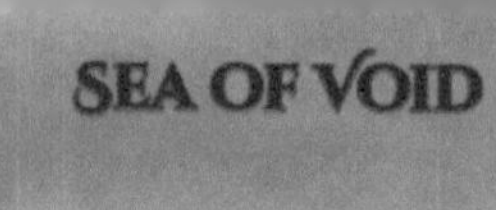

SEA OF VOID
AKECIA
KIZAR
FALGON
CERITHIA
EXILE
CRIMSON
FORBIDDEN WOOD
ELLORYON
SEA OF VOID
ISLANDS OF DEATH

Chapter I

Blood covered every surface of the forest around me. Glancing at the dead bodies, I ensured my magic had killed each man. No survivors could be left. As the blackness around my vision lessened, the darkness within me still refused to release its grip.

It pulsed through my veins, searing itself into my bones. It wouldn't let go. Not once in the last few weeks has its hold lessened—not since *his* betrayal. I was a shell of who I used to be. Rage and devastation waged such a violent war inside me that no one was safe. I once believed my darkness was a manifestation of my most powerful self, but that was before I felt this white-hot rage swarming within me. All because of *him*. It was a rage that demanded vengeance and insisted I punish all who had wronged me. It burned so fiercely in me that not even the gods were safe from my wrath.

If I ever found a way to the stars, I would unleash this rage upon them for giving me such a cruel fate, for allowing me to know what it was like to have Cassius and then taking it away. Neither the gods nor Crimson would be allowed to live happily while I lived like this—a weapon.

These last few weeks have been spent killing Cerithian enemies. Nothing had made me feel better. Nothing would until I could kill Cassius. Not until I could drive my viper-handled dagger through his heart. A noise behind me interrupted my thoughts. A man was trying to crawl away from where all his companions had been slaughtered. I watched him for a moment before taking a step toward him.

"Why did Falgon come onto our territory?" I asked him.

The man was struggling to breathe as he bled from a large chest wound. I felt nothing as he bled out at my feet. His mouth opened to say something, but at first, nothing came out. He tried again and managed one word—a word that made my blood run cold.

"Cassius..." the man coughed blood. His eyes turned vacant as he died at my feet, but the grip on my dagger tightened at the mention of Cassius. No one had said his name in front of me since the day I left the clearing.

Madness lurked at the edge of my mind, waiting and watching for a moment of weakness so it could take over.

Something as simple as hearing Cassius' name was enough to tip me into insanity. The gods knew I was barely holding onto the tiny shred of myself I had left. What did that man mean by uttering Cassius' name?

It made no sense unless Cassius had sent Falgon to capture me so he could kill me himself. That didn't sound like Cassius, but then again, I didn't understand how Cassius' mind worked. If he wanted to kill me, he could come and try himself—coward.

As I glanced at the faces of the dead men, all I could picture was them as Cassius. The blood bond on my arm sent a sharp, angry pain through me every time I imagined him dead, but I ignored it.

I stepped over the dead Falgon guards, their blood sticking to my black boots as I headed toward Cerithia's castle. My horse, Kaida, waited for me out of harm's way. She didn't shy away from me, even drenched as I was in enemy blood. Her white coat stained red as I climbed onto her back.

There was something unforgiving and tense in the air of the forest, but I paid no attention to it because I was used to it. It followed me. No matter where I went, I never felt right. My eyes darted around the darkness, searching for Wisp out of habit, but she had abandoned me too.

She never left Cassius' side in the clearing, and she never appeared again.

As if my darkness anticipated feelings of sadness and confusion, it buried itself deeper into my mind, refusing to let me feel those emotions.

Just as I started to urge Kaida forward, I saw her. The woman with golden skin and eyes the color of the stars stood in her black lace gown, watching me oddly. I watched her as she stood in the forest, staring at me like she always did. She never spoke, but she always lingered around me.

Just like Wisp, this woman was unseen by anyone else, which only made me question my grip on reality even more. Maybe that day in the clearing took more than Cassius and my friends from me—maybe it took my sanity too. Her pretty eyes flickered to the dead fae around me before a deep frown tugged at her lips.

I could practically feel her disappointment in me, so I looked away without saying a word. I had convinced myself that this woman wasn't real, so trying to talk to her would shatter any semblance of sanity I had left. At this point, though, it might be an improvement over my current reality.

I nudged my horse into a run, turning away from the woman. Numbness and nothingness coursed through my mind and body as Kaida raced through the forest of Cerithia, where Falgon guards had attempted to sneak in. My chest tightened at the sight of Cerithia's castle in the distance. Dread filled me as I got closer, but like every other emotion, I pushed it aside. The castle was beautiful with its pale gray stone walls and blue flags. Even at night, the air was hot and sticky, reminding me of Exile.

The memory of Exile made my throat tight and itchy with sadness. My chest grew heavy with the grief of losing all my friends and questioning their very existence.

I had been so stuck in this grief when I first arrived that I couldn't allow myself to go there again. I had yet to emerge from the darkness that swallowed me whole the first time. My eyes drifted behind me to see if the woman was following me. She wasn't, but I could feel her close by, watching me from out of sight.

When I returned to the castle, I put Kaida away before heading in through the side door. My father, Jesper, and the queen were waiting for me when I entered. A sigh escaped me. I had hoped to avoid them by using the side door.

"You're dripping blood on the rugs," the queen gasped, disgusted. As if she hadn't ordered me to kill those men.

My black eyes darted toward her, but I didn't say a word. I had hardly spoken to anyone since being back. My father stepped forward a half step before stopping. My darkness hummed at the sight of him frightened in front of me. He tried to hide it; they all did, but I could sense it all around them. They were terrified of me.

My father and his family all kept an arm's length away from me, as if I might explode at any moment and kill them all. I smirked to myself, as if that would save them. I could kill them all from across the realm if I chose to. Jesper was the only one who didn't seem afraid of me. His handsome face was always smiling at me, but I found him unpleasant. He was always so happy to see me, and I didn't trust that.

"Thea, are you alright?" My father's voice wavered. "Is this blood yours?"

I shook my head before glancing at my half-sisters walking up behind our father. Tally and Mae reminded me of Princess Flora. Their pretty, sun-colored hair was perfectly straight, and their bright blue eyes reminded me of the summer sky. They gawked at me like everyone always did, as if I were a monster. There was no denying it anymore, though. That's exactly what I was.

They were the true daughters of my father, and it was clear that we were not the same. They had the parties, the clothes, the parents, and the smiles. I got none of that. I was simply the bastard daughter of the king, and I did not get such privileges. No one celebrated my return. No one told me I had been missed. No one touched me.

"Girls, stay back," Gwyn, my stepmother, spoke as if I would kill them.

The girls stopped immediately and stared at me.

"Thea, did you do what I asked?" My father raised his dark brow at me.

I nodded. For some reason, I did not mention the guard uttering Cassius' name because I didn't even know if it meant anything significant. At this point, I believed I had probably imagined it, just like I imagined the woman with star-colored eyes.

"How many guards were stationed?"

"Twenty-one," I muttered.

The queen scoffed, making me turn my attention back to her, which she shrank away from. She was always so rude for someone who was terrified of me.

"You killed twenty-one men by yourself?"

I didn't respond because I hated her. No, my darkness hated her. As soon as I returned with my father and saw her and my sisters, I hated them. My mind might not remember why, but something deep inside of me did.

She did not hide her distaste for me. Gwyn referred to me as the bastard of Cerithia, and my father did not stop her. It was clear what my position in this kingdom was.

"Gwyn," Jesper said, his glare sharp. "Do you need Thea to demonstrate her powers to you firsthand?"

He was always sticking up for me, and I didn't ask him to. I didn't need him to. They stared at each other for a long, awkward moment before everyone turned to me again.

"Am I dismissed?" I muttered.

"Yes," the king whispered, and they all watched me walk away without another word. I headed down the stairs to where the maids and servants lived—where I lived. Just before going into my room, my eyes lingered on the black door at the end of the hallway, as always.

It caught my attention every time I came to my room. Without thought, I walked to it quickly. The closer I got to the door, though, the more the air filled with an almost suffocating feeling. I struggled to approach the door. Slowly, I placed my hand on the knob and tried to enter the room. As usual, it was locked. It had been each time I tried to get in. The physical effect of being close to this door was unbearable, so I turned and headed into my bedroom.

As soon as I was in, I stripped off my blood-soaked clothes and bathed. No thoughts ran through my mind as I watched blood and dirt circle the drain. My mind was in a constant state of confusion. Nothing made sense anymore, and I tried to stop piecing together what my life was before I lost my memories. When I walked out of my personal washroom, my eyes scanned the ridiculously small bedroom that was mine. Seeing that nothing was amiss, I decided to rest.

My body protested as I lay on my extremely uncomfortable bed and stared at the crack running along my ceiling. The walls were chipping from age, and an odd color of pale yellow had started to show through.

This room was more suffocating than my room in Exile had been. Each night, I lay here and stare at the cracks in the walls, and each night all I can think of is how much I missed my home. The gods were sick fucks, making me think Exile was my prison, but Cerithia felt worse than anywhere else. Crimson had at least pretended to like me. No one here could even muster up enough fake affection to make me feel welcomed.

My family did not seem to miss me. Sybil and the twins were dead. The man I loved did not want me back. He had never been my savior like I thought; he was my captor. I was just too starved for love to notice. But now my eyes were open, and my heart was closed off. I noticed the way those in Cerithia treated me—like I wasn't anyone of importance. I noticed the cold looks and the fear in their eyes. No one here trusted or liked me, but I didn't feel sad about it. I didn't like it here either.

I turned to my side and stared at the dried, black flowers on my nightstand. They were out of place here, but they were the only thing that made me stop thinking about this new prison I was in. I wondered where they had come from. Had I collected them when I was younger? Did someone give them to me?

I yawned as I tried to fight sleep. My heart's pace quickened because it knew what would happen when I closed my eyes, and I wasn't sure if it was because I was happy about it or tortured by it. I sighed and closed my eyes, knowing my broken mind would show me Cassius.

CHAPTER 2

"*I* *could make you happy.*" *Jesper smiled at me as I tried to find a way over the wall my father had built around the castle to keep me in. I turned to him and raised an eyebrow.*

"A future king does not want a bastard daughter." I frowned as I looked for a branch to help me climb over.

"I don't care about all of that," he sighed. "You kissed me; I thought you liked me."

Intent on ignoring him, I reached for the next branch, only to find it missing. I rolled my eyes heavenward, realizing my father must have cut the branches off the trees so I couldn't climb them anymore.

I turned back to him. "Your family would never approve, and neither would mine. Besides, no one wants me. I'm broken and tainted." I repeated the words my stepmother had said about me when she thought I couldn't hear. Even though I knew they were true, it still hurt when she said them.

"I don't care," he ground out. "I want to try."

"You aren't my type," I said as an excuse. I didn't know what my type was, but Jesper Alcove was not it. Sure, he was handsome, but that was as far as the appeal went.

He scoffed. "I'm everyone's type."

I scrunched my face at his comment. He said things like this a lot, conceited prick.

"Well, not mine."

"Why not?"

"Do you even know how to defend yourself? Do you know how to climb a tree or sneak through the woods at night? Can you make a joke?"

"None of that matters. I'm going to be King of Kizar one day." Jesper was fit, handsome, and rich, but no matter how many times I kissed him, it didn't ignite a spark in me. I felt nothing toward him.

"It matters to me," I said, rolling my eyes. "You're boring."

He paused for a moment, a hurt look on his face. It quickly changed to anger. "And you're just the king's bastard daughter," he spat angrily.

My mouth hung open as I searched for something to say, but it shut when I couldn't find the words. Jesper needed to understand that I only kissed him to see what it was like. There was nothing behind the kiss except simple curiosity. I did not feel anything for him, and that was because he was an entitled prick.

"I'm sorry." He pinched the bridge of his nose. "That was cruel."

"What are you two doing?" Tally walked up, glaring at me.

"I'm trying to get over this damned wall Father built so I can watch the blood moon."

"If you leave the castle grounds, I will tell my mother," she sneered. "They forbade you from going."

"Don't do that, Tal. I'm going to go with her; you'll get me in trouble too," Jesper announced. Well, this was news to me because I wanted to go alone. "You can come with us. Have a little fun and not be so boring."

His eyes flickered over to me. Is this why he suddenly had a change of heart? He wanted to prove he wasn't boring.

"I'll go if you are." Tally smiled at Jesper, who smiled back at her. I rolled my eyes. Gods, please give me the strength to never fall for a man as boring as Jesper Alcove. I would rather be alone.

"Why do you want to go see the blood moon so badly?" Jesper asked.

"It's my favorite night of the year; it calls to me. The beauty, the mystery, the stories of wishes coming true. All of it... intrigues me."

"What stories?" Tally scoffed.

"You mean you don't know?" I asked smugly, glad that I had the upper hand in something for once. "The blood moon is supposed to know your true desires, and sometimes it will grant them to you. Maybe love or fortune. I like the thought that something out there knows what I truly desire and could grant it to me."

"That is not true. It's just a stupid moon. Nothing but bad things happen on the blood moon," Jesper huffed, but continued to follow me.

I frowned. Every year, I asked the blood moon for the same thing. I wished for someone who would love me—someone to build a real life with. A mate.

I stopped talking and headed to my favorite spot.

"We shouldn't be out here," my half-sister muttered somewhere behind me. When I turned toward her, her pretty blue eyes paled as she looked at the dark forest around the castle.

"Then go home, Tally."

Her eyes shifted to Jesper before returning to me.

"No."

I didn't like the way she only followed when he was near. Jesper was not my boyfriend, but it was clear he had affection for me. On the other hand, it would be nice for him to stop bothering me so much. Tally's dress tore as it snagged on a downed log. I was the only one of us who dressed appropriately for trudging through the forest, in my trousers and boots.

The darkness made it hard to see the tree limbs blocking the path, and I could feel them pricking my skin and leaving abrasions. I didn't care much. Tonight was the blood moon, and I wanted to see it from my favorite spot. I turned around when I heard Tally whimper in pain. Jesper scooped her up and held her close to him as he walked. My eyes took in the sight of them. They looked good together.

I shook my head and continued walking up the hill. It was forbidden to leave the castle at night. Our father had always driven it into our heads and the heads of our fae that we would die at the hands of monsters if we were caught outside the walls at night. I had been sneaking out for years and had never encountered a monster. I was starting to think they were made up. I smiled to myself as I saw the field just ahead.

I pushed through the branches and stopped at the small clearing that led to the cliffside. We could see for miles and miles here. The blood moon was so red and beautiful that it nearly stopped my heart. Beautiful crimson red covered everything the moonlight touched. It was such a beautiful color, but I never spoke of that in Cerithia. It was a color that represented our biggest enemies, but something about it made my heart race.

"It's kind of creepy," Tally whispered as Jesper set her down next to him. My gaze flickered at her in annoyance.

"It's beautiful," I said sharply as I turned back to the moon. It appeared so large that I felt like I might be able to reach out and touch it.

"It is a little creepy." Jesper glanced back into the forest before meeting my eyes. "I feel like we're being watched." His hand ran through his dark blonde hair as he glanced around us.

I felt it too, but nothing stood out to me in the darkened woods. I wish they would have just stayed back at the castle. They were ruining this night for me with their complaining.

"You guys may go back to the castle, but I wish to stay for a little bit."

"Are you sure you'll be alright out here by yourself?" Jesper asked.

I turned to him and stared at his hand holding Tally's tightly. I thought he would protest me staying out here by myself or at least pretend to care as he claimed to.

"Yes."

"Ok." His tense shoulders sagged as he and Tally walked into the dark forest without me. My eyes lingered where they disappeared. I should feel more upset that they left me, but I knew where I stood with my family. As the illegitimate daughter of the King of Cerithia, I was not royal by any means.

All my father had to do was accept me as his daughter, and I would be considered royal blood. He hadn't, though, and I was losing hope he ever would.

Tally, Gwyn, and Mae all pretended to be civil with me, but I could see the hatred in their pale blue eyes when they looked at me. Maybe that was why I was surprised when Jesper approached me instead of Tally. Everyone in the kingdom knew who I was to the king, and most stayed clear.

My focus returned to the blood moon, and I smiled as I sat down on the grassy cliff. This was nice, quiet, and peaceful.

The villages in the distance started putting out all sources of light. They believed it would keep them safe from monsters that lingered in the woods. Tonight was the most dangerous night of the year, according to what we had been taught. Monsters would kill and eat anything that moved, but again, I had never seen these monsters.

My eyes shifted down the cliff as I scooted a little closer so I could throw the flower petals off the side and watch them drift down. My face turned up to the blood moon, and I asked it for the same thing I did each year. A mate, a man I could love and build a true life with.

I shifted slightly when I heard a small noise behind me. I turned, expecting to see Jesper standing there, but I didn't see anything. Someone or something was watching me.

I pulled a dagger from its hiding place in my boot.

"I can hear you. Come out, you coward." I stood and backed away from the cliff.

I half expected nothing to happen, but then he stepped out. The man was taller than any man I had seen in our kingdom. He wore all black except for his cloak, which was dark red—or maybe it just looked that way in the blood moon. He kept his oversized hood on, but I could feel his eyes on me.

"A coward, huh?" he said with a chuckle. I should feel scared. Why didn't I? I gripped the viper-handled dagger in my hand tightly as he stepped closer.

"I will kill you if you get any closer."

"Oh, I believe you would try, little viper." His voice was deep and reverberated off the forest and dirt around me. Something about it instantly soothed my tense body. I glanced around the woods to see how many others there were, but I couldn't make out anyone else. My eyes shifted back to him.

"Why are you out here?" I demanded with as much confidence as I could muster.

"I could ask the same of you." His voice was soft, like he worried I would spook easily.

My gaze narrowed at the hooded man, but I didn't respond. His golden eyes shined brightly from under the hood, making me lose my thoughts altogether.

"Watching," he finally muttered.

"The blood moon?" I turned toward the moon for a brief moment before looking back at him.

"No." I gasped when he was only a few feet in front of me. The stranger had made no noise as he snuck up to me. I should not be out here talking to this man. "You."

"Me." I stilled at his confession. I should run. I should run and scream. If he thought I would be an easy target, he was very wrong. I was a good warrior. My father let me train with his guards because I was not a woman of royal blood.

"You come here often." It was a statement. "Alone, without protection. There are monsters in these woods."

"I've done just fine by myself," I argued weakly.

He let out a soft chuckle again and took a step forward.

"Have you? Or maybe someone else was watching out for you?"

His question confused me. Who would be watching out for me in these woods, and how would he know? My hand gripped the dagger tighter. His golden eyes dropped to the blade in my hand, and I swore he was smiling.

"*Are you implying that you have been protecting me?*" *I scoffed.*

He took another step closer to me. An overwhelming urge to see his face overtook me. Why was he being secretive? I traced the outline of him, hoping something would tip me off to who he was. He was dressed oddly. He definitely wasn't from Cerithia.

"Someone should protect you," he said. "Monsters would love to get their hands on you, little viper."

"Are you a monster?"

"Yes," he said confidently and without hesitation.

"Show me your face. Do I know you?" Gods, why did he seem so familiar?

"No." He turned his back on me and took a step away. He tensed, turning to the forest, and sighed like we were being interrupted. I glanced where he did, but I didn't see or hear anything. When I glanced back to where he was, I had to step back in surprise. He had moved directly in front of me again. His large hand pushed my dagger away from him.

"I will not hurt you." His golden eyes pierced into mine, and I felt no danger from him.

I believed him, and it was stupid. I didn't know this man. I normally had good instincts, but they were all over the place right now.

"You told me you were a monster," I whispered. His scent filled my space, and I wanted to bury my face into his chest and inhale deeply. He smelled like forest and rain, two of my favorite things.

"I am, but never to you."

I opened my mouth to say something, but he sighed heavily as he turned to look into the forest again.

"Get back!" Jesper yelled from the tree line. His panicked voice startled me out of whatever trance I was in, allowing me to realize just how close the stranger was to me. He must have enchanted me.

Sensing the danger I was in, my dagger flew forward, and the mysterious man grunted at the force of it settling into his stomach. Strangely enough, the sight of it made me want to apologize to him for some odd reason, but I didn't. The viper-handle protruded from his stomach. I backed up, and Jesper's hand wrapped around mine and pulled me close to him. The hooded man groaned softly as he stood up straight and yanked the blade from himself.

"What the hell were you doing?" Jesper hissed at me through clenched teeth. "He was practically flush against you."

I dropped my hand from Jesper's and glared at him. He had left me out here without protest. I didn't need him to rescue me from a man who didn't seem to want to harm me. Jesper grabbed my hand again.

"You left her out here alone, on the blood moon," the hooded man said loudly. His gold eyes flickered to where mine and Jesper's hands connected, and I swore they swirled with black.

"She didn't mind," Jesper retorted. "And I came back."

I could hear something else shifting behind the hooded man in the woods. My eyes strained in the darkness to see what it was. Jesper glared at me like this was all on me. I mean, I guess it was. I was the one who insisted on coming out here. I had never had issues before, though. Maybe it was the blood moon. Then a noise caught my attention, and I slowly turned. My eyes adjusted just as a monster started to appear from the dark woods behind the mysterious man.

The monster stood at least three feet above the stranger. Its skin was covered in thick, dark fur. Its arms were so long that they dragged on the ground as it slowly crept forward on its back legs. The monster's long, pointed ears twitched as it watched us. The beady-red eyes didn't blink as they emerged from the woods. The creature snapped its jaw, showing the rows of pointed teeth.

"Behind you!" I warned.

"Get her out of here," he demanded at Jesper, who had froze when he saw the red eyes watching us.

Suddenly, the creature moved. It was so fast that I would have died if I had blinked. The hooded man pushed me out of the way just in time, almost as if he anticipated the attack, and speared the monster with a sword I never saw him carrying. I tumbled to the ground with a loud, hard thump, and my head bounced where it landed. Dazed, I struggled to lift it. Once I did, I saw that Jesper had retreated into the woods without me. Asshole.

The monster lay next to me, dead. The man was hovering in front of me a moment later as I sat up. His hand brushed the hair off my face as his eyes traced over me, looking for wounds. The backs of his hands were tattooed, but I couldn't make out what they looked like.

"Are you hurt anywhere?" His hands held my head gently. My gaze shifted over his shoulder when another one of the creatures came from the woods. It was easy to spot in the dark with its glowing red eyes.

It all happened so fast. Something inside of me stirred as the monster headed straight for the mysterious man. I opened my mouth to warn him, pointing at the creature that was racing toward us. Before I could get any noise out, fire exploded out of my fingertips, burning the monster into ash before it ever reached us.

Panic filled me at the realization of what I had just done. What the fuck was wrong with me? I didn't have magic; I didn't. I glanced at the man, confused. Fear laced every part of me; fire magic was not common. It was considered elite. If I had elite magic, my family would hate me.

"I guess you didn't need me to protect you," he chuckled.

I could hardly think as I stood up and began running through the woods, back toward the castle of Cerithia. I stumbled and tripped with deep pain consuming my head. Gods, I was hurt badly. I had just lifted my hands to see if there was any trace of fire magic on my skin when I heard something behind me. I went to grab my dagger but realized I had left it embedded in the hooded man's stomach. Great.

Fearing another monster, I turned and started blindly punching and scratching at my attacker, only to be subdued with little effort.

"It's alright, little viper," he grunted as he caught my wrists and yanked me flush against him—again. This was beginning to become an annoying habit of his. He lifted me before walking quickly. "You're hurt," he said angrily.

I closed my eyes tightly, trying to keep myself from throwing up. Jesper had left me for the monster to eat and saved himself. I knew he was a dick, but gods, I hadn't realized he was such a coward. I opened my eyes after the nausea had settled, and I tried to see the man carrying me, but it was no use with his hood on and the darkness of the forest surrounding us.

"You saved me even though I stabbed you."

I was slightly worried that if I reminded him that I had stabbed him, he would retaliate somehow. I could not even defend myself against a mouse right now. He laughed loudly, and something about it made me feel warm all over.

"You did stab me. But in your defense, you told me if I came any closer, you would. I guess I should have listened." He paused for a moment. "You could stab me a thousand times, little viper, and I would use those same knives to kill anyone who meant harm to you."

I swallowed hard as my mind tried to come up with a response to that. What did someone say to that?

After a brief pause, he continued to walk. I used these few minutes to rest my head against his chest, letting the scent of rain and forest surround me.

"I don't have magic," I whispered as I looked up at him. Tears of confusion filled my eyes.

He stared intently at me.

"That was your first time using it?"

"Yes." I glanced away. What did this stranger think of magic? Did he hate it like my father?

"Well, little viper, I'd say your elite magic was triggered because you were in danger," he sighed as he kept walking.

Elite magic.

I was going to be sick.

"I was worried you were going to get hurt," I confessed. "That is what triggered it."

I felt his body stiffen as he continued to carry me. I could feel him staring at me, but I couldn't bear to look at him just in case I saw disgust for magic.

We walked in silence for a few more minutes before I finally saw the castle break through the tree line. He couldn't take me there. He would be killed immediately, and the thought made me feel a way I didn't like.

I could see Jesper and Tally standing close to the castle wall, pacing. Jesper glanced up and began running toward us the moment he saw us.

The man carrying me tensed. His grip tightened momentarily, but he eventually loosened it and stood me on my feet. I was wobbly, but I would be alright. I turned to the hooded man, desperate for him to stay a little longer and to hear his voice once more.

"Will I see you again?" I whispered.

"I'm not sure."

I frowned.

"But who will protect me when I sneak out again?"

I didn't need to see him to know he was smiling at me. I could sense it. I could feel it.

"Maybe you shouldn't sneak out." His amusement was evident in his tone.

"But I will." I wasn't lying, either. I would probably be out here tomorrow. "I can't count on him to save me." I pointed to Jesper over my shoulder.

"You are strong enough to save yourself, little viper. You do not need a man to do that for you."

He was both so sure of himself and so sure about me that I could feel myself believing it too. I raised my hand to slide his hood off, but he moved from my reach and grabbed my wrist. I frowned up at him, then gently pushed my hand toward his face, and this time, he didn't stop me. My fingers met stubble on his chin. My thumb rubbed his lips, feeling them curve into a smile. He turned my hand and pressed a soft kiss to my palm before letting it go. Then he placed the viper-handled dagger in my hand. Hesitantly, he lifted his fingers and brushed my braid over my shoulder.

"Your magic was a beautiful thing to witness. Never be ashamed of it," he whispered as his fingers tucked a stray curl behind my ear, causing a hot sensation to burn where he touched.

The man leaned forward and pressed his lips to mine briefly. Gods, I wondered if he could hear my heart pounding. Kissing Jesper had never felt like that.

"I hope our paths cross again soon, little viper," he said as he turned and ran toward the trees.

My chest ached as I watched him run away. What if I never saw him again? I watched as he turned when he got to the tree line. I could see his silhouette as he grabbed his hood and pulled it off. What a little shit. I bet he was smiling to himself too.

My mind snapped back to reality when someone yanked my arm roughly. I looked up to see a guard, and behind him stood Tally, Jesper, and the king and queen. Shit. How much had they seen? Did they see the hooded figure? Did they see me touching his face? Him kissing me?

I suddenly became very lightheaded, and my eyes felt fuzzy. I didn't pass out, however, until after the queen backhanded me across the face for sneaking out. As I felt her hand connect with my cheek, everything went black. I welcomed it, though, because maybe the hooded man would meet me there in my mind, in my dreams.

CHAPTER 3

Again. Again. Again. I lunged forward and stabbed the makeshift target I had made. Sweat ran down my face and stung my eyes in the unbearable heat of Cerithia. My viper-handled dagger pierced with perfect precision each time, and my heart raced with adrenaline as I envisioned Cassius as my target. He was standing in front of me, and I returned the favor of killing him.

My body did not like envisioning him dying. It did not want to stab him or kill him. But this has been my only focus since returning to Cerithia. The sharp pain in my chest subsided after I ignored it long enough, but the burning of my blood bond was enough to make me stop.

I forced the sadness away and replaced it with images of Cassius being so cruel to me in that clearing. I repeated his words like my own sick mantra. *Who could love a monstrosity like you?* His hateful words fueled my darkness. It made me stronger. There was no time to grieve everything

I lost, and I knew it. If I let myself think about it too much, I would fall into the darkness and never resurface.

The darkness wanted to take over; it wanted me to allow it complete freedom. It felt like something new lurked inside of me, and it was evil. Not only did it want to level Crimson, but it also wanted to punish the gods. It wanted me to level Elloryon with a flick of my wrist. Everyone should feel as horrible as I did.

How could the gods allow me to live in a realm where Cassius did not want me, did not love me back? A sinking feeling overtook me as I tried to stop my thoughts.

The more I pushed the hurt and confusion away, the more I felt lost. There was nothing else to replace it with. Cerithia had not filled the void of losing Crimson or Cassius.

"Thea?"

I turned quickly and found my dagger pointed at my father and Jesper. They both took a hesitant step back before I dropped the blade to my side.

"What are you doing? The sun hasn't even come up yet." My father glanced at my makeshift target before looking at me. My eyes found Jesper. He had been nothing but kind to me since being here, but all I could do was think of how unpleasant I found him in my dream the night before.

"I couldn't sleep."

"Still?" My father glanced over me as if he were looking for something. I nodded but said nothing else. He always seemed to be analyzing me, as if he was expecting to see something. "It's been weeks," his words faded off, and I knew he wanted to question why I was still so... out of it. I could not seem to get acclimated to Cerithia, no matter what I did. I wish I could feel like I belonged here.

"I'm training. What do you want?" I sighed, annoyed that they were bothering me this early. There was a reason I came out here before everyone else woke up.

My father watched the dagger in my hand, like I would reach out and slice him open. There was no connection in my heart to him, to the castle, or to this family. No one had tried to make me feel welcomed. When I first arrived, I was shown to my tiny room and left to rot away. My father and Jesper had treated my return more like an interrogation. They wanted to know everything about Crimson. What were their armies doing? Did Cassius speak of war? What did I know about everything? When I didn't have the answers they sought about Cassius or his army, they seemed disappointed in me. They eventually stopped coming to see me altogether when I couldn't give them anything.

Even now, my father and Jesper stand far away from me. I felt as though they feared me more than they liked my presence. I hadn't expected fae to rejoice, but I expected someone, anyone, to say they had missed me.

My eyes shifted to behind my father, where the woman with star-colored eyes had appeared. I shook my head and closed my eyes tightly. She wasn't real. I was seriously fucked up in the head. My eyes snapped open when Jesper spoke.

"Training for what?" He raised his brow, ignoring my irritation.

"To kill Cassius," I huffed, ignoring the stabbing in my chest. My blood bond burned at my words, but I didn't let them know that something twisted in me each time I thought of Cassius dying.

"Very good." My father gave me a weak smile. "That makes me so proud to hear."

His words should have made me happy, but I felt nothing. My eyes shifted once again to the woman who stood watching, and this time, Jesper's eyes followed. Her bright eyes glanced over me, pausing on the blood bond on my arm, and I swore she smiled slightly at the sight of it.

Jesper looked right through her because she wasn't real. He turned toward me and watched closely, like he could see the cracks in my armor. He looked at me like I was broken and barely functioning. The woman looked concerned for me. She always seemed to be looking at me as if she cared about me and could see my sadness that no one else seemed to.

Did anyone notice how utterly lost I was? Did they not realize that my own reality was shattered and I couldn't fit the pieces together in a way that made sense? I was so...empty. A thickness overtook my throat, but I swallowed it down so my father couldn't see how tortured I felt. No one seemed to understand the hell I faced. And to make matters even worse, I felt like every part of me from Crimson was slowly dying. Each day that passed took me further from myself and closer to a monster controlled by madness.

They don't understand the price I paid by losing Cassius. It was as if he had given me a reason not to be completely lost in my darkness. But now that I was without him, I had nothing to tether myself to as a war waged inside of me. I was slowly being lost inside of myself, and no one saw it. My pain was visible, but no one here seemed to care enough about me to help. They were letting me drown in my own devastation, betrayal, and madness.

"Is something wrong?" Jesper took a small step toward me. "You keep looking at something."

I glared at his movement, and he instantly stopped. The dagger in my hand was gripped tightly to help ground myself. I did not like talking about Cassius with them.

They refused to let me go to Crimson to kill him. My father had said I was not ready, and the Cerithia guards would need me to train them for war. It was stupid, but it felt like my father was keeping me away from Crimson for another reason too.

"Jesper, leave us. I want to talk with Thea." My father frowned at me, like he could finally see how utterly broken I was.

Jesper hesitated at my father's demand but left without protest. I felt awkward as my father stood there staring at me without saying much at first.

"Did you want to walk the grounds as we talk? You used to enjoy that." His green eyes filled with sadness at his statement. I nodded as I put my dagger in its sheath. Guards followed us at a safe distance.

Cerithia was hotter than Crimson was. I found it nearly unbearable to wear my green cloak here, but I did because it brought me comfort. My mind was blank as my eyes looked anywhere but at my father. My fingers picked at the loose thread of my cloak as I waited for him to speak. Birds were starting to chirp in the distance as the sun rose, and I would have found it peaceful if I was not so worried about what my father wanted to tell me.

"I apologize for how things have been since your return. It was probably not the big welcome home that you had expected from us, but I want to explain why so that maybe you can understand our perspective on things."

I glanced at my father, relieved that he wanted to tell me anything. My mind swarmed with hardly any thoughts since Cassius betrayed me. Most days I went through the motions of what I needed to do, but at the end of the day, I could not recall details from anything I did. Time has moved slowly since being here.

"It is partially my fault that you fell in love with Cassius." His confession had me snapping my gaze to his.

"You were the best warrior that had ever come from Cerithia. I was so proud that you wanted to become the captain of my armies. You were always so clever that I thought you could handle the mission I sent you on."

My chest tightened, desperate to find out any information about my life that was not tied directly to Cassius.

"You trained for months and months before you went, and I had no doubts that you would be successful. You were the perfect assassin—beautiful like your mother, powerful too, but tactical like me. I thought I was so clever to have you weasel your way into Crimson with the pretense of pretending to love Cassius. You were to use him, get information, then kill him and return."

"I was a spy?" I questioned.

My father nodded before he continued.

"Months passed by, and we had stopped hearing anything from you. I thought you couldn't get correspondence to us, so I waited. But as time passed, I realized something was wrong. We tried to send guards to Crimson to get you, but none of them ever returned. Then one day, you appeared in the throne room, claiming to love Cassius."

My father's disappointment was clear in his voice, and shame filled me.

"You told me he was not a monster. How Crimson was this magical place, and you didn't think we should be at war with them. I couldn't believe my own ears. I begged you to stay in Cerithia and not go back, but you refused. Gods, I felt so disgusted having to tell the fae of Cerithia how my own daughter had chosen Crimson. It was a betrayal that no one here has forgotten. I admit that things have never been good between you, Gwyn, and the girls, but that just put an even bigger wedge between all of you."

"So that is why they don't seem happy I'm back," I sighed.

"It's been a difficult time for us to adjust to your return, but I am happy to have you at home." He gave me a small smile. "Besides, a few months later, you came back panicked. You told me that Cassius had enchanted you and your view of Crimson, that everything you thought about him was not your own thoughts or feelings. I had never seen you so terrified of another fae as you were of Cassius that night."

Enchantment. Is that what he did to me during the trials? It would explain why I felt so drawn to him. It explained why I still had these unforgivable feelings for him, even though he killed me.

"So, you came home, and you fought harder than I had ever seen you fight before. You never did tell me how you learned of the enchantment, but you told me that you understood why Cassius was known as this heartless, cruel male. You wanted to kill him; that is why you were in Crimson the day he killed you. You wanted to end him, but he got to you first."

Gods, Cassius had been manipulating me through my dreams since before I ever left Exile. My mind raced with memories of us, trying to understand when exactly he had enchanted me. Was it in my dreams, or perhaps it was the first time he spoke to me at the trials? Is that why everyone in Crimson treated me so kindly? It was all fake.

"I still don't understand why he would make up the trials and pretend to care for me," I confessed.

"That bloodstone holds great power, Thea. It was gifted to me by your mother, and Cassius wanted it. I must admit that what he did was the cleverest plan I have ever seen concocted. He killed you, not knowing that the gods would be angry because your prophecy had not been fulfilled. He didn't account for the god, Mikel, being furious with him when he came from the stars. Cassius was cursed by the gods that day."

I stopped walking.

"Cassius was cursed?" That couldn't be right. I was cursed. I had no memories.

"Yes. The gods were furious with him for taking your life because your prophecy hadn't come true. Your power is unheard of, Thea. The gods had big plans for you, and he ruined them. Cassius probably assumed he could charm his way out of repercussions, but Mikel didn't listen to anything he had to say."

"But I lost my memories; how does that curse Cassius?"

"Mikel thought he was sparing you the pain of Cassius' betrayal, but there was another reason he took your memories. He did it to make breaking Cassius' curse harder for him. I also believe that he was only trying to wipe Cassius from your memories, but he wiped everything by accident. It was Cassius' intent for you to choose him and give him the bloodstone, thereby breaking his curse," my father sighed heavily. "The curse causes Cassius to lose parts of his elite magic for every year that passes without you breaking his curse. He also cannot take the throne or create an heir for Crimson. Essentially, he is useless to his kingdom if he cannot take over the crown."

The revelations had my mind reeling. "That was why he wanted the stone so badly," I said. "What would have happened if I gave it to him?" I shook my head as I realized how close I had been to giving him exactly what he wanted that day.

"His powers would have multiplied, and he likely would have begun to slaughter the other kingdoms. Crimson wants all of Elloryon to be ruled by one king, and the only way they can do that is to get rid of the rest of the royal bloodlines."

Gods, I felt so stupid.

"Cassius is powerful, Thea. His elite magic is unheard of, but some fae think he has a second magic. One that can manipulate the minds of others. I don't know if it is true, but I do know that he used either that or an enchantment against you. Whichever it is, it has worked multiple times."

"I feel stupid," I confessed. "I have caused so much chaos unintentionally."

"Well, I do not hold it against you, but I must warn you that others in Cerithia do not share my forgiveness. This will be a hard journey here."

"I understand." I nodded as the sun beat down on us as if it were punishing me for almost betraying my family. "I will do my best to not get upset about it."

"I know you have asked to go to Crimson to kill Cassius, and I have not been willing. It is only that I fear you will fall for his manipulation again, Thea. I fear losing you. I also know..." he paused, almost unsure of what to say next. "I also know that killing Cassius is the only way to get your memories back."

The thought of killing Cassius made my stomach churn. It made perfect sense, but I didn't like the thought of it. My father's words sank into me. It had been obvious that he was keeping me from anything war-related, but now it all makes sense. Could I be trusted so close to Cassius without my feelings clouding my judgment?

"I don't blame you, but at some point, you must let me try."

"I promise," he said with a soft smile.

We walked through the small gardens in silence, but now it wasn't awkward. Shame filled me. This must have been so difficult for my family to go through. I had caused so much hurt and heartache for my family and kingdom.

"We sent guards to Exile per your request," he broke the silence. "They found no trace of the town or the tree with the X carved into it that you described. It must be part of the curse, an illusion of living a normal life with other fae before you get your chance to break the curse."

Pain seared into me. Sybil and the twins weren't here anymore. They were gone, and I would never get to say my goodbyes or tell them what happened to me. Tears welled in my eyes at the thought of never hugging them again. My father must have seen my pain because he stopped and wrapped his arms around me, embracing me as I cried about the family I had in Exile.

"I'm sorry, Thea. You have lost everything you knew, but I promise we will do our best to make you feel at home."

★★☽★★

I had never felt more out of place in my life. My father had planned a feast to honor me in front of the kingdom, and I did not want to be here. Everyone stared at me when I walked into the celebration, as if they had hoped I would never show my face here again. Which seemed fitting because not a soul had come over to welcome me back or to say hello.

At first, I hesitated to come at all, but my father insisted that it was good to get me in the public eye again. It was time to try and repair the damage I had done before I was tricked. I was hiding in a corner of the ballroom, where everyone seemed to leave a large space around me. A group of younger fae stood at the food tables, staring at me and laughing. I tried not to show my anger or irritation, but my darkness simmered inside of me.

My father spared no expense in decorating the space with gold and crystals. The amount of food was so vast that I'm sure it could feed the entire city below us, but the smell of the food made my stomach curdle. Most of the guests stood on the outskirts of the dance floor that was in the center of the room. The large crystal chandelier dangled high above us, with ribbons of blue and gold draping from it to the walls.

The sound of laughter floated all around me. It nearly drowned out the soft music that played. My favorite thing about the space was the flowers. Each table was covered in gold tablecloths, and in the center were large flower centerpieces. The white and blue looked so beautiful.

My father and Gwyn had begun to ignore me only two minutes after my arrival, and I hadn't even seen my half-sisters. Not that they would bring me comfort. I knew my father and Gwyn had to mingle and interact with the others, but I had hoped for my father to at least show me around and help me acclimate. I shifted back and forth on my feet, wondering how long I needed to stay. Would anyone notice if I just left? I stiffened up when I saw Jesper.

Before I could move, he made a beeline right for me, even though I was trying to hide from him.

"Thea, you look remarkable." He smiled sincerely.

"Thanks," I half-muttered. I felt uncomfortable in the light blue silk dress I wore. It showed my scars to everyone. Glancing around, I could see the other fae watching Jesper, and I like they couldn't believe he was so close to me.

"Dance with me." He held out his hand. I went to refuse, but he grabbed my hand and practically dragged me with him onto the dance floor. Jesper pulled me flush against him. It was too close for my liking. Everyone's eyes burned into us, and I felt my cheeks getting hot under the scrutiny.

"How are you enjoying your celebration?"

"I would hardly call it my celebration when only you have uttered a word to me. They won't even come near me."

Jesper glanced around, seeming to realize all the staring.

"You intimidate them."

"They look at me like I'm disgusting, like they hate me." Sighing, I glanced up at Jesper. "Did they treat me like this before I left?"

There was something familiar in the looks of disgust and the contentment of being left alone in a crowd of others. This was not anything new to me, even if I couldn't remember the details. Jesper stared deeply into my eyes, as if he cared about me.

"No," he lied. "They just didn't know you were back, and they don't know how to interact with you after everything."

I felt like he was lying. There was no way that these faes had missed me or even cared that I was gone.

"You must remember that you betrayed everyone here by going to Crimson. They will be standoffish until you prove your loyalty."

"How am I supposed to do that? I already chose Cerithia," I sighed heavily.

Jesper's pretty blue eyes glanced down at me and frowned.

"Give them time, Thea. It has only been a few weeks."

"Why are you so kind to me?" I whispered. He was the only one here who seemed to not care about my betrayal, and I couldn't understand why. Jesper gave me a soft smile.

"I've been given a second chance to prove to you that I can be more. I can give you the life you deserve. I'm not the pretentious prick I was before. I want to show you I can be worthy of your love."

His words were kind, but they made my stomach twist with dread. I didn't want him. My blood bond burned violently on my arm at his words. How could I ever trust someone again?

"You don't need to say anything right now," Jesper sighed. "But you were mine first. Before *he* came and tricked you, he stole you from me. I guess I underestimated how much Cassius was willing to do to convince you that he had a heart. He has a reputation as being a stone-cold, unstable man. Someone like that doesn't know how to love anything but greed and power."

I said nothing. Cassius could never love me; I knew this because it seemed that no one cared about me. Love was not a possible emotion for someone to feel about me; I had learned this the hard way. Even Jesper's words meant nothing to me. There was no way I could trust him.

"Don't tell me you don't agree with me." Jesper's voice was annoyed as his hand gripped mine tighter than necessary. "You understand that Cassius only paid any attention to you because he needed something from you, right? I'm sure he's already moved on to his next victim."

"Stop," I hissed. Jesper was too much; this celebration was too much.

Everyone was gawking at us, and it made me uncomfortable. My chest tightened at the looks of the other fae. I didn't want to ruin trying to make amends with them.

Jesper's hands gripped me tighter.

"I want to hear you admit that Cassius is nothing to you."

"Piss off," I snapped as I tried to leave. Jesper refused to let me go.

"You better get over this unrequited love before we..."

"Is everything alright?" Gwyn raised her brow at the scene Jesper was causing. "Thea?"

"Jesper won't let me leave, and he's making me uncomfortable."

She looked at Jesper, and I expected her to tell him to release me and not talk to me in ways I didn't like. Gwyn's eyes were cold and distant when she looked back at me. Her lips twitched with smugness.

"You will do well to remember that Jesper is royalty and should be treated with respect. Quit making a scene."

Jesper smirked at me when I physically flinched at Gwyn's words. She wasn't going to stick up for me.

"I'm royalty too. He should not be allowed to grab me like that."

Gwyn and Jesper started chuckling.

"You are a bastard daughter, Thea; you are not royalty. You knew your place here before; do not make this harder on yourself by remaining ignorant. You are the captain of the armies, nothing more."

Her words cracked open a deep wound I didn't even know I harbored inside of me. I glanced at them, then at the fae watching the exchange, sneering at me like I was the problem. My chest ached at the faces full of disgust.

"Am I not part of your family?" I asked.

"Of course," she smiled, like she hadn't said such an awful thing to me moments ago. "You need to remember your place because I will not tolerate any insubordination that you learned in Crimson."

"I'm insubordinate because I do not want Jesper grabbing me roughly, and I do not wish to speak of Cassius."

Gwyn's eyes were wild with anger at the mention of Cassius.

"You should probably leave. It has been an overwhelming time for you."

A heavy, dull pain spread through me as I turned from her. I headed for the side door of the room, trying to ignore the stares. Anger surged forward to shield me from the disappointment I felt in Gwyn. I know they were weary of me, but it was obvious that Jesper was out of line, and she didn't stick up for me.

The group of fae that had been gathered around the food table laughing at me earlier all stared as I tried to leave peacefully. My darkness hummed at the fear I felt from them as I got closer.

"Well, if it isn't the Crimson whore," one of them snickered as I was walking by. The insult wasn't meant for me to hear, but my darkness, already upset, surged forward. My feet stopped immediately, and I turned to the woman who had made the cruel remark. The group had stopped laughing when my eyes flashed black toward them.

"What did you just call me?" I took an intimidating step forward, and they all stepped back.

"Nothing," she muttered.

"No, not nothing." I stepped closer to her as my eyes narrowed on her. "Crimson whore."

The woman tried to mask her terror as she straightened herself up and scoffed. This had several of the others in her group following suit. Pretending to be so brave in front of the monster.

"That's right. You are Crimson's whore. You can ask anyone in Cerithia; it's what we all call you."

They laughed, so I, in my maddened state, joined them by laughing along—only they stopped immediately. The brave girl swept her red hair over her shoulder with a look of disgust toward me.

"You really shouldn't have called me that." I stepped closer again. I knew that I should turn and leave, but my darkness refused to let me. It wanted to hurt others.

"Careful, Linea, you don't want the whore to touch you," another woman said in disgust. It was enough to distract me from snapping this woman's neck.

"Out of respect for my father, I will not kill you and ruin this party." I paused for a moment. "But just know that you will not get away with saying any of this. I will hunt you down, and I will cut the tongue from your mouth for being a disrespectful bitch. I will find you when you least expect it. I will not wait for you to be alone or wait as you walk home in the dark. No, there will be a crowd gathered in broad daylight when I come for you." My darkness was in control at this point, and I couldn't stop the threat from escaping me.

"Do you know who we are?" Linea scoffed. The tremor in her voice showed me that her confidence had wavered. "Our families are nobility."

"Noble or not, you will bleed the same as any of the other fae who have died by my hands. The next time you two see me, it will be when my dagger is cutting your tongues out."

I glanced at all of them, allowing my fire mist to swirl around me for a moment before turning and leaving. My anger simmered so violently inside of me that I thought I would burn down the castle if I didn't escape it. I turned and headed for the closest door, needing to get out. As

I ran from the castle, I realized that I felt detached from everything that had happened. My darkness was still in control of me, and I couldn't stop it.

"Thea!" Gwyn had caught up to me outside. "How dare you!"

I didn't respond. Not only because I knew she would not listen, but I also worried I would lose complete control. I knew it was useless to try and evade her. She cared too much about her image to let what I said to the guests go.

"You threatened the lives of two noble daughters."

"It was more of a promise." I glared at her. "I could have done it in there, in front of all your guests."

"You will not do it at all."

"They called me Crimson's whore," I ground out.

"Well, you are. If you hadn't crawled into bed with Cassius, then Cerithians wouldn't call you Crimson's whore."

Her words almost made my fire burst out of me again. She had better stop talking because I could feel myself slipping farther into the darkness.

"I'm your daughter. You shouldn't allow such disrespect toward me."

Her jaw clenched tightly. "You are not my child."

Her words hurt me more than I cared to admit, but only for a moment. My darkness wouldn't allow me to be upset over Gwyn. It gripped me tighter, making my hands clench tightly. My vision pulsed red. Gwyn grabbed my arm and tried to force me back with her.

"You will come and apologize now."

"Don't ever touch me," I said softly, ripping my arm from her.

My father appeared and walked toward us in a hurry.

"Thea? Gwyn?" he questioned. He stopped and took a hesitant step back from the sight of me.

"Your daughter threatened the lives of two noble daughters and refused to apologize."

My father frowned at me.

"Thea, why would you do that?" His disappointment doused my anger slightly.

"They called me Crimson's whore."

My father opened his mouth to talk, but Gwyn stepped forward before he could.

Gwyn's eyes bore into me with such disgust. "You better get a better grip on yourself because I will not let you destroy our image any more than you already have. You did this to yourself by sleeping with that monster, Cassius, so if others call you Crimson's whore, just know you earned that title yourself."

"Gwyn!" my father yelled at her.

At her harsh words, the last of my control left me. I felt my darkness escape me, and I smiled as it crept along the ground toward Gwyn. Without warning, it coiled around her and lifted her a few feet into the air. I forced the darkness to tighten on her, slowly restricting her breathing. I wanted to punish her, and my darkness was urging me to just do it. I could kill her without lifting a finger.

"Thea…" My father's panicked voice made me pause. "Don't hurt her."

I stepped toward Gwyn, and I could practically taste the fear her body pumped out. Stars above, her fear only fueled my darkness more. It took every ounce of restraint I had to pull my darkness back. My body trembled with pain as it tried to claw its way out of me again.

"One day, you'll regret what you just said to me," I promised before dropping her to the ground roughly. My fingers dug into my palms so hard that I could feel warm blood seeping through them.

Gwyn started wailing, and I just stared at her with disgust. My darkness felt pleasure in watching her cry. And, like a monster, I also felt happy about it.

"I will not be treated like this. I did not come here to be treated worse than Crimson ever treated me."

My father whipped his head around, his green eyes full of anger. His lips curled.

"You will never compare my kingdom to Crimson. Everything there was a lie!"

"Well, fake or not, they could at least pretend to enjoy my presence for a night," I said, just to get back at him and his terrible wife.

"Please, you must give us time to try," he begged. "How dare you treat us like this. We are your family."

His words stopped my anger almost immediately. My darkness retreated inside of me enough to allow shame to fill me.

"Is everything alright?" Jesper's voice broke through my guilt and angered me all over again. This started because he was an asshole.

"Thea's lost her fucking mind," Gwyn declared.

Jesper turned toward me and frowned. Tally and Mae were coming up behind him too. They slowed down when they saw their mother crying hysterically.

"What did you do?" Tally yelled.

I ignored her and focused on the way my sisters curled into my father's side for protection. The sight of him holding them safe from me, the monster, made me sick.

"You're a monster!" Mae cried out when she saw her mother.

I gave them a small smile. My darkness swirled around me in an angry vortex.

They were right. I was a monster. I couldn't even keep myself together for one night. I turned away from them and headed into the woods, walking without thought as far as I could. Once I was far enough away from them, a vicious scream tore through me. The pain I felt and the power that I released as a result of it left me in waves, ripping trees from their roots and scorching the forest around me. Power pulsed from me violently. I had never felt so upset with myself. I had never wanted to explode and take everything around me out like this.

I fell to my knees as my power quickly drained from me. Tears filled my eyes, knowing I had probably made things worse for myself here. How could I win them over and prove my loyalty to them if Cassius had damaged me so much that I couldn't even turn an eye to one hateful comment?

I cried because I did not think anything would fill this void I had become. There was no cure for this silence that lived inside of me. Nothing brought me happiness. I looked forward to nothing. Hopelessness filled me and gripped me so tightly that I thought I would die. My lungs couldn't get enough air. My heart palpated, causing a sharp pain in my chest as I tried sucking in a deep breath.

I was dying. I had to be. Desperately, I tried to take a deep breath, but I still couldn't get enough air. Tears blurred my vision as I looked around.

My mind froze in shock as Wisp suddenly appeared near me. It was the first time I had seen her since Cassius' betrayal. She turned away and floated deeper into the forest, her flames a bright white.

"Wisp!" I called out to her, but she flickered farther into the forest, like I was supposed to follow her. I reached out as I kneeled on the dirt, still unable to move. "Please, don't leave me!" I begged her. She kept getting farther and farther away until, eventually, she was completely out of sight.

I collapsed to the ground when exhaustion and panic finally gripped me completely. My eyes started to flutter shut, but not before I saw that Wisp had returned and was floating right next to me. Relieved, I reached for her. But as my fingers neared her bright white flames, everything began to fade. As I lost consciousness, her flames, along with everything else, seemed to be extinguished from my sight.

CHAPTER 4

Yesterday, I woke up still lying on the forest floor. I was lucky no monsters ate me as I slept. Wisp had been gone when I awoke to the sounds of guards stomping toward me. They took me back to the castle. My father had waited at the entrance of the gate and stared at me with disappointment. But he said nothing before turning and walking away.

Exhaustion had kept me in bed all day yesterday. I couldn't stay hidden in my room forever, so I planned to ask my father for something to do.

I slipped on my cloak and boots. I stared at the viper-handled dagger, and flashes of Cassius' face popped into my mind. I tucked the blade into my boot and headed upstairs. My father had not come to check on me. I hadn't left my room since our fight. I felt shame every time I thought of my father's disappointed face.

My darkness tried its best to shield me from my sadness, but it never truly went away. I was feeling particularly down today after another night of dreaming about Cassius. All the smiles, kisses, looks, and hugs made me feel ill when I saw them in my dreams. None of it had been real. Did he feel disgusted at having to pretend to like me? I swallowed the lump of emotion down and refused to think like that.

I tried to seek him out through the bond and my dreams during the first few nights in Cerithia, but he was silent. Even my loud sobs and pleading did not get a response. I'm sure he was ignoring me and taking pride in the fact that I was weak and vulnerable.

My eyes burned with tears that wanted to fall down my face. But deep inside, I knew that I didn't want to feel this anymore. He had killed me. He had cursed me to have no memories. I begged for an answer to his betrayal, only to be met with silence. I needed to forget about him. That was why I was out of my room today. I needed something to do.

I paused on the way to my father's throne room. The queen and my sisters were dressed over the top as they headed for the front doors. Quickly, I headed for them.

"Good morning, queen, Tally, Mae."

The queen was startled when she looked over my marked skin and black eyes.

"Oh, it's you." Her face was passive, but my sisters looked as though they would catch a disease from me.

"I wanted to apologize for my behavior."

They said nothing back to me. I waited an awkward amount of time but realized they weren't planning on saying anything back.

"Are you going somewhere?" I asked.

The queen raised her pale brow at my question. "Yes, we are hosting a luncheon with the noble women in the city."

"Perhaps I could go? I would change, of course." I tried to sound as genuine as I could. I found it difficult to be this close to Gwyn. My darkness hummed as we watched her. It wanted to punish her for her nasty words about me. *Crimson whore.*

"You weren't invited," the queen scoffed.

"But isn't it your luncheon?"

"Yes, your point being?" She didn't hide her irritation at my question.

"I just mean that it's your luncheon, so you could invite me to go."

It was clear my stepmother and sisters didn't like my presence. I wanted to try to fix my mistakes for the sake of my father, but I had no real desire to have a relationship with these three cruel women.

"Keep your distance from me and my children," she spoke with venom.

The queen lifted the skirt of her light blue gown and walked through the doors without saying another word. My half-sisters let out soft chuckles as they followed. I just watched them climb into the carriage. Instead of feeling hurt or angry, my darkness was happy at the sight of Gwyn's discomfort.

After a moment, I turned away from the doors and went to find my father. My family's distance these past few weeks was intentional. They didn't seem to care that I was here, even though I had hoped that maybe they would understand how confused and devastated I had been over all of this. I had hoped they would give me grace as I tried to figure things out.

I stopped at the throne room that my father worked in and knocked. Glancing over the large wooden carving that had haunted my dreams while I was in Exile, I felt dread now, just as I had then.

"What?" he snapped, letting me know I could enter.

I opened the door and poked my head in. His green eyes narrowed on my face before surprise took over his features.

"Thea," he sighed, irritated. My chest tightened as I entered the room. A deep sinking feeling consumed me every time I came in here. I wasn't sure if it was a forgotten memory or if it was because I dreamt of this room while in Exile.

My father stood in his fancy blue robes with his arms crossed, glaring down at me like I was more of a burden than his child. I knew I had messed up, but I felt that I was not the only one to blame for everything.

"I was thinking I could do something here, like a job or something."

My father turned, sitting down on his large, hideous silver throne. It was overdone and gaudy, with large jewels and accents of gold all over it. The tackiness extended to the rest of the area, with the signature color of Cerithia, light blue, hanging on the tapestries around the overly extravagant room. His large crown never seemed to be off his head when I saw him. His eyes looked over me for a long moment.

"You are still considered the captain of my guard."

"Yes, I know," I frowned. "I thought maybe I could do whatever it is that Tally and Mae do as daughters of the king."

He quirked his eyebrow up at me like he hadn't even thought about it. My heart pounded as I waited under his pointed stare. It felt odd that even as his daughter, he didn't consider me to do what my half-sisters did. Royalty or not, I should still be considered family.

"They are royal. You are not." He shook his head. "You still need to pay your debt to us for what you put us through."

My shoulders deflated at his words. I was sick of being here with no purpose, and if I didn't get something to do soon, I would lose my mind completely.

"But you said I was your daughter, that I had a spot here, in my home. It seems like I do not belong here in any capacity."

Something I couldn't decipher crossed his features. His already rigid posture stiffened even more at my words. He didn't like that I had used his own words against him.

"We have a celebration tomorrow night. You can possibly attend if you wish, but you must behave yourself. If you pull anything like you did last time, you will never attend another family function."

I nodded, but I didn't feel any excitement. It felt like he was forced to ask me instead of thinking of me. I was an afterthought. My stomach clenched tightly in disappointment.

I gave a small fake smile and turned to leave.

"Thea," my father called out to me. "You are the captain of my guard, and you will continue those duties. War will fall upon the kingdoms in the near future, and you are the key to winning. You will be expected to take down Crimson and kill Cassius. It is the only way to gain a place here."

"Or you could tell everyone that I chose to come here to fight for my family and Cerithia. Surely that would suffice until war came. Your approval of my return could help me acclimate."

He didn't respond.

I nodded slightly and headed for the door before pausing.

"Does my mother live in Cerithia?"

He stood so immediately at my question that I stepped back away from him.

"She's dead, and we do not speak of her." But he had spoken of her the other day in the gardens.

"B-but..."

"But nothing!" he bellowed before he seemed to realize he was yelling at me. "Your mother betrayed me, Thea. I do not wish to speak of her. She is dead, and I never want to hear you speak of her again. She is a traitor to Cerithia. Like mother, like daughter, I suppose."

I flinched at his cruel words, but my darkness surged forward, wanting to hurt him. It took all of my focus not to let it out. My fingernails dug into my palms so painfully that I wondered if I had drawn blood again.

I wanted to ask more questions. Didn't I deserve to know about my mother? What had she done to betray my father and Cerithia? I didn't even know her name. I didn't know if she was married to my father or if I had another family from her side. My father's hands fisted as he waited for me to either ask a question or drop the subject matter entirely. I nodded.

"I'm going to the city to try and help my memories come back."

"That isn't a good idea."

"Why am I being treated like a prisoner?" I glared. My father obviously realized I was not going to keep being pushed to the side.

"You did a lot of damage with your outburst at the party. I do not think the other fae want to see you."

I deflated at his words.

"Fine."

"You can start training the men if you wish."

I nodded and headed upstairs to change.

I walked onto the training field that was behind the castle and looked over at the men waiting. Dozens upon dozens of them stood watching me in their blue uniforms. I tugged at my blue uniform and sighed heavily as the weight of everything settled on my shoulders. My eyes had become even more black than they had been before, but surprisingly, most of these men did not stare in disgust or malice.

I walked to the front of them and looked over their faces. They looked at me with respect, and that caught me off guard. All of them saluted me.

"Who has been in charge since I...went missing?" I asked.

A man stepped forward. He was tall, muscular, good-looking, and heavily tattooed.

"Me, Captain." He bowed his bald head to me. His dark skin glistened with sweat as he stood up.

"Your name?"

"Jeb," he said, looking up at me with his dark eyes. "I did my best to continue how you trained us. I hope it is to your satisfaction."

"Thank you, Jeb. You will lead today so that I can get acclimated to this role again." Honestly, I had no idea what I was doing. Cassius' words from the day I went to get the witch's bloodstone popped into my mind. *You are a great warrior, Thea. Even without your magic, you are clever, smart, tactical, and strong. You are the best captain of any guard the realm has ever seen—a true leader. You just need to believe that about yourself.*

Even if his words weren't true, they comforted me as I stood there, clueless.

"It would be my honor." He bowed again and came to stand next to me. "Men, let's impress the captain today with our fighting skills."

I watched as the men instantly fell into their places and immediately obeyed. I walked around with Jeb and watched them practice their hand-to-hand combat. I realized that no one used magic.

"Who here has elite magic?" I asked Jeb. His eyes widened at my question, and he looked around before leaning closer.

"Only you. All the other elite magic holders disappeared when you did." My brain spun at his words—all of them?

"Okay, who has any magic?" I looked up when I noticed the men had stopped fighting at my question. Obviously, this was a touchy subject. "Who?" I demanded.

"I–I'm not sure," Jeb stuttered. He was clearly flustered by this simple question. It made me want to push the topic further. Why was everyone acting strangely about magic?

"Very well." I turned to the men. "If you have magic, step to this side of the field." I pointed to my left. "Those without magic will be on the opposite side."

The men looked at me without moving. Then they really pissed me off when they looked at Jeb.

"He's not your fucking captain anymore, so I suggest you start moving your asses!"

That was all the encouragement they needed. The men scattered quickly until only about a dozen stood on my left. But as my eyes caught sight of a familiar face within them, I paused. Leer was trying to hide behind the other fae, but he stuck out too much. He was taller by at least a foot, and I could never forget him.

"Jeb, continue working hand-to-hand with the men who hold no magic," I ordered.

"B-but."

I turned to him quickly and stared at him.

"I didn't ask for your opinion. Do it now."

Jeb clenched his jaw and turned to follow my order. Slowly, I walked to the men with magic and watched Leer practically shake from fear. My darkness hummed at the sight of him, quivering like a coward in front of us. Cerithia men were not allowed to compete in the trials, so how did he? My brows knitted together as I realized Leer had to have known who I was before he forfeited. Was he sent by my father? If he was, why did he apologize?

"In a line," I said.

They listened immediately.

"I want to know what magic each of you has."

I walked down the line, listening to them each speak out their magic, all common. Light manipulation, nature magic, water manipulation—none of it elite. Then I stood in front of Leer, who was last. He stared at me like I would call him out, but something told me not to.

"And you, soldier, what do you have?"

His bushy brows furrowed as he stared at me for a confusing moment. I noticed the sigh of relief he let out.

"Nature magic, specifically plant roots."

"Alright, I will start with you." I pointed to Leer and told the rest to join the others.

My eyes narrowed on Leer as soon as it was only the two of us. His light hair was still in a long braid down his back, but his eyes didn't hold hatred for me like they had at the trials. He also had a scar that ran across his face that wasn't there before. His blue eyes looked over me with fear. Leer looked exhausted.

"Leer."

"Captain," he bowed respectfully.

"What the fuck are you doing here?" I looked around, but no one paid much attention to us, besides Jeb, who seemed to watch me more than he needed to.

"I live in Cerithia," he whispered as he looked around. "I did not know you were Thea Alzara when I was at the trials until you used fire magic. They do not know that I competed in them."

"Why didn't you tell them?"

Leer looked around like he feared something. My eyes glanced around and saw nothing out of the ordinary. Jeb was the only one who watched us. It was clear that he didn't like that I was having a private conversation. Leer's eyes peered at me cautiously as he whispered.

"I was worried for my family's safety." His eyes shifted around us again. He was terrified. This was a completely different man than the one I competed against in the trials. "This is not the place to talk about this, Captain." His pale blue eyes pleaded silently at me. "Please."

All of a sudden, his fear did not make my darkness happy.

"Very well, Leer; please continue training."

He hurried away and didn't look at me again. I would visit him later. I called on other guards to make it look less suspicious. I asked them basic questions, but they all tensed when I asked about their magic. None of them wanted to talk about it. It was odd. They all seemed scared of the topic. After a few hours, Jeb dismissed them for the day and told me they would meet again in the morning.

"Magic is not allowed to be used," Jeb sighed.

"Well, that is stupid. It could win us the war."

"Magic is forbidden here, and if you keep bringing it up, I will have to tell your father," he warned me.

"Do whatever you wish, Jeb, but just remember that I'm the captain, and I don't take kindly to threats."

Jeb said nothing as he turned away and headed toward the castle. I stayed on the training field, trying to sort out what I was feeling about seeing Leer. He had been so cruel at the trials, but the man I saw today looked terrified and defeated. I glanced around me for Wisp out of habit, hoping she would give me any insight, but she was nowhere to be seen.

CHAPTER 5

Standing in front of the mirror in my room, I stared at myself in my newly tailored captain's uniform. Blue did not suit me in the slightest. I had been back to training for nearly a week, and I had not seen anyone from my family during that time. So, I was surprised when Jesper found me and gave me my new uniform, saying I needed to wear it to the meeting tonight.

My eyes stung with tiredness. I was pushing myself too hard at training, but it was hard to stop when it was all I had to keep me sane. My eyes drifted down my uniform, and I paused before lifting the sleeve of my arm up to reveal the communication bond I had with Cassius. I traced the red crown on my arm, stopping at the crack that ran through it. Could he still feel me through this bond? Flashes of him giving it to me played through my mind. I closed my eyes, wishing I could have had a little longer to pretend with him. I knew I shouldn't feel this way. I shouldn't mourn his loss.

Straightening up, I yanked my uniform down over my bond, but the weight of losing Cassius was crushing me.

Sighing, I put my viper-handled dagger into my boot and headed out. Jesper had told me the gathering was in the ballroom attached to the throne room. I hadn't even bothered asking him what the meeting was for.

When I entered the room, a hundred fae turned toward me. I raised my chin, so they knew I was not intimidated by their cold glares. Immediately, I found my family standing at the front of the room. I walked toward them quickly as others gazed at me, but I didn't bother looking around.

I stood at the end of the group next to Mae, who scoffed quietly under her breath. My father and Gwyn were whispering harshly to one another before my father turned and came to me.

"Thea, what are you doing?" His nostrils flared.

"I'm sorry I'm late. Jesper only told me twenty minutes ago."

"It's not that. You can't stand up here with us." He gave me a pleading look.

"Where should I stand?" I glanced to see no other space for me up front.

"You can sit with the commoners." His words made me frown. "Only the royal family can stand here."

My darkness surged forward before I could contain it. My eyes flashed black, and my father stumbled back slightly.

"And I'm not part of your family."

"Not in the royal sense," he clipped before turning his back on me.

Heat filled my cheeks as I stepped down and sat in the front row. The fae sitting closest to me scooted away, so I was alone. I refused to look up when my father greeted everyone. My hands tangled together in my lap as I focused on not being upset.

"We understand there are concerns among the commoners, so we invite you all to tell us what we can do." My father's voice was void of any kindness. He sounded angry that there were complaints. It was a long moment before I heard a fae scuffle up the aisle and stop beside me.

"Your Majesty, I speak for all of us when I say thank you for allowing us to voice our concerns." The old man stuttered out his words. "Our concerns lie solely with the return of Thea."

My head snapped up to the old man, my darkness still clinging to me, making my eyes black. I could practically taste the fear of everyone in here once I glanced up.

"What concerns are those?" Gwyn smiled smugly at me.

"Well, she has been missing for years, presumed to be living in Crimson. And now she is here, in our home, and we are concerned about what her intentions are."

The other fae muttered in agreement with his statement. Why did they all think I was in Crimson? Did my father not tell anyone about my curse?

I looked at my father, but he didn't even spare me a glance.

"Thea is here because the prophet spoke of her killing kings and crumbling kingdoms. She is here to fight for this kingdom and kill our enemies, including Crimson."

His words weren't cruel, but my heart ached slightly at the sound of them. I had hoped he would have told them that this is my home too, and I belong here. Why wouldn't he tell them about the curse and Cassius tricking me? All the fae thought I had been living happily with Cassius for years. There was no way they would ever forgive me for that. Gwyn stared me down as she opened her mouth.

"Thea is paying off her betrayal by fighting for us. If you are worried she is unpredictable, then do not fear about that. Her father has her on a very small rope; she is never out of our sights."

My darkness seeped out of me slowly as I listened to her. It sounded like I was their fucking pet. I stood up, pissed off at how they had not said anything truthful. They could have put an end to this hatred from the other faes by telling them what really happened.

"Thea?" my father questioned me.

"Why are you not telling them the truth? That I did not intentionally betray this kingdom. I was tricked and enchanted by Cassius, and I came back immediately once I learned of it. You are letting these fae think I am a traitor. Do they even know that I was cursed?"

Jesper and Gwyn raised their brows at me before glancing at my father, who stared at me.

"Because you are a traitor, Thea. Whether you feel it was intentional or not, you are a traitor to the crown. Do not ever talk to a member of the royal family in that tone again." His voice was dismissive, which instantly enraged me. My magic was bleeding to the surface, and my skin began to glow with red and orange swirls.

"Witch!" someone yelled, making the room break out in chaos. The fae scrambled from me like I would eat the flesh from their bones.

My father started walking toward me, but unable to face him, I ran out of the room and toward town. My anger was too out of control to talk to him. I knew I would do something that I regretted if I stayed here.

I left the castle and made my way to the main road. My lungs burned as I ran to the city I had not been allowed to visit.

A part of me wanted to see if the fae there would treat me with the same cold indifference that I got from my family and the others at the meeting tonight.

Gods, I missed the cooler air of Crimson. Here, the sun shone so hot that it made everything miserable.

The heat made sweat bead on every part of my skin, and I hated it. It reminded me of Exile.

The path to town wasn't paved in stone but was instead just a carved-out dirt path. I hadn't been here yet since my return, and I had hoped that I liked it as much as the Crimson Kingdom's city. When I got to the outskirts, I stopped and looked at the shambled buildings and homes that lined the dirt roadways. My eyes flowed over the wooden structures that looked in desperate need of repairs. As I moved closer to the town square, the buildings became bigger and were in better condition.

Most of the nicer buildings were made of gray stone, like the castle. I looked around at the fae as they watched me. No one smiled or waved. Instead, they all stared like I was a spectacle, like they were seeing a monster in the flesh.

Silence engulfed everything as those around me recognized who I was. I ignored them and continued to explore.

There was no laughter or music. No dancing in the streets as there had been in Crimson. The only beauty that I could see came from a pretty, vine-covered fountain that was covered in blue flowers. It was the prettiest thing I had seen here yet.

A bench next to the fountain caught my attention, so I decided to sit. It was difficult to ignore the stares because no one seemed to be happy to see me. The reactions of the fae here were the same as those at the castle. All this hatred toward me for what? Because I had been tricked by Cassius? Shame filled me. They clearly didn't care that I was back. If anything, I had the feeling they wanted me gone. Glancing around the streets, I tried to focus on the buildings and shops. Something here would certainly trigger a memory. As it stood, I had no memories at all of my time in Cerithia, except for those with Cassius on the night of the blood moon when we were younger. All my memories were of Cassius in some way or another.

I saw a couple walk out of a small cafe storefront holding a drink that looked refreshing in this blistering heat. I stood, crossing the street, to duck into the shop and get one for myself. As soon as I walked in, all the chatter stopped. Feeling uneasy, I walked up to the man making drinks and gave him a friendly smile.

"Hi, I saw a woman holding a green drink. Could I get the same thing?"

His dark eyes moved over me, and disgust filled his features.

"We're out." He barely paid me any attention before he tried to help whoever was behind me.

"Excuse me, I wasn't done."

His eyes shifted to me and then ran down the red, orange, and black swirls that tattooed my skin. He scoffed with hatred. My eyes darted to others, and I realized that they all held the same look.

I sighed in frustration. This was my home? These are the fae that I chose to fight for.

"We're out of everything that you want. Feel free to leave and run back to the castle. No one in town wants to see you," he spat. Great, another fae who treated me like trash. I looked around, and everyone in the shop was staring at me like I was a monster. It was obvious that they didn't want me in here. This pissed me off because I didn't want to be here either. And yet here I was, fighting for this fucking kingdom that didn't even want me, and I was starting to ask myself why.

"I think I'll have a drink, like I fucking asked." I glanced at him, making my fire magic swarm around me. "I suggest you hurry up before I lose my temper."

This made the other fae gasp. I did not have the same restraint with these assholes as I had with the two noble daughters who spoke poorly at me. Here, someone would die if they weren't careful.

"Chop, chop, prick. I've got things to do."

My darkness hummed at the fear in his eyes and body. But this male did not let it show to the others.

"Well, look at that, everybody; the Crimson whore thinks she has the power here," he laughed, which made others laugh too. Before he could say another word, I grabbed the back of his head and slammed it down onto the wooden counter. The crunch of his nose made me smile. This evil rage inside wanted more pain. My eyes pulsed red.

My fingers grabbed his red hair and yanked him up. I leaned my ear closer to him as if I were hard of hearing.

"I'm sorry, I didn't quite catch that *lovely* nickname you gave me."

"N-nothing," he stuttered.

"Oh, my mistake." I smiled and let him go. My eyes flashed black and made him stagger backward.

"Crimson monster," someone muttered from behind me. I turned, and my eyes found the man. His eyes widened when he realized I heard him. Another man who was disrespecting me. This wouldn't be tolerated, especially when I was fighting for them. I grabbed my dagger and walked to him. Everyone was silent. He tried to run, but I twisted him in my darkness and held him in place.

"Unfortunately, your stupidity has now cost you your tongue."

I roughly grabbed his face with my free hand and pried open his mouth with my magic. Staring into his terrified eyes, I used my viper-handled dagger to cut his tongue from him. His yells only made me feel better. I dropped him to the ground as he sobbed, which was the only sound in the stunned room. I wiped the blood from my blade on his white shirt before heading to the counter again. I no longer cared for the forgiveness of these fae or this kingdom.

"Where's my drink?" I asked the large, red-headed fae. He jumped at my words and started making it. I turned to the horrified faces. Leaning my hip against the counter, I played with my dagger, twisting it in my fingers as I smiled.

"You think that you would show more respect to someone who chose to fight for your homes, fight for you. A woman who could kill you all with a flick of her wrist."

No one said anything, but stars above, their fear made my darkness swarm in a frenzy.

As I looked at them and felt their hatred for me, I realized that this place could never have been my home. Then another, more twisted thought struck me. Maybe I would crumble this kingdom as well, because these ungrateful fucks didn't give a shit about me.

The drink was pushed toward me. I glanced at it and lifted it to my mouth. The sweet liquid hit my tongue. It was delicious. I scrunched my face as I poured it into the trash.

"Tastes like shit," I lied. Gods, I was on a rampage, and I didn't want to stop. "Well, it's been a very welcoming experience; thank you everyone." I glared as I headed out. Part of me hoped someone would say something so I could keep this rage going. As I pushed the door open, my wish came true.

"Crimson bitch," he muttered, like he thought I couldn't hear him. But as soon as I stopped and turned, my face breaking into a wicked smile, the man making drinks realized I had heard. My magic had him wrapped up within a second before he could dart away.

My viper-handled dagger flew from my hand and into his heart, stopping it immediately. My magic released him, and he fell to the floor, dead. I walked back across the room, yanking my dagger out before walking toward the door, but I paused one last time.

"Would anyone else like to say something?"

They all stared in terror.

"I didn't fucking think so."

The sun beat heavily on me as I stepped from the cafe. I looked around the town square and saw everyone gawking at me. Disgust painted their faces.

But I was the one who was disgusted because this kingdom was not kind to me. Something about this place was not right. An intense ache formed in my chest for a place I didn't have, a home.

Everyone on my side of the street crossed it when I started walking. They acted as if they would die if I got too close to them. They didn't hide their hatred for me here. This wasn't the Crimson Kingdom, where they at least pretended to be nice and not see what I really was—a hideous monster that could kill everyone if I wanted to. Here, though, everyone showed their hate and disdain openly, showering it upon me with abandon. These fae didn't care that I had been gone for years. They didn't care that I had chosen to fight for them.

Unwanted, Cassius' words of betrayal entered my mind and weighed heavily on me. *How could anyone love a monstrosity like you?*

CHAPTER 6

I started to head back to the castle but then stopped when I knew no one was watching me. My darkness could feel Leer's magic clinging to the air and wanted me to find him. Why was he fighting for Cerithia when he was scared for his own family's safety if they found out he was in the trials? It didn't make sense.

I followed my darkness to the outskirts of town. His home was one of the shambled buildings I passed by earlier. It needed serious maintenance and looked too small for more than one fae to be living in it. Leer was just getting home with a loaf of bread. He looked over his shoulder like he could feel he was being watched, but he didn't see me as he went inside.

I waited for a while to make sure I wouldn't be noticed by anyone. The dirt crunching under my feet was the only noise heard as I snuck up to his home and peered in the window. He was sitting at a tiny table with two young kids, eating a loaf of bread. I knocked on the door, and when he opened it, he tried to close it in my face. I stopped him easily and pushed my way inside.

"I will kill you if you try to harm them for my mistakes," he sneered as he moved between me and his kids.

"I'm not here to hurt them. I need to ask you questions, and I could tell you were worried about talking with me. I'm sorry to intrude, but it's important."

His eyes looked at me and then at his kids. He sighed in defeat as he gestured to the small couch. I watched him as he encouraged his kids to keep eating, and then he closed the blinds in every window and locked the door. His house was too small for the three of them. I looked at the small loaf of bread they were sharing; did they have more food than that?

Leer came and sat across from me. He looked terrified of me, but for some reason, my darkness did not like his fear.

"I know I treated you horribly in the trials, but my kids need me. So, if you kill me, you'll be killing them too." Leer ran his fingers through his long hair. "Besides, I was told to be mean to you. Nev said you were our biggest competition, and I needed to win that wish. He paid me a large sum to cause you issues, and I needed the money."

Leer looked tired. His eyes were dull and sagged with dark circles. It was a stark contrast to who he was at the trials. He was much thinner, too. Was he ill?

"I forgive you for the trials, Leer," I assured him, even though I never thought I would say these words in my life. "I want to know why you are scared for your family's safety if Cerithia finds out you joined the trials."

"It's forbidden." He leaned back in his chair. "No one from Cerithia may join because Crimson forbade it. Cassius did his best to keep Cerithia out, and I watched him rip another Cerithia fae's heart from his chest when he tried to sneak in. That was before you arrived at the trials this year. But like I said, I needed that wish, so I was willing to die to try and get it. Your father usually handpicks five guards for the trials each year, but this year was different. He sent only two—the man who Cassius beheaded that first trial day in the hallway and the one he killed before you arrived."

"But Nev..."

"Not Cerithian. He's from Kizar. My guess is that your father thought teaming up with Jesper would get more men into the trials, and he was right. I believe your father sent two Cerithian guards so that it didn't look suspicious to Cassius. He sacrificed them so that the Kizar guards were not looked at too closely."

His arms crossed over his chest, like he was nervous in my presence. I wasn't trying to worry him, but he had more information than I did.

"Hadn't you heard of me before the trials? You must have known why the trials even happened."

"I'm not from Cerithia; my wife is. I am from Akecia. I knew of the king's bastard daughter and of her disappearance. I've also heard some of the prophet's telling. Until the trials, I didn't know they were made for you, to help you."

"To help me." I cocked my head to the side as if it would help me understand what that meant.

"Crimson needed you to believe there was a reason to get the bloodstone. A wish granted if you gave it to them." He leaned back and sighed heavily. "If you left Exile and happened to find yourself in Crimson, would you have been willing to go and retrieve a bloodstone if asked? I mean, if the trials never existed."

I pondered his words for a moment. Leer made a good point; I wouldn't have done something simply because someone asked me to. I was more likely to do the opposite.

"Of course not." I picked the hem of my uniform. "Cassius wanted it to break his curse."

Leer frowned at me like he truly felt bad for the situation I was in.

"I don't know the specifics, but I know that bloodstone is important. Crimson wants it."

"For power," I muttered.

Leer looked at me, confused. Before leaning forward so he could stare me in the eyes.

"I think it has something to do with your curse."

"My curse?" I sat up a little more. "What do you mean?"

"I don't think it's for power. If it was, then your father would be using the shit out of it. Crimson... Cassius wanted you to give that stone to him. I overheard some men at the trials talking about it. No one really knows, but I think it's about the curse and getting your memories back."

Leer paused for a long moment, watching me with pity in his blue eyes. "At first, I didn't understand why he didn't just tell you and ask you to get the stone, but then I realized you didn't have memories. You didn't remember him, but he watched you so closely. I remember thinking how odd it was for him to be so cautious about your safety. Cassius Valeska has a reputation for being a heartless monster, cruel even. Why did he care so much for you, and why was it so important that you gave *him* the bloodstone? If it has to do with breaking your curse, then why would he want you to remember?"

"But Cassius killed me, and the bloodstone breaks his curse, not mine." Was everything that Leer was saying true? If it was, why would Crimson want me to remember? Wouldn't they want me to never have my memories? Leer was right about the bloodstone. If it had any power to be used, my father would use it instead of using me.

Leer frowned at me.

"What curse?" he frowned at me. "Cassius Valeska isn't cursed." Leer looked at me oddly. "Why would you think that?"

"My father said that Cassius was cursed and needed the stone to break it." I stared blankly at him, wondering why he was so adamant that Cassius wasn't cursed.

"He's lying to you," Leer sighed. "I don't know why, but if Cassius Valeska was cursed, we would all know of it. Cassius is trying to break your curse."

"Why would he do that? He hates me." I frowned.

Leer swallowed hard.

"He didn't look at you like he hated you. He looked like a man longing for something that he couldn't have."

This didn't make sense. My father had no reason to lie to me. Leer, on the other hand, could be feeding me a lot of lies to get back at me for the trials.

"I don't understand why my father would lie."

"I don't know Thea, but you should be cautious. It seems both of us do not have the full story. I wish I could tell you what you want to know, but I don't have the facts you need. Your father keeps everyone limited on information."

I sat back on the chair and stared at him. He didn't look like he was lying to me. My darkness was not trying to warn me away. Something about Leer's words made more sense to me than anything my family had told me. But was that because I was desperate to understand why Cassius would do something so malicious to me?

"What did you need the wish for?" I finally asked.

His eyes shifted to his kids, who laughed behind us.

"We live in squalor. I can hardly afford to buy a loaf of bread to feed my children. All of my money goes into taking care of my wife, who is ill. Besides, the king hardly pays us and then demands taxes that take almost everything back. It's nothing like what you saw at the Crimson Kingdom. When I got back from the trials, I joined the Cerithian Guard hoping that it would change our situation, but it has only gotten worse."

I glanced at his kids. Both boys looked like him with their blonde hair but had the prettiest amber-colored eyes. No, it wasn't like the Crimson Kingdom. It was as if no one was happy in Cerithia. Before I could ask my other questions, I heard a soft whimper of pain come from a room behind him. He immediately got up and rushed back through the doorway. The kids had stopped laughing as the pained sobs filled the small space. I stood up cautiously and walked to the doorway to see Leer sitting on the edge of a small bed, wiping sweat from a woman's forehead. She was too pale and skinny. Was this his wife? Her hair was dark against the white pillow.

She groaned in agonizing pain. I looked at Leer, and he looked completely devastated. He knew he couldn't help her, and it was destroying him.

"Leer," she whimpered. "It hurts."

"I know, sweetheart." His eyes looked up at me as I walked toward her.

There was an overwhelming sense of sadness as I got near her. She peered at me with dark eyes that held little consciousness. This woman was on the cusp of dying. Something odd pulled me closer, though. Something foreign that I had not felt before. My eyes drifted over her frail body, and with my magic, I could see her sickness coursing through her veins. It was even overtaking her heart, which was nearly covered in a deep, evil blackness. I realized the strange tugging I had felt was death lurking. She was about to die.

"What's wrong with her?"

"Some sort of infection, but nothing can cure it. We've tried everything we can afford. My wish was going to be to save my wife."

Leer didn't bother hiding his emotions as tears ran freely down his face. His pure devastation was evident, and it affected me to see. I sat on the bed next to her, and she immediately reached for my hand, like I was a comfort. Nobody had wanted to reach for my hand in so long, and it touched me in a way that I couldn't quite describe. I grabbed it and could feel how fragile she truly was. Her hand was too cold, and her skin felt paper-thin. I smiled at her when she focused on me. She did not look scared of me, even though I looked like a monster.

"Are you here for me?" she whispered.

I wasn't sure what she meant, so I just responded with, "No."

Her small sigh of relief confused me, but I didn't dwell on it.

I could feel my magic growing in me—it was humming in my chest. I knew what I needed to do. Gathering my strength, I let Sybil's healing magic flow freely from my hands.

I focused on her as red and orange swirled from my body to hers. It ran through her veins and made her whole body glow as I tried desperately to heal her. Not being too experienced with this magic, I didn't know how strong it was. Could it bring someone back from being so close to death? I smiled as I felt her cold hand warm up almost instantly in mine as my magic poured into her.

I continued to hold her hand and smile at her, bending all of my will to this task. Leer's eyes stared at me and his wife. The glow of the magic made the room look like it was brightened by candles. It was peaceful.

The healing magic stopped abruptly, and her eyes softly closed. I held my breath as I waited to see if it had worked.

She seemed to be sleeping, but I did not see her chest rise and fall with a breath.

Leer and I watched her without saying a word. Both of us were too scared to jinx it. My eyes refused to look away from her frail, seemingly lifeless body. Leer's soft cries were agonizing to hear as he buried his face into her still chest. He was pleading with her to not leave him. He spoke of the life they had always talked about, their children, and how he had never loved another woman besides her.

It was too much to witness, so I finally looked away from her. My hand squeezed hers as I tried to understand why Leer and his children deserved this heartbreak. A moment later, I gasped as the woman's hand squeezed mine gently. I blinked slowly when I thought my eyes were deceiving me, but they were not. Her sunken cheeks began filling in, and her loose-fitting nightgown was fitting more like it should. Even her dark hair didn't seem to be as brittle as it had been mere moments before. Then she opened her amber-colored eyes, eyes that matched her children's perfectly. She looked around, confused, but only for a moment.

Something close to relief flickered in her eyes before she reached up and ran her hand through Leer's hair. His head snapped up to see her awake. Leer's eyes widened in disbelief before he pulled her to him and sobbed into her neck. He pulled away and kissed his wife. She returned the kiss feverishly, then sat back to look up at me.

"Thank you," she choked out. "Death was coming for me, and you pulled me back out." She leaned over, and we hugged tightly. Then she pulled back and looked at Leer, who looked at her like he was seeing a ghost.

"Leer," she whispered.

"Larissa," he choked out through a heart-shattering sob as he grabbed her again and held her tightly. Cries escaped them both, and it was enough that the kids came in to see what was wrong.

"Mommy!" They both shrieked and tackled her with hugs. I felt like I was intruding on a special moment, so I stood up and walked out of the room. I stopped at the doorway and looked back at them. What did it feel like to have others care so much about you? To have a family like this? Jealousy bloomed in my chest at the sight of them. I wanted this. I wanted a husband who held me like that. I wanted kids crawling around my bed, laughing. I sighed because I knew that life would never be possible for someone like me. The thought was enough to make tears well in my eyes as I turned away.

I slowly headed toward the front door but was forced to stop when Leer grabbed my arm and hugged me tightly as sobs of relief racked his body. I hugged him back because it was nice to feel like less of a monster, even if only for a moment. Glancing over his shoulder, I saw his wife at the doorway with her two kids, smiling at me like I had hung the stars above.

"I am forever in debt to you, Thea Alzara. You have my undying loyalty for whatever you may need. You gave me my life back, and I can't explain how much this means. Even after how I treated you."

He released me and kneeled before me like I was the queen. His tears flowed freely from him as he gripped my hand in his and kept kneeling.

My mind was reeling with everything, but my ever-present hope flashed through it all. Did he really mean that? He certainly didn't look like a man who was lying to me.

"Tell no one about what I did. If they ask, she got better with whatever medicine you've been giving her." I paused for a moment, then gripped his hand harder. "I forgive you, Leer. If I were in your spot, I would have done anything to save my family too."

I started to turn, but he stopped me again by not releasing me.

"I know about Exile," he said quickly, making me stop immediately. When I turned to him, he still kneeled in front of me.

"What?"

"I know of Exile. I also know that your father told you it didn't exist and that he sent guards to verify it." Leer paused for a moment. "But I also know that he lied to you. He never sent any guards."

The revelation was enough to make my darkness explode into the room, startling his children. They ducked behind their mother and watched me in awe as flames and shadows seemed to fill the air around me.

"How do you know this?" Furthermore, could I trust him?

"Your father had tracked down Exile, but he did it before you came to the trials. I do not know why, but my friend was one of the guards that went on the mission. Afterwords, your father met with all the guards before you started training us and said he would execute anyone who verified Exile's existence or spoke of elite magic holders. Specifically, Kai and Kaz."

My heart was pounding so fast that it made hearing him difficult. Leer frowned at me as I held my chest. My breathing became rapid.

"K-K-Kaz, K-Kai?" I stuttered out.

"We were under the impression that the elitists were with you in Exile, but now your father is trying to cover it up, and I do not know what the reason would be. He's also told the town's fae that you were in Crimson."

"Why are you telling me any of this?" I asked suspiciously.

"Because you saved my family tonight, even after the torment I caused you. I would not have survived this realm if Larissa had died. You gave me everything when you saved her. I am indebted to you, and I will stand by you in any decision you wish to make. As far as I'm concerned, you are my queen."

He bowed his head down, his children and wife doing the same. Something about the gesture was familiar to me, and it brought forth a sense of pride.

But my mind raced with everything Leer was telling me. Hopefulness for my situation bloomed in my chest. I now knew that my mind wasn't broken. I wasn't crazy; my friends were real. But that meant my father didn't want me to find them. Why?

My darkness swarmed around me, making my skin glow brightly with red and orange swirls. Betrayal pumped through me, but doubt still gnawed at me. I wasn't sure if I could take Leer for his word. This could still be a trick.

"I will go to Exile myself and look," I whispered. I kneeled to Leer's level so I could look him in the eyes as I spoke next. My darkness waited to feel his fear as I said, "If this is a trick or you have lied to me, I will come back and kill you, Leer."

Leer's blue eyes stared into mine, and not an ounce of fear came from him.

"I would expect nothing less." He nodded. "I swear on my family and the gods; I am not lying to you."

I nodded as I stood.

"You are excused from guard duty for the rest of the week to spend it with your wife." I smiled at her when she gave me a look of sadness, then turned just as Larissa spoke.

"You made a mistake coming to Cerithia. Your father is not a kind man."

I spoke without turning to look at them.

"I am learning that he is the king and not my father."

Then I left.

Chapter 7

Cerithian guards were constantly present in the hallways. The way they watched my every move made me feel like a prisoner, even though I had chosen to come here. It didn't matter where I was; there was guaranteed to be a guard or two lingering. At first, I thought it was normal, but after talking with Leer, I wondered if they only followed *me* around like this.

I had awoken this morning to my own screams as I dreamt of something I couldn't remember, my head pounding and my body aching with exhaustion. I had tossed and turned most of the night, replaying both my conversation with Leer and how my family had treated me at the disastrous meeting. At points, I would convince myself Leer was lying, but then I always wondered... what if he wasn't?

My darkness had never relented last night. My eyes had remained black, and my swirls stayed bright on my skin. I felt rage, but not rage like I did when I thought of Cassius. No, this rage felt familiar to me, almost as if I had felt this betrayal before.

That was why I decided to see if Leer's story checked out.

The sun beamed through the tall windows of the castle, warming the air so it felt sticky against my skin as I walked through the corridors. My eyes darted to the family portrait in the hallway, making my feet halt immediately. This wasn't my first time seeing it, but it made me feel like shit the more I stared at it.

My father and the queen stood in the back as Tally and Mae sat in front of them. No one smiled in the portrait. Perhaps that was a traditional pose for royalty. I was obviously missing. I wondered if my father would order a new one now that the family was back together, but deep inside, I was sure I already knew that answer.

My father's laughter caught my attention. Tearing my eyes away from the portrait, I headed toward the sound.

This was the first laughter I had heard from my father, and I was intrigued. I walked through the open wooden door to my left, where I had heard him. He sat at a long dining table with my family and Jesper, eating breakfast. I frowned as I took in the sight of them together because

I had not been invited. Every interaction I had with them now would make me question their intentions.

"Thea." Jesper was the one to notice me. His handsome face broke into a smile at the sight of me, and he stood to greet me politely. My insides churned at how he could pretend like he wasn't a complete prick.

"I didn't realize we ate together as a *family*," I said as I stepped toward them. The queen's look of irritation stopped me from continuing but made my darkness happy. It loved to cause her discomfort. "Or should I leave?" I glanced at my father for his permission.

He looked around the table, but his green eyes lingered on Jesper, who gave him a subtle nod.

"Please, sit." He gestured to a chair across from Jesper. The tension around the table made my chest tight. I rubbed the blood bond on my arm as I fidgeted in my seat. "You took off last night?" my father broke the silence.

"I didn't want to hear my family keep the truth from the fae that I am supposed to be fighting for." I glared at him as a servant placed a plate of food in front of me. Something about my family and this kingdom hasn't seemed to make sense ever since I came here.

"We do not need to explain ourselves to you," Gwyn hissed.

"I'm just trying to fathom why my family would not tell the kingdom that I was cursed and not living in Crimson," I spoke with a firm voice as I stared her down.

"Do not start an argument that you know nothing about," my father warned. "We will not explain every decision to you. It is for the best; trust us."

I scoffed. Jeb walked in, glaring at me as he headed for my father and whispered something in his ear. My father's eyes snapped to mine, and I leaned back in my chair, sneering at Jeb. I had a sneaking suspicion that Jeb had just told my father what I did yesterday while in town.

"Thea, you need to stay at the castle from now on. No more visits to town," my father sighed. Did he think I would ever agree to that? I was never going to be a prisoner again.

"You went to town?" Gwyn yelled at me. Her normally pale face had reddened in her anger.

Her words immediately made my magic surge forward. Fire mist wrapped around me in fury because she had no right to say anything. My family all froze at the sight of me, with my power wrapping and twisting around me in an angry buzz. My eyes pulsed with spots of red as I stared down at each one of them.

"Yes, I did, and it was very enlightening. It seems the whole city is repulsed by me. But don't worry, I think I made a very compelling point to the fae of Cerithia." I smiled wickedly.

"What did you do?" Gwyn asked. "Luren, she should not be allowed in public when she looks like that. She makes us look bad." Gwyn glared at me. All I could do was focus on my father's giant golden crown on his head. Those men at that cafe shouldn't have treated me so disgustingly, but I was starting to get the impression that I could be treated poorly by anyone.

"If we tell you not to leave the castle, then you will listen," my father declared. "You killed a man yesterday and cut the tongue from another."

"You stupid Crimson-" Gwyn started, but I gave her a menacing look that let her know if she continued that sentence, she would be dead.

Tally and Mae practically choked on their fancy meal at the news. Tally's hand flew over her mouth as she looked at her mother.

Rage filled me. I did not choose to come here and be treated like trash. Glancing around at my family, I bit back the rage that was coursing through my veins at a violent rate. My fire mist whipped more violently around me, but now shadows intertwined with it—Cassius' shadows.

"Put your magic away," Gwyn demanded, but I just turned my black eyes toward her and didn't look away until she visibly shrank back at my appearance.

"This is your home," my father spat. His words broke something inside of me. I could no longer accept the fact that I had betrayed them, and maybe I should be treated poorly. No, they simply hated me here.

"This is no more a home than it is a prison," I shot back.

They all watched me like I was losing it, which I was. But this was just a small sliver of the rage swarming dangerously inside of me. A rage that started because of Cassius is now being fueled because of this fake family and kingdom.

A moment later, she appeared. The woman with star-colored eyes and golden skin smiled at me as my darkness raged. I stared at her, wondering where she had been.

"Ask them if they will make a new family portrait with you," she demanded of me. No one batted an eye, so they obviously hadn't heard her.

"Will there be a new family portrait painted for the hallway?" I asked, catching them off guard.

"That painting has been hanging there for nearly fifty years; why would we change it?" Tally scoffed.

It hit me that the painting had been there longer than I had been missing. My father seemed to understand why I asked, and a moment of worry flashed across his features before he hardened his face. His hands flew up in defense.

"You did not want to be in the portrait, Thea. You did not like the title of princess. You wanted to be the captain of my guard for the love of the gods."

"Do you really think I will believe that?"

Something deep in my broken memory was struggling, wanting to be free. It was like an itch I couldn't scratch; it became more insistent but never surfaced. Why was my family lying to me?

"Push to be in it," the mysterious woman spoke.

"Well, I would like to be in it now." I pushed to see how they would react.

"Luren," Gwyn hissed through clenched teeth, but I could feel fear from her and my father pumping through them rapidly.

"We will discuss this after you've settled here." He agreed, but I knew it was just to pacify me. Something deep inside my mind knew they would never include me in something like that.

"I want to hear that you will include me in the family portrait. You said I didn't want to be in it before, and now I do. So can we get a new one done?"

Mae and Tally exchanged glances with each other before looking at their mother. Gwyn didn't look to my father for an answer. It was clear that she made decisions without talking them over with him. In truth, I didn't care about being in their stupid portrait, but the more they refused, the more I felt myself pulling away from them.

"We will not be doing a new portrait," she said.

"Of course you won't," I snapped.

The woman with star-colored eyes watched me, and for the first time, she smiled at me like she had witnessed something great. Then she disappeared in a blink of an eye.

"I would still like to go to Exile to see for myself that it doesn't exist," I spoke without looking at my father.

"They are all dead, Thea, and Exile does not exist," Jesper was the one to answer this time. "I sent Kizar guards to the Forbidden Wood where you said they were. They found nothing."

"Maybe they didn't go far enough…" I started to argue.

"They found a large oak tree with the X carved into it. But there was no boundary, no homes or buildings, no Exile. I promise, I made them scour the woods for days. It's not there."

Jesper's voice was gentle, like he was trying not to hurt my feelings. All it did was confirm to me that my father was likely lying to me. My father had already said they didn't find anything at all, especially not the tree marked with an

X. If Jesper had found it, then that meant I was there, and Exile had existed at some point.

I dropped the conversation and ate at this realization. No one said a word. My father had been laughing before I joined them, and now the table seemed so tense. Anger returned to me when I realized that they hadn't actually invited me to eat with them. Couldn't they at least have pretended to enjoy my company? They could have acted like they missed me. My darkness raged a war inside of me. It wanted me to explode at them. It wanted me to demand answers, but I also knew that they wouldn't tell me anything if I asked.

"Did I have friends before I disappeared?" I asked. Maybe they could fill in the gaps for me. There were so many things that didn't make sense, and I trusted no one at this table with me.

Mae and Tally laughed like it was the most ridiculous thing they had ever heard. Then the queen laughed at me. Guess that answered that question. I stood up, my darkness not taking their disrespect a second longer. My hands slammed down on the wooden table to silence them. Our glass plates clunked under the force.

They all froze as the swirls on my skin glowed more brightly. Shadows and fire mist swirled around me in an angry cloud. My fire magic burned the imprints of my hands into the top of the table.

"Is there something funny to all of you sitting here about the fact that I can't remember anything?"

No one spoke.

"Why does my own family think it is acceptable to speak to me like this?" I hissed. No one said anything, but just gawked at me. "Answer me!" I yelled so loudly that the guards all lifted their weapons at me. With a flick of my wrist, their weapons evaporated under my fire mist. Fear now laced everyone's faces. It made my darkness happy to see it.

"Thea, you better calm down now," my father tried to sound authoritative, but it made me chuckle.

"How about you stop letting everyone here disrespect me? Is this why the fae in the city believe it's alright to treat me terribly? Because they know my own family does the same."

"Thea..." Jesper started, but I leveled him with a glare that had him shutting up immediately. I gripped my dagger in my hand.

"I suggest you shut your mouth," I warned him.

"You betrayed us!" My father stood and slammed his fists down too.

"You mean I was tricked by Cassius? You even said he enchanted me, and I figured it out and came back. I fought for you, and he killed me! How did I betray you?"

No one said a word. Liars.

"I suggest you guys start showing me respect if you expect me to fight for this kingdom, because I can still decide not to."

I turned from them without another word and left quickly. I needed air and fast. My darkness whispered that I should hurt all of them as I headed away from the castle and to the woods. If everyone here thought I was a monster and they could treat me terribly, then I would give them a real reason too. I didn't make it far before I heard someone moving behind me.

When I turned, my father stood with his guards. I didn't wait for him to say anything before storming away from him. However, it only took a moment before I heard him catch up to me.

"Thea!" His tone demanded that I stop, but I didn't. I honestly didn't care if he was upset. My eyes flickered around for Wisp out of instinct, but I didn't see her. Where was she?

"Thea." He ran ahead to cut me off, and I glanced at him. "Your behavior is uncalled for. The girls were cruel to you, and I assure you I will talk to them. You must understand that we are all in an awkward position. When you disappeared, you were still not on good terms with us. I thought I could just understand that you didn't mean to betray us and that Cassius tricked you. I thought we could move on like it never happened, but obviously there are still resentments. We will do better as your family to forgive you."

"No one here has tried to make me feel welcomed. Why should I want your forgiveness anymore?" I snapped back as my blood ran cold at his words.

"I want to apologize for how your return has been handled," my father sighed. "We have not made this transition easy for you, and I'm aware that we must do better. Please forgive me for not knowing how to support you."

I fumed at his words. I was his daughter, and he did not know how to make me feel welcome.

"There is another reason why I find it difficult to trust you." My father's green eyes glanced over my shoulder as he seemed lost in a memory. "Your mother betrayed me too. I thought she loved me like I loved her, but I didn't know that she was such a cruel and manipulative woman."

I froze at the mention of my mother. I was desperate to learn anything about her.

"What did she do?"

"Your mother promised me an heir so powerful that the realms would never see another with such magic ever again. My biggest fear back then was not having a powerful heir for the throne, so I agreed. I knew of your fire magic, but your mother had bound all your other magic inside of you when you were a child and didn't tell me. She finally confessed when I noticed how tired and sick you seemed. I begged her to set your magic free, but she thought you would use it to kill her. You were angry that it was trapped inside of you. It was so powerful that it needed energy, and the only way it could get it was to take it from you, from your soul."

"Bayla promised that she would take away the binding spell on the blood moon, but when the day came, she was nowhere to be found. I went to find her and stumbled upon the entire coven, slaughtered. Your mother was a blood witch."

A blood witch. I was a witch.

Cassius' words came back to me from when I asked him about the blood bond. *A blood witch showed me once.* He had been talking about me.

"Bayla killed the entire coven and herself so that your magic could never be freed. She cursed you to die young and never reach your potential. I honestly think she was jealous of your power."

My mind mulled over his words. Did my own mother truly do such a terrible thing to me? There was a chance that what he said was true. I couldn't be sure because I didn't know her.

"So, I'm part blood witch?" The phrase made my mouth dry.

My father nodded.

"The last in Elloryon that we are aware of," he sighed as he stopped to look at me.

"How did the spell break? I mean, obviously, I can use all my magic now, so I was somehow freed."

My father's jaw clenched for a moment.

"I hired every witch, healer, and dark magic fae I could find to free you. That is how you met Sybil. She had always been the best healer in Elloryon, but even she couldn't free you. When Cassius killed you, Cerithian armies were moving into Crimson lands for war. I happened to be there just in case Crimson wanted to negotiate, but I stumbled upon Cassius being reprimanded by the gods. When I saw your lifeless body at his feet, I ran to you. I begged them to bring you back. They agreed, and it was then that I asked them to let your magic free, so that you would not be cursed to die young. Thankfully, they agreed to that too."

"Why would they ever agree to bring me back? Fae die all the time. I'm sure I was not the first fae to die at the hands of someone they loved."

"I believe that the god, Mikel, wanted to punish you for loving the wrong man. They felt disappointed that they had gifted you such power, and you almost let it go to waste—all over a man who had betrayed you without a second thought. You have a prophecy tied to you, and it has not been fulfilled yet."

"Why did they not just kill Cassius for what he did to me?" Something wasn't clicking about this.

"Mikel seemed to think this was a better punishment for Cassius. Killing him would simply allow his soul to move on to his next life. That is not a punishment. They said that Exile would be an escape for you to live in until the curse was broken. Mikel said you could have one chance every year to break your curse. If you chose the wrong side to fight for, then you would die and try again until you got it right. This is the first year you've chosen correctly. You didn't choose Cassius."

My father reached over and squeezed my hand to comfort me. I wanted to rip my hand from his, but I kept my composure so that he didn't realize his slip-up. He just admitted that the gods sent me to Exile. He accidentally let the truth slip out, and my darkness clawed to get out of me and punish him. I would destroy him and his kingdom if I found out all of this had been a lie. The thought made my darkness settle down. A sense of calm overtook me; I finally felt like I knew that Leer was not lying to me. My father was the liar, and it felt good to know that.

"I have another confession." My father frowned. "Gwyn and the girls have never liked you, but that is completely my fault. I hope you do not think lowly of me when I admit I was already married to Gwyn when your mother approached me. Gwyn had been having difficulty conceiving an heir. Your mother knew that it was a weakness of the kingdom, and she exploited it. It was a lapse of judgment on my part, but I do not regret it because it gave me you."

I didn't say anything. Words escaped me as I tried to process everything that my father was saying.

As I glanced at his saddened features, I felt nothing. My darkness practically gagged at his fake love and false concern painted on his face. I swallowed down all the nasty insults I wanted to hurl at him. My mind mulled over my father's words and his slip-up.

"We will try better," he promised. "I try not to blame you for falling for Cassius' lies because I know that you didn't mean to. I've let Gwyn and the girls treat you poorly for my own mistakes. I will be a better father this time,

Thea. I will repair all the damage both Cassius and I have caused you."

"Why are you telling me all of this?"

My father turned and looked me straight in the eyes.

"Because I'm worried that we are messing this up. I do not want to lose you again. Despite what your mother did, I loved her. You are the only piece of her I have left." There was a real sadness that swirled in his green eyes. I didn't say anything back to him.

He turned slowly and began walking back up the path. I watched him retreat toward the castle, but I didn't follow right away. A heavy sigh escaped me as he disappeared from my sight, and I allowed my darkness to creep out of me.

Wisp was there suddenly. She floated around me with her black flames. Something dangerous swirled inside of me as I accepted that my father was a liar. Knowing this new information allowed my emotions to calm a bit and my heart to slow down. Wisp turned white as I started for the castle, and when I glanced at her, she flickered closer to me.

"My father made a big mistake, Wisp. He just admitted that Exile was real when, before, he was so adamant that it had never existed." I sighed and muttered to her, "It looks like I'm going to Exile."

CHAPTER 8

I waited in my room until an ungodly hour of the night. I did not bother attending the event my father had invited me to, and I burned the hideous dress the maid gave me for it. No one in my family came to see if I was coming. No one apologized to me. I doubted my father talked to the girls. But it wasn't going to be my problem any longer. Anticipation coursed through me.

My father was lying, and I was going to prove it.

I wasn't sure if his whole story was a lie or if there was another reason that he wanted me to forget about Exile. Either way, tonight I would find out the truth.

Standing, I slipped on my dark green cloak and strapped my daggers to me. Exile was my destination, and afterward, I didn't think I would return to Cerithia. My thoughts have run wild since this morning. I realized I would not care if I ever saw these fae again. But I would care if I never saw Sybil and the twins.

I glanced around the shitty room and felt nothing but a need to leave this kingdom. Quickly, I headed out of the room and up the stairs. I took my time sneaking out so no guards would see me, but there were no guards in the halls as I slipped through, which was odd. It was too late for the party to be going on, so they shouldn't have been busy elsewhere.

Something in my instincts told me I needed to hurry up and get far from here.

Kaida was happy to see me when I finally made it to the stables. My hand glided over the length of her face before I froze. An odd noise outside caught my attention. Harsh whispering in the dark was moving closer to the stables. I kneeled behind the low wall and waited. Perhaps it was just guards on night duty.

"I saw her run in here," a man whispered.

My body tensed when I realized they were out there looking for me.

"She's going to kill us before we can take her."

"No, she won't," the other argued. By the sounds of their feet, I could tell it was more than two, but no one else was talking.

"Her horse is still here, so maybe she snuck around and kept going to the woods."

I stilled my breathing. It was as if Kaida knew I was in danger and sensed my need for her calmness. She was so nonchalant that she would not attract attention, and her body blocked mine from view. My scalp prickled as I held my breath in order to hear them speak.

It was then that Wisp appeared next to me, her flames burning a bright red. She was warning me I was in danger, but I already knew that. Wisp floated toward me and flashed an array of colors.

I know. I mouthed at her. It's not like I can run out of here. Kaida's ears flattened, letting me know someone was close to me. A moment later, a guard dressed in green popped their head into the stall, locking eyes with me. Before he could speak, my fire shot out and silenced him forever.

"She's here," one of them yelled. I darted.

Moving through the stables, I fled through the back door and into the woods on foot. Wisp floated in front of me, leading me somewhere. I followed her blindly because I couldn't see shit in the darkened forest.

The sounds of heavy footsteps alerted me to the fact that the guards were running behind me. I shot my fire out behind me without knowing where they were in the dark. Their pained screams let me know I hit at least a few of them. All of a sudden, Wisp stopped moving. Her red flames froze, and it made my chest tighten. When I turned around, a small dagger flew quickly at me. Luckily, it barely nicked my arm, but it burned violently.

I continued to run, but my body hummed with something foreign. Fuck. Fuck. Fuck. My magic was retreating inside of me, and I knew this wasn't good. Wisp kept leading the way, but I had to stop. My forehead was damp with a sudden fever that was kicking my ass.

"I can't keep going," I groaned as I leaned over and threw up. Spots overtook my vision. "I don't feel right."

"It's just a little sleepy powder to make you weak." A guard dressed in green appeared beside me. His eyes glanced at me oddly.

"What do you want from me?" I snapped. How did these Falgon guards get close enough to our castle without being caught?

"I was just told to take you." He glanced over at me before looking away. His eyes landed on the other guards coming, and he kneeled down. "Don't worry, you won't suffer for long."

His words were fuzzy at best. I willed myself to focus on him, but it was difficult with the spots in front of my eyes.

My darkness burst out for a brief moment, but it faded before it could kill the guard in front of me.

"Why?" I choked out.

"To start a war, of course," he smiled down at me as I passed out.

★★☽★★

"Crimson's army is breaking through the barriers we had set up as defenses."

My eyes shifted to Kaz. I sighed heavily to control my irritation, but everyone knew I was mad. It was no use trying to hide it. I had just come from the front lines of the battle. I knew how bad it was.

"I know this already. So why did you pull me from the battle for this mediocre news?" I hissed. Someone joined Kaz, but my anger was too focused on him to make note of who it was.

"We found out where he is," he said. I stopped glaring and looked around. I had been waiting to hear these words for seven months. For seven months, this man has caused problems for my men.

"Where is he?"

"Headed toward Cerithia," Kaz spoke confidently. "Leading the army to the castle, we believe."

"Perfect." I smiled as I put my armor back on and hopped on Kaida, racing toward my father's land. Kaz and Kai flanked my sides. I would need them. The captain of Crimson's guard was unstoppable. My men were dying as the man killing them barely lifted his sword to do so. He had to

have powerful magic. Perhaps it was elite magic. My power, my magic could outdo his. Of this, I was certain. I would be the end of the Crimson King's army.

I smiled as I raced through the forests of my homeland. I knew this place better than anyone in this damned realm. I glanced behind me and saw dozens of my warriors following. If I took out the captain, we could push back into Crimson's land and take it over.

After riding for some time, we came to a clearing. I paused at the silence of the forest. It was not right. Not even the birds sang. I held up my hand, and everyone stilled as my eyes scanned the forest across the field. I smiled when I saw them waiting. Even though the sun was setting, I could make out their silhouettes.

Kai looked at me as I shifted my eyes to the clearing edge. A soft whisper moved through my warriors as they prepared for battle. My eyes narrowed when I saw their captain. He wore all black and stood taller than any of the others behind him. I couldn't make out anything else, though, with the armor helmet on.

I led my army. I was always the first to ride onto the battlefield and was usually the last to leave. I was not a coward. My horse was faster than most, but I was surprised when the captain of Crimson's army met me in the middle of the field.

He and I clashed a second before our men did. The sound of swords and armor rang in the cold night air. Magic erupted from some, but not all. My eyes were trained on the captain; he was my only target. My latest mission was to kill him so that I could go about taking the Crimson Kingdom for Cerithia and ending their miserable royal bloodline.

Their captain had struck first, his sword coming down at an angle I wasn't expecting. What an odd technique, I thought. I struck back just as quick, and we both fell off our horses. Our swords fell out of our hands, but before he could get to his, I tackled him to the ground. Our fists connected against each other's armor. I grunted in pain when he slid a dagger into my shoulder.

"Fuck!" I yelled at the sneaky little bastard.

I reached up and yanked the dagger out, then turned it and plunged it into his leg before standing. His scream was drowned out by the clashing around us. He ripped the dagger from his leg as he stood and held it tightly. Impressive. I didn't have time to look out at my men, although I desperately wanted to know how we were faring against the best of Crimson's men.

The captain tossed the dagger at me so hard and fast that I had to use my magic to stop it before it plunged into my neck. For fuck's sake. When I went to turn the dagger toward him, he ran at me and kicked me to the ground. I swept my leg out and knocked him down next to me. I tried to get him pinned beneath me, but he was too quick and strong.

I went to stand, but suddenly he had me pinned with his magic—shadow magic.

"We have the battlefield, captain," someone had said next to him. I glanced around and saw a few of my men retreating into the woods. Damn them.

"Have the men start clearing the dead, Kace." The captain's voice was deep and pleasant.

His magic held me tightly, but I was just biding my time. I could break free from this. I watched as he lifted my dagger off the ground and stared at the viper handle for a long moment. His armor prevented me from seeing his face, but I could feel his eyes on me. In the space of a heartbeat, I was standing up, and the captain of Crimson stood in front of me. He wasted no time reaching for my helmet and sliding it off.

"A woman?" One of the soldiers looked at me with confusion, then back to his captain.

"Where is Cerithia's captain?" my captor asked softly.

"I am Cerithia's captain," I snapped with as much anger as I could muster. My blue uniform was bloodied and dirty, but I stared at him proudly as his shadows swirled around me.

"Impossible. Armies do not have women soldiers."

"Well, then the king of Cerithia must win an award for allowing such equality." My anger was now directed toward my father for making me do this. He hadn't even acknowledged how well I had done in the past few months. Now here I was, being sneered at by the enemy.

He whispered something to the large man next to him, who scurried off quickly.

"Take off your helmet and show me your face before you kill me, you coward," I demanded with as much authority as I could spit out. He laughed. The bastard laughed at me, but his hands slipped off his helmet.

"Is this better?" he asked as he gave me a cocky smirk.

It certainly was not better. I had expected a troll, not—this. His golden eyes held amusement in them as I was trapped against my will in his shadows. His dark hair was chaotic from battle, and his smooth skin glistened with sweat. His jaw was dusted in dark stubble from a few days of not shaving, and my eyes drifted to his strong lips that parted as he gave me a smile.

"Do you like what you see?" His voice held no malice for me. It was more curious than anything. I snapped my jaw shut as I realized that I had been gawking at the enemy.

"Get on with it, prick," I scoffed.

My attitude only made his smile bigger. He took one step toward me without breaking eye contact. I didn't fear dying, and I had no one who would mourn me. The realm would continue tomorrow as if I had never existed in it.

"How long have you been the captain of the guard?"

I stayed silent and did not answer him. His golden eyes watched me thoughtfully. Something was unsettling in the way he looked at me, like I was fascinating. Perhaps he was in shock that I was a female captain. I decided to answer him just so he would stop watching me so closely.

"A few months." Seven, to be exact.

He nodded like he was thinking my answer over in his mind.

"So, you are the reason why Cerithia's guard has improved significantly in their strategy over the past six months?"

It was a compliment, even if he didn't intend for it to be one. I wasn't going to answer him, though. He just stared at me for a long moment before saying anything.

"The real question is, princess, why did your father enlist you in his guard?"

My heart began to beat wildly in my chest. He knew who I was. My eyes narrowed at him. How did he know that when my father and the queen did their best to hide it from other kingdoms? I was under the impression that they did not know of my existence. After all, my father did not accept me as his daughter; therefore, I was not important.

"I'm no princess," I spat, seething at the title.

"You are unlike any princess I have ever met," he smirked when I huffed at the title. "Did you volunteer?"

His eyes looked over me like he was truly confused, as if he wanted to know about me.

"It was a punishment."

He gave me a knowing smile, like he knew I must be a troublemaker.

"It must have been pretty bad," he muttered as he looked over his shoulder. His men were gathering their dead. My eyes followed his, and I watched them gently move my men to the side. Respectful. It was an odd gesture. "You can come to Crimson and fight for me."

"I would stab you the first chance you gave me. I'm no traitor."

"I have no doubt about you stabbing me." A glint in his eye told me he found my answer to be exactly what he expected. "Something tells me that you would be happier fighting with me rather than against me."

He had stepped forward, so we were only inches apart. I would not find this man attractive. A strong scent of rain and forest filled the space around me.

"I would treat you so well, Thea." My name flicked off his tongue like a wicked promise. Urgency filled me; I needed to be away from this man before I forgot he was my enemy. My

chest swarmed with something, like a restless itch that only this man could scratch.

As soon as he turned to look at his men again, I let my fire mist surround me and rip apart his shadows. The captain turned as soon as I freed myself and just stared at me as my tendrils of fire wrapped around him and made him hit the ground on his back. I straddled him as he struggled. His eyes blackened as he stared at me.

I grabbed my viper-handled dagger and held it to his throat. He wasn't trying to escape. I could practically feel his eyes tracing over every inch of me. Why didn't he fear me?

"Fire magic, I forgot," he breathed. He growled when I pushed my dagger harder against his neck.

"Impressive, isn't it?" I smiled wickedly at him. "Any last words, Captain?"

He looked me in the eyes as his own eyes swirled with black and gold. He gave me a lazy smile, as if he thought I wouldn't slice his throat. I'm sure that smile had gotten him out of plenty of situations, but I wouldn't hesitate to kill him.

"I don't think you want to hurt me, little viper."

I pulled my dagger back slightly as he stared at me oddly. No, this couldn't be him. I put my dagger against his throat again. That tugging in my chest only became more intense as I looked down at him.

"How do you know that name?"

"Because I gave it to you." He tried shifting. "You stabbed me in the stomach with this same dagger," he said, chuckling like this was funny. "A dagger that I gifted you, by the way."

My eyes looked over his face, and somehow I knew he was telling the truth. I found this dagger in the woods one day when I was much younger. I thought it had been good luck, but this made more sense. He gave it to me. The hooded man from my past was now my enemy. Why had he saved me that night? My hand reached up and ran across his stubble without me thinking about it.

His eyes stared at me for a long moment, distracting me from my mission. I shook my head, trying to clear it. After all, it was my duty to kill any of the Crimson guards, but even as I thought about it, my dagger fell from his throat.

"You never came back," I frowned.

"Did you miss me, little viper?" he frowned back as I stood up and looked down at him. I turned away and ran into the forest, confusion filling me. When I was far enough away, I released my fire magic from him. Gods, when I fucked up, I fucked up big. Oddly enough, I felt the stirring in my chest get worse the farther I ran from the man with haunting golden eyes.

CHAPTER 9

My eyes cracked open slightly. It was still nighttime, but I was no longer in the woods I had been in when I lost consciousness. It was impossible to tell how much time had passed. Minutes? Hours? I closed my eyes tightly as I lay bound on the hard ground. I didn't want to tip off the men that I was coming out of whatever they had drugged me with.

"This is not a good idea," one of them said in a panic. "What if Cassius sees us? He will rip our limbs from our bodies." The mention of Cassius' name had my heart pounding instantly.

"He won't see us. It's the middle of the night." The one who picked me up in the woods sighed, annoyed.

"Something doesn't feel right about this. Thea was never cruel to us," the first man spoke again.

"Get a grip on yourself. We've already done it. It's too late."

I held my breath as I waited for them to keep talking, but they didn't for a while. I could hear them walking around as if they were looking for something.

"How are they going to think we're Falgon guards if they don't see us kill her?"

"Because your dead body will be lying next to hers, and you'll be in Falgon colors," the one in charge laughed, but a moment later I heard a dagger ripping through flesh. The sound of the man's dead body hitting the ground close to me made my magic simmer.

"What the fuck?" another guard questioned.

"Someone had to be sacrificed. Besides, it was clear he felt bad for the Crimson whore."

My heart hammered in my chest, but I did not dare move. My magic was starting to come back slowly; I just needed a few minutes for it to get stronger.

"Drag her over here," the one in charge ordered.

Someone grabbed my arms and started dragging me across the hard ground, but dropped me abruptly. I almost opened my eyes to see why, but I got my answer a moment later.

"What do we have here?" Cassius' voice was undeniable.

It had felt like a lifetime since I heard his deep voice. I had forgotten how it instantly soothed me and made me feel warm all over. My eyes closed tightly, remembering the last time I heard him was when he was so cruel to me. It made my insides burn with both anger and sadness. But more than that, it was comforting, and that pissed me off more.

"We were just leaving you a little gift," the Falgon guard sneered, then sighed in mock sadness. "Now you can watch us kill your whore."

I had to fight my instincts to lash out and keep him from killing me, but something held me there. I didn't dare move. My need to understand why Cassius was here overcame my need to live for a moment. My breathing froze completely as I waited to hear what Cassius would say. It felt like an eternity before he finally spoke.

"You aren't Falgon guards," Cassius accused. "I know every Falgon guard, and you do not belong to them. So what kingdom are you from?"

"Falgon," the man declared, but less confidently this time.

Cassius spoke. "I know you aren't from Falgon. Valor would never betray me like this." He paused for a moment. "Let me rephrase that. Valor knows I would rip his body into tiny pieces and feed them to his own mother if he were to ever harm Thea. So, try again."

The guard scoffed in indignation. My insides twisted at Cassius' words.

"It doesn't matter. Are you going to come over here and stop us?" the guard laughed. "You can't cross the border into Cerithia until the curse is broken, you start a war, or you are invited by the royal family."

Cassius didn't say anything, but I could hear enough movement that I knew he was doing something. The crunching of the dirt beneath the guards' shoes let me know that they had moved in front of me, toward Cassius' voice.

"I do not need to cross the boundary to kill all of you," his voice dripped with hatred. "Let Thea go."

I opened my eyes, and they adjusted to the darkness quickly. I could see Cassius' own golden eyes watching me, and I saw relief take over his features when I slowly started standing. Gods, he looked better than I remembered.

"You would die before you could kill all of us; she is ours now," the same guard snarled, not letting any of the other guards get a word in. Suddenly, my darkness surged forward, my magic returning to full strength. Not only could I feel it was upset that I had been taken, but I could also feel it was upset because Cassius was being threatened. I chose to ignore that hard truth for now.

Cassius smiled so brightly at me that it actually made the confusion in my mind lift for a moment. Gods, I hadn't felt anything other than anger, hurt, and betrayal in so long that this new feeling felt so foreign yet so good.

More than anything, pain clung to me. It radiated from me because I didn't know if he was only pretending to care for me. Was he trying to trick me again?

"Don't worry, it's not me you have to worry about," he frowned at whatever he saw in my eyes. Suddenly, Wisp was there. She twirled around him, her color a vibrant green. "Thea has always been strong enough to save herself."

It took the five guards only a moment for Cassius' words to sink in. They all turned, and their fear instantly wrapped around me, sweeter than anything I had tasted in a while. It made my darkness hum with anticipation. They reached for their weapons, but before they could even grasp the handles, my fire exploded out of me. Maybe because Cassius was here, or maybe I had lost my mind, but with the release of my magic, I let my darkness take over.

Like the blood in my veins, it coursed through every inch of me, seeping completely into my bones and flesh. It dug its claws into me with such a beautiful pain that I knew it wouldn't let me go for a long time, if ever at all. The marks on my skin glowed brightly, and my vision pulsed red as I stared down the men. All of them shrank away from me, and I chuckled softly. This only made their fear worse.

"You really shouldn't have done this," I said softly. My own voice sounded somehow off—somehow not myself. "Who sent you?"

"Fuck you, Crimson whore," the blonde one spit at me.

I moved so fast that he didn't even have a chance to blink before I was in front of him, driving his own dagger into his stomach. Our faces were only a foot apart as I smiled and ripped my dagger upward through his flesh. The light vanished from his eyes as soon as my blade pierced his heart.

"I don't care much for that nickname," I smirked as he fell over, but another guard was already running at me before the first guard had even hit the ground.

I turned and ducked from his violent swing, plunging my dagger into his throat. The gurgling sound he made had my darkness happy. As his body slid off my blade, I turned to face the last three men, covered in the blood of their comrades. One of them took a step backwards at the sight of me. Smart move, but it was too late to let them go. My darkness wanted vengeance for what they did to me. With a single thought, my fire mist exploded from me and wrapped up the one that tried to run. Then my darkness stepped in and took hold of my fire magic, tightening the grip I had on him until his body exploded from the pressure.

"For the love of the gods!" one of the men cried out at the sight of me as I slowly turned my red eyes toward him. Blood dripped from me, but it wasn't mine. I was bored of fighting them, so I flicked my hand and watched their bodies instantly evaporate from my fire. Once they were dead, I took a deep breath and tried to gain control of myself. I felt a strong resistance as my darkness refused to yield.

It dug itself even deeper into me as I felt it frantically looking for something. As soon as I turned and saw Cassius staring at me, my darkness calmed a bit and hummed in satisfaction, like it had found what it had been searching for. Seeing him was like a fever dream—unreal and delirious. As I stalked slowly toward him, he didn't even flinch at the sight of me. My darkness suddenly lashed out of me and wrapped Cassius tightly in the dark tendrils of its magic.

I stared at him, hating the fact that he wasn't showing any fear that I would kill him, yet confused by the absolute joy in his eyes as he looked at me. My head cocked to the side as he watched me, like I was the best thing he could be looking at right now.

"Aren't you scared?" I asked him.

He watched me for a silent moment. It was then that I realized my darkness was not angry. It was not wanting to hurt him at all, and that fucked with my mind. My darkness was happy to see him. It almost felt relieved at the sight of him.

"Of you?" His voice broke through the confusion of my darkness. My eyes stared into his. "You terrify the fuck out of me, little viper."

His words were not full of hate or worry.

"Why can't I feel your fear?"

"You won't kill me, Thea. Your mind might not remember us, but your heart and soul do, and they would never allow you to do it." Wisp appeared in a dark green flame as she saw Cassius.

"Unfortunately for you, I no longer possess a heart."

His handsome face frowned at my words, but they were true. I was empty. Inside of me was dark, tainted, and destroyed by what he did.

A noise in the distance caught my attention. Cassius seemed to hear it too, because his eyes shifted to the tree line where horses were approaching us quickly.

"Looks like your kingdom has come to rescue you," he spoke with venom. When I glanced over my shoulder, I could see both Cerithia and Kizar guards coming. "Let me guess, you are hopelessly in love with Jesper now."

For reasons unknown to me, my anger expanded at the sight of them. I ignored his jab and turned to focus on him again. I willed my darkness to hurt him, but it refused, just like he had said it would. I tried again, harder this time, but nothing happened. With irritation, I let him go. He fell to the ground and looked at me.

"You didn't kill me."

"No, but make no mistake—I will the next time we cross paths. I want to take my time with you, Cassius. I want to elicit the same pain you did in me, and that will take hours."

The horses were getting closer to us. He stared at me with his bright golden eyes and his chaotic dark hair. I didn't want him to mistake this for me giving a fuck about him.

"Consider this a promise of what's to come," I snapped as I gripped my viper-handled dagger and flung it at him. Cassius didn't move. He didn't try to stop the blade like I knew he could have. He grunted harshly when it hit his shoulder. He fell to one knee, his breathing coming out in short, choppy gasps as he grabbed the blade and pulled it from himself.

"You can cross over and come back to Crimson," he spoke in an exhausted voice as he tossed my dagger back to this side of the boundary. "I will let you do whatever you need to if you come back with me. I will take your anger. I will take your hatred. Yell at me, curse me, or stab me if you want, but do not close me out anymore. This is the worst torture you could give me, my love. Being so close to you without being able to have you."

"Crimson is not my home, and I will not believe a word from your mouth ever again."

His golden eyes dimmed. My heart was pounding out of control in my chest. I needed to be away from him before I fell for his pretty lies again.

"Did you do this? Did you have them kidnap me and bring me to you?"

"No."

"How did you know we'd be here?"

"A friend tipped me off, and I came as fast as I could."

A frown tilted his handsome face as I stared. My mind was trying to understand why we, my darkness and I, didn't kill him when we had a chance.

"Why bother coming here?" I hissed.

"Because I am a moth, and you are my flame. I cannot stay away."

I scoffed.

The sound of men talking in the distance had me glancing over my shoulder. The Cerithian guards were almost here.

"I'm sorry to do this to you, little viper."

His warning was too late for me to do anything. As I turned, he wrapped his shadows around me and yanked me over the border with him. Cassius held out his hand in front of me before blowing powder into my face.

"I'll fucking kill you," I promised as my eyes struggled to stay open. Cassius' shadows swarmed around us. His golden eyes stared into mine without failure. He brushed my braid over my shoulder before his shadows disappeared. A moment later, we were inside the Crimson Castle.

"What did you do?" The king's voice sounded panicked when he saw me. "Cassius, have you lost your fucking mind?"

Cassius scoffed.

"I couldn't stop myself," he sighed as my eyes finally closed, and I passed out.

CHAPTER 10

My eyes fluttered open slowly. Fragments of what had happened came crashing down around me, and I sat up quickly. I gasped when I realized I was in Cassius' bed and immediately tried to stand up. The weight of the chain around my wrists is what I noticed first. This prick kidnapped me and chained me to his bed like some kind of ogre. I growled in anger and pulled as hard as I could, but they were attached too strongly. Frustrated, I gave up pulling, and instead, I tested to see how far I could go. The chains let me roam the room freely, but I couldn't go any farther than that.

My darkness sat inside of me, seemingly content despite the predicament we found ourselves in. I couldn't fathom why it was not full of the white-hot rage I was used to. A noise by the bedroom door startled me. Cassius was leaning against the door frame, arms crossed, and watching me.

"You're awake."

"And you're a dead man walking," I sneered.

Cassius smiled brightly at me.

"I've missed your bad attitude, my love."

I said nothing. Whatever his plan was here, I would not engage with it. Turning from him, I sat on the edge of the bed. I hoped he came closer so I could snap his neck.

"Food is being prepared for you. Do you need anything else?"

I ignored him, and after a moment of silence, his soft chuckle disappeared down the hallway. My mind was calm as I sat in a room that felt both comforting and familiar.

That pissed me off. I should be raging. I stood and started pacing around the space. What was he planning on doing with me?

It wasn't long until Cassius appeared in the doorway again, this time with a large tray of food. He used his shadows to move it to the bed, like he knew I would attack him if he stepped foot in here.

"What are you doing?" I snapped. "Planning on killing me once and for all?"

My words made him flinch, as if I had slapped him. Cassius rubbed the back of his neck.

"I didn't really think. I was just thinking of you leaving and going back to Cerithia. It was too much to bear. So, I don't know, I took you." He shrugged.

My eyes flickered at Wisp floating by him in her happy, dark green flames. I didn't say anything to him for a moment.

"You know I am going to kill you the first chance I get, right?"

"I would expect nothing less," he said, giving me a sad smile. "Call for me if you need anything."

"You are the last fae I would call for anything."

Cassius' golden eyes dimmed, but he left me alone. Wisp floated outside of the room. I picked up the bread from my tray and threw it at her.

"Glad to know that you were never on my side."

Her flames turned white, but I turned my back to her and sat down on the bed.

Did my family know that Cassius had me? I'm sure they would find out once they reached the border and I was gone. Shit. The guards were in Falgon uniforms. They would probably send guards to Falgon to rescue me, not Crimson. I pushed the plate of food off the bed, making a mess on the floor, before crawling under the covers.

I hated how the blankets smelled of Cassius, yet I wanted nothing more than to breathe in his scent. Flustered,

I sighed heavily and sat up in the bed, glancing at the doorway. No one was there, but I could hear faint talking from somewhere close by. I stood and walked toward the doorway, trying to hear the conversation, but it was useless.

I tried to clear my mind but couldn't move my gaze from the bed. Flashes of Cassius and I together plagued me. Gods, this was fucking torture. Tearing my gaze away, I started pacing around the room, wondering what Cassius wanted from me.

"I see you didn't want the food." His voice stopped me in my tracks. I turned to see him standing at the doorway, just out of reach. His eyes glanced over me as if he were looking for wounds before they found my own. My chest ached at the sight of him. This was not how I expected to see him for the first time after his betrayal. A flash of stabbing him back made me flinch and look away.

"So, you did plan the kidnapping," I sighed.

"No. I told you I was tipped off by a friend."

I forced myself to look at him again because I didn't want him to know that he held any power over me. Would he enchant me again, or would he use whatever dark magic he had to trick me?

"You haven't come to kill me yet; why?" His question confused me.

"It isn't because I didn't want to. My father didn't think I was ready," I sighed. "I can kill you now if you'd unchain me and let my magic free."

Cassius glanced at the chains and smiled, like he knew something I didn't. Gods, he was too handsome for a man who murdered me.

"Maybe your father is scared to have you close to me," he smirked.

"Why would that scare him?" Would he admit that he would enchant me?

"Because you might remember me and decide you made the wrong choice in the clearing."

"I didn't." I crossed my arms and watched him closely. My darkness still couldn't feel any fear from him, and I couldn't understand why. "My father knows my loyalties lie with him."

Cassius' eyes flashed black as he straightened up, clenching his fists.

"I'm more interested in knowing if you let that little weasel, Jesper, manipulate you into having feelings for him."

It was my turn to stand tall and glare.

"Fuck you."

"You have, many times, my love." Cassius gave me a smug smile.

"You are a bastard!"

"So I've been told." He took a step toward me.

I stepped back away from him. He watched me move away and kept coming closer, but I matched each forward step of his with a back step of my own, causing him to pause and frown.

"Have you had more memories of us?"

"No," I lied. "Even if I did, I know none of it was true. I know the truth of what happened."

Cassius chuckled loudly before looking at me.

"No, you don't." He stepped forward again, but I had nowhere else to go. I was pushed against the wall. "You want to know how I know you don't know the truth?" Another step forward. My heart raced as he stalked me like prey. "Because you would be here, in Crimson and with me, if you knew the truth. You would be sleeping in our bed tonight. You would be begging me to touch you just how you like. You would be calling out my name to the stars to let them know who owns your body, Thea."

I pressed my thighs together, refusing to let him see the effects his dirty mouth had on me.

"You are fucking delusional."

"And your breathing is heavy, and your eyes are turning black, Thea. You like when I say things like this to you."

I snapped my mouth shut. He stepped forward again, so he was only about a foot from me.

"Do you really think you can stay away from me?" he demanded an answer. He leaned down so we were eye level, his arms caging me against the wall. "If you want me, you can have me," his voice dripped like honey in my ears.

My eyes bounced between his. All the words he spoke in the clearing that day crashed down around me, and I burst into tears. He was tricking me again, or was he? My overwhelmed mind and heart couldn't tell the difference anymore. My heart thought he might mean these words, but my brain told me he didn't.

"My love..." Cassius tilted my chin up to meet his eyes.

I tore my face from his grasp, crying out, "I know you enchanted me into believing that you actually loved me, and I know that is what you are doing now. I know why you want the bloodstone, and I will never give it to you. I would rather die with no memories than remember what you did to me."

Cassius stumbled back, as if my words slapped him.

"Why do you think I want your bloodstone?"

My bloodstone? It belonged to my father.

"To free you from your curse."

Cassius' eyes widened.

"My curse," he muttered. "Who told you that?" His brows furrowed.

"My father."

"I see." He looked at me again, although now with no emotion. "And you believe everything the King of Cerithia tells you?"

"I believe him more than I believe you."

Cassius stared at me for a long moment before he turned and left the room without a word. I waited for him to come back, but he didn't. Hours went by, and I lay in his bed, staring at the ceiling.

Late into the night, I turned to my side, trying to stay awake. I let out a startled scream, jumping up from the bed. The woman with star-colored eyes was standing in the room, watching me. Her dress was a dark crimson red this time. I closed my eyes and shook my head.

"You aren't real," I whispered. "What is wrong with me?"

"Well, for starters, you talk to yourself a lot." The woman's voice was soft, like a melody. My eyes snapped open, and I looked at her.

"You've been watching me; why?" I looked at the woman closely. "If Cassius sent you, then you can fuck off."

She smiled. Gods, she was beautiful. Her black hair was in loose waves, and her star-colored eyes shone brightly against her dark skin.

"Cassius doesn't know I'm here."

"So, he knows who you are?" I questioned.

"Yes," she sighed.

"What do you want?" I stood straight to show her I wasn't scared of her. Her eyes took in my new stance, and she gave me a small smile.

"I want you to break your curse, so I'm here."

"Do I know you? Why would you care about me?"

The woman watched me carefully before taking a hesitant step away from me. I couldn't sense fear from her, but I was wearing magic-binding cuffs, so I couldn't tell. After studying her face for a moment, though, I realized that she looked... scared of me.

"My name is Ardella, but you may call me Della if you'd like." Her name sounded familiar, but I could not remember why. I could tell she was watching me for any sort of reaction to her name. When I didn't give one, she continued. "I'm the goddess who is responsible for your curse."

Her confession had me frozen in my spot. Everything around me seemed to stop as her words sank into me.

"You're the goddess who cursed me?"

"Well, my brother did, but it was my fault," she said with a frown.

It didn't matter that she was a goddess; I charged at her. All the anger I had been harboring about my life escaped me. How could she be so fucking cruel to me? I launched at her, but she disappeared a moment before I would have tackled her. Instead, I hit the floor, knocking the wind from myself. Fuck. I groaned as I stared at the ceiling from my back. Della peered over me.

"Cassius warned me that you would try to kick my ass if I told you who I was. I guess I should have listened." She smiled. "I see why you and Cassius work so well together."

"How could you do this to me? Why did I deserve such a cruel fate?"

Her smile disappeared.

"It was not intentional," she said, reaching out to help me up. I grabbed her hand and sat on the bed with her. "I'm trying to right my wrongs, but unfortunately, my brother tied my tongue with magic. I cannot tell you any-thing directly."

I sat silent for a moment, allowing this news to slowly sink in. "What did I do to your brother to make him do this?"

"Nothing. He was only taking his anger out on you. It is me he is angry with. I did an unforgivable thing, and

I fear I destroyed anything compassionate about Mikel." Della glanced around the room. "What Cassius did in the clearing that day triggered Mikel, and he refused to look at the situation without thinking of his own trauma. His emotions overwhelmed him, and he reacted by making stupid decisions," she sighed before continuing. "And now there is no way to take it back."

"I'm guessing you won't be telling me who I should believe among all of these liars."

"I wish I could, but part of breaking your curse is you making that choice freely." Della glanced over at me again. "If I could go back in time and change what happened that day, I would."

"Well, I don't feel close to understanding anything. Every interaction I have with my family and Cassius only confuses me more."

"I can't imagine," she frowned. We sat in silence, both of us seeming to be lost in our own minds. Della glanced at me.

"You have a prophecy to fulfill; do you know what side you are fighting for?"

Her star-colored eyes stared into me, like she was trying to communicate some unspoken words with me.

"Obviously Cerithia." I held up the chains on my wrists. "Why did you come here?"

She frowned. "Cassius was not supposed to take you, and I wanted to make sure you knew you needed to return to Cerithia."

"So, Cerithia is the right choice?" I found this truth disappointing, but I refused to acknowledge why I felt that way.

"I did not say that. You must go back so that the prophecy will happen. Cassius wants to explain things, but you are not in a space where you will listen, and you won't be until you are in Cerithia learning the truth of all of this." As the words left her mouth, there was a sadness that filled her face.

Della reached over and gripped my hand tightly in hers.

I felt tears at the corners of my eyes as I told her, "But I feel so confused about everything. Nothing makes sense."

"I can't tell you anything except that Cerithia holds truths that you have not discovered yet. The pieces will start falling into place, I promise. But I don't think you will truly make the right choice until you learn what secrets Cerithia holds." She stood up, like she was about to leave. "I must go before my brother knows I'm meddling. I will continue to try and get memories through, but it's difficult. You can head back to Cerithia anytime you want."

I held up my chains.

"Kind of hard to do that."

Della chuckled, which confused me.

"You haven't even tried to escape, have you? Cassius would never lock you up. The chains you're wearing are not magic-binding. You can leave as soon as you decide to."

My cheeks heated at this truth. I hadn't tried to leave.

Della turned around but paused. The air filled with thick tension as she turned back toward me.

"I am sorry for the pain you will endure, but I have no doubt that you will succeed no matter how hard the circumstances are. You are strong, like your mother."

I opened my mouth, but she disappeared.

I was left alone, staring blankly at the wall. When I shifted on the bed, the chains rattled, and I held up my hands. I could feel my darkness swirling inside of me alongside my fire magic, but it did not feel suffocated.

I brought forth my inner heat, causing the chains to slowly melt from my skin and drip onto the bed, leaving molten pools of metal behind to harden. I kept my mind on the task at hand and refused to explore the idea of why I hadn't thought to try using my magic. Slowly, I stood up and cautiously walked out of the room, expecting to see guards watching me. Surprisingly, there were none. It was going to be incredibly easy to escape. I knew that guards lined the horse stables, so escaping on foot was my only option. My heart pounded, and anxiety laced my insides as I made my way out of the castle and into the surrounding wilderness. My lungs burned with determination to get back to Cerithia, but not because I missed it. No, I wanted to break my curse. And Cerithia was the first step to doing that. I needed to fulfill the prophecy so I could make sense of my life.

Flashes of Cassius' sad gaze earlier entered my mind unbidden, which made my feet slow down. I couldn't understand why he took me or why he wouldn't bind my magic. Was he not scared of me at all? Suddenly, Wisp appeared in front of me as if she were trying to stop me, but I ran right through her vaporous form.

In the distance, I heard Cassius yelling for me. I could feel my darkness suffering as it begged for me to turn around, but Della's words swarmed my mind. I needed to go back to Cerithia and learn the truths I missed. So, I kept running.

Chapter II

It took days of traveling, but I finally made it back. I never thought I would feel happy about seeing Cerithia's castle until that very moment. I was exhausted. Sweat drenched my clothes, and my feet were blistered from running. What did my family think had happened to me?

A guard appeared in front of me as soon as I stepped through the tree line, staggering to the gate in the wall of the castle. His body stiffened, and he blinked rapidly as if he couldn't believe it was me.

"Captain!"

He hurried over and tried to help stabilize me, but I swatted him away. The guard led me inside and escorted me straight to the throne room. The queen's eyes frosted over as soon as she saw me.

Yeah, she looks devastated that I was missing.

My family stood at an entrance off to the right that I knew led to a ballroom. They were all dressed impeccably. Each one of them wearing a crown upon their head. The other side of the door was loud with fae and music. I stopped when I realized that they were having a party. I guess I shouldn't have been surprised, though; they had never cared about my well-being before.

"I see you all were devastated that I was missing," I hissed.

"Oh, don't be so dramatic. We figured you ran away at your own accord." Gwyn rolled her eyes. "You look fine."

My eyes shifted to my father, who stood there like a coward, not saying a word to his wife in my defense. I did not look fine; I looked like hell.

"We're glad you're alright, Thea, but we can't stop royal duties. Besides, we knew it had to be Falgon guards, and you would be able to handle yourself."

My head cocked to the side as I stared at my father. The contradicted everything Gwyn just said.

"Falgon guards?" I asked against my better judgment.

"Of course, who else would it be?" he scoffed. "We saw their dead bodies at the Crimson border."

"Crimson," I spoke. "Crimson would make the most sense. Besides, Gwyn just said you all thought I ran away."

They had to have sent guards to the Crimson border first, which meant they thought I ran to Cassius.

"Luren, we have a party." Gwyn gave him a look that said he needed to ignore me.

"If you thought it was Falgon, why did you go to the Crimson border to find me? Especially if you thought I ran away." They were lying to me.

Gwyn and my sisters gave my father a look that let me know I was asking too many questions. My father's green eyes shifted from me to the space behind me. I turned to find Jesper there, only a few feet away.

"We were tipped off," my father lied. My darkness could taste the deep fear he was trying to hide from me, though, showing me the truth behind his words.

"By whom?"

"Damn it, Thea!" My father's voice echoed in the small space around us. "You do not get to question me."

"Why not? Did you even send guards to find me besides the ones you sent to the Crimson border?"

"For one, you're his bastard child." Gwyn's blue eyes met mine. "You don't get to question anyone. Now go away; we have things to do."

"Fuck you," I hissed at her.

When he spotted me, his face hardened, and Gwyn began whispering harshly to him.

My lips curled into a smirk as I stared at their horrified faces. I'll show them what happens when you treat me like shit. I didn't hold back my darkness as it violently tore out of me, causing the swirls on my skin to glow brightly. My eyes shifted to red as my darkness began ripping the decorations off the walls. Guests started yelling and screaming as they ran for the doors. *Not so fast.* I used my darkness to slam the large wooden doors shut, trapping them inside with me.

Their fear filled me, fueling my magic.

My father started toward me, but shadows crept out of me, creating a barrier he could not get past. He was yelling something, but I couldn't hear him through the rage pumping through me.

Gwyn's frantic movements caught my attention. My eyes flickered at the guards, who had all raised their weapons at me. Like that would stop me. In the blink of an eye, I stopped all the chaos my magic was causing. I stood at the front of the room, breathing angrily. I waited until the fae started calming down. Slowly, they stopped yelling and running. They peered at me as I watched them as calmly as I could pretend.

"You fucking monster!" Gwyn started toward me, her guards following in tow. I almost laughed when she thought she could do something to me. It was time to remind them who the fuck I was and why the gods chose me to fulfill the prophecy. I waited for her to try to slap me. When she did, I grabbed her wrist and yanked her to me.

"Thea!" My father was now rushing toward me. I turned Gwyn around and pulled out my dagger. My father stopped moving and paled as I smiled at him. Jesper stepped toward me with his hands up, showing he wasn't a threat. None of these assholes were a threat. I let him get close.

"Thea, I know you're upset, but let everyone here go and talk to us privately," he begged. I pretended to care about what he said, but all I wanted was for him to feel comfortable enough to get closer.

"Fine," I said, and shoved Gwyn so hard that she fell to the floor with a loud thud. She cried out in pain, and I hoped I had broken a bone. Jesper stepped closer. Perfect. I swung my dagger, slicing a cut across his cheek. He grabbed his face as blood poured between his fingers. He looked at me like he couldn't believe what I was doing. Idiot.

"Stop her!" Gwyn yelled to the guards.

I smiled as Jeb came at me. He swung his sword violently at my head, but I dodged him. Before he could lift his sword again, I kicked him in the chest, making him fall backward. Another guard took his place, and I killed him with one stab to the side of the neck. Jeb was back up and charging at me. This time, he was more controlled as I deflected his sword with my daggers.

Jeb was good, but I was better.

I spun away from him and moved closer to my father and Gwyn. Guards immediately surrounded them, and I smiled, completely unhinged. Gods, it felt good to let my darkness out.

"They can't protect you from me," I warned.

Tally and Mae curled into my father as if he could protect them. Jeb sent another guard after me, but I was tired of this. I turned and stabbed the guard in the chest, ripping my blade down so his insides spilled out.

He groaned as life slipped away from him. My eyes pulsed between red and black as I turned to a crowd of terrified faces. I sneered at them before waving my hand, evaporating every weapon that was pointed at me with my fire magic. I heard someone call me Crimson's whore somewhere in the crowd. When I glanced around, two faces caught my attention: Linea and the other noble daughter who had been cruel to me. I smiled when I met their eyes. It was one of them who called me the name. Too bad they didn't learn their lesson. They tried to run, but my darkness burst forth and wrapped around them. Their screams filled the space.

"I told you I would come for you in a crowd. Which one of you said it?"

The noble daughter whose name I didn't know immediately pointed to Linea. I tossed the other girl away. My darkness held Linea as I cut her tongue from her mouth. Her crying filled the space, and all I could think about was how much I hated every fae in this kingdom. Maybe I should kill them all right now. I tossed her to the floor and watched everyone to see who would come for me next. No one moved.

"Now that I have everyone's attention," I said calmly. "I hope this was a nice reminder that I can gut every single one of you in here by myself. If you think I will continue to tolerate your shitty attitude toward me, think again. I don't care if you are noble, commoner, or royal." My eyes flicked to my family. "I will not hesitate to put you in the ground. Does anyone have anything they'd like to say to me?"

No one dared breathe too loudly as I glanced at them. Leer stood in the back of the room with a proud but terrified look on his face.

"I didn't fucking think so. Sleep well." I smiled innocently.

My father didn't dare come at me this time. I walked out of the room slowly, heading toward my shower to wash the blood from me.

CHAPTER 12

"*D*o you always have to be so damn difficult?" Cassius glared at me.

I rolled my eyes as he moved toward me, but when he turned me toward him, I saw the humor in his eyes. I smirked at the look on his face.

"I do love when you give me attitude, my love." He leaned in and kissed me softly. "I was thinking that we should stop pretending you're a prisoner here," Cassius spoke as he pulled away.

His declaration made my smile disappear as golden eyes glided over my face, waiting for me to say something.

"What does that even mean?" I whispered, too scared that my voice would give away the excitement I was feeling.

"I want you to stay in Crimson because you want to. I want you to choose me." His emotions were raw and unfiltered. It may have even been the first time I saw fear in Cassius' eyes. "When I think of you leaving me, my whole body aches with

longing for you. The gods and the stars above know that I would be nothing without you, Thea. They created me to love you, and I intend to do that whether you love me back or not."

Cassius continued in his worried state.

"I never stood a chance. You had me the moment you called me a coward in the woods on the night of the blood moon. You've consumed my every thought since that day, and I've dreamt of a life with you. You are everything I never knew I longed for, Thea, and it terrifies me that you could leave. Not even the gods could keep me from you. So please, put me out of this torment and tell me you'll stay. Even if you do not love me back, stay, and I'll spend a lifetime treasuring you and making you fall in love with me."

Cassius seemed to realize he was rambling and closed his mouth. Through my magic, though, I could feel his overwhelming emotions bubbling up and taking hold of him.

I paused for a moment to allow the silence to fall before whispering, "You've lost your mind..." His shoulders slumped in disappointment at my words, "...if you really think that I do not already love you. My heart and soul chose you long before my mind caught up."

Cassius' mouth seared mine in a breathtaking kiss.

My eyes shot open, and I stared at the ceiling of my bedroom, Cassius' words haunting my thoughts. How could he be so convincing? I sat up in bed, my chest heavy with longing for a man I couldn't have. My dreams had become my own personal hell. There was no relief from the torment of his betrayal. Ever since returning to Cerithia a few days ago, I hadn't stopped thinking about Cassius.

The way he looked at me and smiled in my presence made my insides clench. I couldn't understand why he didn't fear me. Stars above, I was sick and twisted to long for the man who had ruined my life. But there was a burning deep inside me, a rage because he acted as if he didn't kill me.

Gathering my emotions as best I could, I stood and dressed in my guardsmen's uniform. Training would be a great distraction from Cassius—and from the fact that my father hadn't been seen since I ruined his party. The reminder made me smile.

It was easy to fall back into a routine of training with the guards when I never wanted to sleep and didn't have anything to distract me. The guards saluted me as I walked along the front of the fields.

"Who would like to challenge me today?" I asked. A guard stepped forward, and we prepared ourselves for a fight. I was distracted by thoughts of Cassius today, more than usual. It might be the day a guard wins against me.

My face turned at the impact of the guard punching me in the face. Shit. I blocked his next punch, ducking low and punching his stomach. The guard crumpled to his knees, and I pulled my dagger and held it to his heart.

"Dead," I sighed.

The other guards grumbled at my victory. I allowed one challenge a day, and if a guard pulled a death move on me, the men could have two days to themselves. No one had beaten me yet.

I grinned at the men as they all muttered under their breaths and got back into formation.

The men liked the way we trained, and happy guards would be more loyal than mistreated guards.

"They can't afford to take a day off." Jeb looked at me disapprovingly.

"A day off will not lose us this war." I rolled my eyes.

"It's not how we do things in Cerithia," he argued again. "This is something I would expect from Crimson," he said, speaking loud enough for all the guards to hear.

All the men stopped their hand-to-hand combat and glanced between us at Jeb's insult. My fire flickered over my skin momentarily before I regained control. Turning toward Jeb, I took a menacing step toward him. He took a step away.

"Jeb. I will say this once, and I hope it makes it through that very thick skull of yours. I'm the captain; you are not. So, I would not say stupid shit to me unless you want to be demoted or beheaded." His eyes widened, and I could see his dark cheeks redden from anger and embarrassment. "And if you think comparing my tactics to Crimson's guard is an insult, you are dead wrong. You've never seen how ruthless and powerful they are."

Jeb opened and closed his mouth like a gaping fish out of water.

"Now leave my sight."

Jeb scurried away without saying a word or looking back. My eyes glanced at the rest of the guards, who all stared at me. Leer was the only one smiling, but if he liked how I handled that, then I'm sure the other men did too. It was clear that Jeb did not treat them well while I was gone.

"Because Jeb irritated me, and I do not take orders from him, you all may have the rest of the day to yourselves!" I announced.

The men immediately stopped what they were doing and got in line formation, all of them saluting me. Once dismissed, they hooted and hollered as they dispersed.

"You know the men will be loyal to a leader who is fair," Leer sighed close by. "They might all fall in love with you if you keep being so...nice."

"I'm giving them a balance." I nodded. "I understand you all have lives outside of this place, and family is important."

"What will you do with your free time?" Leer asked as we started toward the castle. He worried for me. His wife, Larissa, had him bring me small treats almost every day. Today it was a delicious, sweet bread that I couldn't wait to devour. They were the only two friends I had here.

"Probably sneak around and get in trouble," I shrugged.

Leer laughed but shut his mouth quickly when Jeb and my father strode toward me.

"Go," I ordered Leer, and he didn't argue.

My father's green eyes glared daggers into me, and Jeb's smug smile had me rolling my eyes. He went and tattled on me. I crossed my arms over my chest and waited for them to get closer.

"Thea, is there a problem?" The king questioned. He stayed far from me. It was the first time that we had been near each other since I lost my shit.

I shook my head. "No, no problem."

"Well, Jeb said that you are being unmanageable."

My eyes flickered over to Jeb slowly. He was becoming a real pain in my ass, a problem that I was about to get rid of if he didn't back off.

"I'm supposed to be managed. Why?" I called my father out. He had used a poor choice of words, and his fallen face let me know that he realized his mistake. "I am the captain."

"Not managed, but Jeb has been the captain for seven years. He knows what he's doing."

"Well, now that's debatable." I narrowed my eyes at him, and his face looked ashen. Did he really think I would be deterred if he went and tattled on me? "The men would feed him to the monsters in the woods in a heartbeat. They have no loyalty to a dictator."

The king's eyes widened, and his face reddened at my words. One thing I learned in the past few weeks was that my father hated free will and choice. He told fae what to do, not caring about the impact it had. Fae in Crimson did the opposite, and their guards were loyal to a fault.

"If you really don't think I can manage the men, then maybe we let them vote on who they think should be captain."

Jeb looked at my father, then at me.

"You're that confident?" Jeb hissed. "They would never choose a fucking psycho bitch as their leader; they are being nice to you because they pity how easily you fell for Cassius' lies!"

My father looked at me, his calculating eyes scanning me for a reaction I wouldn't give. I tisked at Jeb, letting him know I thought he was a complete idiot.

"Tomorrow, the men will decide who will continue as captain of the guard," my father agreed. "We are getting ready for the biggest war in Elloryon history, and I need to know my men are loyal to their leader, that they trust them." His face almost looked pained at the idea that I was the one they trusted more.

His green eyes glared at Jeb, then back at me. The king stalked away, leaving Jeb and I alone. I flashed my black eyes toward him, and he let out the smallest startled cry.

"You really shouldn't have done that, Jeb. Consider yourself a dead man walking."

Jeb scrambled quickly away from me; his bravado was gone without the king there to protect him. I chuckled at his retreating form.

I didn't want to go sit in my cramped room by myself, so I headed to the woods to clear my mind. It had been easy to avoid my father and my "family" these past few days. They didn't seek me out, and I didn't bother them either. I wondered if this was how my life had been before I went to Crimson. What had I done to occupy my time before? Maybe I had hung out with Sybil and the twins.

"Gods, this is fucking torture," I muttered, bored.

★★☽★★

The next morning, the men stood in line formation, confused because the king was standing with Jeb and I. The king was never here. This was definitely not something he deemed important.

"Yesterday, it was brought to my attention that you may not approve of your captain, Thea, leading you." The men all looked around confused. "Jeb feels that you may feel more comfortable with him keeping the title. So, today I ask that all of you make your selection of who you'd like as captain by standing behind them."

The men looked around at each other but stood without moving. I nearly chuckled at how ridiculous this was. There were a few who would choose Jeb, but I was confident the majority would choose me.

"Now, would be good," my father growled, and Leer was the first to leave formation and stand behind me. That was the only encouragement the men needed to move behind me. Two soldiers went to stand with Jeb, but it was clear that he wasn't even close to having my leadership skills.

"Well, Jeb, that is settled. Thea will be the captain of the guard," the king sighed, narrowing his eyes at him, as if he had expected a different outcome.

"I want Jeb gone," I demanded.

My father turned to me.

"He's an asset."

"He's a liability. He's undermining my every move. How can we prepare for war when he's trying to divide the men?"

"He will back off." The king narrowed his eyes on Jeb.

Jeb's jaw was so tense, I thought it would snap. He glared at me with a promise to destroy me. Too bad for Jeb, because he would be dead soon. I wasn't letting him continue to fuck with me, and my father wouldn't do as I asked.

"Fine," I agreed, knowing what I had planned.

"We expect to see you for family breakfast in an hour," my father said to me. I couldn't hide the shock that crossed my face.

"Alright," I nodded.

The king walked away, and the men got into line formation. Jeb stood next to me, still tense. I glanced at him.

"Join the line formation; I don't need a babysitter."

Leer was holding back a smile as Jeb did what I ordered. The men stared at me with respect, and it made my chest swell.

"Actually, Jeb, you are on blade-sharpening duty," I dismissed him. "I'm sure all of you are not used to hearing praise, but thank you for trusting me as your leader. I promise not to abuse my power, unlike some fae." I glared at Jeb. "As a token of my appreciation for each of you, I will again be giving you the rest of the day. Rest, relax, and spend it with your family. We will resume training tomorrow."

The men saluted me before cheering as they left. Jeb glared at me from the small armor shed.

Dick.

CHAPTER 13

I'd be lying if I said I wasn't a bit nervous, but I was more curious about my father inviting me to a family meal. I didn't bother dressing up and wore plain black clothing. As soon as I entered the dining room, everyone at the table turned to me. They all put on brave faces, but my darkness hummed at their fear.

I sat away from them. Jesper was the only one who glared at me. I said nothing, hoping they didn't expect an apology. Food was placed in front of us, and I slowly ate the meat as I stared at them.

"Thank you for coming," my father struggled to say, making me smirk. They didn't want me here. They must need something.

"What do you want?" I asked, shoving bread into my mouth. "You don't invite me to meals, and you wouldn't start now, not after I ruined your party. So, what do you want?"

My father glanced into my eyes.

"We've received word that Falgon is planning to move into our territory again. We'd like you to scout their troops and see if you can determine if they're planning an attack."

"All right."

"You'll do it?" He seemed surprised.

"Why wouldn't I? I'm the captain. It's my job."

"After you ruined..." he paused. "You seemed angry with us the last time we were all together."

Well, that was putting it lightly.

"I am, but I have a job to do, and I want to break my curse." My eyes bore into my father as I mentioned the curse. I still didn't understand everything, but that was the only reason I was still here. But one thing was for certain, I hated this kingdom and these fae at the table. A scouting trip would give me the break I needed from Cerithia.

"We'll send some men with you."

"No." I stood. "I'll go alone."

My father's jaw clenched. He wasn't used to being defied or spoken back to. I grabbed my roll and looked up at them.

"I'll be back when I figure out what's going on."

I didn't wait for them to say anything. I walked out of the room and heard their harsh whispers as soon as I left, but I kept walking.

★★☽★★

I was happy to leave Cerithia, even if only for a short while. The atmosphere had been intense since my kidnapping, and I hadn't been able to uncover any new information. I felt stuck.

I set up my base camp a few days ago and had been watching Falgon's castle for two days. I noticed their guards were becoming scarcer, the number patrolling dwindling each day.

Something was clearly wrong. I felt it the moment I stepped onto Falgon territory. Even the forest was eerily silent tonight—the kind of quiet that made the hairs on my neck stand on end, as if sensing I was being watched.

My father's instructions had been vague, almost as though he was desperate to send me away. I nearly turned back to Cerithia when I realized something was off, but I didn't. The truth was, I'd rather face whatever was coming than return to the dullness of life there.

Glancing around the darkened forest, I saw nothing. Just as I shifted my focus back to the castle, I caught a slight movement deep in the trees.

Dammit. They knew I was here. I began to creep toward the castle to see what was happening.

"Don't move." The voice came from behind me. I turned to see dozens of guards now standing in the forest, surrounding me. "We will shoot you."

My eyes darted around, counting about thirty men. I hadn't even heard them approach, which was honestly impressive.

"I could kill you all without lifting a finger," I warned.

"We know," the captain sighed. I noticed that his green uniform had a white crest over his heart. "But you don't need to do that."

Before I could ask him why, a sharp pain made me cry out. One of the men behind me had shot an arrow into my arm. I turned, my fire mist surging forward and killing the man quickly. Whipping around, I killed half the men with a swipe of my hand before I started to feel something foreign pumping through my veins.

My fire magic stopped immediately. Damn it.

"You poisoned me?" I glared.

"We just needed you to not kill us all. It will wear off."

I threw my dagger at him, killing him instantly, and then smiled at the irony.

"I don't need my magic to kill the rest of you!"

The commotion made by all the men yelling and charging at me was so loud that it made more men come sprinting from the castle. I started running into the forest as they chased me down, picking them off one at a time with my daggers. As I ran, I ripped the arrow from my arm. Sybil's healing magic was trying desperately to heal me, but it couldn't.

I kept moving toward Kizar lands, with Falgon's army following. Somehow, though, a guard managed to get in front of me. I readied another dagger to throw at him, but he dropped his weapon.

"Thea, please stop; we don't want to hurt you!" He held up his hands in surrender.

I froze at his gesture. His eyes moved behind me before he moved out of my way.

"Little viper."

Cassius' voice drifted through the cool night air. My body stiffened at the sound of it. Great, the arrow was going to make me hallucinate too. Either the stars were torturing me, and I didn't understand why, or my sanity had snapped for good.

I turned quickly, not expecting to see him. I blinked rapidly when I saw him standing in the forest. Cassius was a vision in his black uniform. His golden eyes glowed in the dark, and his dark hair was chaotic, like he had been running his fingers through it.

"Little viper," he spoke again. This time I realized I was not hallucinating. I gripped my viper-handled dagger in my hand as I ran at him.

Cassius had expected my attack. He pulled out his own daggers and blocked every stab I tried to make. Not once did he try to attack me back.

"Thea, stop," he demanded between my strikes. When I didn't listen, he cursed under his breath. Suddenly, our daggers tangled with each other's, making them fall from our hands. Cassius looked up at me to speak, but I swung my fist and punched him in the face.

He stumbled backward, grabbing his cut brow. Blood dripped down his face as I ran at him again. I was not giving up. This was all his fault. Cassius dodged my attack, grabbing my wrists and yanking me flush against him as we tumbled to the ground. He cushioned my fall and quickly rolled us, so I was pinned under him. I was determined, though. My darkness would not stop me this time. No, it had retreated inside me with my other magic. The guard's attempt to subdue my magic would only help me kill Cassius.

"My love, please stop," he muttered as I thrashed around under him. His grip loosened, and I punched him again, making him fall off me. "Fuck!" He grunted as he held his nose. I stood and prepared myself for him to charge at me, but he just stared at me without moving. Something somber filled his features. I hated the way he stared at me with his empty eyes. The look of longing was worse than a punch to the face.

"Fight me," I demanded. "Let's finish this once and for all."

"No," he said, shaking his head and looking away from me as if he couldn't bear to look at me. I glanced around to see Haden, Kace, and Zade watching our exchange. Gods, I hadn't seen them since the trials. They all watched me with blank, uncomprehending stares. I couldn't stand to see their faces, so I glanced at Cassius.

"Quit being a coward and fight me, Cassius. I promised you I would kill you, and you still sought me out. So now be ready to die."

His golden eyes glanced around us as Falgon guards watched the exchange; all of them had laid their weapons down. His shoulders slumped as his eyes found mine again. My chest tightened at the odd gesture. I wouldn't allow myself to fall for whatever this was. Cassius would use it to break me, to kill me.

He frowned at me before he tossed down his weapons and fell to his knees in front of me. His long exhale filled the silent space around us as his eyes closed tightly. Wisp floated behind him, her flames a normal shade of blue. She wasn't warning me against him, but I knew she was not on my side. She loved Cassius, not me.

"Pick up your weapon and fight me!" I demanded through clenched teeth. My rage pounded in my ears as I stared at him kneeling in front of me. Cassius shook his head. If he thought I wouldn't kill him, he was mistaken. If he thought I would fall for this act, he was stupid. Something about his submission to me made my insides twist with agony. I hated this. Desperate to understand why he was doing this, I glanced around us as if someone would speak up.

"Kill me if you must," he whispered as his haunted eyes found mine.

"Cassius..." Haden started to say, but I was already running toward him. I tackled Cassius to the ground so he was lying flat on his back as I straddled him, my dagger pushed into his throat. A single drop of blood ran from his neck. And yet, he didn't fight me.

"Come home," he spoke softly. "Please."

I sharpened my gaze on him, looking for the cruel, malicious man he had been in the clearing. His lips parted as his eyes glistened.

"I am home," I lied. I would never give him the satisfaction of knowing how terrible Cerithia had been. Della had said I needed to be in Cerithia to learn the truth. I hadn't pieced together enough to understand what the truth was yet.

"I've missed you terribly, my love."

Tears filled my eyes because I knew his words weren't true, but they still made time slow down around us as we watched each other. My teeth sank into my trembling lip so that he couldn't see how much he affected me. Cassius' hands rested on my hips, and I waited for him to hurt me, but he didn't.

"Stop," I demanded. "I will never fall for your lies again."

He winced at my words.

"Come home with me; fight with me there. Yell at me, hurt me, hate me, but do it in our home," he tried again.

"Cerithia is my home."

"Liar," he snapped. "Even you know that is not true."

His words and actions were confusing me. Why wasn't he trying to hurt me? I hated that I didn't know if this was a trick, even though he had betrayed me already. The dagger felt heavy in my palm as his words sank deeper into my doubts. It was clear that he was trying to enchant me. I shook my head, trying to get rid of these unwanted thoughts.

"Have they treated you well in Cerithia?" He kept pushing it. His eyes scanned over my face for any trace of the lie

I would tell. "Did they welcome you with open arms? Do they treat you as well as Crimson did?"

How did he know what to say? All the cruel interactions I had with my family came crashing around me. My stomach sank at the harshness Cerithia had shown me. *Crimson's whore.* It made me hesitate and question if I could kill him. Everyone had been cruel to me. No one wanted me, but I didn't want him to know that he was right that day in the clearing. *Who could love a monstrosity like me?* The answer was no one. Not even my own family.

"Yes," I forced the lie out.

"Oh, my little liar, you will never convince me that Cerithia has been kind to you." His eyes darkened.

"Shut up," I demanded as my blade pushed more into his neck. Wisp twirled around us in a frenzy. Was she worried for me or Cassius? "Why are you in Falgon?"

"Because I cannot cross into Cerithia without dying or being invited because of the curse. This was the only way to get to you and tell you to come home with me. You killed the first Falgon guards we sent to get you. You disappeared from our bedroom before I got a chance to talk with you again."

The Falgon guard who had muttered Cassius' name to me as he died flashed through my mind. My body went rigid as I realized that it was Cassius who had sent the men for me.

"Why? So, you can trick me and kill me again?"

Heartache filled my already tight chest as I watched him closely. This small interaction was somehow making me feel something other than rage and devastation. I knew what he was saying was impossible to believe, but my darkness obsessed over each word he spoke. I didn't know what to do. My lips parted as I tried desperately to slow my racing heart.

"I never tricked you," he pleaded. "The only ones tricking you are your family and that little bastard, Jesper."

"You killed me," I hissed. "Cursed me."

"I know," he frowned, closing his eyes tightly, and laid his head back on the ground.

I pushed my dagger into his throat harder, making him shut the fuck up.

"I was not planning on killing you tonight, but I will enjoy it. I will be happier when I know that you do not exist in the same realm as me." I leaned down closer to him, so our faces were inches apart. "And I will kill you in the name of Cerithia." Cassius' eyes bounced between mine as I leaned over him. Quickly, he pushed forward, kissing me by surprise. The motion caused my blade to nick the skin on his neck.

I pulled back, confused, and lifted my blade over my head so that I could plunge it into his heart. My breathing was too quick, and I thought I might faint. Even as I readied to stab him, he didn't flinch. His hands squeezed my hips tightly, like he just wanted to feel me, as he watched me with a yearning in his golden eyes. The bond on my arm suddenly burned so violently that I thought I would drop my dagger. Leer's words bounced around my mind. *He looks like a man longing for a woman he can't have.*

"Any last words, Cassius?" I breathed out softly.

His hands moved from my hips to my thighs.

"I love you, Thea," he whispered. "It was an honor to be yours, and I wish things had happened differently. Maybe our next life will not be so cruel to us."

A lump formed in my throat as tears filled my eyes. I felt paralyzed by his confession. A tear rolled down my face as I stared at him.

"I will wait for you in the next life." His hand brushed the stray curls from my face. Then he closed his eyes and waited for my blade to pierce his heart. The blood bond burned so painfully that I was losing the grip on my dagger. Doubt swarmed me, even though I knew this was likely another trick. Something about his words had given me mixed emotions. I had expected cruel words or a fight, but not a confession of love. My darkness was swarming inside of me again. It was frantic at what I was doing. It didn't want me to do this.

My movements stopped because I couldn't do this. Gods, was I this starved for love that I was quick to believe Cassius' words, or did something deep inside of me remember him, not allowing me to hurt him. Before I could conclude my thoughts, Wisp decided for me that I would not be hurting Cassius. Her form suddenly shifted to yellow, causing me to look away from Cassius.

The sudden change in her mood made me pause. She seemed to be expanding so vastly that I was in awe. Then suddenly, Wisp rammed me so forcefully that I was knocked from Cassius. I lay there dazed for a moment, then groaned as I lifted myself up off the ground slightly. When I glanced back at her, she had created a wall between Cassius and I. She was protecting him.

I glanced around but didn't try to move toward him again. Relief filled me that I did not have to make the decision to kill him right now. He stood at the same time I did, but he just watched me without moving. He didn't question why I was flown from him as he glanced at Wisp like he could see her. His eyes glanced around him, where she circled him. He could see her.

All this time, at the trials, he could see her. Gods, why did he act like he couldn't?

"You see her," I accused. His tortured eyes found mine.

"Of course I see her," he whispered. I hadn't expected him to be honest. "She is attached to my soul."

What the actual fuck was going on? Wisp was mine. She protected me; she was supposed to be my friend. My jaw tightened as I refused to show my betrayal to them. Was she working with him this whole time?

"Come home with me," he begged, but I shook my head. "You belong with me, Thea. Please, I just want you back in our home, in our room, in my arms, and with me."

"I can't!" I yelled at him. There were still so many things that didn't make sense. She was loyal to Cassius, and her betrayal pumped hurt through me. Before I could see their reaction, I turned and ran toward Kizar's border, hoping Cassius couldn't cross there either.

Tears blurred my vision as I tried to understand what had just happened. I could hear them behind me, but I was almost to the safety of Kizar. Sobs racked through my body so violently that I wondered if the gods themselves could hear my pain.

"Little viper!" Cassius' voice echoed through the forest. I shook away the comfort my darkness found in his voice. It was difficult to see in the dark as my eyes blurred with tears of anger and sadness.

"I dreamt of you before I ever met you in real life," Cassius called out to me just as I crossed into Kizar. His confession made me stop. The air was difficult to breathe in, and I wasn't sure if it was what he said or what just happened. I turned slowly, wetting my dry lips. He walked toward me cautiously but stopped when he saw that I gripped my dagger tightly in my hand.

"When I was a child, I dreamt of a girl with wild, dark curls and eyes as green as the moss in the woods. I told no one about it. I thought you were just some random fantasy, but you never went away. For years, you came to my dreams, and I just watched you from the shadows. I found myself excited to go to sleep as the years went by because I would get to see you, the girl with no name. I think I memorized every line of your face, every curve of your body, the way your voice sounded in my dreams. I was drawn to you before I ever even met you."

My hands trembled at what he told me.

"I didn't know you were a real woman until your mother came to me. I thought the dreams were my own mind torturing myself with someone I could never have."

I searched his eyes for understanding. Cassius took a small step forward with his hands up slightly, showing he meant no harm to me.

"You look just like her, except her eyes were blood red," he smiled softly at me. "I was outside, wandering the woods one day. It was as if something had called me there, but I couldn't explain it. It was an overwhelming need to be in the forest. Then I saw her, and at first, I thought she was the girl from my dreams. I could tell that she was a blood witch, and I knew the risks of going toward her, but there was a pull coming from her. I did not fear her."

I found myself wanting to believe his words. I took a step back as if it would shield me from him.

"Bayla," he said lightly. "She smiled at me when she looked into my eyes. She told me that she knew of my secret—that I dreamt of you. Bayla told me it was her daughter I dreamed of, but she refused to tell me your name or where you lived. I remember asking her what she wanted, and she told me she had seen visions of you and me in the future, that I would fall hopelessly in love with you," he chuckled and ran his hands down his face. "Bayla said she wanted to meet me once just in case she could not witness our love firsthand. I thought she had lost her mind, but she made me promise that I would never stop looking until I found you."

"Why?" my voice shook as I spoke.

"She said we would save each other." His shoulders slumped as he glanced into my eyes. "I started traveling to different parts of the realm as soon as I was old enough and could control my shadow magic. Every night I snuck out, and I searched for you." His lips had a slight smirk, as if he were remembering a precious memory. "I found you a year before I first talked to you on the night of the blood moon. Gods, I knew your mother was right about falling hopelessly in love with you when I saw you for the first time outside of my dreams. You were practicing throwing daggers at a tree, mad at the realm for some reason, and I couldn't stop watching you. I returned every night for a year hoping to see you again. I even left one of my viper-handled daggers for you to find one night. Then I realized who you were. I tried to stay away once I realized you were King Luren's daughter, but it only seemed to make my longing for you worse. Do you know how much torture it is to long for someone you have never met before?"

I shook my head, not knowing how to take this information. "My mother liked you," I said, cocking my head to the side, trying to understand.

He nodded slowly.

"She seemed... pleased with me. I somehow got the feeling that she was making sure that I was a good fit for you. Bayla told me to protect you, and I didn't know what she meant by that until years later. I think your mother knew what was going to happen long before it did. Even if your mother had not come to me, I know our paths would have crossed. It was destined."

My chin trembled as I tried to hold in my emotions.

"Why are you telling me this?" I whispered. "It doesn't change anything."

"Maybe it does," he frowned. "I keep hoping that one day I will tell you something about us that will magically trigger your memories. I pray to the gods, the stars, and any being out there that will hear my plea that you will stop looking at me as if I am your villain. That you will stop looking at me like you do not love me anymore."

"You are my villain!" I stared him down. "How could I love a monstrosity like you?" I spit his own words back at him. He visibly shrank away from my venomous words. Cassius opened his mouth to say something, but he shut it and said nothing else. A pained expression overtook his face as he looked down at his feet.

"My mother was obviously wrong about us." The words tasted sour coming out of my mouth. Cassius swallowed hard as Wisp appeared next to him. He glanced at her, and I swore I saw a sad longing in his eyes. After a moment that felt like forever, he finally looked back at me.

"One day, you will know how wrong those words are. You are angry with me, and it's making you skew your reality in Cerithia because you fear you will have nowhere to belong." His golden eyes narrowed on me as he squared his shoulders. "Well, I hate to break it to you, little viper, but you will always feel that way until you are back home with *me*. I am your home. I am where you belong." He pointed at his chest.

"Why are you doing this to me? Just stop with the lies," I begged. He was confusing me. I had been so sure of my anger and bitterness toward him, but each time I saw him, my walls were breaking. He had admitted to killing me and acted as if it weren't a big deal. My eyes met his. I didn't hate him like I hated my father and Jesper. The hate I had for them burned with a vengeance inside of me. But when I looked at Cassius, it wasn't vengeance that burned, it was a longing to understand why he did what he did.

"When you go back to Cerithia, I beg you to please look at your family and everything around you clearly. Do it for yourself, for your own safety. They cannot keep up any sort of charade with you if you stop turning a blind eye to their behavior. Della was right; you need to find out the lies and secrets of Cerithia before you will ever truly choose me. I know you are confused, and I wish I could tell you everything right this second."

"Then why don't you tell me?" I asked.

He frowned. "Because I can see it in your eyes that you are terrified of me. You are not in a place where you will believe anything I have to say without wondering if I am lying. You need to spend more time in Cerithia to truly understand everything. You are supposed to come to the conclusion that you love me on your own, and I think I keep making this harder for you. I'm making you more confused instead of letting you do this." Cassius looked pained as he watched me. "Della said I was forcing this too much. She said that I needed to let you be angry with me for killing you, to let you process all of this at your own pace. I thought she was wrong, but when I look into your eyes, I know she's right. I just miss you so much that I keep trying to rush it."

I turned away from him because my resolve was breaking. My sniffling seemed deafening in the silent forest.

"I have never been your villain. Gods above, I know I am a monster, but I am *your* monster. I will destroy every fae that has kept you from me, even if I must burn this whole fucking realm to the ground. I will do it for you, for us. I would do almost anything you wish. But the one thing I will never do, even for you, is give up on us."

When I turned back to him, he was gone, and my chest felt as if it were caving in.

Chapter 14

I had returned late the following night. My father was not expecting me back until tomorrow, so I would need to find an excuse as to why I was back. Uncertainty filled me as Cassius' words played over and over in my head. I decided that I would not tell my father that Cassius had been there. Quietly, I headed in the direction of my room. Before I could walk down the stairs, though, I heard my father talking. Glancing around to ensure the guards were not watching me, I darted farther down the hallway.

I paused at the open door where the sound was coming from and listened. My eyes narrowed when I heard Jesper's voice answering my father. This was an ungodly hour to be having a meeting.

"Do you think she is ready?" Jesper asked.

"Yes," my father sighed. "We can't keep putting this off. Thea needs to kill Cassius and King Rylan sooner rather than later. Once she does that, we can start talking about taking over the other kingdoms. Cassius must be her priority. We cannot wait for him to weasel his way into her heart again." Shame filled me with my father's words. As much as I hated myself for it, Cassius' words had affected me.

"She couldn't possibly believe it again," Jesper scoffed. "He killed her. You heard all those nasty things he said to her that day. There is no way she could have any affection left for that monster."

It was silent for a long moment. It was the queen who broke the silence.

"It's clear that Cassius is up to something. Why would he say all of that to her? He wanted to throw us off. I do not trust him or her for that matter."

"Gwyn, Thea remembers nothing," my father sighed, irritated. "You weren't there; he destroyed her heart and had no hesitation in his voice. She pleaded for him to stop, and he just kept going. Maybe he meant it. Perhaps everything had become too much for him."

My brows creased. Why was it so hard to believe that Cassius had meant what he said that day? Gwyn made a scoffing noise.

"Pull your head out of your ass, Luren. That man was up to something, and I do not trust Thea in the slightest. She knows something; perhaps this was an elaborate plan they concocted together. Did any of you consider that? Maybe she is here because he wanted her here to ruin us from the inside out."

They remained silent. My heart thumped painfully fast in my chest. Why would she think I was working with Cassius?

"I don't think he would send her here intentionally. Cassius would never be so reckless with her, but I do agree that he was probably up to something."

Their words had me taking a step back.

"Thea is a smart girl; she will start to ask questions. How will we proceed with that?" Gwyn demanded.

"We will face the questions as they come up. She wants to see effort from us to be a family. We cannot have another incident like the ball."

"I cannot, will not, pretend to be happy to see her," Gwyn sneered. "That Crimson whore is not my child; she's yours, you deal with her."

Anger bubbled up so quickly that I almost lost control right there because my father did not stop her cruelty. Hearing the term Crimson whore triggered a memory of the night I had been kidnapped. The guards kept calling me that. My blood ran cold at the realization that it had been Cerithian guards that had taken me. That is what they called me here. Uneasiness settled inside me.

"You better watch yourself, queen. I will not allow you to treat her or talk about her like that." Jesper's voice was soft but menacing.

"Still so obsessed with the king's bastard daughter, Jesper? I'm sure your father would be happy to hear that his only son is sticking up for the woman who betrayed both Cerithia and Kizar."

"Thea did not betray my kingdom; she broke my heart. There is a difference. Remember that her betrayal of Cerithia was a direct reflection of your poor treatment of her," Jesper raised his voice at Gwyn.

"Gwyn, that is enough. You will not make Thea's transition harder than it already is," my father demanded. "She chose Cerithia. We have never been in this position before, so you will shut up and treat her kindly. I will not allow your hatred for her to ruin this for me. We have already almost lost her, and you're lucky she was willing to believe my stories."

I turned after they remained silent. My skin burned hot with anger. I could not decide if I was in disbelief, enraged, or just hurt. I just knew that I needed to get out of here and think.

Quickly, I darted out of the castle in a spot where the guards did not linger. My legs burned as I ran through the forest until I was far enough away to allow my darkness to take over. Fire burst from me as a vicious scream tore from my throat. I vented my frustration to the gods.

Cassius had been so adamant that Cerithia was not kind to me. The conversation I had just heard replayed in my mind. They worried about Cassius and me working together. What did that even mean? Darkness crept over my skin as my magic fed on my emotions, causing my orange and red swirls to glow brightly. I felt it as it settled deep within my bones and latched onto me, with no intention of releasing me.

Crimson whore.

My darkness tightened its grip on me even more at the insult. She had no right to say that about me. What secrets were being kept from me? What would be the reason to kidnap me and make me think it was Falgon?

"Thea?" I turned and saw Jesper frowning at me. I jumped, upset at myself for not hearing him coming. My arms crossed over my chest as I glared at him. "Are you alright? The guards said you looked upset." His eyes traced over the trees on fire before returning to me. "What happened on your mission? You shouldn't be home yet."

I ignored him and hurried to go around him. Jesper grabbed me and pulled me back around so we were facing each other. My fire magic chose that moment to make an appearance, causing him to drop his hand instantly.

"What did you hear?" He narrowed his eyes on me. His normally friendly face was nowhere to be seen. I faked ignorance.

"What are you talking about?"

His jaw clenched tightly, but he wouldn't say anything, just in case he gave me any hint that there was a conversation going on that I shouldn't have heard.

"You are clearly upset. You lit the trees on fire, and your skin..."

I ripped my arm from his grasp and narrowed my now black eyes on him.

"You are not my king. I will not answer to you."

"Not yet, but you will," he threatened, but I didn't understand. "Did something happen in Falgon?"

My body tensed slightly at his question, but I doubted he noticed. His eyes traced over me like he could read me.

"Something happened," he stated, watching my reaction very carefully. The dirt crunched under his foot as he dared to step closer to me.

"Nothing happened." I rolled my eyes to hide my discomfort. "I came back because Falgon's army was not preparing for an attack."

I started to walk away again because my darkness wanted to snap Jesper's neck.

"Is there any reason we should be concerned about where your loyalty lies?"

This made me stop and look back at him.

"Who else would I be loyal to?" I questioned.

"Crimson," he didn't hesitate, but I saw the instant regret on his face. He hadn't meant to say it, but it was too late to take it back.

"Why would I be loyal to a kingdom that tricked and used me?"

Jesper's eyes darted around us as if he were looking for a way out of this conversation. But I waited for him to answer me.

"I don't know," he said. "Forget I said anything."

I turned from him and made my way back to the castle, heading for my room. I wouldn't forget that he was concerned that I could be loyal to a kingdom that had betrayed me.

As I made my way through the halls and reached the corridor, Wisp appeared. She was flickering in front of the black door near my bedroom. Her green form changed to red and black as I stepped toward her. I could see nothing different about the door this time, but something felt... wrong.

"It's locked," I whispered to Wisp. "I've tried almost every day to get into this door."

She stopped moving at my words but then wrapped herself around the handle of the door, popping it open with a soft click.

I immediately gasped and stopped moving as the chill of the room instantly coursed through me. Something evil seemed to press down on me, and I wasn't sure if I should be going in there. Wisp twirled around me as if she were urging me to trust her.

Taking a deep breath, I slowly pushed open the door and stepped into the dark space. As soon as I stepped inside, Wisp slammed the door shut behind me. I turned and panicked, trying to open the door, but it was locked.

"What the fuck are you doing?" I yelled, but Wisp was gone.

I leaned my forehead against the door and took a deep, calming breath. Once ready, I turned and faced the space behind me. My fire magic surged forward, lightly illuminating the small, dark room. Cautiously, I walked forward so that I could see what was so important that this room had remained locked.

My nose itched at the dust that covered everything. As my eyes adjusted to the light, I noticed the room was basically empty except for a large wooden table in the center of it and a small desk against the far wall. I glanced around to make sure no one lingered in the dark corners. It felt as if I was being watched, even though I saw no one. Other than the table and desk, the room was oddly empty.

I took a look at the table and noticed a large map sprawled out on it. At first, it looked like a regular map of Elloryon, but I froze when I realized it included Exile. I looked closer. Not only did it show Exile, but it was very detailed. It showed where every building was. The makeshift stage was there, the shadow boundary, and even, marked with a star, mine and Sybil's home.

How did my father have such a detailed map of Exile while there was still a border around it? My hands traced over the shadow border until I saw the X on the tall oak tree that marked my escape route. This was just more confirmation that Leer had been telling me the truth.

"I don't understand," I muttered to myself.

My father had been so adamant that I made up Exile as part of the curse. Wisp's blue glow caught my eye, letting me know she had returned.

"How does he know what Exile looks like?"

Wisp did nothing but float in the corner of the room. Panic started to seep in again because I couldn't think of any reason that was good enough to explain why he would have this. My hands tore the map off the table, and I rummaged through the papers on the desk, desperate for any information they might yield. Most of the papers didn't make sense until I saw the words 'the creek will dry, and the forest will die' scribbled onto one of the pages.

Scanning the rest of the page, I realized it was a contract of some sort. A name I couldn't read was at the bottom of the contract, along with Gwyn's and my father's signatures. Quickly, my hands scrambled through the other pages and found another contract, this one detailing an attack on Exile. My heart pounded as I read the details of the plan. Men would come to Exile in the night and slaughter anyone outside their homes.

Flashes of the attack that killed that mother and her young child flashed into my mind. I had done everything I could to save them, but my father and Gwyn had killed them. Tears pooled in my eyes at the reality of what I had just discovered. My family was responsible for why Exile had begun to fall apart. They were responsible for the deaths of the elite fae there, for the drying up of our creek, and for killing our forest. These contracts proved they had hired witches or some other magical being to harm us. After all, who else could dry up rivers and cause forests to die?

Wisp's sudden, quick movement caught my attention, and I realized my fire had slowly crept from me with my rising emotions and was now swirling around the room in a fury, threatening to ignite the furniture and papers around me. My emotions were overwhelmed again. The contracts in my hand crinkled as my hands balled into fists. They had lied to me. All of those moments where I felt I didn't fit in here suddenly made sense. It was as if my body and heart knew that this was not where I belonged.

I knew my family had never cared much for me, but I still thought this was my home. How could it be, though?

"Did I ever have a home?" I sobbed quietly at Wisp.

She flashed a bright orange.

"I don't understand why my own family would do this!" I cried into my own hands. I had never felt lonelier and more confused than I did at this very moment. It felt like I was caving in on myself because every foundation I had made to rebuild my life was now crumbling underneath me because of lies and deceit.

Suddenly, I felt something foreign creep into my awareness. It started like a small tug in my chest. I could hardly feel it. But the urgency and pull of it became too intense. I glanced up to see if it was Wisp, but she was gone. My eyes focused on the stone wall across from me. My magic had all swarmed in front of a small section of it, gathered in a single spot as if it were trying to get through to something.

Crossing the room, I ran my hands over the stone wall, not feeling anything. Just when I was going to give up, my finger brushed against what felt like a scratch in the stone. I leaned down to get a better look at it. The mark was carved deeply, as if it were intentional. As soon as I touched it, my head began to pound so violently that I fell to my knees, clutching it with both hands. Suddenly, I felt my magic swarm from me, covering the entirety of the room around me without me willing it to do so.

I tried to focus on what was happening, but my head was pounding too hard as the magic pumped from me too quickly, seeming to take all of my energy with it. Then, just as fast as it had left, my magic swarmed back inside of me. Catching my breath, I looked up and glanced around the room, realizing that it was now completely different than it had been moments before.

Instead of being surrounded by bare stone walls, I was now surrounded by cells.

Scanning around the room, I realized that some sort of enchantment had shielded them from me. And now it was broken.

Slowly, I began to turn in a circle. The cells were small, dirty, and all empty except for the one in the middle. I gasped and jumped back in surprise when I saw that a woman was standing there, staring at me with piercing brown eyes. Her gray hair was unkempt, and her skin was pale. She looked as if she had been in here for a long time.

"Thea," she muttered in a soft voice. "Thank the moon."

The phrase was odd. I stood and approached her cautiously. Even though my magic swarmed inside of me, it did not warn me of danger. Once I was close enough to see her aged face smiling at me, I stopped.

"Do I know you?"

The woman frowned.

"A long time ago, I was family to you." Her eyes glided over my face as if she were seeing an old friend. "I'm sorry, but I can hardly believe my eyes." Her tone was soft as she cocked her head to the side. "You look just like her."

"Who?"

"Your mother," she smiled. Her words formed a pit in my stomach as she continued. "Bayla told me to wait until you came to me, but I got worried that she was wrong, so I came here searching for you. I was discovered, though, and Gwyn and your father locked me in here. I thought I would die in this cell."

"My mother is dead. You are mistaken." Disappointment coursed through me.

"I'm not mistaken, but Bayla was right, per usual," the woman chuckled softly as she spoke of my mother. "But it's alright because you found me anyway."

"Who are you, and how did my mother tell you this if she is dead?"

"I'm Rosaline," she said, pausing to watch me for a reaction. Her name felt familiar, but nothing could tell me why. "I had a son once, Killian, and he was your mother's fated mate."

My mind was racing. This woman knew my mother and could help fill in the gaps I didn't understand. My father had painted a terrible picture of her, and I had always felt like it wasn't true.

"Bayla and Killian married, but he died before she could bear an heir for the coven. It was your mother's duty as Queen of the Blood Witches to have an heir. That is where your father came into the picture. The letter will explain it to you."

"The letter?"

The woman nodded.

"I came here to give it to you, but your father took it. Good thing it was only a copy. Bayla always said to expect the worst outcome and be prepared. Smart woman," Rosaline said with a smirk.

"My mother was Queen of the Blood Witches."

"Yes, so I guess that makes you the queen now, even though you are the last blood witch that we know of. I don't think anyone escaped the slaughter of the coven." A deep frown took over her friendly face.

"Your mother started having odd visions of you as an adult when you were still a child. She had never had the ability to see your future, so she thought she was cursed at first, but then Killian came to her in a dream and told her that she was being blessed by the gods to see your fate so that she may change it."

"How did he visit her if he was dead?"

"Mates can visit dreams, even if one is dead, as long as the other is waiting for them before moving on to the next life."

Cassius had said he met my mother. Did that mean she saw him in her visions too? If she had seen the horrors he would do to me, then why didn't she kill him to change my fate?

"Bayla always told me when she had a dream about you, but never the details. I think she feared for my safety. That is why she wrote a letter and said you would come to me in the future, and I must give it to you."

"So how do we get to the letter?" I asked.

"You break me out of this cage, and I can handle the rest," she smiled. I nodded as I scanned the woman with my magic once more for danger. My darkness wasn't alert to anything, so I used my fire magic to melt the locks off. The door popped open, and Rosaline smiled as she scuddled out.

"You might feel queasy," she warned as she lifted her arms, and a white light appeared in her hands. Rosaline grabbed the ball of light and stretched it wide enough to step through before dragging me into it with her. A moment later, we appeared to be in a bookstore.

She was right; I did feel queasy. My stomach rolled, and I closed my eyes tightly, trying not to hurl all over her store. Rosaline reached out to help steady me.

"This happens all the time to others who travel by light. There is nothing to worry about; it will pass." She patted my hand softly. I nodded as my darkness crept from me and absorbed some of her magic for us. This would come in handy.

"Did the enchantment stop you from using your magic to break free?" I asked, trying to distract myself.

"No, it was only used to keep anyone from finding me. They had a witch come and put a magic shielding spell on me."

"Are you a witch?" I asked, unable to tell. I opened my eyes as my stomach settled. She turned to me and lifted her white hair to reveal her pointed fae ears.

"No."

My head spun as I glanced around the dimly lit room, stepping in slow circles to take everything in. My fingers brushed the old leather-bound books as I passed by the shelves, leaving dust behind. I was sure these books had not been touched in years and found it... charming. I liked the thought of something untouched by the cruel realm of reality.

"Come."

She led me through fancy velvet drapes behind the counter and down a short hall until we reached an iron door. Her wrinkly hand grabbed a singular key from her pocket. The top of it having a skull on the top of it.

A sense of lightness flowed through me as I eagerly followed Rosaline. I wanted to learn anything new. I followed her in after a small light sprang to life and illuminated the space. It was cold and smelled of an unpleasant wetness.

Rosaline picked up a small, blood-red box and struggled to pop it open.

"I loved your mother as if she were my own daughter. I wish she and Killian were still here, but I like to think they are in the next life together. It brings me comfort. Now that you are getting closer to breaking the curse, I will always have a part of her through you too." She smiled as she handed me an envelope.

"Bayla tried to protect you from your father, but she couldn't."

"My father?"

Rosaline squeezed my hand with sadness painted in her eyes.

"Read the letter. I will be back when you're done."

Before I could say anything, the woman seemed to disappear before my eyes. I glanced around the small, dingy space before opening the letter gently. My heart pounded at the thought of what I would learn from my mother. What was so important that she had to write it for me?

Slowly, I unfolded the pages.

My dearest Thea,

Writing this letter is so painful, knowing that if you read it, I will be long gone. The thought of not seeing you grow into a powerful woman makes my heart physically ache. As I write this, you are picking flowers in the garden, and I watch you in wonder. You are everything that I could wish for—smart, brave, kind, and powerful.

I hope that you forgive me for what I confess to you in this letter and know that I did everything for you. I love you more than anything, but sometimes love brings us to do things that we do not wish to.

I am sorry that I caused your life to be hard. It is my fault that when you are older, you will die for the choices I made. I have sealed your fate to be so difficult. When my mate, Killian, died, I was so lost in grief. But I knew I needed an heir to make sure the blood witches continued. The thought made me sick, but your father approached me, and he was so kind. Trusting him is what gave me you, and I will forever be grateful, but it was the start of my own downfall.

I had visions of Elloryon being destroyed as soon as I fell pregnant with you. I went to the gods with the vision, and we made a bargain. A bargain that I now wish I wouldn't have made because it was the start of your downfall as well.

Because you were born on the blood moon, it only made your magic expand into something incredible to behold. Your father was terrified of you. Terrified of what you would be-come. It was clear, even as a baby, that you would be unstop-pable if you wanted. He wanted to have you killed because your magic was too much for him to handle. I refused to allow that, so I made him a deal. I would put most of your magic in a cage inside of you, keeping just your fire magic free. I used a binding spell that would keep you safe from showing how much magic you had. I did not tell your father about the dark magic inside of you. The one that takes magic from others and allows you to have it too. But gods above, I was so proud of your abilities. I was never ashamed of what you could do.

But the binding spell will need to be redone as you get older, and your magic expands. If it doesn't, it will kill you. The spell only allows me to undo it on the blood moon. My plan is to let your magic free this blood moon and not rebind it like your father is demanding.

When you were a small child, I started having visions about your future. At first, I thought they were just nightmares, but then Killian visited me in my dreams, and I knew he was trying to warn me. All the visions showed me dying and you growing up without knowing that your magic was stuck inside of you. If this happens, you will grow up sick. Your magic will start to take from you and your soul in order to fuel itself. That is, if I cannot free you first.

I have seen so many versions of your death in my dreams that I do not understand what my visions are trying to tell me. It is not always death, though. I have also seen you happy with a family of your own. It is almost as if both versions are true, but how can that be?

I wished to every holy being that I could give you more clarity of what your future holds, but it is as if you die several times, and I cannot understand why. Every decision you make will impact you in a significant way, but your prophecy will come true. You do not have a choice in that, but you will have a choice in who you fight for. I have only told one soul of your prophecy, and that is Brim. He will not speak of it until he must, but when the gods will it, he must tell it.

If I could give you one piece of advice, it would be this: never, under any circumstances, trust your father. I have never seen as much evil and cruelness in one fae as I see in him. He has a gift of making those around him think he cares and has good intentions, but he does not care for anyone but himself. If you are reading this letter, I know you are back in Cerithia. Find Brim; he will help you understand the prophecy and perhaps give you more insight. Do not tell your father of this letter, of Brim, or of Rosaline.

Also, you must know that my bloodstone is for you and you alone. With it, you will have unlimited energy for your powers. It is the most important thing I could leave you. You need the bloodstone. Find it, keep it, and do not, under any circumstances, let your father have it.

Killian was such a wonderful man that I wish he could have been your father, but I did what I needed to for the coven. I wouldn't trade you for anything, Thea. You will always be my greatest love and accomplishment. But I think I will carry the guilt of who I made your father and binding your magic inside of you into the next life and each one after.

Even though I am no longer here, please remember that you are strong, powerful, and unbeatable. You do not need anyone else to save you; you have always been strong enough to do that yourself.

There is a man with golden eyes who will watch you in the future. I do not know who he is. I have never met him before, but he seems to be important to you. He holds answers for you, but I have also seen him kill you. I do not know what his significance is to you, and even though I saw him kill you, I cannot bring myself to hate him. I will seek him out for myself and see.

You have all my love,
Mother

My head swarmed with so many questions. My eyes scanned her perfect penmanship, wanting to take in as much detail about her as possible. I paused at her confusion about my many deaths. My mother had seen my curse and the ways I died. She also saw Cassius in these visions, but she did not fear or hate him.

"I have a portrait for you," Rosaline said from behind me, startling me. She held up a small, framed painting, and I took it. It was of her, Bayla. My eyes could not look away from my mother. It was as if I were looking at an image of myself. The only difference was her red eyes, like Cassius said. I gasped when I saw the red and orange swirls on her skin; they were the same as mine. I took in the man next to her. He was taller than her, with kind brown eyes and dark hair. Killian. I glanced at Rosaline.

"They look happy."

This made her smile.

"They were. I don't know if I ever saw anyone so in love." Her hand grabbed mine and squeezed it tightly. "You are so much like her, Thea; it's like the gods gave me a piece of her back."

"I wished things had been different." I frowned at the image.

"Your mother came to understand the meaning of the visions before she died. She knew of the curse, and she had met Cassius."

"She envisioned him because he killed me. His significance was that he cursed me."

Rosaline shook her head.

"Your mother eventually found the answers she sought, but this letter was already written," Rosaline said with a smile. "Bayla never shared what she found out about Cassius, but I do know that she did not hate him."

"Then maybe she didn't understand what he did."

Rosaline gripped my hand.

"She knew, Thea. She knew everything before she died. Bayla knew she would not see you grow up, but she was at peace with it after meeting Cassius. She said you'd be in good hands with him. You must be so confused, but you need to trust your instincts. There is a reason you hate it here, and do not hate Cassius as much as you try to convince everyone."

"Why would you say that? You don't know what I feel about Cassius."

"It's plain as day on your face that you *think* you should hate him because he killed you, and maybe you feel shame that you don't. But I'm telling you that you *need* to trust your instincts. If you don't hate Cassius, then figure out why." Rosaline gave me a sad smile.

"Do you think I am a fool to have feelings for him still even knowing that he killed me?" I whispered. I was fighting with the idea that I did not hate him like I should. I wanted to forgive him, and that made me feel pathetic.

"No. I think your mind doesn't remember, but maybe something in your heart does." She frowned at me. "Trust yourself, Thea."

I nodded as I stared at the portrait of my mother. My instincts wanted me to forgive Cassius.

"You should go before your father tries to find you. Keep the portrait," she smiled. "And Thea, I think you know that this is not your home. But I think you are too scared to admit it, so I am telling you that it is okay to feel that way. Blood does not make a family."

I glanced down at the image of my mother, and when I glanced back up, I was no longer in the bookshop. I was standing in the hallway of Cerithia's castle. I rushed inside my bedroom and shut the door.

My body collapsed on my bed, and I stared at the dingy space, realizing just how small and unkept it really was.

The silence of my room brought me no comfort. I just wanted someone, anyone, to help me understand. Everything my mother said in her letter was the opposite of what my father told me, but now I wondered if he had read the letter he took from Rosaline and crafted his own version of the tale. Rosaline told me to trust my instincts, and those instincts told me that I didn't want to be here. I wanted Cassius, even if I couldn't understand why. So I would trust those instincts and figure it out.

Cerithia and Kizar would crumble with the prophecy, that I knew for sure. My father, Jesper, Gwyn, and Cerithia would crumble at my hands because they had all lied to me. They had attacked Exile. My father and Jesper were using me. I would not bow. I would not bend. I would not break at the hands of men who didn't truly care about me.

CHAPTER 15

I woke up the next morning groggy and sore from lack of sleep. My mother's words and Cassius' had replayed in my mind all night. After what I had learned last night, I didn't think I could even pretend to be civil with my father anymore. My darkness had crept over me as I lay in bed and was now refusing to let go of me. My mind was spinning as a result of the decision I had made. But to pull it off, my plan had to be fool proof. I couldn't just slaughter my family because I would still have an entire kingdom to face afterward.

I knew I could level Cerithia with a flick of my wrist, but I would never do that. There were too many innocent fae who lived here. My plan was to stay out of sight today and sort through my thoughts. When I snuck out of my room, it was with intentions to go get food, but then I saw Wisp. My heart began to beat rapidly in my chest because

I had learned that she started showing up when there was something she wanted me to find.

She flickered quickly to me, twirling around me with her flames a stunning shade of purple. Wisp finally stopped moving around me and floated a few feet in front of me. Anguish spilled from her and wrapped around me tightly, making it hard for me to breathe, almost as if she were hugging me in her own special way. When she switched back to a dark green, I knew it meant she was happy.

Once satisfied with herself, she flickered away from me and back down the hallway she had been headed toward. My feet were following her before she could summon me. She moved slowly, letting me know she was worried there was a chance we would run into someone else. My eyes scanned around the corner, and I sucked in the small gasp that nearly escaped me.

Lavtan, the chief adviser to the king of Crimson, was walking into the throne room with my father, Jeb, and Jesper. What was Cerithia's enemy doing meeting with the king like this?

There were no guards outside, which I found odd. My suspicions were raised. I slowly slipped forward and peeked into the crack of the door they had left ajar. There was no mistaking Lavtan's cruel face once I saw him standing over my father's map of Elloryon, which he had sprawled out on a table.

"How are you managing, Thea?" Lavtan asked. I couldn't understand why he would be here and ask about me. Maybe he had been sent by Cassius to check on me?

"She won't be a problem," Jesper sighed. "She hasn't told us she remembers anything, so maybe being away from Cassius has stopped the memories."

"I have found out that Cassius is not planning on attacking Cerithia. So, if you're waiting for him to start a war, you'll be waiting forever," Lavtan spoke. "Cassius is worried that starting a war will make Thea come kill him without giving him a chance to talk to her, so he is avoiding it."

"We will declare our plans at the meeting of the kingdoms. Are you sure it will be safe to take Thea?" My father questioned Lavtan. "Is Cassius planning to steal her away?"

"As far as I can tell, he has no plans to try to take her. He hasn't spoken a word of her since she chose Cerithia. It's almost like he doesn't care anymore." Lavtan spoke so casually, but his words were still a dagger through my heart. "What of the other elite magic fae?"

My ears pricked at the question. Was he referring to Exile? Wisp turned black, letting me know that she didn't like this conversation either.

Jeb spoke this time. "As far as Thea knows, we checked Exile, and no one was there. She thinks that she just made them all up."

"She will want to see for herself at some point. She's a persistent bitch. Make sure they can't be found."

They glanced over the map for a few silent moments. My fire simmered in my chest in anger, heating me to the point that sweat beaded on my forehead. Gods, I didn't know if I could hold out much longer on my plan to kill them. My darkness didn't urge me forward at the thought, so it must have agreed with me that there was more to learn.

"You didn't see her compete this year," Lavtan sighed. "She is much stronger than she was seven years ago. When they were together, she was immediately drawn to Cassius, and he could hardly stay away from her either. You better get her over that attitude if this is going to work."

What was going to work? Lavtan continued talking about Crimson's defenses, guard patrols, and border patrols, proving that he was a traitor to Crimson. My body seethed at this news. It didn't surprise me that he was a traitor. He had treated me terribly at Crimson.

"Well, we wouldn't be in this rushed position if you had done your fucking job," King Luren snapped at Lavtan.

"I tried everything to get her not to finish the trials. I gave her the worst team for the maze. I practically handed her to Riven, and the idiot couldn't finish the job. I even invited Flora to the castle to try and seduce Cassius, but it did nothing. Nothing got to her this time. Even Nev fucked it up when he tried to handle her. I told him exactly where she was and how weak she was, but she still got free."

"Because Haden turned his back on Kizar!" Jesper growled. Haden, he was something else. I smiled at the thought of him betraying Jesper to help save me. Lavtan nodded slightly as his cruel eyes drifted around the men in the room.

"We may have lost Haden, but I have a new ally in Cassius' kingdom. He will do anything we ask, even kill Cassius if I say so." Lavtan's words chilled me. Who was betraying Cassius? Was it Kace, Zade, or someone else?

"I've been thinking, and I believe it's time Kizar and Cerithia form a powerful alliance," Lavtan said with a smile. "Make a spectacle of Thea at the meeting, but do not make it seem as if she's a prisoner. Make everyone in that room feel like she wants to be there." Lavtan's warning rang through my head. Wisp flashed a series of random colors, trying to get my attention. "You better have control over her."

Just then, I heard footsteps coming down the hallway and darted into the darkness of the corner. My lungs burned as I held the air inside, trying to make myself as invisible as possible. The queen and Tally walked past me and into the meeting room before shutting the door completely, cutting me off from whatever was going to happen next.

Fuck. I needed to get out of here.

I glanced around, but Wisp was gone. Taking that as a bad sign, I headed to my room. The castle's normally fresh flower scent was gone, replaced by night and rain as a storm raged outside. Lightning ruptured through the night sky, mirroring the war I was feeling on the inside. I now knew for certain that Cerithia only wanted me as a pawn, but learning about all the scheming that Lavtan had done over the course of the trials was appalling.

Cassius and the rest of Crimson had no idea Lavtan was betraying them. Part of me wanted to race to Crimson to tell them, but my senses took over. If Lavtan had worked so hard to serve me on a silver platter for Riven and Nev to kill, then that must mean that my father and Jesper both really wanted me dead. Why else go through such trouble to kill me?

At least Cassius and Crimson had tried to keep me alive. My mother was right. I should've never trusted my father. Out of nowhere, an onslaught of memories hit me, and this time I fell to the floor, groaning at the pain that came with them.

I saw Cassius smiling at me. Then the Crimson King hugged me tightly as I wore a dark red dress. After that, Cassius again, but now he was laughing in the place he called our home. Then it switched, and Cassius was holding a dagger to my throat, still smiling.

I gasped for breath as the visions slammed into me, but I felt like the room had been stripped of all air.

When the final memory invaded my thoughts, it hit me with such force that I almost blacked out. I saw Cassius again, but this time he was cradling me in his lap as he whispered that he loved me with tears streaming down his face. Then he raised his hand with a dagger in it and stabbed me through my heart.

My lungs finally sucked in the air they were desperate for as hot tears streamed down my face, but I wasn't sure which memory was making me cry. An overwhelming feeling of uneasiness now filled me.

Wisp appeared in the corner of my room in her normal blue shade.

"I still can't believe you never let me know that you were tied to Cassius' soul and that he could see you."

Her flames turned white, and that anguish from earlier came rushing back. She didn't respond verbally, but I knew she couldn't talk. Gods, I was starting a fight with my only friend. I glanced at Wisp and frowned.

"I made a mistake in the clearing that day, didn't I?"

She flashed bright orange.

"Stay orange if I should have chosen Cassius."

Her color stayed orange, making me feel stupid for falling for my father's words.

"Did Cassius actually stab me? Did he curse me?"

Wisp's color burned bright orange, still making me more confused. Why did Wisp think I should have chosen Cassius even though he killed me? I opened my mouth to ask another question, but she disappeared. Wisp was gone. The newfound knowledge had my darkness raging inside of me. I knew I couldn't kill my father yet, but that didn't mean I couldn't take revenge on someone. Quickly, I slipped on my cloak and grabbed my daggers.

★★☽★★

My footsteps were silent as I entered a quaint home close to the castle. Jeb wasn't here yet, which gave me time to snoop through his things. His home was a mess. Dishes were piled in the sink, and dirty clothes were strewn in a corner of the bedroom. It was clear a woman didn't live here. It looked exactly as I had imagined—a pigsty.

I rifled through his belongings, searching for anything useful. He had nothing. A small noise outside caught my attention. My darkness stirred with excitement, signaling Jeb's arrival. My eyes were still pulsing red, but my dark green cloak concealed the glow of my skin. I pulled up a chair and placed it in the middle of the dark living area. Jeb walked in a moment later, unaware of the danger awaiting him. He turned and locked the door, which made me smile to myself.

Too late for that.

Jeb set his things down and flicked on the light, freezing when he saw me sitting nonchalantly with my dagger.

"You might be the most unaware man I've ever met," I sighed as I stared him down.

"What the fuck do you think you're doing?" he snapped. My smile widened as his fear washed over me. He was terrified.

"I think you know why I'm here, Jeb."

"You can leave now, and I won't tell your father what you've done." His eyes darted to the drawers scattered across his already filthy home.

"You're going to tell me why Lavtan is helping my father and Jesper try to kill me."

"Fuck you."

"I hoped you'd be difficult." I stood and kicked the chair away. "It just makes this more fun for me."

Jeb backed up to the door, his shaky hand fumbling to unlock it without my noticing. My darkness slammed the door shut as he managed to open it.

"I won't tell you anything," he said, squaring his shoulders, as if that would make me back down.

"We'll see," I smirked.

Jeb charged at me with a small dagger, swinging it in quick, violent jabs. It was easy to dodge as I stepped aside and kicked him in the back, sending him crashing into the wall. He turned quickly, expecting me to approach him, but I was content to draw it out. He slid down the wall, dazed.

"Tell me," I demanded.

He shook his head, so I walked over to where he was slumped against the wall and stabbed his thigh. Jeb's painful yell echoed in the small space.

"They don't want you to break your curse," he gasped, breathing heavily.

"Why?"

Instead of answering, Jeb stood and readied himself for a fight. If he wanted to do this the hard way, so be it. I moved forward quickly and swung my daggers at him.

Jeb managed to keep up with my swings, even nicking my forearm in the process. However, his movements were slowing due to his wound.

I punched him in the face as he swung and missed, sending him stumbling back into the wall with a groan.

"Why!"

"Because you would run to Cassius," he breathed heavily. "You would never choose us."

My red eyes narrowed on him.

"So Cassius didn't kill me?"

"No, he did," Jeb groaned. I walked forward and stabbed Jeb's other thigh, frustrated by his vague answers. "He killed you!"

"There's something I'm not understanding about all of this, and I know you know what it is, so start fucking talking."

Jeb shook his head.

"You can kill me, but I'm not betraying my kingdom," he said, sliding down the wall in defeat.

"I was hoping you'd put up a better fight," I replied, kneeling out of his reach just in case he tried anything. "It won't matter, Jeb, because I know enough. I will be killing my family and Jesper. Cerithia will crumble, and when it does, your honor will die with it."

Jeb's nostrils flared as he glared at me. I stood and glanced down at him.

"Look at how pathetic you are," I sneered. My darkness wanted out, and I finally let it free. "I barely lifted a finger to overpower you. I didn't even need my magic."

My darkness crept toward Jeb, unseen, wrapping around him. I heard the sickening sound of bones breaking as he cried out for help.

"I feel a little bad that you'll miss me destroying this kingdom and killing my father. You're going to miss quite the show when I fulfill the prophecy."

Jeb tried to speak, but my darkness was squeezing him too tightly. I forced it to ease up.

"You'll never win. You and your precious Cassius will both fucking die!" He spat blood toward me, causing my gaze to flick up to him.

"My precious Cassius." I nodded, acknowledging that Cassius had always been the right choice for me, despite him killing me. "Thank you for confirming that he means something to me."

"I hope your death is slow and painful, you stupid fucking bitch!" Jeb's attempt to appear fearless only highlighted his terror.

"How long until you're begging me for death?" I purred, leaning down to see how mangled his hands were from my darkness.

His jaw clenched, signaling that he was done talking. I lifted him with my darkness and set him down in the chair.

"Unfortunately for you, Jeb, you're the first one I've gotten my hands on to kill, and I have a lot of anger built up inside me."

That was the last thing I said to him as I stepped forward and stabbed him in the stomach, twisting the blade before pulling it out. My darkness crushed the bones in his legs and arms, causing him to cry out. I cut off his fingers, one at a time. It only took two before he begged me to kill him, but I ignored his pleas and finished with all ten. Blood pooled beneath him in the chair. Fuck, he was losing a lot of blood. I summoned my fire magic and burned his finger wounds shut. Jeb was sobbing.

"Have at it," I told my darkness, which lashed out and crushed Jeb's whole body painfully slow. The sound of his bones breaking was absolutely disgusting. I flinched as my darkness drew it out. A moment later, it dropped Jeb to the floor, leaving a jumbled mess of his body. Dead. My darkness swarmed around me in a frenzied joy. I considered burning down his home but decided instead to make sure my father knew how painful Jeb's death was. With one last glance at Jeb, I left his home and headed to the castle.

CHAPTER 16

I headed for a side entrance close to the training fields, creeping across the grounds to avoid being seen by any guards. As I got closer, I saw the silhouette of a man standing in the field, and my heartbeat quickened. Cassius? I moved swiftly toward him, but I stopped when I realized who was actually there.

Jesper gave me a small wave. Disappointment weighed heavily on my chest as I continued walking toward him.

"Where did you come from?" Jesper asked with a smile.

"I went for a walk and saw someone standing here. Curiosity got the better of me," I said carefully, my darkness ready to kill him at any moment. Killing Jeb tonight wasn't enough to satisfy my need for vengeance. I knew the soft moonlight concealed Jeb's blood that was splattered on me.

Jesper's smile brightened as he pointed to a blanket and food. "Do you want to have a midnight snack out here under the stars with me?"

"Do I have a choice?"

His smile faltered, and I hoped he felt like the slimeball he was. I sighed as I sat on the opposite side of the blanket from him. He sat and smiled brightly at me. I could see how I had been drawn to him before Cassius came along. He was handsome, and his smile made him look innocent, but I saw the monster lurking in the depths of those eyes. He handed me some food and poured drinks. Part of me wondered if I should kill him right then and there.

But I was curious about why he was out here and what he would say to me.

"I wanted to apologize for the way things have gone since being back," he said.

"Okay," I muttered, unsure of what to say. My family must have sent him, knowing I no longer trusted my father.

"I feel protective over you. I forget that you could kill us all if you felt like it," he chuckled instead of showing disgust at the magic I wielded. His hand instinctively touched the large gash I had given him. My dagger pressed against my leg in my boot, a silent reminder that I could end this liar too. "Your father can be a difficult man to get along with."

"Stop calling him my father. He is the king, not my father."

He nodded in agreement, his eyes turning to the sky as he ate his snack.

"Before Cassius, it was me, you know. I was the one you were in love with." His lie sounded so genuine, but I knew better. I had never loved this monster in front of me. How could he sit here and lie like this, knowing they had tried to kill me in the trials?

"No, I did not," I scoffed.

"Yes, you did. We were to be married, but then Cassius came along and tricked you. He stole you from me."

Uneasiness filled me. Why was he pushing this so hard?

"You are not anything I want from a husband," I said, my tone dripping with clear disgust.

The moment I insulted him, his entire demeanor shifted. I almost smiled as his true self surfaced.

"Well, too fucking bad," he glared. "Your father will be announcing our engagement at the meeting of the kingdoms."

"Luren would never allow that," I hissed, but I was filled with fear. I couldn't get married to someone like Jesper.

Especially now that I could see the evil that lurked under his fake friendliness.

"Showing a united front between our kingdoms will elicit a new sense of power for both of us. You will be my wife, but your father still has the ultimate say."

"Why would you ever agree to that?" I scoffed.

"The kingdoms will never stop fighting over you, Thea. If you are married to me, then I will have your perceived power on my side. They will not mess with my crown."

I was to be a pawn again.

"I would rather die than be tied to you," I snapped. "I will not marry you."

"You will not have a choice." His eyes were now enraged and full of hatred. "I will force you anyway I can. You will be mine, and that is something I can throw in Cassius' face for the rest of our existence."

Through the haze of anger in my mind, my senses alerted me to something moving near us. My ears perked at the rustling of bushes in the woods. My eyes darted toward the sound, but I couldn't see anyone there. I held my breath, hoping to hear the noise again. When nothing appeared, I let my attention fall back on Jesper.

"Cassius would not care," I said, but I knew the words sounded untrue.

"Do you think I don't see how you're acting lately?" Jesper cocked his head to the side, analyzing me. "I know something happened. Did you speak with Cassius?"

"Of course not," I said to him like he was an idiot.

"Your father is too blinded by greed to see how much you hate it here. He doesn't see the way you recoil when he says you will fight for Cerithia. But make no mistake, Thea, I see everything you do, and I know that you hate this kingdom, your family, even me. You can't fool me."

"You're right. I fucking hate you, I hate my family, and I hate the fae of Cerithia. But that does not mean I will not fight against Crimson. I hate them more." My darkness hissed at my lie.

The rustling sound in the woods caught my attention again. I focused once again on the darkness. This time, my eyes landed on the silhouette of a man standing at the edge of the woods, just in the shadows. The man was too short to be Cassius, but it was clear that he was watching Jesper and I.

"I don't trust you," Jesper scoffed.

"I don't fucking care." I turned to him. My magic was ready to reach out and burn him alive.

"There is a meeting in a few days that the king and I will have to attend. You will need to be there too, as the captain of the Cerithian army. You will be on your best behavior."

I needed to kill them before that meeting. The stars would fall from the heavens before I married Jesper.

My focus, however, was now elsewhere. I only nodded in response, not truly listening anymore. My eyes were fixated on the shadow in the tree line. Maybe I should tell Jesper we were being watched. Immediately, I dismissed that thought. Hopefully, whoever it was, was here to kill Jesper.

My attention refocused on Jesper and what he was babbling about, but a freezing gust of wind came through, chilling me instantly.

"I'm going to bed." Jesper stood. "Guards are watching you, so don't even think about taking off," he snapped.

My eyes drifted back to where the shadow had been, but I didn't see the man anymore.

Jesper waited for me to respond but turned in a huff and left when he realized I wouldn't be. As soon as his steps faded away, I headed straight for the woods.

"Hello?" I called out into the now silent woods. "I saw you... Who are you?"

Nothing responded. But as I looked around, I noticed that there was frost clinging to the nearby trees. Only one fae that I knew of had the power to do that.

"Haden?" I whispered harshly for him, but he was long gone.

I waited in the woods for a few minutes, but he never showed up, so I headed back to the castle, trying to understand why Haden would be here. He was from Crimson. Was he spying on Cerithia? I continuously glanced over my shoulder all the way to the castle just in case he came back, but he didn't.

Near the end of my walk, I turned around to see Wisp hovering in front of me. She was flashing black and red in front of me, almost as if in warning. I paused, puzzled. Was she warning me from Haden or was something else out here?

Feeling uneasy, I hurried into the castle, realizing only too late that it was an ambush she had been warning me about. As soon as I entered the doors, guards grabbed me and restrained me. One of them punched directly against my temple, making me dazed for a moment. Before I could even evaporate everyone with my fire, Jesper stepped forward and twisted magic binding barbs into my wrists, making me cry out in pain. Jesper, Luren, and Gwyn all stood against the far wall and watched what was happening.

My darkness and magic simmered inside of me, wanting desperately to kill all of them. Once I was bound by Jesper, the guards quickly let me go. Before they could stop me, though, I grabbed my dagger and plunged it into the neck of the closest one to me, then stood, full of rage, and headed for Jesper. I was still lethal, even without my magic.

"If you harm him or us, we will kill everyone in Exile," Gwyn sneered at me. Her threat made me stop heading for Jesper and turn towards her instead. By this time, my eyes had turned red, and my skin glowed with swirls of red and orange.

"What did you just say?" I demanded an answer.

"We will kill every elite magic fae in Exile if you do not cooperate with us," Luren said so casually.

"I should gut each one of you right now. I do not need my magic to kill everyone standing here."

Gwyn stepped back at my promise.

"They will be dead before you can ever reach them," Jesper scoffed. "If you harm any of us, the guards in Exile have orders to kill them—painfully."

Relief filled me that Sybil and the twins were alive. I knew I hadn't made them up. But gods, I had failed them over and over again. I lowered my dagger.

"Very good," Jesper said with a smile. "I told you she was acting weird." He glared at the king and queen.

Seething with hatred, I stared each of them down in turn. "I should have gutted all of you tonight instead of Jeb."

"Jeb?" My father glared.

"He was too easy to kill. I should have slaughtered all of you while Lavtan was here."

My father rolled his eyes.

"You are too much like your mother—always watching and scheming."

Something about his comment made me so angry that the grip on my dagger tightened until it was painful.

"Everything was a lie, wasn't it? The day I came to get the stone, you fed me lies about this being my home and you being my family. I know you had Cerithian guards kidnap me. It was not Falgon or Crimson."

This made all three of them look surprised.

"They called me the Crimson whore, which is only what fae in Cerithia call me. I also know that you hired witches to fuck with Exile. I saw the contracts."

No one answered me, but I knew that it was them. Gods, I would have destroyed this whole kingdom if my magic wasn't barbed inside of me. Cassius had known that Cerithia was not kind to me because this was how they had always treated me.

"You'll get over it," Jesper sighed, irritated.

"You tried to kill me on Crimson lands to start a war, and you think I'll get over it?" I took another step toward them. "Why on Crimson lands? If Cassius hates me so much, it would not make any sense to kill me on *his* lands to start a war." The thought that struck me next was so unbelievably painful that I almost couldn't say it out loud. "Unless he doesn't hate me at all."

My father stepped forward and tried to grab me, but I swung my dagger at him, slicing open his cheek.

"You stupid fucking bitch!" he yelled, clutching his bleeding face. Seeing him in pain pleased me, and I smiled at him, making him step back with wide eyes.

"I should have killed all of you when I discovered your schemes. You tried to get me to fail the trials, and you've been lying to me. I want to know why."

"If you don't stop talking, we will fucking kill you and try this again. But before you come back from Exile this time, we will slaughter Cassius and his entire family. You will be ours no matter what," Gwyn snapped.

"I will kill you first," I promised her. "Actually, I think I'll kill your daughters first so that you will really suffer." I smiled when Gwyn's face paled. "And anyway, Cassius would have you all slaughtered before you could hurt him."

Gwyn had made a very big error in her threat. She threatened to harm Cassius and his family, which let me know that they were important to me as well. They feared my feelings for him, even though he killed me. I knew that I was still missing a large piece of the puzzle, but it was starting to come together. My instincts were telling me I should have picked Cassius.

"If you do anything against our wishes, we will kill Sybil and the twins slowly and make you watch. As for Cassius, he would never see our spies coming. He would be dead before he realized what was happening," Luren threatened.

I said nothing as I stared at them. I was so angry. My thoughts were racing, but I knew one thing: I had to act now.

Turning to the three guards behind me, I threw my dagger into the heart of the closest one. As another guard rushed at me, it took little effort to overpower him, using his own sword to kill him. The last guard tried to flee, but I ran after him, grabbing him by his hair and yanking him back. My dagger slit his throat, and his blood spilled onto the king and queen. Once the guards were dead, I turned back to my so-called family. They had backed themselves against the far wall, as far from me as they could get.

"Don't worry, I'll let you all live," I snapped. "But make no mistake, it is only because you have control over those in Exile." I also wanted to mention that it was also because they had insiders in Crimson, but I pretended as if I didn't care. "You might as well kill me, because now I will never fight for you."

"You will obey us, Thea. We will not allow you to die and start this all over again. If you are here, then we know that you will not be in the hands of our enemies. So, you will stay, and you will fight, or you will lose everyone you love."

With one last black-eyed stare as full of threat as I could manage, I turned and stepped over the dead bodies of the fallen guards and left the room, leaving the bloody prints of my boots behind me.

They had said nothing as I left, probably knowing better than to tempt fate any more than they already had tonight. I hurried to my room and slammed the door shut, my chest aching so painfully that I thought my heart would burst. My magic swarmed inside of me, causing an uncomfortable ache that was bottled up and unable to free itself because of Jesper's binds. However, mixed with all of the pain and confusion was the relief of finally knowing some of the truth.

Wisp appeared close to me; her color is a bright green. She was happy that I knew the truth, but now what would happen? I had no magic. I couldn't risk killing those in Exile because of my fuck-up. My hope for the future deflated. All the realizations of Cassius and me had come too late, I was stuck in this hell.

CHAPTER 17

The hot spring I sat in was relaxing my sore muscles, and it was nice to wash off the dirt from war. I heard a noise coming through the forest. I cocked my head to listen and froze instantly when I realized that it was the sound of footsteps—heavy footsteps—and they were coming closer to where I was. Before I had time to react, an armored figure appeared at the tree line. It was Cassius. I grabbed my viper-handled dagger, but he only smiled at me as he began to strip.

"How the fuck did you find me?" I hissed as I watched him step into the hot spring with me. "I will stab you."

"Easy, little viper. I don't feel like fighting today, and I'm unarmed." He winked at me as he sat across from me, then dipped below the water before resurfacing a moment later with his dark hair dripping down his handsome face. His golden eyes stared at me for a long moment.

"We are in a war, and you want me to just forget that so we can relax together?"

"I would really enjoy a little break from pretending to hate each other." He smiled at me when I scoffed.

"I'm not pretending anything. You are my enemy."

He moved closer to me, not the least bit affected by my threat to stab him if he got close enough. His hand grabbed my dagger and pushed it away from him with little effort.

"Are you sure about that, little viper?"

"Someone will see us." Was the only retort that fell from my lips.

"No, they won't," he reassured me as he pried the dagger from my hand and set it on the shore. "We have both been working hard, so let's take the night off from this war garbage and relax in a hot spring that we both stumbled upon by accident."

I kept my eyes on him as he sat next to me and closed his eyes. I could stab him now while his guard was down, but I didn't reach for my dagger. I just stared at the handsome face of the man I was born to hate but, for some reason, didn't.

"I can practically hear you trying to talk yourself into stabbing me, Thea." He opened one of his eyes to look at me.

"What are you doing?" I questioned. "You think because you have a handsome face that I will be fooled?"

He opened his eyes and turned to face me.

"So, you do think I'm handsome?" His smile was a perfect masterpiece for making women swoon at his feet.

"Not really," I lied. His deep laugh reverberated around the silent forest.

"You are even more interesting than I thought." He smirked as he moved toward me. "You're also a very bad liar."

"Are you flirting with me?" I asked, unsure whether to put steel or interest in my voice.

"If I was?" His eyes swirled with blackness. I was treading a very dangerous line. My back hit the edge of the spring as I moved away from him. He had followed in tandem, but then he stopped a foot in front of me. Lines were beginning to blur as he moved closer to me. Inch by inch, he crept forward. I knew I should stop him. I knew I should leave. I just couldn't, though. He stopped when his lips whispered against mine.

I stared at him as I leaned forward and closed the space between our mouths. It was all the encouragement he needed to pull me closer to him. His hands wrapped around my waist and pulled me over his lap as he sat back. My naked skin skimmed over his, and it instantly sent a wave of anticipation through me. His stubble scratched and tickled as *he kissed down my neck, and a soft moan escaped me. His hands gripped me tighter.*

"I like those little noises you make," he growled. "I want to hear more of that, Thea."

The next day, I awoke with the determination to do my best without my magic. I was intelligent and trained as the captain of my guard; nothing could stop me. I knew that before I could do anything effective, I had to get information, so I decided to steal it.

Breaking into the king's office was too easy. No guards protected it unless he was in there, and he was currently in the city doing something today with his family. Fine with me. I wasn't sure what I was looking for, but I knew there had to be something in here that I could use. My eyes glanced over the map he still had spread out.

When I walked up to it, I looked at all the land of Elloryon. My eyes took in Crimson before sweeping across the map. The Forbidden Wood was easy to spot. I traced my finger over the creek that I knew flowed through Exile and breathed heavily when I didn't see it marked on the map.

I sighed in frustration. I didn't know what the hell I was looking for. A sudden flash of blue let me know that Wisp was back. She had been lingering near me all night but was gone when I awoke.

"I'm assuming you were with Cassius."

She ignored me and twirled around my father's desk. I moved to it, yanking open the drawers. Mostly it had ledgers and contracts.

"I don't see anything useful."

She practically slammed into the top left drawer, causing the desk to rattle. I narrowed my eyes on her.

"Easy," I whispered. "We can't make a mess."

I ripped the drawer open, and at first, it seemed normal, but then I realized it was too organized compared to the rest of the desk. I pulled everything out, but it was just blank paper. Well, that was odd. Suspicious, I pressed my hand against the bottom of the drawer, and it shifted up, revealing a secret compartment. I pulled out dozens of letters.

Some of them were a faded yellow from being here so long. I opened the first, and my heart raced.

King Luren,

It appears Thea has not made it long enough to be a threat this year in the trials. It will make you happy to know that Cassius is a mess if you want to declare war in his disheveled state.

Lavtan

What a prick. I ripped open another letter.

King Luren,

Thea is doing exceptionally well in the trials this year. However, she is injured, and I've made sure the next trial will be impossible for her to get through. I do expect her demise soon, so get your witches ready to attack Exile before next year's trials. If we weaken her before the trials, then maybe we can find a way to stop this madness once and for all.

Lavtan

Lavtan's betrayal has been going on for years. I opened another letter, craving the information.

King Luren,

I do not write this with good news. Thea has done better than ever in the trials this year, even with the attacks on Exile. Expect that she will be coming for the bloodstone. I hope you have a plan to get her to choose Cerithia. Cassius has weaseled himself into her heart again. It's obvious that she is infatuated with him. She will choose Crimson, so do something!

Lavtan

Wisp turned black, as I assumed she was reading over my shoulder. Lavtan and my father had made sure I failed every year. Pain shot through me as I slammed my fist down on the desk.

King Luren,

Crimson is in good standing with every kingdom besides Cerithia and Kizar. Jesper would be an easy alliance to form, and he's young enough to manipulate. The only way you will gain control over all of Elloryon is with Thea. The prophet has made sure everyone knows she is dangerous, but without her, you do not stand a chance. Elloryon would do better with one king, and that king should be ruthless like you. If you want to take over, then you better start by forming an alliance with Jesper. His father, King Halon, is very ill and should be dead within the next few years.

Lavtan

Lavtan had been using my father like a puppet to start wars. My father, of course, was either too stupid to see it or he knew and was using Lavtan to his advantage. Lavtan wanted to destroy Elloryon, all because he's a selfish prick. I glanced at Wisp as I struggled with what to do. Sighing, I took the letters I read and slipped them into the waistband of my trousers. Wisp turned a bright red, and I didn't know what that meant.

"I have to take these," I whispered as I started to put things back. "Lavtan, Jesper, and Luren want to destroy Elloryon, and I won't let them. I won't be a part of this."

Her color turned dark green, letting me know she was happy. I froze when I saw a letter with my writing on the front, addressed to King Luren. I grabbed it and shoved it in my trousers too. I took my time putting his drawers back perfectly. My heart was heavy with disgust. How could this man be my father? I glanced around the throne room as anger gripped me. Lavtan and my father had made sure I failed the trials. They knew I'd pick Cassius over them, but that only made me more confused.

Knowing that Cassius killed me and cursed me, why did they think I would still choose him? What did they know that I didn't? Uneasiness settled over me as I hurried down to my room. Wisp floated in the corner.

My heart ached, and my chest tingled with anxiety as I asked her a question that would surely hurt my feelings.

"Do you think Cassius actually loved me?" I whispered. Wisp froze at my question.

She flashed orange. Relief coursed through me.

Sighing, I slipped the letters from my trousers. I grabbed the one in my writing and opened it.

Father,

I have written you countless letters about my time in the war and have not received a word back. I can only assume you do not care about my well-being or the fact that I'm the best captain Cerithia has ever had leading them. Which is disappointing to know that nothing I do will make you care. So, this will be my last letter. If I'm killed in battle, please put my body to rest in the forest next to water so I may find peace for once in this gods-forsaken life. And if this is to be my last correspondence, I hope you feel the guilt of my death for the rest of your days.

Captain Thea Alzara,
The daughter you gave up on.

My lips tilted into a smile at my signature. I knew this must have angered my father because he had kept it over the years. Then my heart realized all the sadness I had written into this letter, and I was sure it never got a response anyway.

The contents of the letters weighed heavily on me. Something about them just didn't sit right. My father and Jesper wanted to take all the other kingdoms down. Even though I knew they had troubles with Crimson, why would they destroy Akecia and Falgon? Simply for land was a selfish thing, and I could not allow them to kill thousands of innocent fae for their greed. At this point, I didn't know if the prophet foresaw me crumbling all five kingdoms or if I would only crumble one.

Maybe the meaning was behind the letters. If I didn't say anything, then my father would expect me to destroy all the other kingdoms and kill their kings. I have no issues with any other kingdoms, and I wouldn't be doing that.

"I'm giving these letters to Cassius or someone from Crimson at the meeting. I can't let my father do this. This would be a lot easier if you could just tell me what the hell I am not understanding about all this shit."

She turned a melancholy gray as if to say she couldn't, which I knew already.

"There are things that I'm not understanding correctly." I glanced at her, and she turned a bright orange. "Do I give them to Cassius at this meeting? What if he tells everyone that I betrayed them?"

Orange burned brightly around her, letting me know that I had the answer I had been waiting for. Lavtan was from Crimson, and I hoped Cassius ripped that man's head from his body. I turned to ask Wisp another question, but she was gone. I closed my mouth with irritation. I did not understand why she kept going to him. It was part of the reason I knew I was missing something. She was supposed to be my friend, and she sought him out instead.

I sighed, knowing that I would have to give Cassius the letters somehow at the meeting, and hoped he cared enough to warn the other kingdoms. Even if he exposed my betrayal, I was fine with the consequences of dying.

I kneeled next to my bed and cut a hole in the side of it, slipping the letters inside among the stuffing.

Was it worth the risk? Yes, if it saved innocent fae throughout Elloryon. If I died trying, then at least I tried to do good before I died.

CHAPTER 18

Jesper and the king had ignored me since they barbed my magic inside of me. That was three days ago. I was thankful that I did not have to pretend to care for them any longer.

The king of Cerithia was equally as silent as we rode through a darkened forest in the carriage on our way to the meeting of the kingdoms. I stared out the small window and wished they had let me ride on my horse instead of sitting in this painful silence. The letters I had shoved into my trousers practically burned against my skin with every bump on the road.

I was sure I could get these letters into the hands of someone who would care. When I asked what kind of meeting this was, I was ignored. So, I kept my mouth shut. The king had made me take off my cloak and leave it at the castle, stating that he wanted everyone to see the colors of his kingdom on my uniform. In reality, though, it was so they could see that I belonged to him.

My jaw clenched tightly as the bumps irritated the magic barbs winding around each of my wrists like a bracelet. They wouldn't stop bleeding, and my skin burned and itched badly.

I perked up when I saw a white castle in the distance after riding for nearly a day and a half. We were visiting a new kingdom, and I thought it would be exciting to at least see something new. There was snow on the ground here. The bare trees were covered in frost, making the boughs bend downward toward the ground. It was stunning, even if the air was too cold and there were no flowers. The cold instantly made me think of Haden.

The town surrounding the castle was charming, with its lovely cottages and a light dusting of snow. The fae here stood and watched as our carriage passed by, most with light hair and bundled in large clothing. I took in their happy faces as they walked the stone streets. They appeared to be happier than Cerithia fae.

My fire magic didn't seem to enjoy the cold temperatures, but gods, this place was beautiful.

My breath was visible in the carriage due to the drop in temperature. Snow flurried around us, and I couldn't help but smile. It felt like a dream.

"The kingdom of Akecia," the king said, breaking the silence as our carriage rounded the front entrance. The Crimson Castle, with its black stone, was always stunning, but this castle, with its dominating white stone, was a close second. My mouth hung open as I craned my head back to admire the grand building. Snow fell on my face, and I closed my eyes, savoring the peacefulness of this place. I didn't know what awaited me once I entered through the doors.

My cloak would have been nice in the cold winter air, but we were ushered inside before I was done admiring outside. I stood to the side of my father as a man approached us. He wore all white with an icy blue crest over his heart on his robes. I shook my head—a perfect target.

"King Luren and Prince Jesper, welcome to my home. We were all sorry to hear your father has become more ill, Jesper." This was their king?

His hair was white as the snow outside, but he was only my age, if not a few years older. His beard was large but trimmed nicely. His dark eyes turned to look at me, and he stepped back slightly at the sight of me.

"Thank you for hosting, King Sybrien." Jesper bowed. "Are the others here?"

"Yes, we are all ready to start." His eyes shifted to me again, and confusion filled his expression. I tried to give him a small, reassuring smile, but he turned away from me quickly. "Follow me."

He headed down a long hallway. Everything was so... white. Silver also adorned some fixtures, but the castle definitely reflected the snow outside. It was not decorated with expensive things like the one in Cerithia. It was somewhat more modest, even though they could likely afford to decorate it expensively. The king of Cerithia followed King Sybrien first, then Jesper, and then I walked behind.

We made our way across the grand floor of a beautiful room and towards a large set of double doors. The guards on either side pulled them open as we approached. Discussions that had been going on ceased immediately when we walked in. My eyes instinctively landed on Cassius first, like they could sense him before I registered it. His eyes were black as they immediately dismissed my presence.

I would be lying if I said my body had no reaction to seeing him. Something bloomed deep in my stomach at the sight of him. My darkness practically purred when I glanced at him, which only confirmed that I made the wrong decision by choosing my father. The King of Crimson stared at me with a deep crease in his brows. Then I saw Haden, Kace, and Zade standing by them as well. I looked away from them quickly before my feelings could show on my face. Emotions immediately stirred in my chest, making my darkness swirl.

Wisp chose this time to make her appearance again. Or maybe she had come with Cassius. She swirled around him in her pretty, dark green color, happy to see him. His hair moved slightly at the breeze that she made, and his eyes finally found mine. I still didn't understand how he was the only other fae who could see her.

I was actually thankful that the magic barbs were on at that moment because my darkness would have left me at the sight of them. Knowing what I did now, I realized that I should have gone to Crimson with Cassius when he asked me to.

I was almost ashamed for him to see me like this, with my face still cut and bruised by the guards that held me down the other night. My eyes shifted to the others grouped here. All five kingdoms were in attendance. My heart was beating so loudly that I wondered if they could all hear it. Maybe that was why all of them were staring at me right now, not because of my black eyes and glowing swirls on my arms.

My father sat in a chair next to Jesper and pointed for me to stand next to them. I did as I was told. My eyes immediately shifted to Cassius again as he whispered to his father. Then I met Haden's eyes as he stared openly at me, frowning as I stood stoic. The king had drilled it into my head this morning that I would be on my best behavior. My darkness was clawing at my chest, wanting to go to Cassius. It was painful.

King Sybrien stood and held his arms up, calling attention to him. "Thank you all for coming to this meeting of kingdoms. Today, we are here to discuss the rising violence between Crimson and Cerithia in hopes of deterring them from the path of war. To hopefully find a peaceful solution, so that we may all stop losing men and resources."

This made all the kings nod their heads, except for Luren and Jesper.

"If the Crimson kingdom concedes the land they stole from us, then we will consider not declaring war," King Luren spoke.

"Land that we took back because you broke the peace treaty between us in order to steal it in the first place," Crimson's king answered back. "We will do no such thing. It has been nearly three hundred years. It's time to move on."

My eyes shifted to Cassius when his black eyes flickered at me. He held my gaze without any sort of emotion, his cold indifference shielding whatever he was thinking. It made a shiver run through me.

"We will give you the land," Cassius said, making his father pause. My father's interest was piqued. "You can have the land if you give me Thea."

My darkness vortexed inside of me at his offer. But it wasn't upset; no, it was happy. It wanted my father to hand me over. My eyes were locked on Cassius. I could feel his longing for me as he watched me.

"Thea belongs to me," my father snapped. "The only way she will go to Crimson is to put an end to your bloodline. If you want to continue this war talk, then so be it. You will not, cannot, win against Cerithia's forces."

"And what of Kizar and Cerithia's war?" King Sybrien asked.

"It's done," Jesper spoke. "We have come to a mutual agreement fit for both kingdoms."

The other kingdoms were clearly surprised by this information. Whispers spread like wildfire through the men. I could feel Jesper touch my hand and went to pull away from him, but he gripped me to the point of pain. Cassius' face finally broke from cold indifference at seeing the touch. Anger now coated his handsome face. Jesper pulled me down so he could speak to me.

"If you make a scene, I will destroy Exile and everyone still in it."

My chest tightened, and my mind was slowly retreating from all the hateful comments I wanted to spew at him.

"What agreement?" someone called out.

"A marriage bonding our two kingdoms in power," King Luren smiled directly at Cassius and the Crimson Kingdom. "Jesper and Thea are to be wed soon."

Crimson's king stood up from his seat and glared. It was just then that Cassius' shadows burst from him, and he headed straight for Jesper but stopped before reaching him. Disgust filled me at the declaration. I did not want to marry Jesper. Turning toward him, he gave me a look filled with warning.

"You cannot be serious," the King of Crimson snapped. "That's low even for you." He was so angry that it caught me off guard, but I saw him looking at me with pity in his eyes when he said it.

Meanwhile, Cassius' anger filled the entire room we were in. My darkness fought to escape when it felt his emotions. All the kingdoms frowned at the scene unfolding. Cassius closed his eyes tightly, as though he were trying to compose himself. When he opened them again, they seemed to be staring right at me.

Jesper pulled me into his lap and wrapped his hands around me. His mouth brushed my ear as he chuckled so softly.

"Look at Cassius right now and tell me that isn't worth all of this."

Cassius looked devastated.

"He may have stolen you from me, but it's my bed you will sleep in, my surname you will take, and my children you will bear." Like hell I would.

"You make it sound as if he cares about any of that," I replied. Jesper's eyes narrowed, but he didn't respond.

I tried to stand, but his arms gripped me tighter into him.

"If you make a scene, you will lose everyone in Exile," Jesper hissed at me. It immediately doused my fight. "That's right, Thea, Sybil, and the twins can be saved if you put on a good show." I didn't fight him. "Good, now kiss me," he whispered.

I turned toward him but paused.

"Or I'll send my spy to slice off Cassius' head, then the rest of your little friends over there." I knew Cassius would have Jesper in pieces before he could do anything. But I still had to put on this show because the safety of others depended on it. I now had a reason to behave, and that reason was to get back to Exile.

I leaned forward and crushed my lips to his. He gave me a low moan of approval and deepened the kiss. This felt so wrong. I didn't even close my eyes as Jesper kissed me—all for show. He pulled away, and I turned forward. My blood bond caught fire as soon as my eyes landed on Cassius, and I had to smother the flames on my sleeve. Cassius' eyes were closed tightly as his shadows swarmed around him. His hands balled into fists at his sides as he turned from us. I could see the rapid rise and fall of his shoulders. His father was saying something to him.

"We heard the prince of Crimson is also in the works of a marriage," the King of Cerithia smiled directly at me. "Princess Flora of Falgon?"

My eyes shifted to Cassius, but he didn't look at me. My heartbeat echoed loudly in my chest as I waited to hear if he was marrying someone else willingly.

"Cassius does not wish to be married at this time, and we in the Crimson Kingdom value choice and free will." He was clearly making a jab at my father. "Why are you starting rumors of Cassius looking for a wife?"

"You value weakness, King Ryland," he snapped back, but said nothing about the rumor allegations.

"I'll marry Thea," Cassius declared loudly. "Should we ask her if she'd rather marry me or Jesper?" He snapped viciously at my father. "I would tread very fucking lightly if I were you, Luren." There was an unspoken statement that passed between them. His declaration made my stomach clench tightly.

"You disrespect me by using my first name," my father hissed.

"You are not my king, and even if you were, I don't respect you enough to ever address you formally. In fact, there is only one royal member in your family I respect, and that is Princess Thea."

Gods, his words were affecting me. My cheeks burned as everyone seemed to be watching me. I tried to shield how I was feeling.

"She is not a princess," my father snapped. "At least not yet."

My father's jab made Cassius take an angry step toward him, but he seemed to realize what he was doing and stopped.

"So, you're saying that you will not declare peace with Crimson? Do you want war?" King Sybrien asked.

"Nobody wants war! The choice is not ours. Crimson can still concede our land back to us and admit their wrongdoing. We will give them a little longer to change their minds before we go to war. But if we do declare war, then we will expect the other kingdoms to make their alliances with us or with the heathens of Crimson."

"This is not our war," the King of Falgon scoffed. "You would make enemies out of all of us but Kizar?"

"If you do not stand with Cerithia, then you will fall just as the prophet spoke." All the kings' eyes shifted to me. "Thea has made her decision, and that is to fight for Cerithia and Kizar."

I wanted to scream that I didn't choose them.

"We are to believe that this woman is capable of all this destruction?" Falgon's king looked at me with skepticism. "She has taken a beating from someone, obviously, yet she can kill us all with a single flick of her wrist. I don't believe it."

Jesper pushed me up so forcefully that I stumbled in front of them. I now stood in the center of the circle as the leaders of the kingdoms looked over me like I was nothing spectacular. Except for those from the Crimson Kingdom, who all looked like it pained them to see me like this.

"You want a show of Thea's magic?" Jesper asked as he glared at me.

They all hesitated.

"Of course, Thea won't hurt anyone. Right, darling?" Jesper demanded a verbal reply.

"Of course," I said. I didn't want to hurt anyone. Well, except Jesper and my father, that is. Even with Cassius so close, I didn't feel the urge to hurt him anymore.

"Alright, Thea, darling, show them why they should fear you," he smiled. I could only stand there and look at him like he was an idiot. Did he not remember I was in magic-barbed cuffs? "Thea?" he said, irritated.

I lifted the sleeves of my Cerithia captain uniform and showed my magic barbs. Jesper stood and came over to me, unwrapping them with more force than necessary. As soon as they were off, my fire mist shot out of me without permission, knocking Jesper back forcefully. It did not like to be contained like a caged animal.

"We thought you would all feel more comfortable knowing she was barbed," Jesper lied through his teeth. "If you harm me or your father, I have guards on standby to slaughter every last one of them," he whispered as he gave my cheek a soft kiss. Jesper sat down and nodded for me to give them some sort of show.

I rubbed my sore wrists for a moment, then did as he asked. My fire mist snaked across the ground toward each king, but it didn't touch them. Instead, my fire mist rose up and around each of the kings so that only the five of them and I were in my trap. All their eyes widened with fear, except for the King of Crimson. He smiled proudly at me. I lowered my fire wall and saw that all the guardsmen had weapons drawn at me. I ignored them as I pulled out Haden's ice magic from deep within me.

I let it seep out of my hands and freeze the flowers in the room before moving to the guardsmen's weapons. They froze instantly. It was then that I felt Cassius' shadow magic surfacing around me, and I let it. Dark swarms of shadows grew and surrounded me in a black tornado, making my hair whip around at the force of it. My eyes met Cassius through my shadows, and his sadness nearly floored me. I turned away from him, and my eyes met King Sybrien. My healing magic hummed in my veins like it could sense that he needed it, but I didn't do anything about it yet. I don't think they wanted me to heal others. Instead, I closed my eyes and felt my invisible tendrils of darkness move throughout the crowd of men in here, looking for new magic to pull from. I smiled when I felt the first one.

I thought I was pulling shapeshifting from Kace, but instead of turning into the small animal I had seen him become at the trials, my body instead morphed into a large bird, and I shot up to the ceiling of the castle room we were in before dropping back down as myself. I needed to pull as much magic as I could from those around me while I had the chance. Using the excuse of showing off my powers was a perfect cover-up for it. The more I pulled, the more I collected inside of me. My darkness called out to me to keep taking. *Take. Take. Take. Power. Power. Power.* I closed my eyes and found my next magical victim quickly.

Looking around, I focused on a guard from Kizar staring at me in horror. I smiled at him as his elite magic pumped into my veins. As soon as I had made contact with him, though, a pulse shot out of me, radiating throughout the room, stopping everything in its tracks. The fire, the shadows, and even all of the people had stopped moving completely. I looked around us at everyone, frozen in time as I walked to him.

"You have elite magic." He looked at me with terror as I spoke it.

"They do not know. I will be killed."

"Your secret is safe with me," I assured the guardsmen of Kizar. He immediately bowed to me. "How long does this last?" I asked.

"When I do it, I can only hold it for fifteen seconds at most. This is longer than anything I can do." He stood and looked around at everyone, running his hand through his dark hair. "It only freezes this moment; outside of this room, everyone will be moving at a normal rate."

"What a wonderful gift." I smiled at him, my compliment taking him by surprise. I then moved away from him and unfroze the room. Then I played with this new magic again. I refroze everyone but kept my focus on keeping King Sybrien with me. He looked around the room as I walked toward him.

"What the fuck did you do?" he asked, as he tried scooting away from me like I was going to murder him. "Get back, Thea."

"You're sick." I could see the sickness under his skin and in his blood. Just like I could with Leer's wife. I could sense death close to him too. My comment made the king freeze. Did he know? "You're dying."

"I have been for quite some time," he sighed and relaxed slightly. Knowing this news made me sad for a man I did not know. "Only my wife and I know, so how did you find out?"

"I can see it." I pointed to his neck. "I can heal you, but you must not tell them what I've done. I don't think they want me helping potential enemies."

"Why would you even offer? My kingdom will never stand with Cerithia or Kizar. I am an enemy. I am on Cassius' side, always." I admired the truth from him. Even though I was his biggest threat, he didn't hide his distaste for me and Cerithia. The honesty of others is what I missed most about Sybil. She had always given it to me, even when I didn't think I needed to hear it.

"I am not a monster," I sighed. "Do not declare a side today. Hold off if you can before siding with Crimson." I grabbed his hand, and he tried to yank it away but stopped when he felt the healing swirls of orange and red as they moved into his skin. His eyes widened in shock as my magic did its work. When I pulled my hand away, tears filled his eyes.

"I feel...normal."

"It's gone." I smiled, and he looked over my face.

"We were all hoping you would side with Crimson, Thea. Cerithia and Kizar will only take more and more. You picked the wrong side."

"So, you choose the right one and stick with Crimson. I will not slaughter innocent men and women for greed. You have my word."

I walked away from him as I unfroze the room. Everyone looked at me, none the wiser, not realizing that their world had just stopped. Cassius' eyes, however, narrowed on King Sybrien as silent tears streamed down his face before shifting to me for an answer, but I gave him none as I pulled the next magic to me. Once it was mine, I reached in front of me, and light shone brightly from my hand, creating a small, floating orb. I grasped it and stretched it wider, like I had seen Rosaline do, then stepped into it, only to appear across the room a moment later.

Jesper smiled at me like he was proud of me, when in reality, he should fear me. I sensed more power and pulled in two other types of magic that were looming in the air. I stopped for a moment when I became disoriented. At first,

I thought it was too much magic pulling at the same time, but then I heard them. Voices were speaking loudly into my mind, seeming to come from nowhere and everywhere all at once. I pulled out of that magic instantly. I looked around and found the guard I had pulled it from. He was standing next to the king of Falgon. Once again, I froze everyone in the room except for him. He raised his weapon, and I stopped.

"What magic did I just pull from you?"

He stilled.

"I don't have magic," he growled.

"You have elite magic." I raised my eyebrows at him. "The voices."

He lowered his weapon and frowned at me.

"That's magic? I thought... I thought I was losing my mind. I shut them out. I thought they were all coming from my own mind."

"Is it someone else's thoughts, maybe?" I questioned.

"If it is, I don't know how to use it." His eyes stared at me oddly.

"Tell no one you have this gift. It will put you in danger," I ordered. He nodded in response. I unfroze the room again and made to show my other new power. I lifted my hand, and all the loose metal in the room rose up into the air. I let it hover for a moment, then I dropped it, causing a resounding crash to echo throughout the room.

Then I reached out and pulled the last magic I could sense in the room. I looked at the servant standing in the corner where it came from. She had elite magic. I released her powers and filled the room with butterflies and flowers before making it smell like rain and night. Illusion magic could mess with the senses. I could do so much with this one that I didn't show all its glory.

Finally, I turned toward Jesper and felt exhaustion cloud over me. Too much magic and energy were being used. I was now running out of time to use the magic I had acquired. I couldn't miss out on the only chance I had to make a difference. I looked at Haden and swept my arm out so that the whole room froze again, everyone but him. I took a step toward him, and his sad eyes glanced around before landing on me. I was getting weak; this magic was draining me too quickly.

"You were spying on me in the woods. Why?" I glared at him. "Did Cassius send you to hurt me?"

Haden's face fell at the accusation.

"He would never hurt you." His face scrunched with disgust. But he had hurt me.

"Why?" I demanded.

"To make sure you were alright; don't worry, I let him know how well you were doing while having a date with Jesper." His anger and disgust caught me off guard.

"You don't know what you saw," I said with a frown. The magic still pulsed inside of me, but I knew it was fading. I needed a minute to gain enough energy to use it once more. Quickly, I returned to where I had been and unfroze the room. Haden glanced at me oddly.

"Is that enough of a show?"

"Yes." Jesper smiled proudly and stood with the magic barbed cuffs. The sight of them hit me like a hammer, and I instantly froze the room, crying softly. All I could think of was heading back to the loneliness of Cerithia. I turned and walked to Cassius. His face was set in a hard, unforgiving expression as he stared at where I had been standing.

"I don't understand why you would do this to me. I don't want the pain and confusion of loving you any-more." I leaned my forehead against his hard chest and sobbed. I didn't want to be this monster. My fists rest-ed against his chest too, and my blood seeped onto his uniform from my wrists. Rain and forest filled my lungs, making me relax when I should be repulsed by him.

"Help me understand all of this."

I could pull his dagger from his sheath and kill him, but I wouldn't...because I still fucking loved him. I reached up and ran my fingers across his cheek. As soon as our skin made contact, though, memories hit me so violently that I fell to my knees as they flashed through my mind. But none of them were new. No, they were memories from our time during the trials.

A moment later, I heard the room bustling again. I hadn't meant to stop the magic from keeping them frozen.

I glanced up from where I was kneeling and crying to see Cassius' golden eyes locked on mine. He looked at me, kneeling and crying at his feet, then to where I had been before returning to me confused. I dropped the dagger on the floor, the noise ricocheting around the room.

I froze the room again quickly, but Cassius blinked at me. Reaching into my trousers, I grabbed the letters. It was now or never. I reached out, and he took the letters from me with confusion plaguing his features. I ripped them from his hand and shoved them into his shirt to hide the letters from Jesper and my father.

"Lavtan..." I started to tell him, but the magic started fading away. The noise of the room cut off my sentence. "Forgive me." I wanted to apologize for not going to Crimson with him when I had the chance. I knew it was right now. Cassius and Della had been right, I needed to understand the secrets of Cerithia before I could truly see what was going on.

"My love," he whispered so softly as his shadows swept out and caressed my cheek gently before I was yanked backward by my arm.

"That's enough magic fun for today, darling." Jesper wrapped the barbs tightly around my wrists again, making it nearly impossible to hold in the pain it caused. Blood dripped from my wounds as he yanked me up. He hugged me so tightly that it was crushing me, but to others, it looked like a loving embrace.

"I guess another punishment when we get home will be in order since you think you can use magic without permission," he hissed, so only I could hear. This time, he slid his hand over my cheek and gripped the back of my neck, as if he might kiss me.

"Please stop," I begged quietly.

"You should have thought about the consequences before disobeying me. What did you say to him?"

"He was frozen too," I confessed quietly as Jesper pulled my face to his and kissed me softly.

"If you tell everyone here whatever pathetic declaration you had for Cassius, I will lessen your punishment," he whispered to me.

No, he wouldn't. I looked past him to the ceiling above me and waited for someone to step in and save me from this monster, but they wouldn't. To them, he looked like he was proud of me and giving me praise.

"I'll take my punishment," I answered back.

"You see how no one came to help you, Thea? Because no one gives a fuck about you," he laughed into my ear. I'm sure it looked like he was giving me a very long hug to everyone else in the room.

"I didn't expect anyone to save me," I whispered.

"Oh, but you hoped *he* would," he said back. "And that ends today. You will become my wife and belong solely to me."

"I know."

Silent tears fell out of the corners of my eyes as Jesper pulled me to him for a kiss, making a spectacle out of it. Fear trickled into my mind as I thought of what he would do to me later, what my father would do to me, but I said nothing else because he hadn't threatened Exile again and I didn't want to remind him.

"Cerithia and Kizar are now allied and will fight against anyone who does not declare loyalty to us. Thea only showed a fraction of her abilities to you all. There is no way to defeat her," the king of Cerithia spoke as he stood. "I hope you all think this over seriously."

Jesper turned me so my back was pressed into his chest and forced me to look at Crimson.

"This is the last time you will ever see any of them," he whispered in my ear. "Alive, at least." Jesper released me. "We hope to see all of you at our wedding," Jesper called out to the room.

I could see the king of Crimson saying something to Cassius as shadows swarmed dangerously close to where Jesper and I stood.

Haden looked at me in a way I couldn't understand. Cassius stared me in the eyes before closing them tightly in defeat.

Jesper then proceeded to drag me through the castle by my wounded wrists. Before we walked out the front door, Cassius' shadows swept over my face with a gentle touch.

The gesture calmed my frantic heart. But it was short-lived because Jesper tugged me forcefully into the carriage and then kicked me when I tried to sit on the bench. I fell back to the floor and didn't move.

The ride back to Cerithia was silent and tense. I tried to push the fear I was feeling away, but it wouldn't let me be. Maybe the gods above would show mercy on me and end this suffering. I didn't dare to sleep the whole ride home. Fear wouldn't let me close my eyes. As soon as the carriage stopped back at the castle, Jesper grabbed me by the throat and tried to drag me inside, but I shoved him and started running. I was too weak to get far, both from using magic and not sleeping.

Jesper tackled me to the ground a moment later. I swung my arms frantically to get him off of me, but he grabbed them and pinned me down. His blue eyes were void of any sort of emotion as they looked at me in hatred. I still thrashed under him, yelling and crying to be let go.

"You will never embarrass me like that again." He grabbed my jaw so tightly that I thought it would break, making a painful sob tear through me. I couldn't let him take me into the castle. A surge of terror had me headbutting him. Jesper fell from me, holding his bleeding nose, as I stood and started running again.

It only took a moment before he caught up to me. He grabbed my wrists again and hauled me over his shoulder with little effort. He walked past my father, the queen, and my half sisters, who all looked like I was getting exactly what I deserved. I pounded on his back and kicked my feet, but it was for nothing.

I was still crying when he led me to a part of the castle I had never been to before. It was cold, and the air felt heavy and wet.

Jesper opened an iron door and tossed me onto the stone floor without regard to my safety. I landed with a horrible popping sound around my wrist, causing me to yell loudly in pain. Jesper moved around the room, doing something for a moment, before grabbing my wrists and tying them together, then to an iron circle embedded into the wall.

He straddled my legs as he ripped my Cerithia uniform open. My instincts started kicking in when I thought he was going to touch me against my will. My darkness expanded inside of me so much that it caused physical pain in every fiber of my body.

"If you move, this will hurt worse for you," he growled as he pulled a knife out. "What should I carve into your flesh? This blade is special, Thea. It has just enough poison forged into it to make you weak and not think clearly. It will make you more manageable for the rest of our lives."

I twisted and turned, but the sharp sting of the knife had me calling out into the darkness. I stopped moving as best I could, but he did slow strokes of the knife into the flesh of my stomach. When I thought I would pass out from pain, he turned me over and cut me there too. The punishment felt like it went on for hours. The cutting had been the worst part, but the times when he got bored with that and administered hits and punches weren't far behind.

I could feel myself drifting in and out of consciousness. Would I die? I had to be bleeding too much to survive this.

I didn't want to survive this. After what felt like forever, my swollen eyes watched Jesper walk out of the cell I was in and lock me in it.

"Now, every time you see yourself in the mirror, you will remember how fucking useless and pathetic you are. I want my face to haunt you in those moments so that you won't ever make this mistake again."

Then he was gone, and I was left in the cold darkness to suffer alone. Always alone.

CHAPTER 19

No one came for days. I wasn't sure if it truly had been days or if it only felt that long because of the pain and darkness of the cell. My head pounded harshly, and my whole body burned with pain. Finally, I heard the door of the cell open, but I couldn't see who was coming through my swollen eyes. I curled into a ball, trying to make myself small and shield myself from an attack I knew would be coming again.

"Darling," Jesper muttered softly.

I was shaking uncontrollably, whether from shock or the cold—I wasn't sure. Maybe both. When his fingers touched me softly, I cried out, terrified. He lifted my face to his, and I could barely make out his features through the damage that had been done to me. The smell of whatever he had recently eaten clung to his clothes, making me feel nauseous with hunger.

I whimpered softly at the small movement I made. Jesper's fingers brushed my blood-crusted hair from my face.

"You're filthy," he tisked at me, as if I could help it. His lips pressed to mine quickly before standing up and grabbing something. Cold water drenched me when he tossed a bucket toward me. I cried out for someone to help me, and it only made him laugh as I trembled on the ground. Every shiver felt like a knife gliding across my skin.

I heard loud footsteps coming toward me again, and I curled myself into the wall to get away from Jesper.

"I think you need more time to think about your behavior," he spoke somewhere near me. Then he walked away from me and locked me in the cell again. I begged for anyone to please save me, even if it came in the form of death. My stomach growled violently, and my head pounded from pain and hunger.

I closed my eyes and hung my head, my hands still tied to the iron circle in the wall. Yes, death would be a mercy. I cried to the gods and stars above, but no one came as I fell into darkness again.

★★☽★★

Jesper shook me awake, and I had no idea how much time had passed since he had been here last. A day or two, maybe.

"Still alive," he sighed, like he wasn't sure.

I couldn't even open my mouth to say anything. He untied my wrists, and I fell to the floor without having the energy to catch myself.

"Pick her up and bring her to her room," he told someone. My head bounced and flopped as they carried me with little gentleness. I was so far gone in pain that I couldn't really feel it anymore. I was numb. I felt my bed as the guard lowered me to it.

"Fuck, Thea." It was Leer. "Are you alive?"

I nodded slightly, but he didn't say anymore when someone walked in behind him. Jesper.

"That's all, now go," he dismissed Leer, and the door shut. I felt the bed dip somewhere next to me, but I couldn't even open my eyes to see if I was about to be attacked. He didn't say anything as his fingers traced over my face softly. "You rest. When I come back, I'll have the maids run you a bath."

My head swarmed with thoughts, but none of them made any sense. The poison was making me feel ill and confused. Then, like a light beckoning me through the darkness, I saw him. Cassius stood in my broken mind, holding out his hand for me. I grabbed it as he pulled me along in the darkness. I couldn't see where he was taking me, but I knew it would be better than here.

Suddenly, the darkness faded, turning into his bedroom at Crimson. He laid me down on the bed before lying down next to me without saying a word. I could feel tears pricking my eyes as I stared at him.

"Why are you crying?" he whispered to me. His hand gently pushed my wild curls from my face.

"Because I wish this was real."

He just pulled me to him and wrapped me in his arms as an answer. This wasn't a memory or a visit to my dream. This was my broken mind trying to escape the hurt and darkness by making a scenario where Cassius saved me. I buried my face in his hard chest and breathed in the familiar scent of rain and forest. I had missed him terribly. He wrapped the dark green blanket around us and gave me a kiss on the forehead.

"Let's sleep until you feel better, my love."

I nodded as I dozed off into a peaceful sleep.

★★☽★★

When I woke up, I was confused about being in my room in Cerithia. Had I not been in Crimson with Cassius? I didn't feel much better than the last time I had been awake, but my eyes could crack open a bit more. I froze when I saw Jesper sitting in a small chair next to me, like he had been waiting for me to wake up.

"Thea." He stood so he could grab my hand and kneel next to me. "Fuck, I thought you were going to die."

I was confused by his worry.

"Your father would have killed me."

That made sense. He didn't care if I died, just that he didn't die consequently. I tried swallowing, but my throat felt dry and itchy. How long had I been asleep? I couldn't even muster up the strength to ask.

Jesper looked over my face thoughtfully as I looked around confused. He gave me a small smile, like he cared about me. If I had my dagger and strength, I would have slit his throat open.

"You haven't been conscious for nearly a week, darling."

A week. I didn't say anything because I couldn't and I didn't want to. I could feel my eyes wanting to close and rest again, but Jesper lifted me up and out of bed. I cried as my body ached. Maybe he was taking me back into the cell now that I was awake. Instead, though, he carried me up the stairs. My eyes drifted closed but opened when a door opened. A hot bath had been drawn, and it smelled like lavender.

"Let's get you cleaned up." He helped me stand on shaky legs as he pulled my ruined uniform from my body, turning me so I could see myself in the mirror. I immediately looked away from the blood and bruises, but Jesper moved my head back toward the mirror.

"You don't like your tattoo?" He gave me a wicked smile. My eyes drifted to the words carved into my stomach: *useless crimson whore* marred my skin. "The back one says 'traitor' if you are curious," he laughed.

And everyone thought I was the monster of Elloryon. I held the tears in, no longer showing them I was broken and weak. I would be fine after I healed. Besides, I had already decided on a plan. I would sneak out and head for Exile to free them. I needed to do that as soon as I could ride a horse again. Then we would get the fuck out of here and never return.

I flinched when the hot water scalded my cuts and bruised skin. Shit. Jesper sat in the bathroom with me and stared at me as I washed myself off. Was he worried I was going to run? I couldn't even walk on my own. I stared into his eyes for a moment, and I decided then and there that I would plunge my dagger deep into his heart and stop it one day soon. Even if it cost me my life, it would be worth it.

"Care to share your thoughts?" he sneered.

I shook my head.

"You're lucky your friends from Exile weren't there anymore. I was so angry; I would have slaughtered all of them if they had been," he said so coldly.

"Gone?" my hoarse voice whispered.

"My guess is Crimson killed them as soon as you chose Cerithia. They would have never let you rescue them, especially since they would all follow you into battle. They are loyal, if anything, but only to you for saving them the first time. Can you imagine elite magic fae in our war? We would be unstoppable." His cold, unforgiving eyes stared at me. "I guess we are unstoppable with you. Your demonstration of magic was absolutely perfect."

"You guys lied to me. You never had elite magic fae."

"We needed you not to go crazy on us," he shrugged.

"And now? There is nothing stopping me from killing all of you." My eyes coated over with blackness. Jesper just smiled at me.

"Don't worry, we improvised." He ran his fingers through his blonde hair. "The elite fae have families in Cerithia still. We have guards stationed at every home, ready to kill them if you piss me off."

"You found all their bodies in Exile?"

Tears fell from my eyes. Jesper had to be lying. Cassius would never do that to me or to them. Would he? Jesper wouldn't lie about killing them, or even taking them. It would only give him more power over me.

"No, but my guess is they burned them in their homes. All the structures had been lit on fire. Such a shit hole."

The structures were all burned. He really did go to Exile just to slaughter them. Sybil and the twins' faces flashed into my mind. I pictured them standing in the small home in Exile as I headed for the trials. I would give anything to go back to that moment. Tears fell silently. Crimson couldn't have done that. There was no way that Cassius would do that. He had elite magic.

I would still go and see for myself if they were there or not. I would not take Jesper's word for anything.

"Our wedding plans are coming along nicely," he smiled. "Soon you will be my wife, and we can put all this trouble you created behind us."

"When is the wedding?"

"A week." He cranked his neck and popped it. "Don't worry, it's customary to send invites to all kingdoms when a royal member gets married. Crimson should be getting their invitation today."

"I do not care."

"Yes, you do, but I like that you are willing to lie about it now. Maybe my punishment was effective." He stood up and walked to the edge of the tub to stare down at me. His eyes narrowed on my face.

"You will get fitted for your wedding dress today. A traditional Kizar gown, but in gray instead of white. Since you spread your legs for that Crimson trash."

"So, what if I did? Are you a virgin?" I hissed.

"No, in fact, I slept with your sister, Tally, this morning."

"You're a fucking pig."

Jesper moved quickly. He grabbed my head and pushed it under the water. I thrashed as I tried to fight him off, but I was too weak. He let my head come up a few moments later. I had been gasping for air so desperately that I had inhaled water. My lungs burned as fear spread like wildfire in my veins.

"Do not test me, Thea. You will not win." The sleeves of his shirt were soaking wet. "I will have consorts through our marriage. You will bear two heirs for me, and that will be the end of our sexual relationship."

"Will I be allowed a consort?" I spat back just to piss him off.

"What do you think?" He glared at me for a moment longer, then yanked me from the bath. "I think you're clean enough. Let's get you fitted for a wedding dress."

CHAPTER 20

The wedding planning kept my body busy for the next few days. There were so many questions and things others wanted my opinion on, but I honestly didn't fucking care about any of it. I usually pointed to whichever option I found to be the ugliest. After all, this wedding was not mine. I didn't care what color the flowers were or what food we ate. I didn't care if I wore white or not.

My eyes darted to Jesper as he and Tally emerged from a storage room together, clearly having just fucked. Tally's blue eyes met mine and gave me a sneer, but Jesper walked over to me with a frown.

"I didn't know you were up here."

"Like that would have stopped you," I muttered. "I'm over all the questions about planning the wedding. I don't care about the details."

I thought he would get angry with me, but he nodded. His blue eyes darted around the room at the dozens of fae planning our wedding.

"I'm sick of all the questions too. I'll tell the planner to decide," he agreed.

Well, that went better than I thought.

"I don't understand why you don't just marry Tally." I wasn't angry because he liked my sister or was sleeping with her. No, I was angry because I was being forced to marry this monster. Why did I have to give up my future for him? He looked at me for a long time, then sighed heavily.

"Because Tally doesn't have magic and you do. My children will hopefully inherit your abilities, making them feared." He paused for a moment, like he wasn't sure if he should continue. "And I want to throw you in Cassius' face for the rest of our existence."

"Like he cares."

"Oh, he cares because Cassius hates losing, and you were the ultimate prize."

With that declaration, he turned and followed wherever Tally had gone. I watched after him and felt all those emotions of him doing this to me before resurfacing out of nowhere. He had always been an ass. I had never really cared if I settled for someone like him because I thought he was as good as it would get for me. How wrong had I been. Cassius made me realize what it felt like to be cared for. Cassius showed me what love should feel like. He was the reason that I knew I deserved more than this shitty life my father had given me in Cerithia.

Jesper was delusional to think I would let him use me to breed children. He was not getting anywhere near me. I would kill him before he touched me in that way, or I would gladly die. Either way, it was a win for me. Had I ever been with another man besides Cassius? A violent longing burned in my chest for him. I wanted Cassius. My instincts told me that none of it had been a lie, so why would he kill the woman he loves if not for betrayal? Cassius was right, he did feel like home, and I was missing that feeling terribly today.

Sadness returned as I headed outside, my mind ruminating on missing Cassius. My father had stopped me from training the guards until after the wedding. He said he couldn't risk me tainting them with my rebellion, whatever the fuck that meant. I didn't understand why everyone thought I would be more easily managed when I was married. If anything, I would become even more rebellious. I smiled at the thought. I would make Jesper's life a fucking living nightmare, my father's too. That would be the sole purpose of my life—to bring destruction down upon them all from within these walls.

I had already decided the first time my father laid his hands on me that I would do whatever I could to make the walls of Cerithia and Kizar crumble at my feet. I would not win a war for them. I would not be their monster. I would be on my own, and I would burn the realm that thought they could treat me like trash. I would take everyone down with me.

I smiled to myself as I walked through the woods within the wall of Cerithia. I wasn't stupid enough to disobey today. Not when tomorrow was the big day, the day I was going to Exile to see for myself if everybody was really gone, and if they were—the realm of Elloryon would crumble with me as I gave in and lost my mind.

I paused at a small, run-down shack in the forest. I looked around to see if anyone was near me as I moved toward it. It was falling apart, and I knew it couldn't be inhabited, but I was still curious. I had not ventured into the forest here before, so I wasn't sure why I felt like this shouldn't be here. It seemed somehow... misplaced.

Maybe that was what drew me to it. The wood planks that made the walls were vertical to the ground, but some of them had rotted away with time. This allowed me to see that there was nothing inside, but that didn't stop me from continuing into it. I assumed the roof was also made of planks of wood, but I couldn't be sure because of the moss covering it. The thin door was ajar when I reached it. I peeked inside and saw nothing, but I still couldn't stop myself from taking a step through the doorway.

Once my whole body crossed the threshold, I froze. The shack had suddenly transformed into a stunning yet quaint home. I looked around the space and saw that it was now the size of ten shacks. The floor was pretty hardwood, with beautiful rugs spread across it. Two large chairs faced a roaring fireplace that held little knick-knacks on the mantle.

I turned and saw artwork hanging on the walls. So much that there was no room to hang another piece anywhere. I took a hesitant step forward so I could see the handcrafted wooden table and chairs that sat in a small space by the kitchen. Who lived here? How had they enchanted this space to be hidden so well?

"Thea," a frail voice from behind, startled me. I turned to see a man sitting in one of the chairs by the fireplace that had been empty a moment ago. How had I not heard him? He was small—at least two feet shorter than me. The gray hair on his head was scraggly, and his beard was unkempt, like he didn't know what a brush was. His clothes looked handmade and old, stitched with patches and threadbare on his papery skin. I held my breath when he turned slightly to me, his cloudy white eyes surprising me. He was blind.

"How did you know it was me?"

He scoffed.

"I expected you days ago, child, but better late than never, I suppose." He waved his arm to the other chair by the fire, and I took it. Nothing told me I should feel in danger. In fact, I almost felt like I belonged here.

"Should I know who you are?"

"No." He turned his head to the roaring fire. "We've never met."

I looked at him for a long moment, trying to decide what I should ask first. He started rocking his chair slightly as I stared speechlessly at him.

"Then how do you know my name?"

"Everyone knows who you are, Thea," he scoffed, like it was ridiculous that I didn't know that. I glared at his bad attitude, not that he could see it. "Don't look at me like that."

My face dropped immediately, and he laughed loudly. The high-pitched cackles echoed in the small space.

"A seer may be blind, but we see all."

A seer, I had never met one that I knew of. I smiled at him as I leaned back in my chair and rocked in tandem with him. Something about this quaint space made me feel calm and safe.

"You are troubled," he frowned. "I feared you would be after the prophecy revealed itself, but I did not know it would cause so much deception and betrayal for you." He turned to me. "I'm sorry I revealed the prophecy, but as a seer, I did not have a choice. If I had, I would have never spoken about your identity."

I stopped rocking immediately. This was the man who had revealed the prophecy. This was the man who saw what I was to become and terrified everyone by revealing it.

"You are responsible for the prophecy," I muttered, not sure how I was actually feeling. "You're Brim?"

He nodded at his name. "No, I am not responsible for anything. I am a mere vessel for the prophecy. It chose me to speak the words, but that is the extent of my doing in all of this. Being a seer is not a job for the faint. We must tell our visions, even if it is not always for the best."

"And what did the prophecy say of me?"

"No one has told you?" He looked truly appalled. "That's a bunch of shit." His choice of words made me chuckle loudly. He smiled at the sound.

"I have heard bits and pieces of it, but no one has revealed its entirety. I know that kingdoms fear me, fight over me, and even think I'm a monster because of it." I frowned as I said the words out loud. He rocked silently for a moment.

"They are all idiots," he finally declared. "The problem with prophecies is that they can be interpreted to suit anyone's needs, being misconstrued and twisted into what they are not. I suppose that is part of the allure of a prophecy. Sadly, though, I am not in a position of power or authority to try and tell them that they are wrong."

"Did anyone interpret it correctly?" I asked.

"Yes," he sighed thoughtfully. "Although I cannot reveal who, you must discover it on your own and draw your own conclusions from it."

I nodded as a response.

Clearing his throat in preparation, the old man began to speak in a measured cadence, using a tone that elicited my full attention.

A day in which a decision was to be made—a choice that only results in death
To be reborn is to be freed from a cage they inhabited
She will be the end of all we know
Destruction to the kingdoms of Elloryon
A power will be awakened by a knife's blade
She will hold the fates of everything

Those should bow to her magic, for there is none like it; it is unmatched and unbeatable

Elite magic so grand that even the heavens above and hells below do not know where it belongs

She will not fail, so be wise, for she will determine fates

And all should bow to Thea Alzara, for she possesses power that will make kingdoms crumble and destroy all we know. She will kill kings.

His words wrapped around my mind. That could mean anything. I admit that it didn't sound great for me. It made me sound... unstable.

"It sucks, huh?" he sighed. "So much left for interpretation."

"They concluded I was a monster from this," I muttered.

"Like I said, idiots," he scoffed with disgust. "They do not like that you hold this power, Thea. They will always see you as a threat, and make no mistake, a threat you are. But that does not mean you are evil or bad. Maybe Elloryon needs a little... restructuring. But change scares others and is generally unwanted. It also makes men in power do stupid things."

"I have witnessed that firsthand," I nodded. "You can't tell me anything else?"

"Afraid not." He stopped rocking. "Some will see power and crave it. Others will cage it, tame it, use it for pointless things, beat it to submission... Then there are those who will protect it, love it, and be in awe of it, but still know to be cautious. Just remember that not everyone sees your power as a way to cage you."

I looked at this frail man in front of me and felt a connection that seemed to have been forged long before we met today. Perhaps we had met in a different life. Or maybe he was the only one who could see me without having to even look. He seemed lost in thought as I watched the crackling fire.

"Fine, you twisted my arm," he said suddenly, surprising me and making me sit up straighter in my chair. "This prophecy cannot be fulfilled until you break the curse."

"But–"

"Your mother unintentionally cursed you with the binding of your magic, but Cassius freed you from that curse long ago."

I shook my head, trying to form a question to ask. Freed me, he had freed me?

"I don't understand."

"You are not the only cursed soul in this, Thea." He turned his cloudy, white eyes toward me. "Cassius was the one who angered the god, Mikel, not you. I believe Mikel was trying to give you mercy by taking away the memories of Cassius' betrayal."

"So, this is Cassius' curse?"

"You are both cursed."

"Does Cassius know that it belongs to both of us?"

"Cassius is a clever man, but it doesn't matter if he knows that particular fact. He knows how it must be broken, and that is what matters. Your prophecy happens because you are able to see the truth of others on this journey, which allows you to save both Cassius and yourself."

"Cassius needs my bloodstone, doesn't he?"

Brim's cloudy eyes shone brightly.

"Yes... You figured that out?"

"I've been piecing together information, and it all circles back to the bloodstone. My father told me Cassius was cursed too. He said Cassius needed my bloodstone so he could take his crown and bear an heir. He claimed that Cassius would lose part of his elite magic every year that passed if I did not break the curse, and that it would only break once I gave him my bloodstone. Is that true?" I frowned as I glanced toward the large flames of his fire.

"Your father is a master manipulator. Cassius is not cursed in such a way."

"Then how is he cursed?"

Brim's cloudy eyes stared into the fire.

"He must watch the woman he loves look at him like a villain. He watches you die over and over. I would say that is a terrible fate."

"But he killed me. I do not understand why everyone thinks it is justified. He loves me, but he stabbed me. He was cruel to me in the clearing." That was the one piece I couldn't understand. If he killed me for a good reason then why was he so cruel to me?

"Love makes us do things we do not always want to. Sometimes, we love someone or something enough to hurt them in order to save them. You still haven't actually talked with Cassius. That is another part of the curse: he is the only one allowed to tell you the truth. He must tell you himself why he killed you and why that cursed you with no memories."

I opened my mouth to beg for more information, but he held up his hand to silence me. I didn't dare breathe, as he seemed to be trying to hear something.

"You should go. They are looking for you in the forest," he whispered. "Best of luck to you, my dear."

Then, as if I hadn't been in his home at all, I fell to the forest floor on my ass. I was sitting inside the shambled shed alone. No trace of his inviting home around me. Although I could smell the fire on my clothing. Heavy footsteps sounded close by, and I stood up quickly. My head poked out of the shed, and Jesper stood ten feet away, with a handful of guards behind him.

"What the hell are you doing?" he snapped.

"I was exploring the forest." I stepped out of the shed, and he grabbed my hand, dragging me back toward the castle in a haste.

"I was told I couldn't leave the wall, not the castle grounds," I responded to his silent anger. "Is that wrong?"

"No, of course not," he sighed. His fingers gripped me tightly. "I just get worried when I don't see you for a while."

"Can you stop hurting me?" I groaned as his fingers dug into my barbed wrists. Jesper looked over me before irritation took over his features.

"I'll do whatever I want to you."

He gripped me by the back of my neck and shoved me toward the castle, making me fall into the tall green grass.

He was one who aimed to cage me. He feared my power and hated me for it. The fear I could understand. After all, I could change an entire realm with a flick of my wrist if I chose. I, Thea Alzara, should be bowed to.

Through the haze of pain, I smiled at the words of the prophecy. I would have loved to see the faces of everyone when my name was called out.

My eyes caught sight of Haden standing in the forest of Cerithia as he watched Jesper forcefully rip me up by my hair. What was he doing here again? His clenched fists were covered in frost as he watched Jesper hurt me. Quickly, I glanced away because I didn't want Jesper to see him. When I glanced back, I saw Wisp floating by where he had been standing.

Haden was gone, and within a moment, so was Wisp.

My eyes drifted to the training fields, where I spotted Leer. He was watching me, relief on his face that I was alive. I needed to go see him and his family tonight.

CHAPTER 21

Jesper had kept me close to him all day. His hand was clasped tightly around mine, as if he feared I would be snatched away at any moment, and I worried why he had this sudden attachment. Hopefully, he will leave me after dinner like he normally does. I ate in silence with him and my "family" like we did almost every night. Tally was staring at Jesper with a smile. Every now and then, he would look up and return it to her.

Good—hopefully, she'll keep him busy after dinner so I can make my escape. I would make a quick stop at Leer's home, then head to Exile. I knew that I would probably be caught sneaking off, but I had to try. I needed to know if my friends were still alive. I couldn't wait any longer to go. Exile depended on me, and I would not give up on them until I saw the truth for myself.

After dinner, everyone stood and went their separate ways. I thanked the stars as I watched Tally and Jesper disappear down the same hallway, then hurried downstairs to grab my cloak and daggers before sneaking back out to the hallway. Guards had been watching me closely, so I knew I probably wouldn't get lucky enough to avoid them.

I crept silently up the stairs, only to be met with two guards. As soon as they saw me, they were on edge.

"Where do you think you're going?" one of the guards asked.

My eyes darted around to see if there were others. There weren't.

"I'm sorry," I said quickly as I stepped forward and killed one of them. The other immediately attacked with his sword. Stumbling forward, I fell face-first into the wall. Pain radiated from my eye. I turned and barely dodged his sword. The force of his swing made him stumble slightly, giving me an opportunity to stab him in the back.

He slumped to the ground. I wasn't sure if he was dead, but I didn't stay to find out. I ran from the castle before anyone saw the bodies.

My horse snorted at me when I turned the corner of the stables, like she was pissed off that I hadn't come to see her. I pet her as I snuck her out of the stable, then walked her deep into the trees to picket her while I went into the city. I couldn't take her to Leer's home; it would look suspicious.

"I'll be back for you shortly," I assured her. "Be quiet."

I turned and ran toward Leer's house, thankful that he lived on the outskirts of the city. When I got there, I walked in without knocking.

"Thea!" Leer jumped up and wrapped his large arms around me, squeezing me to near death. "I thought you were going to die."

"I'm sorry for barging in." I breathed a small breath as he let me go. His wife, Larissa, gasped when she saw my face. I glanced away from her. "You said you were in debt to me, right? I've come to ask a favor of you."

"Anything," he nodded.

"I want you to take your family far from here. Take anyone from Cerithia that you care about and leave."

Confusion was clear on his face.

"But..."

"No, please don't argue. You and your family need to leave. War is coming, and Cerithia will be destroyed."

"What will you do?"

"I will destroy it, Leer. I cannot, will not, stand by and destroy other innocent kingdoms because Jesper and my father are greedy bastards. I will take Cerithia and Kizar down with me if I must, but you have a family that you just got back. I don't want to see you killed because my father will gladly sacrifice all the guardsmen for greed. So, I need you to leave and never come back."

He looked at his wife, who shared the same worried expression.

"Leer, I don't want to lose you," Larissa whispered. "We should listen to Thea; she is our only friend here. I trust her."

The words warmed my cold heart. He looked back at me with wide eyes. I could see all the questions forming in his mind, but I couldn't answer them. I didn't have the time.

"Where should we go?"

"Crimson. They will gladly let you live there."

"Our biggest enemy?" he frowned.

"They aren't monsters there, like the fae in Cerithia or Kizar. They will not kill those who seek refuge from my father or Jesper. I know they won't. You saw how happy everyone was there; it's nothing like here."

"No, they wouldn't harm us," he said. "We will go tonight."

"They will be searching for me in the woods soon. You need to go now and not stop until you are in Crimson."

"Alright," he nodded. Larissa was already running around, throwing their belongings into bags.

"I must go. Travel safe." I looked at all of them. Leer grabbed my arm and turned me back to him.

"If you ever come back to Crimson, find us. You will always be welcome in our home." He gave me a tight hug before I nodded and left. I would never return to Crimson again. My father would make sure of that.

I ran through the darkness and into the forest, where my Kaida waited. She was standing silently.

"Good girl," I whispered before climbing on her back and urging her to run.

★★☽★★

When we entered the Forbidden Wood, it was just sunset. I could feel the adrenaline start pumping through my body as anticipation and dread filled me. I was worried about what I would find—or not find. Once I spotted the large tree I had carved an X on to mark the shadow border, I dismounted from my horse and told her to stay.

It turns out I didn't need the marker, though, because the shadow border was no longer there. Almost scared to look, I turned my gaze to where the town should be.

A cry caught in my throat. I could see the remains of Exile across the meadow. "No!" I cried as I ran to the burned buildings, hoping to see something—anything—that would let me know the inhabitants were still alive. I paused at the green door that marked where mine and Sybil's home once stood. It was half burned, and now it led nowhere. It was the only part of our home that still stood.

All the structures had been destroyed a while ago, but the smell of burning wood still clung to the air. I turned and looked at the dead grass and the dead trees—everything just felt... dead. Exile was gone.

So where were the elite magic holders that had resided here? My mind flashed to Jesper telling me that Crimson must have killed them to prevent them from fighting in the war. He hadn't been lying. Crimson had killed them all; everyone that I held dear was now gone forever because of them. It had to be Crimson. My father and Jesper had no reason to lie about Exile being gone. They would have taken them prisoner and used them to control me. Fear trickled into my mind. I couldn't take a betrayal from Cassius. My darkness wanted to take over to shield me from these dangerous thoughts, but it was stuck inside of me.

Disgust, anger, grief, and confusion filled my every breath and tainted my insides with the strong need for revenge. Someone would pay for this. Someone would answer for taking them from me. All of them suffered and died because of me.

I had failed them, and it made me want to kill someone, anyone. Darkness clouded my thoughts as I looked at the destroyed town that I used to hate so much but where I would now gladly live the rest of my days.

Sybil's and the twins' faces haunted me. They hadn't deserved this. They deserved to get out of here and be with their families too.

Justice, they deserved justice.

I turned and made my way back out of the village, then headed straight for my horse. I climbed on her in a numb haze, not sure of my next step.

I let Kaida lead me, and as the fates would have it, she headed toward the Crimson Castle.

If Cassius was there, I would kill him. I would slit his throat if he told me he had done it. I couldn't even process the emotions I felt at the sight of the castle looming in all its dark glory. There was sadness, for sure, and yet happiness was somewhere in there as well.

This place just called to me.

Home, my mind called it, and I had to shove those thoughts aside as soon as they appeared. I had no home. I belonged nowhere. I pressed on and rode through the towns without looking away from the castle. It was my destination, my only purpose tonight. When I got to the gates outside of the castle, the moon was high in the sky. I jumped off my horse, and she immediately ran to the stables where Cassius' horse stood. She had missed him.

"Don't mo—" I tossed my dagger at the guard who dared try to stop me. Dead. *Kill them all.* My mind was on a rampage. I looked at the guard running at me with a sword and felt my fire magic begin to simmer, but it couldn't break free. Instead, I tossed my dagger at him, hitting the Crimson crest on his uniform dead center.

"Cassius!" I yelled for him so violently that the ground vibrated. I knew he heard me. How could he not in the dead silence of the night. I paced in front of the castle, my eyes burning with fire and shadows. I watched the door, waiting to see him walk through it. I had already retrieved my viper-handled dagger. I was willing to die tonight if it meant justice would be served.

It was then that Cassius stepped out of the castle doors and stopped immediately at the sight of me. He was wearing black trousers and a loose-fitted black shirt. Suddenly, he was running to me, like he couldn't believe I was there. Instead of embracing him when he reached me, like he probably hoped I would, I tackled him to the ground and straddled him. My dagger was instantly at his throat.

"Little viper?" he asked in a confused voice. "Is this a dream?"

"Where are they!" I bellowed at him. His dark eyebrows pulled into a confused expression, and his golden eyes traced over every line of my face. I could hear guards coming, but I paid no attention to them. Cassius was my target. I could hear swords being unsheathed.

"If any of you hurt her, I will kill you myself," Cassius barked at them. His declaration confused me, but I didn't release my dagger from his throat. His golden eyes didn't leave my face, like he was worried that if he looked away, then I would be gone.

"Thea?" It was the King of Crimson who spoke, but I still didn't look away from Cassius.

"Where. Are. They?" I spoke with so much hatred in my voice. "Did you kill them all?"

"My love, I don't know who you are talking about."

"Do not call me that."

"It's a habit," he frowned. A light briefly shined on my face as a door nearby was opened, and I saw his eyes widen in shock. "Who the fuck did that to you?" I had forgotten about my cuts and bruises. I knew they had been bad, but I hadn't even looked in a mirror since Jesper forced me to read the words carved on my stomach. Cassius' big, calloused hand brushed against my face, and I pushed my dagger into his flesh harder. He dropped his hand and looked at me like he could feel my pain.

Rage was all I felt at that moment. He didn't get to pretend to care about me now. Not ever again.

"Where is everyone from Exile?" I demanded.

"Why do you think I would know?"

"Jesper came to get them, and he said they were gone. I came to see for myself, and no one was there. So where are they, Cassius?"

His face turned cold in the blink of an eye. Disgust contorted his face at the mention of Jesper, and his body was suddenly angry and tense under me.

"So, you thought it was me? Or did your precious fiancé blame me, and you believed him? Or is he your husband now? The date on your wedding invitation slips my mind at the moment."

He was jealous. I pulled back slightly at his onslaught of jabs, my emotions still raw from the abuse I had suffered.

"Why would Jesper lie about them not being there?" I hissed. "He would have told me that he killed them; that was the whole reason he went to Exile. To punish me by slaughtering them! That leaves you, did you do something to them?"

I hadn't realized Cassius' hands rested on my hips until his fingers gripped me tightly. I hated that it felt warm and comforting.

"What could you possibly do that would warrant the slaughter of Exile?" he questioned. His body tensed at my questioning.

"Because of you," I whispered. I didn't elaborate on what I meant, but he just stared at me oddly. "Just tell me if you killed them." My voice broke. "I cannot continue without knowing."

"Maybe you should ask your father or fiancé again. They are the ones who despise elitists. They will not even allow magic to be used on their lands at all," he hissed back at me. "You really think I'm capable of slaughtering them? I'm not a monster, Thea. I hold elite magic; did you forget that?" he said my name so angrily, and it sounded so wrong coming from his mouth.

We stared at each other for a long moment before he huffed out a deep breath.

"I do not understand you," he said, sounding so confused. "You chose Cerithia, yet you use magic to freeze a room so that you can kneel and cry at my feet. The letters you gave me... you betrayed your own kingdom for Crimson. I beheaded Lavtan myself for everything he did to you." Cassius looked so sad, but I didn't have an answer to give him. "Then you come here and think I'm capable of doing such an atrocious thing, but the man you chose to marry has left you looking like this." He waved his hand at my bruised face. "You turned your back on me and closed me out without ever giving me a chance to defend myself."

"I didn't choose him! I chose you, and you betrayed me." I could feel the tears stinging my eyes, but I didn't want them to fall. I had begged him through our bond and called to him in my dreams. He never showed up. Cassius' hands gripped my hips tightly at my declaration. My heart fluttered when I looked at his handsome face, wondering why he didn't come for me in our dreams.

"You're getting married to him in three days." His eyes looked away from me. "You didn't choose me."

"You don't know what you're talking about," I scoffed. "Did Haden tell you of his last visit? How cruel Jesper was to me? Do you think I would choose a man so awful?"

"Yet you are tying yourself to that monster forever? A man who puts his hands on you like this?" He touched my face softly.

"What was my alternative, Cassius? Stay here and marry you? You forget the fact that you stabbed me through my goddamn heart!"

Hurt, shame, and guilt are what I saw flicker across his face as he stared at me. Gods, why was I being cruel? Because I was angry at him. I still loved him, but I was angry at how everything had happened.

"I am a slave, no matter where I am. Someone will always try to cage me, use me, or betray me."

"I didn't kill them," he whispered as his eyes broke their contact and his hands fell from me. I pulled my dagger from his throat. For some reason, I believed him. I didn't need reassurance from him. So, if he hadn't done it, then what happened to them?

I straddled him still, even though there wasn't a reason to. I had put my dagger away. His eyes found mine, but there was nothing I could decipher in them.

Then suddenly, his shadows swarmed around me, holding me tightly as he stood up. They tightened on me like a vice.

"Go ahead and kill me," my voice wavered slightly. "Death will be a mercy compared to what Jesper will do to me when I go back."

"I would never hurt you, little viper." His back was toward me.

"You killed me."

"I know," he answered. "And I'd do it again."

My eyes flickered at everyone watching us; their eyes were all sad. Even the king frowned at me, like I was in the wrong. I felt like I was in the wrong. His shadows caressed me like they missed me as they released me.

"You shut me out, my love, and you never gave me a chance to explain why I killed you. You will not let me into your dreams, and you refuse to come home. I do not know what to do anymore. Stay here, please. You do not need to go back to them. I will protect you."

"I can't stay," I whispered. If elite magic fae had families in Cerithia, then I had to try and go back for them. I would not fail Sybil or the twins ever again. If I couldn't save them, then I would save their loved ones. I had to find out what Jesper or my father did to them.

My response made Cassius' shoulders slump. He released me a moment later and started walking to the castle. Panic set in. That was the only thing I felt as I realized this would be the last time we were likely to see each other.

Anger and hurt burned through me, and I ran at him, shoving him hard from behind and making him stumble.

"No, you don't get to walk away!"

"Thea." He looked so hurt. "Please stay. He will never lay another hand on you again. Why are you allowing them to do this to you? I can keep you safe."

I shoved at him again, but it was a weak attempt. There were so many things I wanted to say and do, but they all slipped my mind as I glared at him through tear-filled eyes. He looked at me like I had lost my fucking mind, and I probably had. I was angry that I couldn't stay.

"What are you doing?" he asked, his nostrils flaring in anger.

"This is all your fault! How could you be so fucking heartless? You have destroyed me. You have made me beg the gods to take away my suffering, even if it is in the form of death."

His eyes flashed black.

"I am trying to fix this, but you do not want to stay."

"It doesn't matter. I'm giving you the chance to end all this talk of war and suffering by killing me right now. So do it."

"No," he growled. "What the fuck have they done to you to make you think death is the only escape?"

"You mean what did you do?" I hissed. "You broke me more than they ever could." That was the truth.

His eyes faded from black to gold in an instant. It was the truth. I loved Cassius and his words in the clearing had broken me. I *was* angry at him for that even if I still loved him.

"My love..."

"I'll see you at my wedding," I said, just to see his reaction to me marrying someone else.

I turned and started walking away. I was leaving my horse. She deserved to be here, and she looked happy.

A moment later, I was tackled to the ground as Cassius jumped on me, flipping me over so that I was on my back. This time, he was straddling me. His friendly golden eyes, however, were gone and replaced with unforgiving black-ness.

"If you think I will ever let you belong to another man, then you severely underestimate my affection for you." His voice was laced with possessiveness. "You are mine; I do not care if you hate me. You can hate me for what I did, but I will *never* apologize for it. But you can hate me here, you can hate me in our home. One day, you will forgive me. Do you know why? Because you fucking love me, Thea. Even now, you cannot stay away from me. Even knowing that I took my dagger and pushed it into your heart, you still want me. Admit it."

He laid his hand over my heart and felt it beating wildly in my chest. Gods, he had lost his fucking mind and I loved to see it.

"You're as psychotic as they said you were," I spat back at him.

"Only you bring that out in me." He glared down at me. "I love you. Is that what you want to hear? I love you so much that everything feels wrong when you are not nearby. I crave you as if you are the air I need to breathe, and I am slowly suffocating without you. I have been yours since the first moment I saw you in my dreams, and I will die belonging to you. Please stop shutting me out. Let me see you in your dreams. Let me make this right." Then I saw the glistening in his eyes. He was holding in tears. The emotion was too much.

"I have called to you in my dreams, and I begged you for an explanation, but you never came!" I yelled, so mad I could stab him. "You left me. You are the one who shut me out."

Suddenly, he was tense on top of me. When I turned to look at him, his eyes were staring at my wrist. His grip loosened as he traced his thumb over the crack in the blood bond.

"It's broken," he whispered. His eyes stared at me like he couldn't believe it. "How long has this been cracked?"

"It broke when you told me of your betrayal."

He shook his head like he was confused, and his grip tightened on me like I would slip away from him.

"It's been broken this entire time." His eyes shone bright gold as he looked down at me. A bright smile spread over his face, confusing the fuck out of me. My stomach clenched at how beautiful he was. "All this time, I thought..." he swallowed down the emotion that was forming inside of him.

"Please, don't. I have to go back to Cerithia," I sobbed. I needed to save the families of the elite fae. If he kept talking, I would stay, and they would be slaughtered. That would make me a monster if I allowed them to be killed. "I have to go, but I do not want to."

Cassius' eyes stared into mine and he must have seen something pleading back at him because he let me go. I ran until my lungs burned and sweat beaded on my back. Then I ran some more. I paused as I kept heading toward Cerithia. I didn't want to go back. I wanted to stay here.

I froze when I felt it. I lifted my hand and watched black shadows swirl around my wrist, caressing me, holding me. I turned and saw Cassius in the far distance, watching me. He pulled the shadows back, bringing me with them.

I tried to fight them, but I was weak and unable to do anything. I was in front of him in only a moment. His whole body was rigid, and his face was menacing. Almost angrily, he stepped forward and pressed his lips against mine, claiming me. Before I could react, he stepped back and let me go.

I started running for the border, but his words stopped me.

"I'll see you at your wedding, little viper." He didn't sound angry. He sounded...happy. I kept running. My body and heart begged for me to turn around and take Cassius up on his offer. It would destroy me knowing I didn't protect Sybil's family, so I kept running.

CHAPTER 22

I reached Cerithia's castle a few days later. I steadied myself before I stepped through the gate, knowing that someone would be waiting for me. This couldn't be put off forever. Cassius' words tortured me. His face had haunted me the entire trip back to this gods-forsaken place.

My clothes were torn and soaked with sweat, and I felt like I could pass out from exhaustion. My bed sounded like heaven if I could get there undetected.

When I stepped through the gate, no one came for me. My chest filled with anxious tension. I would not get away with this. I had been gone for days. I walked into the castle and was met with an eerie silence. I scanned my surroundings looking for anything out of place, but there was nothing. No one lurked around corners or in the dark. There were no guards standing in the hallways.

I hurried down the stairs to my room. Once there, I shut the door and locked it. A deep breath escaped me, and with it my fear. Only for it to return two-fold.

"You've been gone an awfully long time, darling." Jesper was lying in my bed when I turned.

"Jesper," I acknowledged him but said nothing else.

His blue eyes cascaded over my filthy clothes, then over my sweaty face. Did he know where I had gone or who I had seen? How could he know? Something in the way he was so calm let me know that he knew. A shiver of fear ran up my spine.

"Where were you?"

"I had to see Exile for myself. I had to see they weren't there or see if I could find their bodies," I muttered as fear swirled in my stomach. He stood up and took a small step toward me. I backed up until I was pressed into the door. My dagger was in my boot, but I knew I wouldn't be able to get to it before Jesper got to me.

"You didn't believe me," he frowned.

"I couldn't believe it unless I saw it. They were my family for the last seven years."

He nodded slowly as he looked over at me. Jesper's eyes paused on my wrists to make sure my barbs were still in place.

"You shouldn't have left, but I understand your curiosity."

My eyes looked at him. He was being too agreeable. Why wasn't he beating me into oblivion? This was almost worse. He was toying with me. Jesper reached out and swiped the sweaty hair from my forehead. I shook at the small touch. My breath came out shaky, giving away my worry.

"I gave you a chance to tell me, yet you weren't completely honest," he tisked.

"I—" The back of his hand cut off my words. His hand wrapped around my throat and slammed me back so roughly that I thought he would crack my skull open on the wooden door. I held onto his forearm, trying to release some of the pressure from my throat. I even reached towards his face and scratched deep grooves into his flesh, but it did nothing to stop him. Jesper's handsome face had contorted into a hideous monster filled with jealousy and rage. My fingers scratched and clawed at him more in hopes he would drop me. Nothing I did seemed to faze him, though. My fire magic surged forward, but couldn't break free of the magic barbs. Fear laced every fiber of my body as I thrashed around, desperate to run straight back to Crimson if I needed to.

"Crimson," he hissed. "You went to see him. Even after all the punishment from last time." He tossed me into my two-drawer dresser, and it shattered under my body. I cried out as the pain shot through me. Something sharp stabbed into my leg, blood spewing from the wound as my adrenaline pumped through me.

"It wasn't like that!" I yelled, but his fists rained down on me without mercy.

"I don't care!"

He pulled something from his pocket, and when I saw it was rope, I tried to crawl away. But he gripped my ankle and pulled me back. He tied my hands easily to the bedpost above my head as I sat on the floor.

Then he pulled out his knife.

I screamed for him to not do it, but that only made him smile. Terror ran through me and seized any ability I had to fight. I closed my eyes tightly and screamed to both the heavens above and hell below to save me.

Cassius, please come for me. I begged silently. Cassius, please save me—take me away from the pain. Jesper's knife carved into the inside of my thigh, and then he moved to the inside of my forearm. He took his time again, and when he was done, I was barely conscious. I closed my eyes and drifted into darkness, but I was awakened by a bucket of hot water.

I bellowed out in pain as the heat scorched my cuts. Then another bucket hit them, and I couldn't even cry anymore. As I lay on the floor, I wondered if this would be my end. Sometime later, he stopped and left the room after saying something that I could not comprehend in my state. I stared at the cracked ceiling of my room, and my confused mind started counting the nails before darkness beckoned me into it.

My Cerithia uniform was dirty and torn from fighting someone in the Crimson army. His sword technique was impeccable, and I was having a hard time deflecting the blows. We were ambushed in the woods by Crimson's guard. My eyes had immediately scanned the red uniforms, looking for his black one. I hadn't seen it.

We had been battling for nearly an hour. The sun had retreated behind the mountains, and the temperature had dropped significantly. Our numbers were dwindling, but so were theirs. I grabbed the dagger from my boot when his last blow knocked me to the ground. I turned quickly and sank my blade into his chest. His dark eyes stared at me, and his red hair whipped in the breeze as he fell to the forest floor.

Fuck.

I stood and turned, stopping when I saw that Cassius stood directly behind me, holding my viper-handled dagger only inches from my heart. Shit. I had thrown it at someone earlier and had not yet had the chance to retrieve it.

"Point," he whispered, before he handed me my dagger. "I do believe that is five points, so I win."

"I never agreed to five points being the winning number," I growled. "You ambushed us."

"No, this is not my guard," he sighed. "Illusion magic," he whispered as I looked back out and saw the dead men wearing gray uniforms. Kizar guards. Why had they attacked us? I turned back to Cassius, who had a mischievous glint to his smile.

"You owe me a surprise." His eyes twinkled with delight.

"I owe you fucking nothing," I scoffed. I started turning to leave to help the few men left fighting. He grabbed my hand and turned me back.

"I love it when you pretend to hate me, little viper; it only makes this more fun for me."

"Who said I was pretending?" I retorted.

He threw his handsome face toward the darkened sky and laughed loudly. My mind held onto that sound so I could never forget it. Cassius' laughter was my new favorite noise.

"I look forward to my prize." His pretty golden eyes gleamed.

"Well, you'll be waiting forever. The hot spring was as far as you'll ever get with me."

He frowned for only a moment.

"You don't have to keep running from this, princess." He smiled when I pointed my dagger at him. "I think you enjoy this as much as I do."

"You are my enemy," I reminded him and myself. My heart was racing so rapidly in my chest that I worried he could hear it.

"An enemy that you kissed twice." His eyes gleamed brightly. He reminded me every time we saw each other. Which seemed to happen often these days, like he was following me. Then he started this stupid game of how many times we could have killed each other. I did like this game, but I wouldn't admit it. I had panicked in the hot spring when he touched me, and I liked it too much, so I got out and ran before anything could happen. But I would be lying if I said that kiss, and the way his body felt against me didn't haunt my mind.

"Then I left because it was a mistake," I lied.

His eyes looked over my face, then smiled, like he knew I was a damn liar. He leaned forward.

"Something that feels that fucking good isn't a mistake, little viper. It's a divine intervention written in the stars above."

His words made me blush, even though he had been flirting with me for months. Cassius' eyes softened as he looked at me. His fingers came up and gently brushed my wild curls from my face.

"Blushing for me, Thea?"

I looked over my shoulder at my men. They had finished off the Kizar guards and were doing a walk-through. They didn't seem to see me behind the tree yet, but they would quickly. When I turned back to Cassius, he had moved closer. His chest was nearly flush with mine, but I could only focus on how handsome he was when he looked at me like that, like he really did care about me. My body swayed toward him ever so slightly, like it was begging for his touch without my permission.

"I look forward to whatever my surprise will be."

"You'll be waiting forever."

"I'd wait forever if you made me," he said, his voice soft, as if it were a true promise he was making.

I turned and walked away from him before I did something stupid, like kiss him again. I looked over my shoulder as he watched me walk away before turning and disappearing into the trees behind him. I stared at the spot and felt that stupid heart of mine wish he had stayed.

I ignored the feeling in my chest every time I thought about him for three days. It only made the feeling worse, though. It was like Cassius was calling to something deep *inside me that I couldn't even see—something only he could. No form of distraction had worked. Even touching myself felt lackluster. Cassius was the only one who could satisfy this need I had.*

I owed him a prize; it made me smile. I stared at myself in the reflection of the water. That is why I was doing this, I told myself.

A prize for almost killing me the most. It didn't mean anything. I could convince myself of this lie. I stared through the trees and watched his guard's camp. He hadn't been that far from my camp, so it took me no time to find it. It was like he wanted me to be able to find him. I had watched him disappear into a large black tent and not emerge again. That had been an hour ago. I had been trying to talk myself out of this since then. I was nervous, so much so that my palms were sweaty.

I should be cold with the little clothing I had on under my button-up cloak. I had left my hair down but slipped the oversized hood on. His men were on patrol, but they disappeared from sight, and I knew it was now or never. I hurried from the tree line and straight into his tent. I stared at the large bed he had there. He was sleeping on his back with no shirt, and my eyes instantly drifted over his tattooed skin.

My heart pounded in anticipation as I moved slightly closer to the bed. I could stab him right now, which would be a million points because I had infiltrated his tent. I shook my head and took one more step forward, but suddenly he sprang from the bed and jumped at me. He gripped me and pinned me to the bed with a dagger to my throat.

"Ok, I'll leave." I tried to tease him, but he let go of me instantly and stood up.

"Little viper?" He looked around like he wasn't sure if this was real life or a dream. "You snuck into my tent." His voice held a note of awe in it, which made me smile.

"I could have killed you four times over. I should get double the points for that." The nervousness I was feeling made my voice waver slightly. Cassius' eyes drifted over me, and I felt my body tremble at his gaze.

Realization set in his eyes, making them glow in the darkness of his tent.

"Is this my prize?"

I swallowed hard and nodded, too scared to say anything. I had never seduced a man. Not like this. I had gotten a few kisses, yes. Nothing more, ever. I stood up as he sat on the edge of his bed, watching me. Slowly, I unbuttoned my cloak. On the last button, I took a deep breath as his golden eyes swirled with blackness. Here goes nothing. I let it fall open.

A loud hum of approval filled the tent when he saw my lack of clothing. I slid the cloak off and let it pool at my feet. Cassius' eyes never left me. He watched every movement like he needed it to breathe.

I took a small step forward. He still hadn't said anything, and I had never done this. Did I misread this? Maybe he didn't actually want me in this way. Maybe it was just harmless flirting for him. Heat covered my cheeks as doubt crept in, making my chest tight with worry.

"I should go," I whispered and grabbed my cloak.

"I don't think so, my love," he ground through clenched teeth as he picked me up and hauled me to the bed. I yelped and dropped my cloak.

He sat on the edge with me straddling his lap. I could feel how much he liked this when his hard length pressed against me. His hands ran over my bare back and hips. I didn't know what men thought was attractive. Every part of me was filled out and curved. I had been worried that he wouldn't like what he saw, but his eyes drifted over me and turned black. His big hands squeezed the flesh of my ass as he pulled me tightly against him.

"Kiss me," he demanded.

I did so without hesitation. My lips parted for his tongue as it pushed into mine. My hands ran over the stubble on his chin before running through his dark, chaotic hair. He hummed in approval when my hips moved at their own pace, tearing his mouth from mine so he could kiss down my neck. His stubble scraped against my sensitive skin, leaving red marks.

I sighed heavily into the silent tent when his tongue ran over my nipple before sucking it into his hot mouth. His teeth and tongue teased it so perfectly before moving to the other.

"Cassius," I said with a plea.

"Does my little viper like this?" he purred as his hands grabbed my breasts and he brought his mouth back down to tease them. My hips rolled faster against him, and he finally grabbed me, pausing my movements.

"Gods above, give me a minute," he groaned. "You're killing me."

My cheeks flushed.

"Sorry, I didn't mean to hurt you."

His face snapped up to mine with an odd look.

"That's not what I meant. I mean, it feels too good, and I need a minute to collect myself," he reassured me softly, but his eyes bounced between mine.

"Oh." I felt my cheeks redden even more. Gods, I was going to mess this up.

Something flicked over his face as he turned us over and laid me on my back. His mouth found mine as his hand slid down my body. He didn't bother pulling off my underwear.

He shredded them with little effort. My hips bucked up when his fingers slid over me.

"So wet for me already," he said, eyes gleaming.

I swallowed hard as his fingers teased me softly before sinking deep into me.

"Fuck," I moaned into the air.

"You look so pretty like this, my love."

His fingers moved slowly, his thumb rubbing me so perfectly that I could feel a weird sensation building up inside of me. It felt like I was climbing and climbing, just waiting for the right moment to free fall from high above. I realized I was making whimpering noises and shut my mouth. His fingers stopped as soon as I did, though. My eyes flew open and I glared at him.

"Don't you dare hide those noises from me, Thea. Those are mine, and I want to hear every fucking one of them fall from that pretty mouth of yours."

I nodded, and his fingers moved again, making me moan with pleasure.

"Good girl," he hummed in approval at my noises. At this point, I didn't even care if anyone else heard me. The climbing sensation kept on rising until an orgasm tore through me at his praise. I called out his name as his fingers slowed down their movements to prolong my waves of pleasure. My arms

crushed him against me as my hips rolled into his fingers to ride out my orgasm for as long as I could.

"Fucking beautiful," he growled as his lips crushed mine. He removed his fingers and crawled over me, then nestled between my thighs, giving me soft kisses for a moment until I was able to open my eyes again. His handsome face looked at me like I hung the moon and stars.

"Are you sure about this?" he whispered softly, stroking me in reassurance.

"More than anything." Nothing had ever felt so right in my life. Everything about Cassius made me feel safe.

He lined his hips with mine and kissed me hard.

"It's going to hurt at first."

He knew I had never done this before. And when I thought he would slowly sink into me, he did the opposite. Cassius thrust his hips so quickly that I cried into his neck as he shredded through my virginity. He didn't move as I adjusted to him. His lips pressed soft kisses on my neck, my lips, my jaw. He was distracting me from the sharp pain I was feeling.

He stayed still for a minute, then slowly lifted himself up on his hands, looking down at me with lust in his eyes. He then gave me a soft kiss before laying all his weight on me. I moved my hips, testing out how it would feel now. The pain had faded and, in its wake, left nothing but pleasure when I rocked my hips against his. Cassius took the hint when I started moving, and his pace increased into strong strokes. How had I never had the urge to see what sex was all about? No wonder everyone was so preoccupied with it.

"Fuck," he whispered so softly that I nearly missed it.

His rough hand grabbed my thigh and adjusted it so I was wrapped around his hips. His fingers squeezed my flesh so tightly that I hoped it left bruises.

"Cassius," I pleaded, but I wasn't sure what for. I needed more, I needed less, and I needed to be somehow closer to him. His fingers grabbed my jaw tightly and forced me to look up at him. His eyes were black as night, beautiful and haunting.

"When you cum, don't you dare hold back. I've dreamt about hearing your moans for years, Thea. I want to hear them all. I want to hear what I do to you."

My eyes closed tightly as his words soaked deep into my bones and clawed out of me through waves of pleasure. A deep groan left my throat as soon as I felt the start of my orgasm racing through my veins. My hands fisted the blankets below me as if they would help me not fall into bliss.

"Yes," Cassius ground out as unintelligible noises fell from me. His hips picked up tempo as they slammed into me. His breathing became shallow and short. I was a whimpering mess below him as his own release roared through him.

He collapsed on top of me and held me tightly. Wetness pooled in my eyes, and I wasn't sure why. I wasn't sad. I felt an overwhelming sense of satisfaction and happiness. Cassius rolled off me, and I turned my face away from him so he wouldn't see the emotions I was having for no reason.

"My love?" He questioned me as I turned my head. "Did I hurt you?"

"No."

I stared at the cloak on the ground. Well, I guess this is the part when I get up and leave. I slid off the bed and grabbed the cloak, slipping it on.

"What the fuck are you doing?" he asked, almost in panic.

"Leaving." I looked over my shoulder at him. "We both got what we needed."

Anger covered his face.

"You think that I was chasing you just to fuck you and send you away less than a minute later?"

"I don't know," I admitted. "Is that all you wanted from me?"

I had turned so I could face him. The harsh lines of his face softened when he saw the worry all over my face. I didn't know how to do any of this. Everyone always tossed me aside after they got what they needed or wanted from me. I wouldn't blame him if he did the same thing. He stood up quickly and grabbed my face so he could give me a deep kiss.

His hands slid the cloak off my shoulders, and he lifted me effortlessly off the ground before setting me under the blanket on his bed. He crawled in next to me, rubbing his hands over my hips and thighs.

"Now that I know how fucking good we are together, little viper, I don't think I can ever let you go." He gave me a lazy smile.

"It couldn't have been that great for you. I don't have any experience." I looked over his features to see if a flicker of agreement would pass over them, but nothing did. Cassius' fingers stopped rubbing my naked skin.

"You have no idea how feral it makes me to know that I'm the only one that's done this with you, the only one who knows what you sound like when you cum, the only one who knows what you feel like. Nothing ever has or ever will compare to how good you feel. No one could ever hold a candle to you, Thea." He stared into my eyes. "Tonight was better than anything I could have ever imagined, and I have imagined all the things I've wanted to do to you for years."

I knew he meant it.

"I have not even looked in the direction of another woman since I first laid eyes on you, and I don't plan to ever look anywhere else but right here."

CHAPTER 23

I woke with a jolt, feeling oddly overwhelmed by my memory. When I went to sit up, I remembered where I was. I wasn't with Cassius. He wasn't kissing me or telling me things I wanted to hear. I was tied to the bedpost and bleeding from my punishment at the hands of Jesper. My body ached so badly from lying on the hard wooden floor.

I turned towards the door and waited for what felt like hours for him to come through it. When he finally did, he paused at the doorway and waited for my eyes to look at him.

"Today is our rehearsal; our wedding is tomorrow. It's customary for all royal families to attend tonight. Although I assume Crimson will not want to. You will behave yourself, or I will kill Sybil's husband and children tonight. You're lucky I didn't kill them for your last stupid mistake."

He came over and untied me roughly. His hand grabbed mine and led me upstairs to the large bathtub he had brought me to last time. Once again, Jesper stared at me the entire time I soaked. He had carved his name into my thigh and forearm. I didn't say anything about it, though. I wasn't going to give him the satisfaction. So, I stayed silent the entire time I sat in the tub. Flashes of Cassius and I took up all thoughts in my mind.

"You're awfully quiet today."

No response from me. I took my time scrubbing the sweat, dirt, and blood from my skin. His blue eyes watched me curiously, like he thought I would attack him at any moment.

"Your wedding dress has been altered. You will now have sleeves to hide your wound," he said, speaking as if I were pleased by this. My face was still riddled with cuts and scrapes. I also didn't care because I knew that this wedding was a joke. The whole thing was a twisted display of power. I knew that following along would let both Jesper and my father think that I was going to obey.

I would do my best to do so, to lull them into a false sense of security. Then, I would cut both their heads off when they least expected it. That was my plan. Maybe I would kill them as they slept tonight.

"Say something for fuck's sake," he growled.

"No." My black eyes narrowed on him. "Is that better?"

He sighed heavily but didn't get angry. When I got out of the tub, he led me back to my room. Blood and water still coated the floor. I turned when I heard Jesper behind me. I backed away when he planted a kiss on my lips. Disgust was probably plain as day on my face.

"Don't do that tomorrow or tonight," his voice strained.

"If you think I'm going to pretend that I like you today or even on our wedding day, you are more stupid than you look."

His nostrils flared as his hands fisted by his sides. I widened my stance, readying myself for the strike I was sure was coming.

"Did you ever think that you could have learned to love me? You didn't need to make all of this so difficult."

"Did you ever think that you could have married someone who actually liked you? I will never harbor any feelings for you other than hate and disgust. You are a weak man."

He backhanded me, and I fell into the wall, but instead of showing him the agony I felt, I laughed.

"Point proven. You are a coward."

Jesper stared at me like he wanted to strangle me, but he turned and left instead. Worry clawed at my insides. I didn't want him to think he could just touch me whenever he pleased after tomorrow. I might have to kill him sooner than I originally thought. Thinking about it made me smile.

A flicker of relief ran through my arm, and I looked down at the contrasting feeling. My eyes stared at the blood bond that Cassius gave me. It no longer had a crack in it. He fixed it.

The relief disappeared after a moment. I stared at the bond, feeling unsure. Why did he fix it? I focused on the blood bond for hours, but nothing ever came through it. Finally, I lay down, pretending like I wasn't about to go to a rehearsal for my own wedding tomorrow.

★★☽★★

I scanned the beautiful dress I was wearing. The fit across my chest was perfect and if this were any other occasion I would admire it more. The sleeves that were added were odd and the lace fabric irritated my wounds. I grabbed the hem of them and ripped them off. My hair had been pinned back, and my make-up was overdone. It was as if they thought they could get rid of the bruises and cuts. They didn't. I sighed heavily as I looked at myself and unpinned my hair, letting it cascade down my back.

"I look stupid," I scoffed. Then I laughed because I didn't want to feel pretty. I hoped I looked like a troll walking down the aisle. My eyes had been green earlier, but

I focused on the mirror long enough that they shaded over red. My swirled tattoos were faded, but if I could make them glow, I would. Anything I could do to be rebellious tonight without doing it outright, I would try.

I had even replaced the nude lipstick with dark red that reminded me of Crimson. My heart squeezed briefly. Would he show up today? He said he would see me tomorrow.

Jesper had told me it was custom for the royal families to be present for the rehearsal dinner and then attend a feast in our honor. I wondered if any of the families would show after my father and Jesper had been complete assholes at the meeting of the kingdoms.

My father came to the doorway then, dressed in his finery and ready to impress his guests.

"Ready?" My father asked.

"Sure."

He turned and walked out. I told him he could walk me down the aisle the day my corpse was in the ground. He didn't argue. I grabbed the ugly blue flowers the wedding planner had picked out. They were Cerithia blue, but I didn't care much for them. They looked like flowers you would give to a sick friend, not for a wedding or rehearsal.

They were perfect.

The most awful music was playing. It was beautiful and romantic, which was the complete opposite of how I felt on the inside. I was tempted to just run down the aisle and get this rehearsal over with, but I had a different approach. I walked unbearably slow, just like I would tomorrow. I didn't bother holding the flowers up; they dangled in my left hand. My eyes scanned everyone in attendance. The kings of the other kingdoms were all here, except Crimson.

Disappointment coursed through me. I didn't want him to witness this, but I had also just hoped for a glimpse at his handsome face. I could see the disgust on their faces as I walked down the aisle. I looked like I had been beaten to a pulp, which technically I had been.

The air outside was hot but not unbearable, and the sun shined brightly on the large blue and white flowers that lined the aisle. The decorations were pretty, but nothing to my taste. I preferred dark colors, like black and crimson red. My heart pounded sadly in my chest. Not that long ago, I thought maybe Cassius would be the one I walked down the aisle toward, but now when I looked, all I saw was a monster disguised with blonde hair and pretty blue eyes.

Jesper smiled at me, like he was truly happy to see me. I wanted to glare, but I didn't. My mind flashed to Cassius.

I would have married him in a heartbeat, but he hadn't asked to marry me. Dread filled the sadness. I didn't want to belong to Jesper.

I didn't want to live with him, kiss him, sleep with him, or bear his children. One of us would end up dead soon enough because I couldn't live like that. I needed to save the families of those from Exile before I killed Jesper.

King Sybrien stared intensely at me as I walked slowly. His dark eyes looked as if he were trying to communicate something to me. The chairs reserved for Crimson were empty next to him.

Cassius said he would never let me belong to another man. So where the hell was he? He had once told me he was feral with the thought that he was the only man to know what I felt like; did that cross his mind anymore? Had he forgotten how good we were together?

I glanced around and silently pleaded for anyone to ruin this rehearsal.

The band restarted the song as I took my leisurely time getting down the aisle. My eyes looked over everyone present. I didn't have a single friend here. No one. Jesper held out his hand for me when I was close enough. I hesitated for only a moment before I slipped my hand into his. His skin was soft and warm as he held tightly to me. We faced each other, but my eyes looked anywhere but at him.

The priestess started the rehearsal, telling us how it would go and what we were to say in response. I couldn't even focus on her words. My mind called out to me, asking why I wasn't running. Leave him, it seemed to say; we do not belong to him. My darkness swarmed inside of me, trying desperately to escape. Jesper squeezed my hands in his softly and brought my attention to him. He gave me a breathtaking smile, but I knew the monster that lurked under it.

I didn't give him any sort of response. I kept my face passive and indifferent through whatever spiel the priestess was saying.

"I, Jesper Alcove, take Thea Alzara to be my wedded wife..." I blocked out his voice. My heart pounded in my chest. Would I be able to recite those words out loud? I didn't care who interrupted this rehearsal, but I wished someone would. I didn't want to do this. I would rather die than be tied to this prick.

"Thea?" Jesper barked softly. "It's your turn," he said gently, but there was a warning in it.

"I, Thea Alzara, take..." I couldn't spit out the words, even though this was only a practice. My eyes focused over Jesper's shoulder and widened in surprise to see Della standing close by. Her dark skin was peppered with faded freckles over her nose, and her star-colored eyes shined brightly as usual. Her black hair was styled perfectly. She was breathtaking.

This time, I realized she wore a small, dainty black and silver crown on her head. I realized she was wearing a crimson red dress instead of her usual signature black.

She frowned at me as I stared at her dress. My head pounded when a memory of Cassius escaped.

"You and me, viper, we're what the stars and gods created the realm for. Happiness, belonging, and love." Cassius smiled at me. He wore beautiful black and crimson robes that were far fancier than I had ever seen him in. "I belong to you, and if anyone thinks they can take you from me, then they sealed their own death for thinking such foolish things."

The noise that ricocheted through the crowd stopped my memory immediately. Jesper had been grasping my hand to the point of pain, but I hadn't noticed because of Della. King Sybrien had accidentally knocked over a flower vase, shattering it.

"Oops." He frowned up at Jesper. My heart plummeted because, for a split second, I thought Cassius had shown up. My eyes flickered at King Sybrien when he gave me a small, friendly smile and made a gesture I couldn't quite understand. Was he warning me of something? My eyes flickered around the crowd, but I didn't see anything unusual.

"Try again, Thea," Jesper demanded.

"I..." I swallowed hard. "Thea..."

Jesper's eyes were wild with impatience as I stumbled with my words, but it wasn't intentional. Something odd soaked into my thoughts, and it was like I couldn't think of anything for myself. I stared at Jesper as my mind went completely blank. Then my eyes flicked to Della as she moved closer to us.

I will find a way to stop this. Just stall a moment longer; her voice spoke into my mind. *He is late,* she sighed, but I didn't understand her. I watched as she moved down the aisle. No one else turned to watch her.

"What the fuck are you staring at? If you think I won't punish you tonight because our wedding is tomorrow, you are mistaken," Jesper whispered harshly.

I ignored him.

Della smiled at me when she turned my way. Her hands lifted slightly, and the sun started to disappear. Everyone stared into the darkening sky. I could hear mutters from guests wondering what was happening. She lifted her hands up more and focused on Jesper and I.

Don't move, Thea, she spoke into my mind.

I went deathly still. Then a bolt of lightning struck at the base of the arch that Jesper and I stood in front of, immediately setting it ablaze.

Our guests gasped.

"How'd you do that?" My father questioned me.

"I didn't do anything," I snapped back.

Tell him the gods and stars must not be happy about this union, her voice spoke to my mind.

I snapped my eyes back to her.

"It appears the gods and stars do not condone this union," I called out to my father with a genuine smile. His face paled at my words.

"Well, that ruined the whole rehearsal," Jesper growled, but his eyes darted around like he was looking for the goddess who had ruined our rehearsal. Jesper was terrified, I realized. He looked at me oddly.

"Where were we?" he spoke. What a persistent fuck.

The priestess fumbled her words as Jesper squeezed the bridge of his nose. When he glanced up at me, I could tell he was about to lose his shit.

"Forget it!" He threw his hands up, defeated. "We all know how a wedding works. I'm sure it will go better tomorrow. Let's just go inside and eat." His eyes darted around us again, looking for a reason for the sudden change in the weather.

Thank the stars. The guests practically ran inside the castle and into a smaller ballroom that was transformed overnight into a beautiful space for a celebration. Tables filled the room with stunning flower centerpieces, golden tablecloths, and food that could feed the whole city. Jesper held my hand in a death grip and led me to the front table.

"Don't think I didn't notice how happy you were that we were interrupted. You will not get so lucky tomorrow," Jesper whispered. "And if you walk that slowly down the aisle again, I'll snap your legs and give you a reason to be slow."

"Don't worry. I'll be on my best behavior," I scoffed. His hand gripped mine so tightly that I cried out. "How did you do it? Your magic is barbed inside you."

I just smiled at him. I wanted him to think I was still able to get some magic out. He stared at me, terrified.

Another crashing noise made him drop my hand. King Sybrien had knocked over another flower vase, shattering it.

"For fuck's sake, can you not break something for five minutes?" Jesper snapped. The king didn't acknowledge him. No, he was staring right at me with a big smile on his face. Why was he so fucking happy? The lights of the ballroom began to flicker violently. Instinctively, I glanced around for Della, but she was missing.

Darkness enveloped the room for a brief moment before the lights flicked back on, revealing Cassius and several other men, who now stood in the center of the ballroom.

CHAPTER 24

A black vortex swirled quickly around Cassius and his guards. My heart nearly stopped. He looked around the crowd before his golden eyes found mine. King Sybrien gave Cassius a subtle head nod, but I saw it.

"Sorry, I'm late," he said, smiling toward Jesper. "You wrote the wrong time on my invitation. An honest mistake, I'm sure."

"What the fuck are you doing, Cassius?" Jesper's guards had already lifted their weapons, but Cassius paid no attention to them. His eyes lingered on my face, tracing over each bruise and cut. His gaze snapped to Jesper with deep hatred. My eyes shifted to Haden, Kace, and Zade behind him. They were all looking at me with no emotion. How was he here? He said he couldn't cross into Cerithia lands without dying, unless it was war. For fuck's sake, was he declaring war right now?

I shifted my attention to Cassius when I felt his eyes on me.

"My gods above, Jesper, I didn't know you could afford such a pretty dress." Cassius' smiled at me. "You look stunning, my love, but gray does not suit you. This would be perfect if it were crimson red."

"Leave," Jesper warned.

"I was invited," he smiled. Realization set in. He could cross the border if he was invited. In Jesper's desperate attempt to be petty, he gave Cassius an opening to come to Cerithia. "Besides, I'm not here for the wedding festivities. I've come for my prisoner. I'll leave once they are handcuffed."

Prisoner?

Did he mean me? It had to be. I glanced around as if I would find an answer to my question in the crowd. My father was glaring daggers at me as if I had concocted this whole thing. Jesper was losing his patience, but Cassius looked amused by the whole exchange. Please take me out of this hell.

"What are you talking about?" Jesper glared at Cassius, enraged by this intrusion.

Cassius looked around at the crowd and sighed heavily. His golden eyes turned black as his shadows swarmed around him. He was putting on a show; why?

"A few days ago, Cerithia broke the peace treaty," he declared.

An uproar ensued in the crowded room. Jesper froze tensely next to me. That was a very big accusation to say out loud. Had guards snuck onto Crimson lands and been caught?

"That's bullshit!" My father cursed Cassius.

"Oh, but it's not," Cassius tisked at my father like he was an idiot. My father's hands fisted at his sides. "You have not declared war, so any unprovoked attack on my land is considered a peace treaty violation, is it not?"

"My men have not crossed into your lands, Cassius. What lies are you trying to spin here?"

Cassius' eyes met mine, and I immediately understood what he was talking about.

Me. I broke the treaty.

"Thea, my love, did you not tell anyone where you were a few days ago?" Cassius smiled smugly at me. "I can tell Jesper probably found out, seeing as your face is covered with cuts and bruises."

"Jesper?" My father questioned.

Jesper said nothing to my father, but his hand squeezed mine so painfully that I whimpered under the pain.

"Thea crossed into Crimson lands, killed my guards, held a dagger to my throat, and threatened to harm me.

She is from Cerithia, and I do believe she is the captain of your guard, is she not?"

My heart hammered in my chest. What was this? Was he going to really sit here and intentionally get me in trouble? What if they did let him take me?

"Yes," my father ground out. Both he and Gwyn looked like they would kill me.

"Tell them, Thea," Cassius said with a sweet smile.

My eyes scanned the angry faces of my father and the queen. But when I glanced at Haden, he gave me a subtle nod and smirk.

"Yes, I did what he is accusing me of."

The other kingdoms whispered as they watched the exchange. I didn't know it was a treaty violation. Not that it would have stopped me.

"You can't just fucking listen, can you?" Jesper snarled at me. He had dropped my hand, but only to smack me across the face, making me fall against the table. A loud gasp came from the royal families. Blood dripped from a cut on my lip that had been split open. Jesper tangled his hand into my hair to stand me up, then punched me so hard in the stomach that I fell flat on my back and saw black edging around my vision.

"If you want to keep your hands, Jesper, I suggest you not touch her again." Cassius' voice was dark, malicious in his warning. A moment later, shadows swarmed around me, lifting me back to my feet as blood poured from my split lip and onto the gray dress I wore. Cassius then stepped to Jesper and grabbed him by the throat, slamming him against the wall.

Cassius whispered, so only the three of us could hear.

"If you ever touch her like that again, I will cut your fucking head off." Then he grabbed his dagger and slammed it into Jesper's thigh before yanking it right back out. Jesper's pained yell echoed in the silent space. No one dared move or breathe. Cassius' chest rose and fell in angry puffs as his black eyes turned to inspect me. Then he turned his attention back to the crowd and stepped toward my father.

"As the treaty states, the land that was violated gets to choose the punishment. Thea will be imprisoned in the Crimson kingdom until her violation is paid off."

"Fuck you, Cassius!" Jesper bellowed. "You are not taking her."

"But I am Jesper, and there isn't a fucking thing you can do to stop me. If you try to keep me from enacting my punishment, then I have grounds to kill you right here, right now. And I would gladly rip you apart. Actually, I think I would let Thea do the honors."

I stood very still. Cassius was taking me. He was taking me to Crimson and away from this nightmare. Even if I were a prisoner, it would be better than being here. Relief flooded me at this news.

"You just can't stand that she chose me over you," Jesper hissed.

Cassius laughed loudly.

Haden and the other guards scoffed at Jesper. Haden glanced over at me and frowned at the sight of me. My eyes flickered to Wisp. She was twirling around Cassius, but I didn't know if this was a good thing yet or not.

"You think that is the face of a woman who chose to marry you? Don't flatter yourself, Jesper; Thea has better taste than a coward who raises his hand to her. Don't you, *my love*?"

His eyes flickered to mine, but I didn't speak.

I could feel a shot of calmness running up my arm. Cassius was trying to soothe me through the bond, but it wasn't working. What if they didn't let him take me? Would I be tortured slowly? Images of Jesper carving into my flesh and holding me under the bath water plagued me. I saw Cassius wince, and I wondered if he saw it too.

His shadows pushed out farther around him, like he couldn't help it. They knocked Jesper forcefully so that he stumbled into the table behind him.

"You have to give a length of time for the punishment." My father stared at me like he would come up and stab me if he could. "A reasonable time."

"Three months." Cassius looked at me.

"Two," my father bit back.

"Deal." Cassius smiled like he got more time than he thought he would. "I guess you'll have to postpone the wedding."

"We can just do it now," Jesper said harshly.

"Over my dead body." Cassius came up and grabbed my hand, his thumb rubbing my skin in a quick, gentle movement. He held up a pair of iron cuffs and then attached them to my wrists.

"Take these magic barbs off of her, now."

Jesper did what he asked but did so roughly that I started bleeding again. Cassius' eyes watched Jesper closely, and as soon as his hands were off mine, he stumbled backwards as Cassius punched him square in the face. He then wrapped Jesper up in his shadows, his smile menacing as Jesper called out in pain.

"I should gut you right this second." But instead, he tossed Jesper across the room. Jesper bounced onto the floor after hitting the wall.

I watched Jesper hold his bleeding nose, his eyes wild with anger. I saw his fingers bent at odd angles from Cassius' shadows. My lips twitched at the sight of him as he cradled his mutilated fingers.

"If you touch him, if you even think about it, I will make your life more unbearable than you could ever imagine." Jesper glared at me.

"Someone's possessive," Cassius whistled mockingly. "Are you ready, little viper?" He spoke the term of endearment just to piss off Jesper, and it worked.

"You have no idea what you've done." Jesper looked at Cassius. "Wait until I have her back and I send pieces of her back to you until there is nothing left of this Crimson whore."

My eyes flashed back to Cassius, who was very still, his jaw and fists clenched tightly at Jesper's threat. Cassius gripped his dagger in his hand, and it was obvious that he was contemplating killing Jesper right then. Before he could move, Jesper was lying flat on his back as Haden's frost shot at him and hit him in the chest. When my eyes found Haden, his face was full of so much anger and rage that I took a hesitant step backward.

Cassius stepped forward, shielding me from Jesper.

"Oh, I know what I'm doing, Jesper. You won't declare war without her. I just bought myself two extra months of preparations for when you do declare. When I return her to you, Jesper, it will be without her magic barbs, and

I hope she uses that chance to rip the limbs from your body."

Cassius returned to me and took my hand in his softly. I could feel my magic stirring as I realized the cuffs he placed on me didn't smother my magic.

"Oh, Luren, I almost forgot. I brought you a lovely gift as a congratulations for your daughter's engagement." He dropped my hand. He got my father a gift. Haden smiled as Cassius grabbed a sack from Kace. Was that blood dripping out of it? Cassius' eyes flicked to mine, and he gave me a menacing smile as he reached into the bag and pulled Lavtan's severed head from it. Cassius tossed it to my father. The disgusting thudding noise of Lavtan's head hitting the table Luren was sitting at made me recoil.

"What the fuck?" The queen screamed.

"I brought your friend to you," Cassius said with a smile as he crossed his arms over his chest. "A traitor of Crimson. Someone who will never help you take what belongs to me again." My father's eyes glanced at me as Cassius walked up to me, his shadows caressing me gently. He leaned in and softly, sensuously pressed his lips to mine.

Before anyone could respond, black shadows rose up and swirled around us. When they disappeared, we were standing back in Crimson. I looked over to see a room full of people staring at me. The king, the queen, Cassius' siblings, and even the guards. They all smiled when they saw me, but I couldn't smile back.

I looked at Cassius, who was staring at me oddly. His golden eyes dim in color.

"How long?" The king finally broke the tension.

"Two months," Cassius answered without looking away from me.

"I was expecting only a month, so that's good." His dark eyes looked at me. "Welcome home, Thea."

But I said nothing. I wasn't sure if I was in shock or if the poison from Jesper's blade still lingered in my mind.

Cassius frowned at me briefly before looking away.

"Let's get you situated," he sighed and grabbed my hand, slipping the cuffs off. I pulled it away from him but followed. I knew where he was taking me, and I didn't want to stay there. I stopped and refused to move when he looked back at me.

"I will stay somewhere else. You are staying in *our* room," he spoke as if he heard my thoughts.

Fine. I would stay if he were not. Anger was simmering in my chest. I started walking again, and he followed me this time. My body burned in agony. The pain of beatings and torture made me ache all over. I needed a hot shower and sleep. My fire mist rose up and swarmed around me, happy to be free. I couldn't control it right now, even if I wanted to. Then I felt it—happiness followed by sadness—through the bond. I turned to see my fire mist swirling around Cassius, caressing him like it had missed him.

His eyes found mine, but I turned away from him and continued up the stairs. I hated that I instantly relaxed when I stepped into the space. It smelled like night and rain. It smelled like home, and that pissed me off. I stopped and turned when Cassius followed me inside.

"You shouldn't have taken me!"

"Thea, you didn't want to go back. That was all I needed to hear from you. You are where you belong."

"They have Sybil's family. They have all of their families, and now they will be slaughtered because you took me!"

"That is why you thought you had to go back," he said with a frown. Cassius moved toward me, but I stepped backward. "My love, they do not have their families. Most of them left Cerithia and came to Crimson and Falgon. They lied."

Emotions clouded his handsome features.

"Are you sure?"

"Yes, I'm sure. I would never let them harm elite magic fae or their families."

Relief filled me. It was just another lie. Fuck, I could have stayed and not endured the beating from Jesper. I nodded and stared into his eyes. Gods, I felt like I was home. But my body and mind ached with everything I had been through.

"You must be exhausted. I will have food brought up for you. Rest. Relax. If you need anything, call for me, and I will come immediately."

I turned away from him and went to the bedroom. My eyes took in the space, and I felt like the walls were closing in. It looked just as it did when I left. I spotted a piece of paper on his bedside table and walked to it cautiously. It was the note I had scribbled before I left to get the bloodstone. My chest felt heavy after seeing it again. Being here was not easy. The memories of Cassius clouded my mind.

I stripped my ruined dress off and stood in the hot shower for a long time, trying not to think of anything. I didn't want to feel at all right now. I wanted all my memories to disappear again so I didn't have to remember what Jesper and my family had done to me. Cassius had saved me, but what happened when he didn't return me?

I shook the thoughts away and wrapped myself in a towel. Once I found clothing to sleep in, I hurried into the bed. It was so large that I could stretch out in it comfortably.

I looked at the ceiling and saw no cracks or nails sticking out. Then I fell asleep.

CHAPTER 25

I hadn't left the bedroom in days. Exhaustion plagued my every waking moment. I thought I had been resilient during my time at Cerithia, that nothing had broken me while I was there. But being here made me realize how truly broken I had become. My nights were sleepless, memories of Jesper beating me haunted me, and my mind constantly made up new scenarios of what would happen to me when I had to go back.

I couldn't go back. Tears filled my eyes and streamed down my face silently as I lay in bed. Emotions flooded me every time I opened my eyes, and trauma haunted me when I closed them. I couldn't get any relief. I couldn't stand to feel this way. A loud sob escaped me as I buried my face into the pillow. I did not know how I could survive this.

"Little viper." I jumped when his voice whispered.

I sat up in bed and refused to look at him. My face was wet and was surely a mess from nonstop crying. My hands tried to wipe the wetness and snot away, like he wouldn't be able to tell. I could feel him staring at me with worry. I was broken. Could they see it just by looking at me?

"You haven't eaten anything."

"I'm not hungry."

He was silent, but I could still feel his presence in the room. I stared at the dark green comforter and tried to block out the racing thoughts. Flashes of Jesper cutting me invaded my mind, and I flinched at the intrusion. I didn't know trauma could hurt worse in the aftermath than it did in the moment.

"Does anything sound good?" he finally spoke. "Whatever it is, we can make it or get it."

"I'm tired," I sighed and laid back down, pulling the thick comforter over my face.

"You've been sleeping for days. I'm worried," he said, his voice laced with concern. "You're losing weight."

"I didn't ask you to worry. I'm not your burden."

Silence.

I wanted him to know that, though Cerithia had been physical torment, Crimson was emotional and mental torment. I didn't know which was worse. I thought I could forgive Cassius after everything I learned, but I was still angry. He should have told me instead of letting my father tell me. My darkness was frozen inside of me. She was not shielding me from all the pain, hurt, and anger I had. Even when I begged my darkness to take away the emotions, she ignored me.

I felt the bed dip down somewhere in the direction I was facing. Part of me almost told him to leave, but a bigger part of me relaxed. I wasn't so lonely now. As if he had been expecting me to react, he waited a moment before the bed shifted again as he lay down.

I closed my eyes and felt exhaustion, forcing me into a nightmare I didn't want to live in.

Jesper always looked the same in my nightmares. The cold, unforgiving face when he carved into my skin in the dungeon was the only expression there.

My eyes looked at all the blood on the ground as my stomach bled and bled. Then suddenly, Jesper was holding me, forcing my face to look into the mirror and see the words carved there. I tried to close my eyes but couldn't. Please stop. I don't want to remember this. Then I saw something reflecting in the mirror from a dark corner of the room. Golden eyes.

My gaze held his as he watched Jesper hold me in place. Then Jesper laughed loudly and turned to where Cassius stood.

"Do you like her new tattoos? I did them myself." He smiled so wickedly that I looked away from him. *"Every time she sees her reflection in a mirror, she will remember me."*

I jolted awake, swinging my arms and kicking my feet wildly. I was crying, begging, and screaming for him to stop.

"It's okay, my love." Cassius was holding me tightly. "It's alright; it was just a dream."

I shook my head to argue. It was a nightmare, a memory.

"He hurt me," I choked out.

"I know." His voice was strained with emotion. "He won't ever hurt you again."

I moved away from Cassius and stood up. His eyes were wet with unshed tears as he looked at me, like he was seeing now how truly fucked up I was. I was not the Thea I was when I left for the witch's bloodstone. I wasn't even the Thea that marched here after visiting Exile. Jesper and my father had broken me since then. I don't feel anything but despair and hatred now. I hated myself for every decision I made.

His eyes turned black when he looked over at me. The anger in his face scared me. His shadows swarmed around him quickly as he walked toward me with quick strides.

My reaction was to make myself small, to protect myself.

I began to shake violently, and I could hear pleading sobs coming from me as I slid down the wall, curling into a ball as he got closer. I waited for his anger. I waited for the pain to come, but it didn't. My sobbing was the only thing that filled the silence of the room. Cassius had stopped moving. I peeked at him. Horror filled his face as he stared at me, a trembling, pleading mess in the fetal position at his feet. I was terrified of him, of everyone, and of everything. Cassius sank to his knees and stared at me.

"What did he do to you, my love?"

I watched the tears fall down his face at the sight of me. His eyes shifted to my arm, and I realized his torrent of anger was not directed at me. It was Jesper's name carved into my skin that had upset him. I had used healing magic, but scars couldn't be erased. His words had been on my skin long enough that they would never fade.

I looked away, feeling disgusted with myself. I pulled my sleeve down and hid my arm from him, staying where I was. My chest heaved with small, choppy breaths. I could hardly get any air in. It felt like I was dying, and part of me wished I would. It would finally set me free from torment. My shallow breathing made me shaky and dizzy. My chest hurt and felt tight. I could feel myself spiraling out of control.

Then the smell of rain and forest surrounded me, and my hazy eyes cleared.

Cassius had come over and lay on the floor next to me. He raised his hand hesitantly and brushed it over the hair on my face. I kept my eyes closed tightly as the tears continued to flow. His rough hand gripped mine, and he lay on the hard wooden floor with me. Even though my darkness was not threatened by Cassius, I still could not bring myself to relax in his presence. What if he was a monster? What if all of this was another lie or trick? Was he enchanting me now?

"I never want you to look at me that way again, little viper," he whispered. "That look will haunt me the rest of my life."

I opened my eyes, and his handsome face was close to mine. I couldn't respond. He closed his eyes tightly, like he couldn't stop seeing it.

Cassius sat up, letting go of my hand before scooping me up and setting me on the bed. So many questions swirled in his eyes, but he didn't ask them. He turned and headed for the door, but that familiar tug of wanting him to stay made me speak.

"It will only be worse when you send me back."

Cassius stopped mid-stride but didn't turn to face me as he spoke.

"I never had any intentions of letting you go back. You're where you belong." He looked over his shoulder at me. "I would take your pain and hurt from you if I could. I thought you wanted to be with him. I thought you chose him over me because you weren't calling to me in your sleep anymore. You weren't sending anything through the bond. I didn't know it had broken that day. I didn't know that you couldn't feel me trying to fight for you, begging you to come home. I thought maybe you were happy, and I would have let you go if you had been. If I had known that the bond had broken, I would have torn through Cerithia or any of the other kingdoms to find you. I would have destroyed the realm for you if I had known what was happening. I know you hate me, but I hate myself more than you ever could. Seeing you so terrified of me makes me hate myself for not taking you."

I opened my mouth to say something, but he stopped me.

"You will never go back to Cerithia or Kizar. You belong in Crimson. Even if you choose to have nothing to do with me, you belong here."

Then he was gone. I looked at the crown tattoo on my wrist. I hadn't been able to feel him or see him because it had been broken, not because he had abandoned me.

Relief I didn't know I needed flooded me, and I drifted to sleep peacefully.

CHAPTER 26

It didn't matter how much I slept; I always woke up exhausted. I had no idea how long I had been rotting away in this bed, but I knew it was too long. Rain poured down outside the window, making me stand so I could get a better glimpse of it through the large windows in the living room. I remembered how beautiful Crimson was as I stared out into the forest.

A movement reflected in the window, and I froze. Someone with blonde hair stood behind me. I immediately began shaking because my mind had already convinced me that it was Jesper.

"Thea." I felt a firm grip on my arm as I was turned around, and Haden's horrified face stared at me. I trembled as tears burst from me because I didn't know how to not be so scared anymore.

"Fuck, I didn't mean to frighten you." He frowned as he pulled me into him and wrapped me in a hug. I buried my face in his chest and cried violently as he held me. I was too broken to care if I was embarrassing myself.

Haden's hand rubbed my back in a comforting way.

"I'm sorry, Thea," he sighed heavily before backing up and sitting on the couch with me next to him. "I wanted to check on you because you haven't left the bed in weeks. Cassius is worried. Everybody is worried."

"I'm tired," I whispered softly.

"No, you're depressed. You've been through hell, and your body doesn't understand that you are safe now, so it keeps you on edge just in case you need to keep fighting."

I sat up and stared at Haden.

"I don't know if I'm safe here, though," I confessed. "What if my father wasn't lying about everything? What if Cassius *did* enchant me or used some sort of magic to trick me into loving him? I don't know what to believe anymore. I'm just so tired. Please, as my friend, tell me if this is a cruel trick. I cannot survive another betrayal from Cassius."

Haden's blue eyes scanned over my face, and I could see the pity he had for me.

"Cassius loves you." Haden frowned. "And I think that you still love him too, despite everything he's done to you. I think that deep inside your broken mind, you remember why he did what he did, and your heart just can't hate him. Your heart knows that he never betrayed you."

Haden was right in so many ways. I couldn't hate him, not really. And I didn't understand why. I sniffed and wiped my nose on my sleeve, then leaned in and hugged Haden. A moment later, someone cleared their throat behind us. When I turned around, Cassius was looking at us. Haden stood up quickly, muttering something about being a dead man.

"I came to check on her and scared her. I was trying to help calm her down," he said defensively, his hands in the air to show he meant no harm.

Cassius' black eyes stared at me relentlessly.

"That isn't your job, Haden. It's mine," Cassius whispered. "I get to comfort her," he said in a slightly injured tone.

"I'll leave," Haden sighed heavily.

Cassius kept staring at me, and I couldn't look at him.

"I'm glad to see you out of bed, but I wish it was me that could have convinced you, not Haden."

"He didn't convince me. I was already up watching the rain, but he startled me, and... well, he tried to help me."

"And did he? Help you, I mean." Cassius glanced over me as if he were looking for something that had been missing for a long time.

"Yes."

Cassius swallowed hard and finally glanced away from me.

"Is that what you need? Someone who is not me to help you. If it is, I will have Haden come back."

When I glanced at him, he was staring at me with a longing that made me sad to see. He looked at me like he loved me, so why couldn't my mind convince me I was safe? I realized I needed to hear it from him. I needed Cassius to tell me he didn't do all of this because he used me. My mind was confused because it wanted reassurance from *him*.

"Did you enchant me when we were enemies? My father told me I came here as a spy for Cerithia, and you used magic to make me fall in love with you. Is that true?"

Cassius stared at me, his face a conflicting mask of emotions.

"Does it feel true?"

I sat silent and thought for a moment before answering. "No, but I feel as if I cannot trust myself to make good judgments anymore."

"You fell in love with me before you ever came here, and when you came, it was not because your father sent you. I took you as a prisoner when you refused to admit you wanted me. You thought we couldn't be together because our families were enemies. I refused to let that be our fate, so I took you." He shrugged like it was no big deal. "You hardly protested. Especially after you found out your father had been slaughtering elite magic fae instead of enlisting them in the armies, like he told you he had been. You *chose* to be here with me."

There were so many questions I had about what he just said.

"You kidnapped me."

"Technically..." he frowned. "But it sounds bad when you don't have the context of our history." He rubbed the back of his neck in frustration, like he was saying all the wrong things.

"So, I wasn't a spy."

"No." His golden eyes glanced over me sadly. "Can I answer any other questions?"

My mind went blank at his request. I knew there were so many things I wanted to know, but now that I had the chance, I was overwhelmed and couldn't think straight.

"You love me?" I whispered softly, almost hoping he didn't hear me. He straightened up as he took a step toward me, but stopped when I backed up.

"I love you more than anything."

"I hate that I think everything you say is a lie." Cassius frowned at me as I stared at him. "Even after I learned what my father did, I still feel angry at you."

Cassius' shoulders deflated at my words, but he didn't look away from me.

"While I was in Cerithia, I had planned to kill you. And I truly think I would have if Wisp or my darkness had not intervened and saved you. Your words to me that day in the clearing have haunted me everywhere I go. *Who could love a monstrosity like me?* My mind truly thinks that no one can, and you are lying to me because you need to use me for something.

"But my darkness does not want to hurt you when you are near. It refused to kill you when those Falgon guards—I mean, Cerithia guards—kidnapped me. It hums with happiness when I am close to you, and it seeks you out every time you are near. My mind only shows me memories of us when we are happy, but my mind is broken, so I don't know if I can trust it."

Cassius opened his mouth to respond, but I held my hand up to stop him, a pleading look in my eyes.

"I am broken," I choked out. "I am damaged and tainted. I feel nothing but self-hatred and pain inside of me. I do not know how to fix myself. Nothing brings me happiness anymore, and I worry that I will never be the same woman

I was during the trials. I thought I was fine. I thought Jesper's beatings and torture didn't break me, but the gods know that I am barely hanging on here."

My sobs were loud as I spoke the words, not knowing if Cassius truly cared or if this was another plan to use me.

"I will help you, Thea. I will gather each piece of you and make you whole again; even if it takes a lifetime, it will be a lifetime together. You do not have to weather this storm alone. Let me be your rock. I know the words you spoke just now are only a fraction of what you are feeling." His golden eyes dimmed significantly. "I can feel every terrible thought and feeling you have through the bond. Please, let me show you just how worthy of love you are.

"My words in the clearing that day were *meant* to hurt you. I needed you to hate me in that moment, because if you had decided to cross the border to me, your father would have killed you before you took a step. I thought I would have the chance to explain myself to you, though. That I could tell you in our dreams or through the communication bond that I really loved you and I was only protecting you, but I didn't know it was broken. I was counting on the fact that we could make a plan in our dreams to save us."

Cassius ran his hands through his hair as he let out a long breath.

"There is another reason I was so cruel to you in the clearing that day, but I will only tell you when I know that you are staying here."

I wanted to demand that he tell me, but I was feeling overwhelmed with everything. I turned from him and looked out the window. The rain was streaking down the windows, but it was Cassius' reflection that I watched.

"We need to talk about everything," I whispered as I turned back to him. "But if I am being honest, I am terrified that you will tell me something that I cannot forgive. If I lose you again, what am I supposed to do? What will I have to live for?"

Cassius frowned slightly at my confession.

"No matter what I tell you, you will forgive me because I did what I needed to save you. Because if I lost you, Thea, I would have to follow you to the stars and into our next lives. I simply cannot live without you." He was so confident in his words. He reached out and gently grasped my hand for a moment. "Take your time, my love. We'll talk more when you start feeling better. I don't want to rush this and mess it up."

His words had calmed me and made my fire mist seep from me in happiness. It crept across the ground until it swirled around him as if it were hugging him. Cassius gave me a sad smile.

"I'm going to sleep on the couch, so I can be here if you need me. If that is alright with you?"

"Fine," I agreed.

Cassius took a hesitant step toward me, and this time, I didn't back up. Once he was in front of me, he brushed the hair from my face before running his hand over my cheek. His eyes stared into mine, and I wished I knew what he was thinking.

At the thought, my head pounded violently as voices muddled my mind. The longer I stared at Cassius, the more the voices narrowed down until it was only his that spoke.

Gods, please let this be the year she remembers us and stays with me. I cannot bear to lose her again.

I shook my head to get rid of his thoughts. I hadn't meant to use the magic I gathered from the meeting of the kingdoms, and it felt like an invasion of his privacy.

"Are you okay?" he asked.

"Yes, I'm just tired." I looked away from him. Cassius walked me to the bedroom and tucked me into the bed.

CHAPTER 27

It had been two days since Cassius and I spoke, but he was always lingering around me. Food and water magically appeared on my nightstand when I woke up each morning. Today, I awoke to a hot bath drawn for me as well as a note from Cassius letting me know that I could come to the dining hall to eat breakfast with him if I wanted.

My chest tightened at the thought of leaving our room, but I was also determined to feel better. I did not want Jesper and my father to have this power over me anymore. More than that, I wanted to learn what I was missing from Cassius. So, I soaked in the bath, trying to force away the memories of Jesper watching me bathe and holding my head under water. When it became too much, I got out and dressed.

As soon as I left our room and walked the hallway of Crimson's castle, I felt terrified. The stained-glass windows shined beautifully across the stone walls, casting rainbows of colors across the ground in front of me.

I could hear the chatter of the men eating as I slowly made my way through the open door. Walking into this space brought back memories of the trials. All the guards stopped eating to stare at me. My heart beat wildly at the attention. Would I always feel this fear?

Before I could feel scared for long, every single guard stood up from their seat to face me. Then, to my astonishment, they all bowed deeply before me.

After they rose back up, Haden walked to me quickly and grabbed my hand, squeezing it. He stepped in front of my eyes so I would focus on him.

"You're alright," he assured me.

"Why did they bow?"

"You'll have to talk to Cassius about that." He smiled as he dragged me to the food. I gathered a plate, trying to ignore the staring I could feel. Instead, I focused on my breathing so I would not become overwhelmed. When I turned, my eyes scanned each face, looking for Cassius.

"He should be here in a minute," Haden said. I nodded as we sat at a table with Kace and Zaden. They both stared at me with big smiles plastered on their faces.

"Hi Kace. Hi Zaden," I spoke softly.

"It's so good to see you again." Zaden smiled.

"Are you feeling better?" Kace glanced over me like he was worried.

"A little." I slowly ate my food as the guards stared at me. I could hear their faint whispers, but I did not get the impression that they were being cruel to me.

They talked among themselves as I ate. I was sure they could tell I was overwhelmed, so they didn't push me into conversations. It was nice to have noise around me, though. My thoughts weren't racing through bad memories like they did when I was by myself.

"So, what have you guys been up to?" I finally asked.

"Mostly training. Cassius has been a little—pissy, so he takes it out on us with our training," Haden chuckled. "Although he has given us a few days off since you've been back, so that's a plus."

Zaden and Kace were chuckling in agreement.

"Anything you want to talk to us about?" Kace asked.

Was there? My mind blanked. So much had happened, but I didn't want to burden them with what I went through. I stared at my plate for a long moment.

"No."

"Well, you'll never believe who moved to Crimson and is trying to be a guard." Haden's eyes widened with his gossip. "Leer."

"Leer made it?" I glanced around the room. "Is he here?"

The guys all stared at me like I was crazy. "I told him to come here with his family for safety. We're friends now."

I glanced over when someone slid onto the bench at our table. My eyes locked with Cassius' as he sat with his plate across from me. My eyes drifted over his face.

"Good morning, my love. I'm glad to see you are feeling good enough to leave our room." He smiled at me, and I almost gawked at the sight. Gods, he was fucking handsome.

"Why does everyone look so horrified?" He asked the guys.

"Thea ran into Leer at Cerithia, and apparently they're friends now." Haden laughed when Cassius' face looked surprised. "She told him to come here to be safe."

"Interesting." His eyes flickered over to me briefly as he took a bite of his food. The chatter of the dining hall had died down, and I could see the guards watching me and Cassius closely.

"Why did all the guards bow at me when I walked in here?"

Cassius choked on his food and had to hit his chest to catch his breath. He glanced around at the men watching us before finally meeting my eyes.

"You're royalty."

Haden raised an eyebrow at me.

"Not really. I'm a bastard child of a king. He never claimed me as his daughter, so I'm not technically royal."

"You're royal," Cassius insisted. "If you don't like it, you can tell them to stop. They'll listen to you."

I nodded in response and took a bite of my food. I saw Cassius look at Haden with a pointed look, and Haden threw up his hands in surrender. He was smiling brightly at Cassius, and the whole exchange seemed odd. Obviously, there was more to this story, but I didn't pry. I listened to them talk about training schedules for a while. Cassius had been running them ragged.

"We have less than a month until war starts. We will need to go scouting," Cassius announced at the table.

"Is war really necessary?" I asked.

"I don't want war, but your father and Jesper will declare it when I don't return you."

"No, they won't," I sighed. "My father is too scared to start a war if I am not in Cerithia. If anything, he will just try to kill me to start the curse over again."

Cassius' jaw clenched at this statement. Kace stared at me so intensely that I had to look down because it was making me feel anxious.

"You're probably right, but we still need to be prepared," Cassius spoke. "You can train with us if you're feeling up to it."

I nodded but said nothing.

"How did you discover Lavtan?" Kace asked as he began shoveling food into his mouth.

"I was snooping around and saw him go into my father's throne room. It was a complete accident," I chuckled softly.

"Lucky for us," Zaden said with a smile.

"Speaking of lucky," Haden smiled. "Where were you last night, Kace? You never came to your bunk." Haden wiggled his eyebrows at Kace and smiled when he refused to answer. "Fine, keep your secrets."

I couldn't help but smile at their banter. I glanced at Cassius when I felt him staring again. His gaze was intense.

"Would you like to go somewhere with me today?" he asked.

"Ok," I agreed.

Haden was smiling brightly at us as we watched each other.

★★☽★★

Cassius was giddy as we rode our horses through the woods. Something about the area was familiar, but I could not place it. After a short ride, we arrived at a small hot spring, and I realized why it seemed familiar. It was the hot spring from my memory with him. Cassius glanced at me and smiled like he was so happy to just be with me.

"A hot spring." I looked at him.

"You love this hot spring," he answered back as the horses stopped.

I slid off Kaida and headed towards the spring. I could feel its warmth without even getting in. Nothing sounded better than soaking in the hot water. My eyes glanced at Cassius as I contemplated whether I felt comfortable undressing in front of him. Could I trust him? My mind waited to see if my darkness would protest, but she did nothing.

Slowly, I started to undress. When I glanced to see what Cassius was doing, he was standing with his back toward me. "What are you doing?" I asked.

"Giving you privacy." His fists were closed tightly at his sides, and his voice was tight with desire. It made me smile as I slipped into the water.

"It's nothing you haven't seen before," I called out. Cassius glanced over his shoulder when he heard the water. He strode toward me, stripping his clothes off too. I couldn't look away from his muscles and tattoos. Cassius gave me a cocky grin as I continued to stare at him, not giving him the decency he gave me.

"It's not polite to stare," he teased.

"I can look away if you want."

"You can look at me; it all belongs to you anyway." He came into the water and sat across from me as I floated in the warmth. It smelled of forest and wildflowers here.

We relaxed in silence for a long time. Cassius never came too close to me. He just watched me from across the spring as I replayed the memory of us here. I glanced over my shoulder, where Cassius had emerged from the woods in his uniform. My cheeks heated as I remembered the kiss.

"Blushing, little viper?" Cassius whispered.

I hesitated a moment before responding. "I know why this hot spring is important."

Cassius' eyebrows shot up.

"You do?"

"Our first kiss," I whispered. "Well, second, technically."

He didn't move. Gods, he didn't even look like he was breathing. His eyes burned bright gold before they began to swirl with black.

"You remember our kiss."

I nodded. Cassius' eyes dimmed a moment later, and I frowned at the shift in his mood.

"What's wrong?"

"I wish you could remember all of it, Thea."

I swam closer to him. The look of sadness that was painted over his features made me want to cheer him up.

"The night we met..." I started, but Cassius sat up straight.

"How much have you remembered?"

"A few things." I smiled. "The night we met on the blood moon, why didn't you let me see your face?"

His tattooed chest rose and fell with deep breaths as he watched me.

"I thought you would recognize me as the Prince of Crimson, and I didn't want you to hate me. I don't know if I could have handled you looking at me like I was a monster if you knew. I liked that you looked at me like I was some type of hero."

"Why didn't you ever come back?"

"I did," he answered. "But you were never there. I didn't realize you had been drafted into the war."

"I remember when you learned I was the captain of the Cerithian armies."

He smiled brightly.

"That may be one of my favorite memories of us."

My cheeks heated again as I stared at him.

"I remember giving you your prize for winning that stupid game."

Cassius' eyes flashed black quickly at the memory. His chest rose and fell in choppy breaths.

"One of the best days of my life," he muttered. "I knew I flirted with you a lot, but I never expected you to reciprocate my feelings, and if you did, I never thought you would act on them."

He smiled at me for a long moment, and I knew that sharing this with him had made him happy, maybe hopeful for us.

"Anything else?" He sounded hopeful.

"No." I shook my head. "I stopped seeing memories when Jesper started hurting me."

"Will you keep telling me what you remember? It's nice knowing that you can remember parts of us."

"Yes," I agreed immediately.

There was a long pause before he spoke again. And when he did, his voice was soft, as if he was worried he would spook me.

"If you ever want to talk about what Jesper did, I will listen."

Gods, I wanted to tell him every hit, cut, and hateful word Jesper ever spewed at me, but I couldn't. For some reason, I felt disgusted with myself that I couldn't fight off Jesper. How can I be this powerful woman who is going to crumble kingdoms and kill kings when Jesper was able to hurt me so badly? I felt weak.

"I don't think it would help," I answered.

"I can see it in your eyes that you hide terrible memories behind them. Every time you look at me, I see all the ways I've failed you looking back at me. You can't hide the emotions you send down the bond, my love. I know that you are hurt deeply, and if you don't get those thoughts out of you, they will eat you alive. Sometimes, speaking about hard things is what we need to do so they cannot hold power over us anymore. Let me carry the burden of your pain with you."

My eyes flickered between his, and my darkness hummed at his words, like they agreed.

I opened my mouth to speak, but nothing came out. Cassius didn't push me to speak; he waited patiently for me to make a decision about what was best for me. Tears formed in my eyes as I looked at him. No thoughts formed, even though I wanted to tell him, so I showed him. Slowly, I rose out of the hot spring, showing Cassius my marred skin. Jesper's name carved into my flesh in two places, along with the insults he carved, had Cassius' face falling as his eyes took in every new scar. I turned so he could see my back, and I cried silently when Cassius' hand touched the word traitor cut into my skin. As soon as I felt him, sobs left me violently.

"Thea…" he choked out.

"I couldn't fight him off. I was too weak, and now I will live with the reminders of what he did to me forever. I can't even look at myself in a mirror anymore."

Cassius turned me, tears falling from his eyes as he pulled me to him in a tight hug.

"He will never hurt you again," he promised. He kissed my head as I sobbed into his chest. After a few minutes, Cassius pulled me back and raised his hand, so his shadows swarmed over me. His eyes never left mine as they moved over every mark on my skin. When he pulled his shadows back, all of Jesper's words were covered in tattoos. Where scars had marred my skin, beauty now covered it. A black forest, crimson-colored flowers, and a blood moon replaced the insults. He had given me the gift of our story to cover Jesper's ugliness.

"Much better," he whispered as he tucked a wet strand of hair behind my ear. I stared at him for a long, tear-filled moment before pushing up on my toes to kiss him. Unlike our first kiss here, this one was not full of lust. It was full of longing and love. Cassius slipped his arms around me and held me to him tightly as he kissed me back.

"Let's go home," he whispered as he pressed his forehead against mine.

CHAPTER 28

I knew Haden was following me. He did a horrible job of hiding in the trees, but maybe he wanted me to know he was with me. After all, he had been lurking around me for the past few days. Today, when I woke up, I finally felt good enough to try and find Leer.

I dressed in simple clothes, not scared of others seeing my scars for the first time in what felt like forever. Nervousness plagued me as I walked the simple road to the town. I was remembering the welcome I had received in Cerithia and hoped nothing like that happened here.

Surprisingly, though, when I got to the city, the fae stopped in the streets and smiled—even bowed to me.

Haden stepped out of the tree line and moved toward me.

"Why are you spying on me?"

"Cassius trusts me to make sure you are safe." Haden gave me a smile. "And you are my friend. I want to make sure you're safe too."

I rolled my eyes and glanced around. After a long walk through the town, Haden finally asked me what I was looking for.

"Leer and his family."

"Are you really friends with him?" Haden frowned. "He was horrible to you during the trials."

"He had his reasons, and I forgave him. He was my only friend in Cerithia."

Haden frowned slightly before grabbing my hand and pulling me to the left. He dragged me through the streets until a cute home with a big green yard stood in front of us. Before I could open my mouth, the door opened, and Cassius stepped out. My heart raced at the sight of how good he looked in his black uniform.

"Thea?" My eyes moved past Cassius to Larissa and Leer.

"You made it!" I smiled and ran to them. They both hugged me tightly. When they let me go, they held me at arm's length to look me over.

"You're in Crimson?" Leer questioned as he glanced at Haden and Cassius.

"I'm a prisoner." I shrugged.

"You don't look like a prisoner." Larissa raised her dark brow at me. I could feel Cassius staring daggers into my back, but I ignored him. "Come in; the kids will be happy to see you, and we can catch up."

"That would be great." I smiled and let her lead me inside.

"I can escort Thea back to the castle when we are done visiting," Leer offered.

Cassius hesitated for a moment, his eyes jumping from Leer to me. "Fine," he muttered as he and Haden turned to leave.

Their home was twice the size of their last, and this time, the furnishings were not falling apart. The kitchen even had fully-stocked shelves of food. The kids came squealing toward me, and I hugged them before they ran off. I could feel Larissa and Leer watching me. When I turned to them, Leer raised his blonde brow at me.

"Why was Cassius here?"

"He was letting me know that he was accepting my application to be a guard of Crimson. He said he hadn't realized that you sent me here."

My heart thudded at the news.

"Your home is lovely." I smiled.

"The royal family gifted it to us." Larissa smiled. "That is part of being a guard for Crimson."

This was a vast change from how they lived in Cerithia. They hugged each other tightly, and for some reason, sadness filled me.

"Now, tell us everything." Larissa smiled and sat me down on the couch. I went through everything I could think of that they missed. When I stopped talking, they both gaped at me from the couch.

"Stars above, Thea." Leer frowned.

"I'll be alright." I looked at them. "I'm so happy you guys are safe. How are you feeling?" I glanced over at Larissa, but she didn't make my healing magic surge forward.

"I've never felt better."

She raised her pretty face up to Leer and kissed him.

I stood. Cassius and I still hadn't talked yet, and he had not made any sort of move on me since I had kissed him at the hot spring. In fact, it seemed like he was avoiding me. I had hardly seen him in two days. It made feel as if I did something wrong.

"I'm going to head back to the castle. I'm still quite exhausted, but maybe we can meet again soon."

Leer stood and told Larissa he would be back after escorting me home. He and I walked in silence for a long time. It was as if he knew I was struggling. Finally, he sighed heavily when we were almost back.

"You aren't alright." He frowned. "What can I do to help?"

I glanced at him and knew he couldn't do anything. Moving my eyes away from him, I looked at the castle.

"Unless you can make my trauma disappear, then there is nothing to do. I want to speak to Cassius, but I feel disgusted with how broken I feel after Jesper's torture. My mind keeps tricking me into thinking I am not worthy of love or Cassius, so he must be using me." Tears filled my eyes even as I tried to hold them in. The past two nights, my mind has reeled with terrible dreams of Cassius killing me. I was struggling with his betrayal and wondering if I was falling for it again. No matter how many times I told myself that Cassius loved me, there was a small voice questioning everything. Just because my father was bad didn't mean that Cassius was good. That's what it kept saying.

I didn't actually think Cassius was a bad guy, but my mind was being such a bitch.

"He cares for you."

"I know, but the confusion is overwhelming."

The words broke my resolve. Tears flooded down my face as a loud sob escaped me. Leer moved to me quickly, holding me tightly against his chest. He didn't say anything to comfort me; he just let me cry, and that was all

I wanted. When I pulled back, I wiped the tears from my eyes.

"I am so lost, Leer."

"Then let him explain, Thea. I'm sure there is a reason for his madness."

I knew I needed to let Cassius explain, but I was scared. I was terrified that whatever his reasoning was, it would not be good enough for me. More than anything, I wanted a reason to forgive him. But fear was making it impossible to move forward. I felt stuck.

"Thank you for being my friend."

"I think I'm the one who should be thanking you, Thea. I owe you my life more than once."

I gave him another squeeze before heading to the castle as he turned to head home.

"Are you alright?" Cassius was standing in the shadows. Had he been out here the whole time? The smell of rain and night hit me as he ran to catch up.

"Thank you," I whispered. "For being kind to Leer and Larissa. They mean a lot to me."

"Anyone that's important to you is important to me," he said sincerely.

"Will you just... stop." My voice echoed around us.

He pulled me back by my arm.

He frowned. "I love you."

My mind didn't want to believe his words, but my heart did. Even though we were making progress, something had shifted in the past two days. My mind had been concocting all these false scenarios of Cassius betraying me, and now I was drowning in negative thoughts. All because he had been avoiding me. It was as if he were chasing away all my doubt by being around, but when he was gone it hit me ten times worse.

He gripped my wrists and pulled me close to his chest.

"I do love you," he said to me. "When the gods decided that I was not worthy of you, Thea, all I could think was to hell with them because you are my heaven and stars. As long as I can make you think I am worthy, then I will die a happy man. I will do anything to show you that I love you. I would do anything for you, my love. Please, just give me a chance to show you and explain to you why I did what I did."

I shook my head. "What if your reason is not good enough? It will destroy me."

Cassius dropped to his knees in front of me. Holding himself to my stomach.

"You are everything to me." His golden eyes looked up at me, and he frowned as tears filled them. "I am nothing without you."

I shook my head.

"What happened in the past two days to make you look at me like this again?" he asked quietly.

"You have been avoiding me and I feel like I did something wrong. My mind is swarming with every negative scenario it can think of, and I can not stop it. I am trying to be strong; I am trying to be in a place where I can talk with you."

"Little viper, that wasn't my intent. I was giving you some space to process. If you want, I will linger around you constantly." He glanced up at me from his knees. "You have to face this at some point. You can't keep running from it, thinking that it will reveal some ugly truth. If anything, I would hope my words and truth bring you comfort."

Gods, he could read me like an open book. I would push this conversation off until the end of time if I could. It was odd to hide from this, but on the other hand, I wanted to know the truth more than anything.

"We'll talk soon," I promised as I backed away from him and headed inside to our room, leaving Cassius kneeling in the dirt.

CHAPTER 29

Startled awake, I quickly opened my eyes. Something felt... off, and my senses were alert, but when I glanced around the dark room, it was empty. Sitting up slowly, I felt an overwhelming sense of urgency. At first, I thought it was the bond, but it wasn't. There was something clinging in the air around me that I had never experienced before.

"Cassius?" I called out, thinking he was close by, but he didn't appear. Glancing around, I couldn't help the feeling of being watched. I stood and walked to the living room, but Cassius wasn't there.

A movement in the tree line outside caught my attention. My body went rigid when I saw her, Della. She stood in the bright glow of her mist, which reminded me of the stars twinkling in the night sky. Her dark hair flowed around her, and she wore a black, dainty crown on top of her head. Her golden skin popped against the darkness of her dress, and even from this distance, I could see her smiling directly at me.

How could she see me so clearly? Then, like a whisper in the wind, I heard her feminine voice calling out to me in my mind.

Come. We need to talk.

I waited for my instincts to tell me not to follow her into the woods, but they didn't. Instead, they told me to go. Still, I hesitated. However, when I saw Wisp with her, I knew I wouldn't be harmed. So, I slipped on my clothing and boots before racing out the door. Quickly, I made my way out of the castle and to the woods. Della stood there smiling at me as I came to a quick stop.

"Thea."

My brows furrowed as I stared at her.

"Where have you been?"

She shrugged her shoulders as her smile widened.

"Around." Her evasive answer did nothing to clear up my confusion. Her pretty star-colored eyes shifted to my left, and I turned to see dozens of wisps near me.

"You can see them too?" I asked, confused.

"Of course. I gifted them to you." Her voice was gentle, but I could feel her power pulsing from her. My head snapped to her.

"Wisp was a gift?" I spoke slowly, trying to understand her.

"Yes." She tilted her head to the side as if she were trying to understand something about me. Her star-colored eyes drifted over me before shifting her attention to Wisp.

"Am I dead? Did I die in my sleep or something? Maybe this is a dream."

"No, neither of those are true." She stepped toward me. "I came because you keep calling to me in your mind. You are troubled."

"Of course I'm troubled. You damned gods cursed my soul, and now I'm living half a shitty life because of it!" She didn't shrink away from my anger or hurt. Instead, Della nodded in agreement, like it was true. "This isn't fair. Why must I be punished? Why must I be the one to suffer? And why would the Goddess of Life come running to me if I called to her? What makes me so damn significant to you and the other gods? Don't you all have better things to do with your time?"

This time her pretty face fell, and she frowned deeply.

"I came because I must. After Cassius killed you, he begged for you back. He even offered his own soul for yours. I had never seen a man so utterly...broken. My brother did not care about his pain and suffering, but I did. And his dismissal of your situation was my fault. I felt somehow responsible. So, I offered something that I had only ever offered once before: part of my soul. I come when you call because you are a part of me, Thea Valeska. Instead of taking your soul as I should have, I gave you part of mine so you could keep living."

My mind was reeling at the information.

"It was all part of the deal, though. I would not take your soul, but to keep the balance after what I had done and break the curse that was incurred, Cassius had to prove that you *truly* loved him, that you would choose him without remembering who he was, and that you would choose him again—even after learning what he did to you. My brother is a sick and cruel god. He made it so that not only are your memories wiped away every time you die, he also ensured that each time you come back, you do not get as many of them back."

Her anger was not directed toward me, but it was palpable. I could also feel her sadness like it was my own.

"Your magic is something incredible. Part of it, you were born with—a power none of us could ever fathom—but the other part of your power is from me. You used it to save Leer's wife. You used it to save the sick King Sybrien. You use it to save others from death. It was not Sybil's healing magic that saved them, as you thought. That magic is not strong enough to do what you did. It was my power of life that you used."

I gave them life back because I had part of a goddess' soul inside of me. My mind was trying to process everything Della was saying, but it was too much. I couldn't even form a question to ask.

Her eyes shifted to Wisp, then shifted to the rest of them.

"They're your guardians," Della confessed.

My eyes followed hers to look at the wisps all changing to vibrant blues, which told me they were happy to protect me, a fact that made me smile. The wisp that always followed me turned dark green when I looked over her.

"These souls chose to stay here and offer you protection instead of moving on to the next life. They want to see you break the curse and regain your memories."

"Why would they do that?" I asked.

"The wisps are souls of elite magic fae that have died."

I froze at her declaration.

"Who are they?" I asked.

"I won't tell you. That is not my secret to share," she frowned. The faint glow from my skin made me lift my arms up to see the tattooed swirls glowing brightly on my skin.

"The wisp you formed the closest bond with is *your* soul."

My eyes shifted to Wisp, *my* wisp. The one that was always lurking and helping me. The one who seemed to like Cassius more than myself. As I watched her green flames, I could see myself within the glow. My wispy form smiled at me. Cassius' words crashed around me. *Of course I see her. She is attached to my soul.* My soul was following its other half, Cassius.

Emotions clogged my throat as I tried to breathe. A sense of sadness washed over me, but also a sense of love.

"Why would they stay behind for me? Why not go into the next life?" I asked.

"Because they care for you and want to see you break the curse. They will move on when you can."

"But I finished the trials."

She scoffed. Who would have known that having a goddess scoff at you could be so embarrassing? My cheeks burned brightly.

"Those trials are not the way to break your curse. The bloodstone will break your curse! You know this." She tossed her arms in the air to exaggerate her point.

"But I touched it, and nothing happened."

"The trials were to give you a reason to want to get the bloodstone, but you must give it to Cassius to break the curse."

Irritation filled me at this stupid revelation. I had to hand Cassius a stupid fucking rock to break a curse he caused in the first place.

"So... My memories rely on handing a damn rock to Cassius. Am I understanding that correctly?"

The goddess tried to suppress her smile.

"Yes."

"Why?" I sighed. "Why can't I just tell him I love him or something?"

She shook her head.

"You don't understand. That bloodstone was your mother's bloodstone. She was a blood witch—a very powerful blood witch. She was a queen before your father had her killed. That bloodstone holds power, but only for you. Gifting something so special to someone will give them some of your power too. Although no one knows that, that is why it's important that you give it to Cassius when and if you decide to forgive him. It is a truly high honor. It will show that you chose to love him even after he killed you."

"My mother caused all of this," I hissed angrily.

"Yes, but she saved you by doing it, Thea. Your father would have killed you if she hadn't barbed your magic inside. *He* is your enemy, not your mother, not Cassius."

Suddenly, Della groaned in pain and fell to her knees. I hurried over to her but stopped when she held her hand up. She looked at me, blood dripping from her nose as she gasped for breath.

"Are you alright?"

"I said too much about the curse," she wheezed. "It will pass."

I watched her as she seemed to be in severe pain, but she waved me away when I tried to help her again. After a few minutes, she took a full breath.

Della's words swarmed through my mind as I helped her stand back up. She wiped the blood from her nose. We stood in silence for a long moment. There was one detail of her story that kept sticking out to me, and I thought maybe she hadn't realized her mistake.

"You called me Thea Valeska earlier." I looked up at her, confused. I had expected her to apologize and correct the name to Thea Alzara, but she gave me a sly smirk.

"Did I?"

"Yes...did you mean Thea Alzara?"

The wisps turned dark green, and the goddess looked at them as if she were communicating without speaking.

"No, I didn't mean Thea Alzara."

Her eyebrows furrowed as her eyes traced down to the crown tattoo on my wrist.

"But that's Cassius' surname." My mind suddenly flashed to Cassius and I standing on a cliffside with a priestess, but the memory was gone just as quickly as it appeared.

"Did he not tell you?" Her confusion made me let out a staggered breath. "I assumed he did."

"I have not let him tell me anything. I am too scared of losing him to find out the truth," I sighed, defeated.

Her eyes moved back down to my communication bond.

"Your marriage bond is visible again."

I lifted my arm and looked over the bond before meeting her eyes again.

"Cassius said this was just for communicating while we were apart," I whispered.

"Cassius is a very clever man," she laughed. "It is not a communication bond. It's a marriage bond. He has one too, but he hides it. It's a red crown—your crown. Just like that is his crown."

I felt dizzy as I lowered myself to the ground and sat, trying to understand everything. This was too much. I couldn't wrap my head around the information she was telling me. Cassius and I were married.

"I'm married to a man who murdered me."

The wisps and goddess all froze at my statement.

"You have to understand, Thea, that what happened between you and Cassius was something we had never had to address as gods before."

"Him killing me?" I glared at her. "I've killed before and have never had the gods come down and curse my soul, or at least I don't remember them doing that."

"We did not curse your soul because you were killed; it was because of who killed you. You need to talk to Cassius so he can tell you what happened."

"Why do I get the feeling that everyone is on his side? Everyone seems to think he did nothing wrong."

"Well, when he tells you, you get to decide if you feel like everyone is justified for feeling that way or if you think we have all lost our minds," Della sighed.

I opened my mouth to argue with her but shut it. She had practically agreed that they were all on his side about this. Della came and sat next to me on the cold ground. We faced the castle and sat in silence. My mind should have been racing with all of the things she told me, but there was nothing. I should have been freaking out, and maybe I would later, but right now it was peaceful inside my mind until one question drifted into my thoughts.

"You said you gave someone else a piece of your soul. Who was it?"

Della's eyes filled with sadness. I could feel it around her like a thick cloud.

"I should have known you two would find each other," she sighed.

"Cassius and I?"

"No, my other death-marked soul." She frowned as she stared at the castle. "His powers developed like yours, but not as strong. It was probably your blood witch lineage that made you so powerful after you received part of my soul."

"The other death-marked soul lives here." I glanced from her to the castle.

"Yes. I'm sorry for everything that happened to you." She glanced at me. "My brother would have never been so cruel to you the day Cassius killed you if I hadn't broken him, if I hadn't betrayed him. It's my fault all of this happened the way it did. I killed the woman my brother loved to save the man I loved, and he cannot forgive me. I do not blame him either, but it is why he thought Cassius should be punished so harshly."

"It's alright." I frowned because she looked so... devastated.

"It's not." She looked away from me. "But if it's any consolation, I will be punished for all my existence to have the man I love hate me. Because I betrayed him too. I am his villain."

Della stood quickly.

"I don't want that." I frowned. I knew the feeling of having the man you love hate you, or at least pretend to. "Who is it?"

"I'm not going to tell you. I have to go. Talk with Cassius; make this right."

As I stood, she vanished into thin air. I turned and glanced everywhere, but she was gone. Wisp—I meant myself—floated around me.

"I'm headed inside." I paused and frowned. A noise in the trees made me freeze. Ducking low to the ground, I looked to see who was coming. Kace walked through a moment later by himself before sneaking back into the castle. Odd.

Wisp twirled around me in her pretty dark green shade. Then she and the others all disappeared into the woods, and I headed inside. I stood in the castle foyer and glanced around, wishing my memories would appear. A noise down the hallway had me hiding in the dark corner.

Haden walked by a moment later with Cassius. They were in a deep conversation about something as they passed without noticing me.

My eyes watched Cassius as he passed. Suddenly, he stopped and turned toward me.

"Is there a reason you're hiding, my love?"

Haden smiled brightly as I stepped out of the shadows and stared at Cassius. I opened and closed my mouth like a fish out of water. My eyes drifted to his forearm, where he should have a marriage bond from me. Heat started in my chest and filled my cheeks.

"Blushing?" He smiled brightly. "Want to share your thoughts?"

My mouth snapped shut, and I hurried past him. When I got to the safety of our room, I let out a long breath. I needed sleep, then I would know what to do with all the information I found out.

CHAPTER 30

My eyes drifted around mine and Cassius' room. I had been rotting in bed all day. How did I mention to him that I knew he was my husband?

A burst of curiosity overcame me. Standing up, I surveyed the room and started digging through things. I found some old love notes in Cassius' drawer and mine, but I needed more proof that we were actually something.

Getting down on all fours, I glanced under the bed and smiled triumphantly at the box as I dragged it out. Opening it, I stared at the portraits of him and I. All of them showed us smiling together. My eyes traced over myself in all of them. I looked... happy. And in everyone, Cassius was looking at me like I hung the stars and the moon.

I kept going through them, each one making me smile more than the last. When I saw the last one, I stared at it for a long time. Cassius was wearing traditional Crimson robes, his crown on top of his head. A red crown tattooed his skin—my marriage bond to him. Then my eyes drifted to the beautiful crimson red dress I wore; a red crown adorned my head, and a crown bond was visible on my wrist.

This was our wedding.

My heart pounded wildly in my chest. We looked so fucking happy. My chest was tight with a feeling I didn't understand. I stood to go find him. Why didn't he tell me we were married? He continued not to tell me anything. The thought upset me. My steps slowed as I realized it was my fault. I hadn't let him explain anything to me because I was a coward. With a new sense of determination, I headed toward the training fields. Cassius was back to working the men all day long.

Della's words circled in my mind.

Husband.

Marriage.

Is this what my mother saw when she glimpsed my future? Is this why she sought out Cassius all those years ago?

Even with the sun shining so brightly that I could hardly see, I knew which man was Cassius immediately. I approached the field, realizing that I hadn't really thought through what I was going to say. Courage bloomed in my chest. I would not back down from this. Maybe learning the truth would set me free to not feel so bad about still wanting Cassius.

My feet slowed when I saw him, shirtless, fighting Haden in hand-to-hand combat. My body flooded with lust at the sight of him. The men in the field recognized my presence immediately and bowed.

Cassius' words from a few days prior hit me. *They will listen to you. You're royalty.* Cassius and Haden stopped when I spoke.

"For the love of gods, stop bowing at me."

Cassius turned to me, his eyes bright with happiness—just like our wedding portrait. My confidence wavered slightly. I could handle this. I could do this.

"Show me your communication bond," I called out to him with a small waver in my voice.

His dark brows knitted together, but he listened to me. Dark shadows swirled around his arm, and a red crown appeared. Something about seeing the mark made my chest tight with longing. He was mine. Thoughts of claiming him as mine plagued me.

A memory flashed before my eyes. *Cassius kissed me on our wedding day. As he pulled away, he smiled and whispered, "My wife."*

I shook the thought away.

"My love, is something wrong?"

Was something wrong? My eyes glanced at all the men watching me and Cassius. My chest tightened with worry at their peering glances. I stood taller and lifted my chin. The move had Cassius smirking slightly.

"Thea Valeska." I narrowed my eyes at him, and his face paled. "That is what the Goddess of Life called me last night when she visited. Thea Valeska, your wife!"

The guards all shifted their eyes to Cassius. My eyes caught on Leer, who was in formation. The news seemed shocking to only him. The other guards, though, didn't bat an eye.

"My…"

"Don't," I sighed. "Communication bond…you mean marriage bonds." I held up the portrait of us at our wedding.

Sadness floored me at the sight of Cassius. He looked so heartbroken as he looked over the portrait. He glanced away from me before swallowing hard.

"I just didn't want to upset you more."

My eyes traced over the portrait in my hands, and I frowned because I couldn't remember. Then, like an arrow through my heart, something snapped inside of me as I looked at him again. The red crown marking him as mine made me feel feral, wild with lust.

"Thea..." Cassius muttered like he knew exactly what was happening to me. It was like an itch that couldn't be scratched unless I touched him. "We should talk first."

I shook my head. I couldn't wait. My magic rose in my chest the more I looked at my husband, simmering just under the surface but longing to burst free. The longer I had to admire him shirtless, with my mark on him, made the need unbearable. My eyes glanced around at the guards still watching us.

"Go, you're all dismissed for the day!" I yelled. Haden tried to stifle his smile, but it was a losing battle as he patted Cassius on the shoulder.

"Actually, take today and tomorrow," I corrected myself.

Cassius smiled this time. The guards all bowed their heads and departed quickly. Cassius watched me closely, as if I were the hunter and he was my prey.

"I want to hear you say it..." I demanded. My darkness swarmed inside of me at the sight of him. It practically clawed at me to go take what was ours. "I want to hear that I'm your mate, your wife."

Cassius' chest rose and fell in quick breaths as he watched me slowly approach him. His pretty golden eyes didn't shy away from mine.

"You're Thea Valeska, my wife. Future Queen of Crimson. My mate. My queen." His voice came out in a rasp.

I couldn't help the smile that tugged on my lips.

"Then kneel for your queen."

Cassius' eyes swarmed with black at my demand. He took two steps toward me before he fell to his knees in front of me. When I was finally close enough to touch, his hands grabbed my hips and pulled me forward so he could rest his head against my stomach.

"Gods above, Thea. I can feel how much you want me. It's almost crippling," he breathed heavily as his hands gripped me tightly.

"Why can't I feel you through the bond?"

His face tilted up to me, a sad look in his eyes. He lifted his wrists, and I saw what looked like thin red bracelets burned into his skin.

"You burned these into my wrists. A form of punishment from that day in the clearing." I traced the red burns softly. Flashes of that day hit me, but they couldn't make this want—no, this *need*—for him to go away. My fire rose up and swirled around his wrist, taking the damage I had done back and making the burns all but disappear.

I stumbled back as the onslaught of his emotions hit me. Sadness, pain, love, understanding, longing, grief, and anger all swarmed from the bond and straight into my chest.

"You took them away, why?"

"I want to feel you," I whispered. My skin was hot, and I couldn't wait anymore. I flung myself at Cassius, knocking the two of us to the ground. Our magic swirled around us, shielding anyone from seeing me ripping the clothes from our bodies.

"My love..." Cassius groaned as my hand stroked down his hard length. Fuck. My heart was thumping so loudly in my ears. I needed to claim him, taste him, touch him. It was all too overwhelming. I leaned forward, my tongue running up the length of him before shoving him into my mouth.

"Fuck," Cassius sighed loudly in response. His fists clenched tightly at his sides. My hand moved in tandem with my mouth, and I could see the muscles of his stomach clenching with each stroke. Cassius wrapped my dark hair in his hands but didn't take control.

His heavy breathing had me pulling away from him. His golden eyes were gone, replaced with black depths of lust and longing.

"I want to cum with you," I breathed quietly as I straddled his hips. Cassius was about to say something, but

I sank down on him, making his mouth tense shut. His hands squeezed my hips as his eyes closed tightly.

"Did you miss me when I was gone?" I asked as I slowly lifted myself up. His eyes found mine, giving me a sexy smile.

"I always miss you, wife."

The word sent a shot of lust straight to my core. The need was already building into something bigger than I had ever experienced.

He sat up and took my mouth with his. His kiss was hard and demanding. I pulled him closer to me so he couldn't stop kissing me. His hands skimmed across my naked back and down my ass, grabbing fists full of flesh, so I was riding him harder. His lips moved down my jaw and neck.

"I fucking missed you so much, my love," he whispered against my skin. His tongue moved over my nipple before he sucked it into his mouth.

"Fuck," I groaned loudly and tangled my fingers into his hair. My hips were rolling slowly into his. It was almost too much emotion, too much want. Cassius' deep exhale hit my wet skin, making me shiver.

"Fuck," he growled as his fingers squeezed my flesh.

He laid back down on the ground and watched as I slid up him and sank back down slowly. His eyes flashed black as his stomach muscles clenched. He closed his eyes tightly and clenched his jaw. I slammed myself down on him.

"Watch me," I demanded. His eyes flew open, and lust shot through our bonds. "Look at how well we fit together, Cassius."

"Thea." It was half a plea and half a wicked promise.

"Did you think about me while we were apart?"

"Yes," he groaned.

"Did you think about me riding you?"

"Fuck, Thea. You're going to make me cum before you."

I smiled down at him, and his eyes traced over my face slowly. Love filled our bond. Suddenly, he flipped us without warning, and I yelped. His hands now held my wrists firmly to the ground above my head. His hips rolled slowly into me. Now he was teasing me, but I fucking loved it.

"I miss hearing you, my love. All those filthy noises you make for me," he whispered close to my face. His lips caressed mine softly, teasing. "Watching you come completely undone by me is my favorite view. Watching you take everything I give you and still beg for more is my undoing."

"Cassius," I breathed heavily. I was climbing quickly. "Please."

"More," he demanded, and his hips picked up pace. "I want to hear more. Give me what I want, and I'll make you cum."

My eyes clenched tightly as his hand snaked to my jaw and held me tightly. I could hear whimpers falling from my lips with each thrust into me.

"Fuck, yes," I groaned when his teeth skimmed my skin and bit me softly. The sensation was pushing me closer and closer to orgasm. He did it again as his hand squeezed my jaw. Our thrusts were frantic, chaotic, perfect.

"Come on, my love. I need you to finish," he begged. "I need to feel that tight pussy clench around me." His hand clenched my jaw. "I want to hear you say I'm yours. Call me your mate, your husband."

My eyes could hardly focus on his handsome face as the cusp of my orgasm teetered on the edge.

"You're mine, Cassius. My mate, my husband, my love."

"Good fucking girl," he growled.

His name tore through my throat as I came harder than I imagined possible. Cassius groaned a sigh of relief as he came with me. His weight crushed me to the ground as we rode out waves of pleasure together. Cassius' face was buried into my neck, kissing softly as I breathed frantically. We lay there for a few silent moments, our hearts beating in tandem.

Cassius pulled back and looked over me, but sadness filled the bond. He pulled away from me and grabbed his things.

"What are you doing?" I breathed.

"Seeing your mark on me made you want me. It's part of the reason I hid it from you. I want you to come to me because you truly love me, because you can forgive what I did."

My eyes watched him closely. The mark on his arm made lust shoot through me again. For fuck's sake, I didn't think I could ever get enough of him.

"Cassius..."

"We aren't doing this again until you're willing to talk to me and listen to my side of the story." He frowned at me. "There is still so much you don't know."

But what if I couldn't forgive him? What if I heard what he said and hated him? I almost didn't want to know because it would make everything so... final. He started walking away as I slipped my clothes on. My chest squeezed tightly.

"You're seriously leaving?"

"I must, Thea. If I let you make me believe that you love me back, then it will destroy me if you decide I'm not worthy of you. There will be no coming back for me if I go through that. If you choose to let me go, I will never be able to recover."

The fear and pain that came through the bond made me stop and let him go. He was right; I would have to face the truth about all of this. Fear suddenly stole my ability to breathe. Slowly, I made my way back to the castle and to our room. There was fresh food on the counter, and someone had cleaned the bedroom while I was out. I laid down in bed and stared at the dark clouds moving in, knowing I was ready to talk with Cassius. I would go to him tomorrow.

CHAPTER 31

"**W**hat do you mean?" I snapped at him. "I don't understand... you're Cassius Valeska? You're the fucking Prince of Crimson?"

His handsome face fell at how angry I was. How could I have been so stupid? Not only was I sleeping with the enemy, but I was also sleeping with the fucking prince who hated my family. Suddenly, I felt sick to my stomach at how much of a traitor this made me.

"Was this some plan? Make the daughter of your enemy fall in love with you!"

Cassius smirked slightly.

"You love me?"

My cheeks flushed with embarrassment. Gods above, just strike me down with a bolt of lightning now.

"No," I lied.

Cassius' eyes shined brightly.

"I love you too, Thea."

My heart beat so frantically at his words. He was the first fae to ever say that to me, and I couldn't tell if he meant it or was just using me.

"I don't believe you." I frowned and looked away. "You should go, and this…" I gestured between us. "Is over."

"My love, please don't do this. I know I should have told you who I was, but I didn't want you to react this way. Our families may hate each other, but we love each other. You can't deny that."

"And what happens now? You betray your family and come live in Cerithia with me? Or you probably want me to betray my family and move to Crimson with you! This isn't ever going to work."

His face fell.

"Please," he whispered. "I waited years for you. Since I first saw you, I've thought of nothing but you. Don't push me away. I love you."

He shouldn't love me. He had no future with me. Not only because he was my enemy, but because I wouldn't be around much longer. Death was coming for me, and I knew it. I should have never gotten involved with him when I knew my future was short. This wasn't fair to him. Guilt settled in my chest.

"I can't do this." I turned my face away from his so he wouldn't see my tears. His sadness filled the air around us.

"Alright," he muttered. "I'll see you on the battlefield."

I waited until his footsteps were gone before I let the sob escape me. Why did my fate have to be so cruel? My head was dizzy, and my body was sore. I wasn't sure I could keep doing this.

★★☽★★

My father's eyes narrowed on me. "What the fuck are you doing here? Why aren't you leading my men into war?"

My body swayed slightly.

"I can't anymore." I frowned. As my father, he should have noticed how pale my skin was and how dull my green eyes had become. Did he notice how much weight I had lost?

"Your sickness?" he sighed. I nodded yes. "That stupid whore-witch did this to spite me!"

I flinched at the nasty names he called my mother, even though I had only ever heard him call her such.

"Binds your magic within you so I can't use all of it." His green eyes looked at me with hatred, because my mother had ensured that my power was beyond his reach. But now, it was slowly killing me. Too much magic had formed inside, stuck, and it was taking from my body. It was taking from my soul.

"If I could kill her again, I would," he spat out at me. I stumbled backward at his words, and he realized his mistake. "I-I mean..."

"You killed my mother?" I whispered. My eyes widened at this declaration. "You said Crimson killed her."

"They did…" he stuttered, but I already saw past his lie. He killed my mother.

"Oh, who fucking cares, Thea? She was a blood witch—the worst of her kind. She promised me an unstoppable heir, then bound your magic inside of you so that you don't become too powerful. Only she didn't tell me that until she was taking her last breath, she had to redo the binding spell as you gained more power. You should hate her; she cursed you to die young!"

"I blame you! Why did you kill her? If you hadn't, she could have saved me." My fire magic was burning hot under my flesh.

"Because she tried to set your magic free one night. But I saw you for what you were—a monster. Someone who would take over the kingdoms with all that power you had. I didn't want your magic free; I wanted it at my disposal. Once I knew what she was going to do, I knew I had to stop her."

I shook my head violently. What else has he been lying to me about? I couldn't believe this man was my father. He was a fucking cruel beast.

His eyes watched me closely. I'm sure he was looking for whatever reaction he could find. Was he planning on killing me too, now that I knew what he had done? My eyes glanced at the queen as she walked in, her cold eyes staring at me.

"What's going on?"

"I told Thea about Bayla."

Gwyn's face soured at the mention of my mother, which pissed me off.

"You told her what the witch did to her; why she's sick?"

He nodded yes, and she narrowed her eyes on me. A cruel smile took over her face. My heartbeat rang in my ears. I was too weak to deal with this.

"I'm glad you're here, Thea. I wanted to speak to your father about the fact that you've been sleeping with Cassius Valeska."

My face paled at her declaration. How did she know? Time slowed, and I was hyperaware of everything happening around me. The fire crackled and filled the room with a slight smell of ash. The way the queen smiled wickedly in her stunning blue dress. The way my father's handsome face contorted to someone who looked capable of murdering his own child. The tension sucked the air from my lungs.

"I didn't know that was him." There was no point in lying about it. I was sure my father was planning on killing me already.

"*Not only are you a disgusting elitist, but now a traitor to Cerithia?*" *My father stomped towards me and slapped me so hard that I fell into the wall.*

"*I didn't know it was him, and when I found out, I stopped.*"

"*A whore, just like your mother,*" *the queen spit at me.* "*We really should just get rid of her like we did with the other elite magic fae. I've been telling you for years that she is just a burden, a problem that never does anything right.*"

My father nodded his head in agreement. I should have told Cassius. I should have told him I was sick. I should have gone to Crimson with him. My fire burned even hotter at the regret I felt. He would never know what happened or why I dismissed him so easily.

"*What do you mean, the elite magic fae? What did you do to them?*"

"*We killed every single one you found.*" *Gwyn smiled at me, and I saw just how truly evil these two were.*

"*How could you!*" *I yelled at them so violently that the floor shook below us.*

"*It needed to be done, Thea. They were dangerous and unpredictable!*" *He stepped toward me but stopped when I grabbed my dagger and held it up like I would throw it at him.*

"You lied to me. You said elite fae were going to be used in our army. You did not tell me you were going to slaughter them all!" Tears spilled from my eyes, but they were tears of fury.

"Calm the fuck down, Thea," he demanded. My only reaction was to throw my dagger at him. It grazed his thigh and embedded itself into the wall next to him.

"All this time, you had me believing I was fighting for the right side. You told me Crimson was going to kill them all."

My father's face contorted with disgust.

"I have elite magic!" I yelled, like he didn't already know. "Cassius was right; you are the monster."

"You are a monster!" he yelled.

"Well, if you're going to kill me, I should let you know that I'm in love with Cassius too." I smiled just to piss them off. My father came at me, his hands wrapping around my throat to strangle me. We fell to the hard wooden floor, and pain radiated through my already fragile body. I just smiled at him before using the energy I had left to let my fire burst out of me. My father and the queen rolled on the floor, their robes on fire.

"Thea!" they called for me. "Save us!" But I just turned and left the throne room, shutting the big wooden door behind me. My eyes stared at the wooden crest on the door as their screaming became louder and flames glowed red *under the door. Guards rushed past me, and I hurried away. My feet stumbled as I found my way to the stables. Kaida neighed at me as I climbed on top of her.*

"Go." I urged her forward, and she took off in a dead sprint. We didn't stop until she couldn't go anymore. What the fuck was I supposed to do now? I had nowhere to go. My horse ran through the dark, seeming to know where to go, even though I had no idea. She continued to run even when I tried to slow her down. It was as if she knew Cerithia was our prison, and we were finally breaking free.

The weight of everything lifted slightly off me the further from Cerithia we got. I had never belonged there, but this was the first time I felt free from it. It was the first time I tried to escape from my father. My horse finally slowed down at a creek, which told me I was in Crimson lands. Tears sprang to my eyes as my father's confession of killing my mother and elite magic fae came back to me.

My ears perked up when I heard footsteps. Before I could grab my dagger, Crimson guards came from the woods with their weapons drawn.

"Captain," one of them said to me.

"Leave me be, or I will not hesitate to kill you," I warned, but I knew that I couldn't fight them off. My body swayed with exhaustion. There was no way to use my magic to save myself. A moment later, Cassius emerged from the woods on

his black horse. Relief nearly floored me when I saw him, but his unforgiving black eyes made me step away from him.

"Good work, Kace. Cuff the prisoner," he said. Prisoner?

The guards did as he asked, and I was too weak to fight them. Cassius' shadows swarmed around me before settling me on his horse in front of him.

"What a turn of events. You belong to Crimson now, little viper. And I don't think I will ever let you go," he whispered against my ear.

Then he took off toward Crimson Castle.

★★☽★★

I gasped for air as I sat up in our bed. The memories swirled inside my head. My eyes glanced out the window and saw how dark it was. I hadn't realized I had fallen asleep.

My chest tightened with uneasiness. My father murdered my mother. Grief and anger swarmed inside of me, waging a war of sadness. I needed Cassius. I slipped out of bed and headed out to find him. He wasn't on the couch like he had been. My first thought was to go to the room he stayed in during the trials.

The castle was kind of creepy at night, when no noises could be heard and no lights were shining. When I got to the door, I crept inside. It smelled like him the moment I stepped over the threshold. My nerves calmed down as I searched for his bedroom. The small hallway only had two doors, and one of them was opened wide enough that I could see Cassius sleeping on his back with no shirt. His arm draped over his handsome face.

I swallowed hard as I snuck in. My eyes drifted over all his tattoos but paused on the 'T' over his heart. Then I saw the marks under it. Six slashes, as if he were keeping track of something—maybe how many times I died.

I shook my thoughts away and slipped under the covers with him. His deep breathing stopped before he lifted his head up to meet my stare.

"My love?"

"Can I sleep in here?" I whispered.

"I'm not sure if that's a good idea." He frowned.

His response devastated me, so I stood up to leave. A moment later, Cassius lifted me off my feet and put me back in his bed.

"What's wrong?"

"I had flashbacks, and I didn't like them." We lay on our sides facing one another, and I traced the tally marks on his chest.

"Of me?"

"Mostly my father and the queen, but you were there for another one," I sighed. "When you told me who you were."

He seemed confused at first, but then he smiled softly.

"When you told me you loved me," he chuckled.

"I didn't quite say that." I rolled my eyes. I scooted closer to him, and he wrapped me up in his arms. I leaned into his chest and kissed his neck.

"My love, I was serious about not sleeping with you until you talk with me." I sighed heavily. It just felt good to be close to him. "Why won't you talk to me? Don't you want to know why I killed you?"

I pulled back so I could see his face.

"Yes, I want to know, but I'm scared." Tears filled my eyes. "I know I should hate you for killing me, but I don't. That scares me, but it scares me more to think that I do not belong with you."

He brushed the hair from my face, then traced a finger down my cheek.

"Do you think I would do something so cruel to you without a reason?" He stopped his movements and stared at me. Our legs tangled together under the blankets.

"No," I answered truthfully. "Or maybe I'm just very gullible."

"Promise me, you'll talk to me tomorrow. I want to take you somewhere, but I must know that you are staying in Crimson first."

I nodded in agreement.

"I've missed sleeping in bed with you," he whispered, and I felt the sadness from the bond.

"How could you visit my dreams when I was in Exile?"

His eyes shined brightly as he pulled me to him tightly. He buried his face in my neck and breathed in.

"Tomorrow. I'll tell you everything."

I nodded and felt my eyes drifting back to sleep now that I was safe with Cassius.

CHAPTER 32

When I woke up in the morning, I stared at the ceiling of the bedroom. Cassius' scent of rain and forest took over the space, even though he wasn't here. I wasn't in a hurry to go find him because I was worried it would only reinforce that I should be leaving Crimson, not staying. So, I laid in bed a little longer before getting in the shower.

The sound of the water drowned out Cassius climbing into the shower with me. His hands wrapping around me startled me as I turned to face him. He kissed me softly before grabbing soap and washing my hair for me. His fingers gently untangled my wild curls. He turned me so I could see his face as he tilted my head back into the water to rinse my hair off. Cassius smiled at me brightly when I opened my eyes again.

"Are you ready for our date?"

"A date." I smiled. "Is that what you were doing this morning?"

"Yes." His eyes flicked down to my mouth before he leaned forward, pressing his lips against mine.

"Aren't you scared?" I whispered because I was terrified. He knew what I meant by my question.

"No." He traced the crown bond on my arm. "I was, but I know you better than anyone. I know you'll understand and forgive me."

Relief filled me with his words.

"Let's go on our date then."

★ ★ ☽ ★ ★

Outside, the weather was nicer than it had been in days. The sun shined, and it made the air perfect as we rode our horses through the woods.

I realized we were going to the cliffside overlooking the waterfall. My heart pounded so fast that I thought it would explode before we got there. The flowers and waterfall were as breathtaking as they had been the first time, but I felt nauseous as I looked around.

This could be the end. This could be everything I wanted, withering and dying before my eyes. We slid off our horses, and I stood quietly for a moment before deciding to sit. Cassius followed my lead and sat down. His eyes stared off into the distance for a while before he looked at me.

"You know, a long time ago, there was a prophet who foretold of a goddess who would fall from the stars. It was before you or I were born." Cassius smiled at the darkening sky as the clouds moved in. "It was said that the gods and goddesses had been warned about a future where Elloryon would be destroyed and ripped apart by the fae. They didn't know what to do to save the fae because they had been unable to save the humans. The gods are not supposed to directly interfere with our realm in significant ways."

I watched Cassius' eyes burn brightly in wonder as he admired the view.

"One day, a woman came to offer guidance. She claimed to have had a vision and knew how to stop the realm from being destroyed. But for her to save the realm, the gods had to grant her a child. Not just any child, but a child touched by stars and who shared the blood of a god."

"It sounds like she was using misfortune in her favor," I scoffed. Cassius' lips twitched as he looked at me.

"Well, the woman convinced the gods after she shared her vision and told them how she knew Elloryon would be destroyed. She also told them she had a vision of her child saving the realm. The gods and goddesses were desperate, so they agreed."

"Seriously?"

"They told the woman that after stopping the madness of Elloryon's destruction, her child would be brought back to the stars to claim their place among the other deities. The woman protested at first but ended up agreeing with them. A power like that was not to be among the fae.

"The woman became pregnant not long after, so the gods waited eagerly to see if the child would be the answer they needed. The woman ended up having a daughter, and she was more powerful than the gods had intended. They feared for the child's safety while she was in her mortal form. So, they bound some of her magic inside of her to keep her from being feared and killed by others."

"Like my mother did to me," I said, frowning.

"Yes," Cassius whispered.

"So would that make her a mortal goddess?"

"Yes, unless she chose to go to the stars and live an immortal life there. Specifically, she's the deity of blood and vengeance."

"Sounds badass." I nodded as Cassius agreed with a soft smile. "So, what happened?"

"The child's mother was killed, but the gods and goddesses did not know of it. So, they did not check on the girl because they thought she was safe under the supervision of her mother. Unfortunately, the girl grew up with her star-blessed magic locked inside her, thinking that she only had elite magic and not knowing the truth. The problem, though, was that a mortal body could not hold that magic for too long before it killed it."

My brows creased as Cassius told the story. Why did this sound so similar to me? When I glanced at Cassius, he frowned slightly at me.

"What happened to the woman?" I asked. I swallowed the lump of emotions forming in my throat.

"The woman fell in love with a mortal man. Eventually, he noticed how tired she was and how she seemed to get weaker by the day."

My heart pounded as Cassius kept talking like he wasn't describing me.

"What did he do?"

Cassius stared at me with a look of longing and sadness.

"He did what he had to. He went to a seer who saw the woman's prophecy of crumbling kingdoms and killing kings. Her prophecy of saving the realm, just as the gods intended. The man asked how she was supposed to be Elloryon's savior if she was dead. The seer said the answer to her freedom was in the prophecy. So, he spent days in that gods-forsaken cabin in the woods and tossed out every idea he could think of."

Cassius paused as his eyes cascaded over my face as if he were writing this very moment into his memory forever. He took in a shaky breath before meeting my eyes.

"Brim shot down every idea I came up with until I finally guessed correctly."

I nodded because I couldn't form any words. He was talking about me.

"A decision to be made, a choice that only results in death to be reborn, freed from a cage, a power awakened by a knife's blade. You had to die."

My eyes widened as he stared at me, waiting for me to process what he was saying. I had to die. To be reborn. I had star-touched magic and the blood of a god in me. I shook my head. This couldn't be true.

"But my father said *he* begged the gods to get rid of the curse when you killed me. That *he* was the reason why I ended up in Exile and could use my magic."

Cassius let out an angry sigh.

"Your father lied to you. He wasn't even there that day until the gods brought him to give him the bloodstone. Your father did not know the true nature of your magic, Thea. He believed it was just elite, but it is far more than that. I still don't think that he believes you are the deity of blood and vengeance. You should have seen him the day that the gods told him what you were. He didn't know any of it."

Anger clouded my insides. My father had lied about everything.

"Your magic needed out before it consumed you." He looked away from me. "I begged Brim for a different answer, but he gave me none. So, I went back to Crimson and stumbled upon war. Cerithia had stormed Crimson while I had been gone, and you were out there fighting. After the prophecy revealed itself, your father wanted to keep you as a weapon, not knowing how close you were to dying. The group of elite magic fae you saved were fighting with you. Sybil, Kaz, Kai, and Fallon, among others. They knew you were too weak to be fighting like you were, so they circled you, helping. I ran across the field to you just as you collapsed to your knees.

"I knew I had to kill you before the magic consumed you completely," he said, his voice breaking as he continued.

"I remember catching you before you hit the ground, and then you smiled at me. You were too pale, and your eyes were turning white. Your magic had almost drained everything away from you. You were being consumed. I had to hurry, and there was no time to explain. You told me you missed me. You told me you loved me as I grabbed your viper-handled dagger. I told you I loved you too." He took a deep breath and looked me right in the eyes.

"Then I plunged the dagger into your heart. Your magic exploded out of you with such a force that trees and fae flew everywhere. Dark clouds moved over us, and lightning lit up the sky. Everything was destroyed around us. I waited for you to open your eyes, but I didn't know..."

He stopped holding my hand and was silent for a long moment. Cassius was breathing heavily, as if he was reliving it. I went to grab his hand, but he didn't let me.

"Gods came down from the stars because..." he looked at me, "I betrayed you. I did what I did because I loved you, and I would do it again, Thea. But if I could go back, I would have had anyone else kill you but me."

He was angry, but not remorseful.

"You weren't supposed to die. You were supposed to wake up. And when you didn't, Della and her brother, Mikel, showed up. They told me how you were a deity sent here to save Elloryon, but I had taken that away because of what I did. I begged the gods to give you your soul back or at least take mine instead. I hadn't meant for things to happen the way they did. You were supposed to wake up and be reborn from your curse.

"They knew I only killed you because of the binding spell, but it was like the god, Mikel, didn't care. He said he was taking you to the stars, but I couldn't let you go. I'm too selfish to let that happen. Della made me a deal instead. She wouldn't take your soul, but to keep the balance, you had to pick me and fall in love with me again. I agreed immediately because I knew I could make you love me in every life. She understood that you had not fulfilled the prophecy yet."

His face turned hard and angry.

"Mikel woke you up from death right then and there. He asked you what you wanted. Either you go to the stars and claim your title as a true goddess, or you choose to stay and fight for a chance at a normal life with me. You didn't even hesitate when you said you chose me. This seemed to piss off Mikel, though. He said if you stayed, you would lose the chance at being a goddess. And yet, you still agreed. Mikel became enraged at your choice and refused to accept it. He said you didn't have a choice anymore; you were going with them to the stars."

My eyebrows knitted together in confusion.

"I don't understand." I frowned. "Is this what Della meant when she said the gods hadn't dealt with a situation like ours before because of what I was?"

He smiled softly as he shook his head. "I told him you were my fated mate, and you had the right to stay if you wanted. This changed everything. Della told me years later that gods and goddesses hold the fated mate bond as sacred above all else. They could not force you to go with them, and you chose me, so they must honor it. If we weren't fated, Della said Mikel would've taken you.

"It was obvious that this angered Mikel further. He kept telling me that I was not worthy of you as a mate. He said I needed to be severely punished for betraying you like I did. Even Della could not calm his wrath. He kept repeating that I was made to protect you and not let harm find you and that I had failed. Mikel was so cold and unforgiving to me that day, even knowing the circumstances." Cassius rubbed his hands down his face as I tried to gather my thoughts about being both a deity and his fated mate.

He waited to see if I would speak, but no thoughts formed, so he kept talking.

"Mikel said it wasn't enough to have you just choose me again; that was too simple. So, he wiped your memories to make it more difficult for me. He claimed that it was to spare you from remembering what I did, even though you would have understood the reasons behind my actions. I still wasn't worried, though, because I knew you would love me again. Then he announced that because you were the last surviving blood witch, your bloodstone would be given to your father.

"The witch's bloodstone that belonged to your mother, the queen, is sacred. You see, covens believe in preserving powers. When witches are born, they use a stone, in this case, a bloodstone, to which they attach their power. When a witch dies, their magic returns to the bloodstone, enabling other members of the coven to guard that magic. That stone holds so much power, Thea, and it's all yours as the sole survivor of the blood witch coven.

"But the bastard, Mikel, gave the stone to your father to keep, just to be an asshole. I still remember the way he smiled at me when I realized how difficult this would be. We had to come up with the trials to give you a reason to get the bloodstone and give it to me. It became so difficult over the years because it seemed like you hated Crimson more and more each time you came back. I still believe that Mikel did something to make you hate me more the longer it took to save you."

"Della told me it was her fault that Mikel was so cruel to you. She killed the woman he loved to save the man she loved, and it destroyed all the compassion he had left." I squeezed his hand in mine. "Besides, Mikel wouldn't have taken me anyway because I still needed to fulfill the prophecy."

"That's just it, though; Mikel was willing to let the realm be destroyed just to punish me, like he *wanted* it to be destroyed. Thank the stars Della talked some sense into him. Maybe he did not want a realm where the woman he loved did not exist anymore," Cassius frowned. "I would have destroyed the realm too if I had lost you that day. I could not bear an existence where I do not have you. One where I must exist without being able to hold you, kiss you, or love you. It would turn me into a monster."

I squeezed his hand in mine.

"It makes sense why I always felt so drawn to you, even knowing you killed me. I thought I was sick and twisted to still miss you."

Cassius stared at me for a long moment.

"Watching you die over and over again, just to come back and not remember me or the life we had started to-gether, is the worst torture. This new curse was not yours, but mine. Loving you so much and watching you stare at me like I was a stranger was the worst part of this. So many times, I caught myself about to tell you I loved you, or I had to stop myself from kissing you. Then you would die, and each time, pieces of me would die too. My father had to drag me out of our room after months because I could not function without you."

Cassius' voice was laced with emotion as he stared at the waterfall. It was clear that he was thinking of all the times I had failed and that he didn't want to go through it ever again.

His golden eyes locked onto mine.

"I knew for a long time who you were, Thea. I think I knew on the blood moon when you stabbed me with that damn dagger you love so much. Your soul was cursed because your fated mate killed you. The gods never had a mate kill the other before, and they could not let me go unpunished. It was the ultimate betrayal in Mikel's eyes. Maybe it is because he lost his mate. I do not know."

My eyes blinked slowly as I stared at him. Cassius was *my* fated mate. I had heard him say it earlier, but the reality of it was just now clicking in my mind. He moved toward me, but I backed up slightly. I needed to process this. He didn't try to touch me again. Cassius watched me closely.

"This is why I dreamt of you, why my mother came to meet you, and why I always find myself drawn to you, even if I don't remember us. It's why I love you even though you killed me."

"It is why you chose to give up going to the stars and stay here to live a mortal life with me. There are times when I feel you made the wrong choice. Maybe you should have gone to the stars because I have not been able to save you."

"You and I were destined to be together," I whispered as my head swarmed through all the emotions of finding out that I never had a choice in loving Cassius. I stared at him, trying to process this. "Does that bother you that we had no choice in who we loved?"

Cassius looked at me as if the thought never crossed his mind.

"No, because we could have ignored it and chosen not to follow our feelings. It would have been easy not to act on them since we were enemies, but we both slowly fell in love. I admit, I think I fell in love a lot faster and way before you did," he chuckled softly. "We still chose each other. We still had a say in it. Does it upset you to know that we are fated?" he asked with pain in his eyes.

"No, and being a goddess sounds boring," I chuckled softly to lighten the overwhelming feelings I was having. "I made the right choice by staying."

Relief filled his eyes.

"You should have seen their faces when I told them that you were my fated mate. I didn't know Mikel could be surprised, but that only made him angrier. Della understood why I did it. She took pity on how destroyed I was. If anyone else would have released your magic that day, we would not be in this fucking nightmare. Della kept apologizing to me, saying that it was her fault Mikel was such an asshole.

"The gods promised you would be kept in a safe place—Exile, as you called it. They let the group of elitist magic holders go with you, so it would seem like normal life. Those fae chose to go with you so you weren't alone, but then started not remembering things either. They also seemed to turn on Crimson the longer they were there.

"Your father has been hiring witches and others to curse Exile, to dry up your water and your food. Everything that started going wrong with Exile was his doing. I'm not sure how he found out where it was, but I think Mikel had something to do with it, or maybe it was Lavtan."

I stared at the waterfall and all of the pretty rainbows in the mist. Fated mate. A deity. I had the blood of the gods and the touch of the stars, but that didn't make me feel as special as knowing I was Cassius' mate.

"It makes sense why I felt so drawn to you in my dreams and at the trials. Every time I see you, there is a pull that I cannot describe."

"I would've torn the realm apart and climbed to the stars to kill that damn god myself if it would give you back to me, so we do not need to keep going through this torture."

Flashes of the day I had the witch's bloodstone in the clearing filled my mind. He had been so worried that I didn't get it, but it was because it would break our curse, not give him power. He had told me I was so close, but he couldn't tell me anything else.

"If I had given you the stone that day in the clearing," I choked out, "this would be over."

"Yes," he frowned. "There are two parts to the curse. You must gift me the bloodstone *and* choose me even after I confess my betrayal."

My mind was still reeling from the fact that Cassius was my fated mate.

"You knew I was your fated mate when we were at war with each other?"

"The moment I saw you in the woods on the blood moon, it was like a switch flipped, and I knew you were it for me. I didn't know what it meant until my father told me," he chuckled. "I couldn't simply tell you that while we were enemies."

"And I obviously knew before I died, since we were married."

"Yes," he smiled. "I'm sorry I didn't tell you we were mates or that we married soon after I took you prisoner. This is where we got married." His eyes glanced out to the cliffside and smiled.

I looked over his handsome face and felt that connection I always had, making him smile softly.

He was all mine.

"I never know how much I should tell you when you come back. It always seemed like the more information I told you, the worse you handled it. Then you started talking about how Crimson and our family were your enemies the last few times. When this all started, I made the mistake of telling you everything, thinking it would be a quick way to break the curse. You took it terribly and died almost immediately because you were distracted. The second year, I didn't even get a chance before Cerithia killed you. Each year I told you a little bit of information, but it seemed like it only made it worse. I thought this year I wouldn't tell you anything and would try to keep my distance. That was probably the worst torture I could have done to myself."

My mind was blank. What did I say to all of this? How was I supposed to act? Relief was the only emotion that sank into my chest. I thought I would have to leave Crimson today if he didn't tell me anything that I could believe.

I looked over at his handsome face. All mine. An overwhelming urge to touch him spread through me. Cassius watched me cautiously.

"Does my family know we are fated mates?" I asked.

He shook his head. "Your family does not even know that we are married. At the meeting of the kingdoms, when they announced your engagement to Jesper, I felt sick. I was so close to killing him, but I didn't because you still looked at me like I was your villain. I didn't want to force anything. Della told me I needed to let you piece together everything on your own after I kidnapped you at the border. She said it was the only way for you to truly choose me."

"How did you know I was going to be at the border when I was kidnapped? You said a friend tipped you off."

"Wisp, as you call her," he smiled. "Your soul."

"My soul is attached to you," I repeated his words to him. Cassius smiled as he nodded. "Della told me who Wisp was."

"You are the other half of my soul, Thea. We are destined to be together. Even if the gods did not destine us, I believe my soul would have searched until it found yours. You are my everything. My heart, my soul, my purpose."

My lips crushed his as he tumbled backward.

Mine. He was mine, and I was his. Cassius held me to him like he never wanted to let go. Like if he let me go, I would disappear. He had been trying to get me back for years. I couldn't imagine what that was like for him.

We lay there in silence for the longest time, just holding each other. My heartbeat was rapid with so much emotion. I sat up, so I straddled his hips and stared at him.

"I missed you so much when I was at Cerithia. I thought I would die," I confessed. "I called for you, begged for you in my dreams to come and explain why you did what you did. Even though I knew you killed me, I was still searching for any reason to understand and forgive you."

Something somber clouded his features.

"As soon as I fixed your bond, I could feel all of it. All the hurt, fear, pain, and moments of happiness and betrayal flooded me constantly. I had already planned on coming to the wedding to plead with you to come home. But then you called to me and begged for me, so I came to the rehearsal. If my bond hadn't broken, you would have known that I didn't mean what I said to you. I thought you were ignoring my pleading."

He had felt it all. I leaned forward and pressed my lips to his.

"I have something to show you that will make you very happy." He smiled as we stood. "Our real date that I was getting ready earlier." He grabbed my hand. "The other reason I was so cruel to you in the clearing."

We climbed on our horses and headed back towards the castle. Anticipation coursed through me as we got closer. Cassius just kept smiling like this was the best day of his life. Instead of continuing to the castle, he turned toward the woods and led our horses down a narrow path around the outskirts of the city.

Cassius' smile widened when we came to a tiny town. I furrowed my brows in confusion as I looked around.

"I don't recognize it."

"You're not supposed to." He climbed off his horse before helping me down. "One last lie I needed to confess."

"Another one?" I raised my eyebrow at him with humor.

"I had to make sure you would be sticking around before I could tell you this."

CHAPTER 33

He grabbed my hand and led me down the small pathway in the town. It was mostly cute houses, some small fountains, and a few shops. It was like a mini version of Crimson City.

"The day you gave the bloodstone to your father, I said horrible things to you. I wanted them to think I didn't care. I didn't want them to use you as a way to get to me, because they would have in a heartbeat, Thea. And I would have done whatever I could to protect you." I looked up to him and felt his sincerity through our bonds. "I couldn't let you choose me once your father showed up at the clearing, because he would have killed you immediately. When I disappeared from the field, I went to Exile. You had told me about it once before, but I couldn't find it. I searched the Forbidden Wood for days until I found it. I swore to you that I would always protect our family, and elite magic fae are a part of that family."

My chest was heavy with anxiety. Did he hurt them? Fated mate or not, I would leave him for that.

"It's alright, my love." He squeezed my hand as fear gripped me. "Because you weren't in Exile anymore, the border had faded. It took some convincing on my part to have them come with me to save them from your father or Jesper finding them. Sybil was the one to convince them. She remembered me while the others only remembered bits and pieces."

Was he telling me that they were here? My eyes looked around as they started emerging from their homes. Elite magic fae lined the street, smiling at me. Tears sprang from my eyes as I saw their faces. They were alright.

"Thea!" Sybil was running toward me with Kaz and Kai right behind her. I dropped Cassius' hand and ran to them. My arms squeezed Sybil and the twins, and my heart exploded with happiness and shock.

"I thought you had died," I choked out. "I thought I had failed you all."

"You've done amazingly. Cassius brought us here to protect us, to save us until we could be out freely without fear of your father and Jesper." Sybil smiled through her tears of happiness. "You picked a good one." Sybil grabbed my face and smiled brightly. All the other elitists came and hugged me as well.

I thanked them. They had chosen to follow me to Exile all those years ago. They had pledged loyalty to me, and some had died because of it. After a moment, I looked for Cassius. He was standing where I had left him, smiling. Love filled my chest when I looked at him. He had done this for me. He loved me. I walked to him and stopped a few feet in front of him.

"Are you happy?" he asked.

"Yes." I felt the overwhelming urge to tell him how much I cared and loved him. There was nothing that I could say. No words would ever be enough to describe what I felt for him. I decided on the most basic form of the phrase. "I love you, Cassius. More than the stars and moon. I will thank the gods every day that they gave me you as a mate."

As the words fell from my lips, something inside me shifted, as if I were exactly where I should be. Cassius' face lit up as he lifted me off the ground to kiss me.

"I've waited a very long time to hear those words fall from your mouth, wife."

The term immediately shot lust through me. Cassius was mine, and nothing was going to change that.

Someone cleared their throat lightly as I deepened the kiss with Cassius. When I pulled away, Kai and Kaz stood in front of all the elite magic holders as they all smiled at me and bowed.

"Captain," they all addressed me. I untangled myself from Cassius and watched them all stand. They all looked at me like I was their hero.

"You should talk with Sybil and the twins," Cassius whispered into my ear as he hugged me from behind. I twisted in his arms and kissed him before stepping away. "I'll be back for you in a little bit."

My heart clenched; I wanted him to stay. He smirked slightly.

"I'll miss you too, but we will have a lifetime together."

I nodded as I headed to Sybil, who wrapped me up in another hug. She pulled away and took my hand, leading me to a nice cottage. My eyes took in the bright space that held so much personality in it. Sybil had decorated the large area with so many herbs and flowers that it looked like a garden.

She got us tea as I admired her cozy home.

"This doesn't seem real," I smiled. "My father and Jesper tried to convince me that Exile didn't exist, that I had imagined it all."

"It was like our memories in Exile weren't our own," Kaz frowned at me from across the table. "Even now, we can't remember what happened right before we went with you. I just know for certain that your father is a bastard."

"We knew bits and pieces, but it all made Crimson look bad," Kai frowned as he gave Kaz a pointed look. "We've never made it out of Exile in the past seven years. Now everything is so clear. Our families didn't abandon or turn us in as we thought."

"How are you doing?" Sybil looked at me with her motherly eyes. "Cassius filled us in on everything that's been happening. He visits us often."

"I'm doing better after today," I smiled as I grabbed her hand. "I finally let Cassius explain everything. So, it's less confusing, but still hard to piece together everything without my memories."

Sybil glanced at the twins saying something without actually speaking. The twins frowned at me. My skin prickled because they looked concerned. Was this going to be about Cassius?

"Just say it. The silence is torturing me." I pulled my hand from theirs and grabbed my hot mug of tea. The smell of chamomile did nothing to calm my nerves.

"When are you going to get the bloodstone?" Sybil was the one to ask. A sigh left me in relief.

"I don't know. I haven't talked with Cassius."

She frowned sadly at me.

"He's going to tell you to not get it." Sybil sipped her tea. "He and I talked about it."

"Well, that makes sense. We can just build a life starting now."

Kaz was the one to grab my hand and squeeze it in comfort. The gesture did the opposite to calm my fears, though. He was not the gentle, calm one.

"No, you need to get it," Kaz whispered. "You can't fulfill the prophecy without it."

I shook my head trying to understand.

"The prophecy hasn't been fulfilled yet, and it won't until you go for the stone. Do you want this to be our life for the rest of our existence?" Kai asked. "Every time you die, we will all be sucked back to Exile. Your father would never stop trying to kill you, us, Cassius."

"Cassius doesn't want to lose you, but if you don't get the stone, we are *all* stuck living half-lives, you included. Do you want a life where you never remember anything from your past?"

I wanted to remember Cassius and me more than anything. But I also didn't want to jeopardize our lives now. However, they were right. It wasn't just me that was being affected by this curse. Everybody that really mattered to me was suffering through it as well. My eyes glanced at them; they were right. The prophecy hadn't been fulfilled. Until

I got rid of Jesper and my father, no one from Exile could live how they wanted. We would all constantly be hiding; Cassius would always be worried about me.

Another thought struck me then that seemed to pierce my heart straight through. We could never have children. They would never be safe. Cassius' family would always be in danger. Tears formed in my eyes.

"You must retrieve your bloodstone. Not just for you and Cassius, but also for all of us who followed you to Exile to protect you," Sybil sighed as tears ran down her cheeks. "It's the only way that we can move on and truly be free."

"I know," I whispered. "But Cassius won't understand."

"Make him," Kai pleaded. "We all have loved ones in Cerithia still being held hostage, so we can never have them. You can't ask us to give up more than we already have."

Hot tears streamed silently down my face. I couldn't, wouldn't ask them to give up more for me. Not when they had already done so much. They deserved their lives back and their loved ones. And I deserved to live with complete freedom.

"I owe you all so much. I promise I'll go for the stone," I said. A knock at the door sounded, making Sybil stand.

"Cassius." She smiled at me. "He truly is such a wonderful man, Thea. By the gods, he fucking loves you."

I smiled because Sybil never cursed. Cassius walked in the door as I wiped the tears from my face. He was holding a bouquet of wild flowers.

"I could feel how sad you felt," he said, frowning as he leaned in and kissed me.

"It's a lot to take in," I answered. "I'm actually really tired." I stood up. Worry overshadowed the happiness I had just felt. I knew I needed to get the bloodstone, but I wished I had more time with Cassius and the elite magic holders first.

"Are you sure?" Cassius frowned. "I wasn't rushing you."

Sybil stood up and smiled at me, giving me a hug, followed by the twins.

"We will catch up some more soon." Sybil looked at me with guilt covering her features. I knew they didn't want to put me in this position, but it was inevitable.

Cassius hugged Sybil before grabbing my hand and leading us to Onyx and Kaida. His shadows lifted me to the saddle of Onyx instead of putting me on my own horse before he climbed on. Kaida followed close behind us. I gripped the beautiful flowers in my hand. Concern filled the bond, and I knew he could tell something was wrong, but he said nothing until we got to the stables.

"Tell me what is making you feel so torn." He frowned as he brushed my braid over my shoulder.

I hesitated before answering, knowing that it would make him upset. "I still have to get the bloodstone."

His hand fell away from me, and he stepped back. Terror filled me from the bond. I stepped towards him, but he stepped back again.

"No," he whispered. "No, you don't need to. We can start fresh from today. I'll tell you every memory I can remember about us."

Tears filled my eyes at the overwhelming sadness he was feeling.

"Cassius, you know that isn't enough. The others can't get their lives back until I get the bloodstone. Do you want me to be responsible for them never getting to find the family they left behind? I can't keep their happiness from them any longer than it already has been. Besides, Brim told me that the prophecy doesn't happen until I break my curse. It must happen to save Elloryon."

"Please..." He turned away. "I cannot lose you again."

"Cassius... I want to remember every detail of us. I want to know what it was like when we got married, when you took me prisoner, and everything in between."

"You can't do this." His voice was harsh, but I knew he was just scared. "I forbid it!"

"I will always be hunted by my father and Jesper if I don't complete the prophecy. And our family will always be in danger. I can feel how much you are constantly worried for me. That is not a way to live."

"I will not let you do this." His eyes flashed black, and anger zapped down the bond. "No."

"You can't stop me." I frowned. "I want to be free. I want everyone not to be tied to me and to be able to live a life all their own. I want to have children with you, and we would never be able to do that if I did not fulfill the prophecy. I do not have an option other than to complete it."

A sharp pang of sadness and lust shot through the bond before anger returned.

"I've lost you six times! I finally have you back, and you want me to let you go back to Cerithia to get a stupid fucking rock."

"Please understand," I cried.

"I understand," he growled. "But it doesn't mean that I'm willing to risk you for anyone else. You have to understand that every time I watch you die, a piece of me dies too. And each time, I don't think I can make it. It took me seven months to leave our room when you died the last time. I'm alone. I'm haunted by our memories. I'm haunted by you wherever I am because I can remember, and you can't. My life stops every time you are away from me."

"Cassius..."

"I need time to think." He turned away from me. "Go get some rest. I'll be back." He hopped on Onyx and rode off.

Cassius' emotions through the bond stopped as he rode into the woods.

CHAPTER 34

As I lay in bed, all I could think about was how heartbroken Cassius had looked at me. I knew the right thing to do was to go get the bloodstone, but I wished there was another way. The selfish part of me wanted to forget it so I could live blissfully with Cassius, but I could never do that to Sybil, the twins, and all the fae in Exile.

They had given up their lives to help save me, and I *would* repay it.

Cassius crept into our bedroom a moment later. The smell of liquor was light in the air. His golden eyes watched me as I sat up to see the state he was in. He said nothing as he slipped off his boots and clothing before crawling into bed. His arms wrapped around me as he held me close to him.

"I'm sorry for my outburst earlier," he whispered as he traced over my face with his fingers. "I would never keep you from freeing those in Exile."

"You're scared of losing me. I'm scared too," I answered softly.

He nodded as his eyes traced over me.

"We will get the bloodstone and make your father and Jesper suffer for what they have done to you."

"I love you." I smiled as I leaned forward and kissed him gently.

"I love you too." Cassius pulled me closer and nuzzled his face into my neck. "It will be nice when you can remember all of us."

I nodded as I held him tightly to me. The warmth of his body lulled me to sleep.

★★☽★★

Where was Cassius? I sat up in my bed and glanced around the room, but he was gone. My hand ran over the silk bedding and felt how cold his side of the bed was. I stood and dressed so I could find him, but paused when Wisp appeared in the corner of the room.

"Where have you been?" I asked her like she would answer me. Her flames were dark green as she floated happily through the room.

When I got downstairs, I planned to head to the training fields, but I paused at the open door of the king's throne room.

"Thea, my dear, how are you?" Cassius' father smiled as he stood, walking to me and giving me a hard embrace. My chest tightened at how different he was compared to my own father.

"I'm alright. I was looking for Cassius."

"Oh, he had to head out on a scouting mission this morning. He'll be back shortly."

I nodded and glanced at the letters sitting on his desk. They were the letters I gave Cassius that day at the meeting of kingdoms. His eyes followed mine, and he sighed heavily.

"I felt so stupid when Cassius showed me the letters you gave him." His voice was hardly above a whisper. "I fear much of this is my fault. I could have stopped you from dying several times if I had paid closer attention to Lavtan. I should have seen through his schemes."

"It's not your fault," I assured him.

"We are so happy you are home, Thea." He patted my shoulder and gave me a friendly smile. "Cassius is such an ass when you're gone." His laughter was contagious.

I glanced around the large room and felt a sense of familiarity. All of Crimson felt right to me. It felt like home. No part of Cerithia had felt this way.

"He told me you would be retrieving the bloodstone." The king broke my wandering thoughts.

"I have to."

"Yes, you do. Cassius felt terrible about how he reacted to you yesterday, but we had a great talk about it. We will always support you and your choices."

His sincere statement made me smile.

"This whole thing must have been so strange for all of you, not just Cassius," I frowned. "I just walked around not remembering any of you, and all of you cared for me still. You know, when I was in Exile and we all believed that you had locked us away there, I wanted to kill you if I ever got the chance. But then, when I met you, you were so...nice."

He chuckled.

"I'm not sure I like being known as nice, but I'm glad you didn't kill me because you could have easily. Maybe your heart remembered that I consider you my own daughter, Thea. And we are family. It makes me sick to think how cruel your father is to you. You are such a wonderful woman, and I'm so glad you were chosen as Cassius' mate."

His face softened at the thought.

"Me too," I smiled.

"Am I interrupting something?" Cassius' voice had me turning to his smirking face.

"Just talking about how big of an ass you can be," I sighed as he stepped toward me. His father chuckled, and so did the guards behind him. He pulled me to him and kissed my forehead. Cassius was covered in mud, and his uniform was drenched.

"What happened to you?"

Haden started laughing loudly.

"Onyx stopped quickly and flung me into a creek." Cassius glared at Haden. I chuckled softly.

"Did you notice any shift in the Cerithia armies?" the king asked.

Cassius shook his head.

"Their borders are clear. I don't think they'd be stupid enough to launch an attack while Thea is here." Cassius paused for a moment. "I think helping Thea get the blood-stone soon would be the smartest move. Maybe a distraction at the border will get their troops out, and Thea can use my shadow magic to travel to the Cerithian castle while they are distracted."

My eyes shot up to his as he spoke.

"Have you thought of this plan since yesterday?" I asked.

"Yes, I want to get it over with so we can put all of this behind us," he frowned. "Cerithia is very reactive with their armies. If we create a big enough distraction at the borders, they'll send their forces to defend them. That would be a good time for you to get into the castle, find the stone, and get back with the smallest amount of resistance." Cassius paused for a moment. "How does that plan sound to you, Captain? You were always better at strategic planning for war than I was."

A sly smirk crept over his face.

"Yes, it sounds fine to me. When should we plan for this? You'll need to help me learn how to work your shadows."

"We'll work on it now," he agreed.

"You'll let us know when you feel ready to go, Thea, and we will make it happen." The king smiled.

I nodded, and Cassius grabbed my hand, leading me out of the room with Haden, Kace, and Zade. They all followed silently before Haden started laughing hysterically.

"You really should have seen Onyx throw Cassius into the creek; it was the highlight of my time in Crimson."

I started laughing with the guys, and Cassius narrowed his eyes at me with a playful smirk.

"You are supposed to defend me, my love, not encourage their behavior."

"I'm sorry," I chuckled softly.

Cassius stepped forward and pulled me to him as shadows wrapped around us. A moment later, the shadows disappeared, and we were deep in the forest.

The sun was hiding behind clouds, and the cold air was telling of a storm headed our way. I glanced at Cassius, who just watched me closely. His dirty clothes were now clean.

"Let's practice with shadows."

I nodded but couldn't turn my attention away from how handsome he looked. His dark hair was disheveled from his earlier excursion. The dark sky only made him look more powerful as he stood confidently in front of me.

"Are you distracted?" he teased.

"A little."

His smile widened, but he got back to business.

"Moving through shadows is quite simple. All you do is summon the shadows and concentrate hard on where you'd like to be."

"That's it?" I asked skeptically. "Seems too easy."

"Try it, but take me with you too."

I nodded as I stepped toward him, but he stepped away.

"Try to take me without touching me; it's harder to do but something that will be beneficial for you to learn. Take us to our cliffside."

I stopped and summoned the shadows forward. They burst from me, swirling around us in a whirl. My mind tried to clear away all thoughts as I focused on the cliff by the waterfall. A moment later, I lifted the shadows back up, but we hadn't moved. Frowning, I tried again, but this time I closed my eyes and pictured it in my head.

When my eyes opened, Cassius was gone, and I was on the cliffside by myself. Shit. A moment later, Cassius appeared next to me.

"You forgot me, my love."

"Sorry, that was harder than I thought."

"Try again."

I did, but again, I moved without Cassius back to the forest we had been in. After waiting a few moments, he didn't follow me, so I went back to the cliffside.

He was smiling smugly at me when I appeared again.

"You need to imagine me coming with you."

I nodded and closed my eyes, picturing Cassius and me standing in the dark forest together, holding hands. This time, when I opened my eyes, he was with me and smiling proudly.

"You always were a quick learner."

"Thanks." I smirked.

Cassius' gaze drifted over me slowly, setting my skin on fire with desire. His golden eyes flickered with black as he took a step toward me, like he was catching his prey. I backed away from him, and his eyes narrowed at the movement.

"Are you playing hard to get?" His husky voice made my heart pound harder.

"Maybe," I whispered, but in all honesty, I wasn't sure why I stepped backward.

"Alright... Let's play this game. I want you to go somewhere using shadows; if I guess where you've gone, I get to have my way with you. I get two guesses."

"And if you don't guess?"

"You can choose a prize." He smiled wickedly because he knew I would still choose for him to have his way with me, but I liked the games we played. My heart pumped lust into every fiber of my body as I tried to think of where to go.

"Alright."

"You have three seconds to leave," he declared. I went to protest... but he started counting. "One... Two..."

I closed my eyes, and the first place that popped up was the training ring Cassius and I used to use in the middle of the woods. When I opened my eyes, it was eerie and fairly dark. My eyes immediately scanned around for him, but he wasn't there. How long would it take him to find me? My stomach clenched as anticipation coursed through me.

A light drizzle of rain started coming down as I waited with excitement for him to appear. Part of me thought he would never think of this place within two guesses. I'm not even sure why I had thought of it. Minutes moved by slowly. Maybe he had no idea where I had gone, and I should go back to the castle.

Both anticipation and doubt coursed through me as I waited, causing an unsettling mix of emotions to overtake me. There weren't many places in Crimson that I could've chosen; he would find me eventually.

Suddenly, his arms wrapped around me, and a small yelp escaped me before he turned me around and devoured my mouth with his. He yanked me flush against him as his tongue shoved its way into my mouth. Cassius was not gentle with me as he lifted me up and pushed me against the nearest surface.

His hips pushed into me roughly, and I moaned loudly as my nails dug into his back. Cassius pulled away and smiled.

"It took me four guesses."

"Then I get to choose…" He cut me off with another devouring kiss. Cassius lifted me effortlessly before walking to the rock wall that had a small overhang, stopping the now-hard rain from soaking us. He gave me one last chaste kiss before setting me on my feet and taking a step away so he could start stripping off his wet clothes.

His eyes darkened as he traced over me as I followed his lead and undressed. I had expected him to devour me with another kiss, but as he stepped forward, he was more gentle with me than I had thought.

Cassius kissed me passionately. His hands gripped my face softly, so I couldn't leave. He pulled me down onto our discarded clothing before crawling over me and pinning me below him with his weight.

When he pulled back, something had changed from hot, searing passion to longing and love.

"I don't want to lose you again," he confessed.

My fingers came up to his face and gently traced his saddened features.

"I am a shell of a man when you are gone, Thea. Nothing feels right, like a night without its stars or a storm without its rainbow; I'm utterly lost without you." Cassius' eyes traced over me as tears filled my own because he feared losing me, and I couldn't guarantee that I wouldn't leave again. I could clearly see the fear he had for my success on his somber face.

"I wish I could take your fear away, Cassius."

He closed his eyes and rested his forehead against mine.

"Sometimes I wonder if your life would have been better if you never met me." His whispered confession nearly broke my heart.

"You can't possibly think that is true."

"Sometimes when you're gone, I lay in bed and think of all the horrible things that I have brought into your life. Maybe you would have been happy with someone else or just living a full life, not this half-life I've cursed you with. All I can think about while you're away is how unworthy I am of you."

Cassius looked away from me as if he were ashamed of himself. I pulled his face back toward me so he could see how genuine I was.

"My life would not have been better without you. You gave me a reason to live; you breathed life into me when I thought no one would ever want me. What I remember about my life before you was no way to live. I would take this half-life with you over a full life without you. Even when I'm in Exile, my heart knows you are missing, and it longs for you."

His eyes traced mine before leaning in and kissing me slowly. Cassius kissed me like it would break the curse. His tongue slid against mine as his hips moved forward.

My moan was lost to the pouring rain. My hips rolled up to his, but Cassius kissed me like we had all the time in the world. He moved against me, causing a delicious friction that had me holding my breath.

"Cassius," I breathed with a plea.

He understood what I wanted as he lifted his hips and pushed into me slowly.

There was no rush in how slowly he filled me. A deep groan escaped him as he filled me completely.

"Stars above, I could die right now, and the heavens could not compare to you, Thea."

His hips slowly pulled away from me before thrusting back in. My eyes focused on him. Cassius' pretty eyes slowly started fading to black as he stared down at me. Something about how gentle he was being was almost too much to handle. His mouth devoured mine as he picked up pace.

"Cassius..." I gasped for air, but I didn't know what I needed from him—more or less?

"Use your words, my love. Tell me what you want from me."

My whole body felt like it was on fire, but it was my love for him that consumed me. My eyes glanced over his face before he rolled us without warning.

Cassius smirked up at me when I started sliding up and down him at an unbearable pace. His eyes drifted down my body, but it was as if his hands were touching me. He let out a groan of approval when he watched where we joined together.

"You look so fucking good like this, Thea. Look at how good you take all of me."

My eyes followed his, and I couldn't help how turned on I was getting. Cassius' hands rubbed over my thighs and my hips, tugging me roughly against him. My orgasm crashed around me, flames bursting out of me as I called out to the stars above.

"That's my girl," he groaned before flipping us again. Cassius leaned over me, just to kiss me roughly before he leaned up. His shadows twirled around him, and I knew he wasn't in control of his magic right now.

"Fuck," I muttered at the sight of him. Black eyes, black shadows, the tattoos on his ribs flexing with each thrust into me.

"I want to hear you again. These noises you make make me want to mark you as mine again, so there is no mistaking who you belong to. A mark that no curse can break... no gods can keep me from you. Do you see what you do to me?"

His shadows slowly crept down his body and over mine. I cried out in pleasure when they gripped my wrists and held me down so I couldn't move.

"Mark me," I begged.

Cassius' eyes were pure black as they raked over me at my plea. I wanted him to mark me, to show the realm I was his again. My magic surged forward, and my fire magic wrapped around him as his shadows moved away from my wrists and toward my chest.

"Cassius," I moaned. When his shadows moved, I glanced over my heart to see a 'C' above it, surrounded by crimson flowers.

"Mine," he muttered as his hips kept surging forward. My fire mist wrapped around his arm, and when it moved, it showed a red viper wrapped up his arm.

"Mine," I repeated.

Cassius leaned over me and kissed me. His tongue tangled with mine as my moan tore through me. His shadows swarmed around us in a frenzy, as if they did not know what to do with all these overwhelming emotions. My fire encircled his shadows as Cassius breathed heavily against my damp skin.

"Cassius..." I breathed as my orgasm crashed around me. I yanked him closer to me, and he stilled as he found his release. We lay there as the rain pounded, our breaths struggling to catch up.

"I love you more than anything, Thea." He leaned back.

Something about his words made doubt creep into my mind. What if I couldn't get the stone? What if this curse was never broken and I had to leave him repeatedly? We lay under the overhang, listening to the rain pelting down all around us. The prophecy still lingered over me like a dark promise of relief from this burden. I knew which kings I would kill and which kingdoms would crumble.

But when would I fulfill that destiny? Would it be as I got the bloodstone? Thoughts raced through my mind as I tried to figure out how all these pieces would fit together and bring me back to Cassius.

"You're very quiet, my love."

I turned to face Cassius and saw how worried he was.

"I feel like you have had the worst of this curse," I whispered. His brows furrowed at my statement. "You have to remember everything, while I live unaware of the pain and sorrow. It must be torture to see me and realize I don't know you at all."

He was quiet as he thought about what I said.

"If this is the punishment I must carry for saving your life, then I would gladly do this every year for the rest of our existence."

"I'll get the bloodstone and fulfill the prophecy so we can live a full life together," I promised. Cassius leaned forward and kissed me before wrapping me up in his arms.

CHAPTER 35

A few days later, Cassius walked into our room with a contagious smile. He was in a better mood than I had anticipated he would be in. I woke up to the wonderful smell of food he had made and brought to bed.

He leaned down and kissed me before pulling back with a big smile.

"Good morning, my love."

"You're very happy." I raised my skeptical eyebrow at him.

"Today is the day we get our lives back, and I can't wait to have you all to myself." He sat at the edge of the bed as I started eating the warm bread and meats he brought me.

"I'm looking forward to it too." I smiled. "Did you always cook for me before?"

"You're a terrible cook." He chuckled when my face fell. "But I was teaching you, and you were getting better."

I nodded as I ate the food. Cassius rested his hand on my leg as he shared breakfast with me. This was a morning routine I could get used to.

"Do you want to hear the plan?"

"Yes."

"We are going to ride to the far border of Crimson and cause a distraction. You'll ride with us there, so you know when to travel to Cerithia using shadow magic. You can take Haden, Kace, and Zade with you when you travel, just in case you run into guards."

"Seems simple enough," I agreed. "Maybe I should go by myself. I can use my magic to get out of there, but having the guys with me might end up being a problem if they are caught."

He mulled over my words and then nodded.

"That's a possibility, I suppose. I don't know how much I like the thought of you going alone, though."

"I can do it. Taking them with me will only make me worry about their safety. If I go by myself, then I can go and get out within a few minutes. Besides, I've only used shadow magic a few times, and if I left one by accident, then I could never forgive myself."

Cassius was silent for a long moment, and I thought he would argue.

"If you think that is best, then I will trust your judgment."

Happiness and pride filled my chest. How lucky was I that my mate believed in me enough to let me do what I think is best?

"I love you." I smiled.

"I love you too, little viper." He leaned forward and kissed me before we stood and dressed.

We met the small group of guards that were going with us in the foyer of the castle. Cassius must have briefed them on the mission because no one asked any questions.

"Does everyone understand the plan?"

The guards all nodded.

"Sorry, I'm late." Kace came running up to the group. His forehead was covered in sweat, and his clothes were disheveled.

"Where were you?" Haden asked. "You never came to the house last night?"

"Out." Kace was a bit annoyed. It was odd to see his bad mood, but maybe he was nervous for today too.

"You know the plan?" Cassius questioned.

"Yes," Kace sighed and fidgeted with the buttons on his uniform. Haden wouldn't stop staring at him intensely.

"I'll move us all to the border," Cassius said as his hand gripped mine tightly. He leaned in and gave me a chaste kiss before shadows wrapped around us. Once the shadows disappeared, we all stood in the clearing that separated Crimson and Cerithia.

As the guards started getting into place, I began to feel uneasy. My eyes drifted around the woods; it felt as if someone was watching us. Cassius had been talking with Haden when he stopped and glanced around the woods too. His eyes met mine as he started toward me.

"Something doesn't feel right," I whispered.

"There's no animal noises in the woods," he frowned. "We should head back to the castle. Something is wrong."

I glanced around at the men and noticed Kace was missing. Haden walked toward us.

"Where is Kace?" I asked, worried he was missing.

"He disappeared into the woods as soon as we arrived." Haden frowned. "He's acting strange. Honestly, he's been odd for the past few months."

Cassius turned to tell the men we were leaving. "Let's pull ba-"

A moment later, a loud explosion had everything around me blurring in a frantic mess. I could see Cerithian and Kizar guards coming toward us, and I threw up a shield as quickly as I could, but then everything went dark as I landed on the hard ground.

Confusion spread through me as I woke up from whatever had attacked me. Wisp circled me with black flames. Something was very wrong. My head pounded so fiercely that I almost fell over as I stood on shaky legs. My eyes looked at the massacre in front of me. Men lay dead; trees were toppled over as if something had exploded.

My mind pieced together what had happened before we had been attacked. I glanced around the clearing for Cassius, but I didn't see his black uniform among the dead guards. Immediately, my eyes focused on our bond, but I couldn't feel anything through it. Fear took over my every thought. I needed to find him.

"Thea."

I held my dagger out but lowered it when Haden stood behind me with Kace and Zade. Haden and Zade were covered in dirt and grime from the explosion, but Kace looked untouched.

"You got your barrier up and saved some of us," Kace answered my unspoken question. "They couldn't get to you because of it."

"Have you felt Cassius through the bond?" Haden frowned. "He's the only one we can't find."

"No." I tried again. "We need to get to Cerithia."

"It could be a trap." Zade was the one to question it.

My thoughts swarmed with images of Cassius being taken by my father. "I must make sure he's alright. I'm going to use magic to get into Cerithia. I'll meet you back here at the border."

"That's not a good idea. You should wait a little bit and see if Cassius shows," Kace argued.

"We searched for him, but he isn't here." Haden glared. "Where were you before the explosion? In fact, where have you been sneaking away to, because you are acting strange?" Haden crossed his arms over his chest and stared down Kace.

"Nowhere," Kace snapped.

Haden looked at him with an odd look, but I didn't have time to stay and argue.

I took a deep breath and concentrated on using Cassius' shadow magic. His powers surged around me instantly, taking me away from the field. My body swayed as the shadows left, leaving me in the middle of the throne room in Cerithia. It was empty when I scanned around me. My ears caught no noise either as I headed for the door.

That odd sensation I had felt in the woods was thick in this room. This wasn't right. Why couldn't I hear anything in the castle? I hesitated at the wooden door, unsure if I should leave. This could be a trap.

I froze when I felt the bloodstone's pulsing energy somewhere close to me. Turning back toward my father's large wooden desk, my darkness searched frantically for it without me asking it to. Would my father leave the bloodstone in here without it being guarded?

I hurried across the room once my darkness determined it was in the top drawer. It was locked when I pulled on it, but I melted the lock with my fire.

There it was, the bloodstone, *my* bloodstone. My body hummed as the power of the stone pulsed through me when I picked it up. It was surprisingly heavy in my hand, and I watched it glow at my touch. My heart raced because I could still break my curse. But first, I needed to find my husband. Slipping the stone into my pocket, I headed toward the door.

It was so quiet in the castle. Something felt misplaced as I waited. I closed my eyes and let my darkness out, telling it to find Cassius by locating his shadow magic. I felt it explode through the castle as if it knew I needed to find him immediately. It scoured the entire building, only to find that Cassius wasn't there.

Where the fuck was he? Something feral and evil snapped inside of me. It wanted our husband and mate now. If something happened to him, I would burn down the entire realm. Everyone would be punished. At that moment, Wisp appeared in front of me, flashing between black and red, letting me know something was wrong. Suddenly, a jolt of emotion came through the bond. It was worry, then an image of the boundary between Cerithia and Crimson. Cassius was in Crimson?

Before I could summon my darkness, it used Cassius' shadow magic to take us to the border. When I stepped through the shadows, I saw Kizar and Cerithia guards holding Cassius, Haden, Zade, and Kace. Cassius looked unharmed, but he was staring at me, bound and gagged.

"Release them, now." My voice startled me. It was laced with a promise of death. My vision pulsed red as the swirls on my skin glowed.

"Do not do anything stupid, Thea. If you do something to harm us, we have the rest of the Crimson royal family and elite magic holders, and they will be slaughtered," my father warned.

Cassius started struggling, trying to break free of his hold. I froze at this news. My heart pounded wildly in my chest. Cassius would be lost without his family. My family. Our family.

"What do you want?" I looked at Cassius, and he shook his head.

"You," Jesper smiled. "We will trade all of them for you, but you have to put these on." He held up magic barbs. I stared at the cuffs and knew I didn't have a choice.

"How do I know you will let them all go if I put these on?"

"We will release them so they can go back to Crimson lands, and we will take you and leave."

"And the rest of them?"

"As soon as the cuffs are on, we will show you them and release them."

Cassius was shaking his head no, but I didn't have a choice. I would never let anything happen to him or Crimson. I could hear him trying to talk behind the gag in his mouth.

I nodded, and a guard approached me cautiously, wrapping the barbs around my wrists. Wisp was circling Kace frantically. Her flames were black with warning. How did Cerithia and Kizar know we'd be here? My eyes glanced at Kace and frowned. Was he the other spy my father had mentioned?

Cassius knocked down the man holding him and ripped the gag from his mouth.

"Thea, don't!"

"It's alright, Cassius," I reassured him as they tackled him.

My father released Haden and the other guards. They all crossed back to Crimson and toward me, but I held up my hands so they would stay back.

"The elitist and royal family... Show them to me, then release them, and I'll come over."

My father's eyes shifted to the woods, and I saw the Crimson royal family and the elite magic holders emerging.

"It's illusion magic; they never had the royal family or elitists!" Haden called out. When I looked back, it was just a bunch of Kizar guards emerging from the woods. My eyes snapped back to my father as he smirked at me.

"Easy, Thea, or we will kill him." Jesper now held a dagger at Cassius' throat.

"Release him, and I'll come willingly."

"Come to Cerithia's side, and we will release him once the guards have you," Jesper demanded.

My eyes met Cassius as he silently pleaded for me not to do it, but I couldn't let him be killed. I would do anything to save him. My feet started walking before my mind comprehended that we were moving. Once the guard grabbed me, Jesper shoved Cassius to the ground.

I sneered at Jesper, but several guards lifted Cassius up and escorted him to the border. Once he crossed, Haden helped him get his bindings off.

"My love, come back over here," Cassius pleaded. "They don't have any other prisoners."

My father scoffed as he looked over me and my magic barbs. The witch's bloodstone hummed in my pocket, reminding me of how close I was to breaking this fucking curse. Cassius couldn't cross over to save me without dying. My eyes locked on him, and I tried to have him understand what my plan was.

Cassius' eyes scanned over my face. I tried to communicate through our blood bond. I needed him to understand that we could get out of this, but we needed his magic to do it. I sent him images of what my plan was.

"No," Cassius said, shaking his head. I knew it was risky, but it was the only way.

"We were so close this time, Thea. So close to you picking our side and getting rid of Cassius for good," my father sighed. "I really thought you would kill him."

I scoffed.

"You did a piss poor job trying to get me to choose you or your shitty kingdom."

My father's face burned red.

"I will always choose Cassius. He is my home."

I felt love and terror surge through the bond, but I didn't break eye contact with my father. He made a disgusted grunt.

"He murdered you, you stupid fucking Crimson whore!"

"No, he saved me," I shot back.

Jesper took a step toward me but stopped when I looked at him.

"It's a shame we must do this over again, Thea. Hopefully, next time you will choose correctly."

Realization hit me. They wanted me so they could kill me. They knew I would never fight against Cassius now.

They were resetting the curse.

"I chose correctly this time," I answered back.

"Thea, please come over here," Cassius pleaded, but I knew I would be killed before I could make it there. My eyes flickered at him.

"I love you with my whole soul." I cried because I didn't know if I would get out of this one.

"Don't you dare say goodbye to me." He started walking toward Cerithia's lands, but Haden and Zade held him back so he wouldn't die by crossing over. "I love you too," he whispered.

"How fucking cute," my father scoffed. "I don't enjoy killing you, Thea."

"You're a fucking liar. I want you to know that one day my blade will stop your cruel heart, but not before I slaughter every disgusting member of your family—Jesper included."

Jesper paled at my declaration.

I focused on the bond, telling Cassius exactly what I planned on doing. He needed to be ready for when I ran. He quieted down at the border, and I knew he understood.

"I think I will enjoy killing you the most, Jesper. I think I'll take my time." Jesper took a step back. My eyes flickered over the guards holding weapons pointed at me. "I will remember each face here, and one day I will make you pay for this." The guards swallowed hard but didn't move.

"Are you done?" My father snapped.

"Yes, but before you kill me, take this as a parting gift." Confusion clouded his face before my dagger flew out and embedded into his shoulder. Damn it, I missed his heart. But I was already running toward Cassius.

CHAPTER 36

Chaos broke out around me as my father and Jesper ordered their men to kill me. My hand reached out toward Cassius. His eyes locked onto mine as his shadows burst out, encircling everyone from Crimson. My eyes focused on the black shadows in front of me. Cassius was all I could think of. Images flashed through my head of the life we once had: getting to be with him every day, loving him, then on to having heirs of our own, having my own family that loved me, having him love me more than anything else in this realm.

A sharp pain hit me as I stepped into the shadows, making me call out in pain.

As the darkness moved from my vision, I realized we were already back in Crimson. We were all surrounded by the royal guard and family in the castle gardens. A loud eruption of happiness spread through everyone when they saw us. An arrow protruded from my leg, but it wasn't a fatal wound. Cassius' frantic eyes looked around for me, and relief spread across his features when I stood twenty feet from him. I couldn't believe my plan had worked. I ripped the arrow from my thigh.

My eyes took in his handsome face. Something like pain flickered across his features, and he stumbled forward.

"Thea," he whispered.

"Cassius!" I was running to him instantly. I tried to release my fire mist to cushion his fall, but the barbs prevented it. Luckily, Haden caught him. The crowd had stopped talking, their murmurs dying down as I slid on my knees to cradle his head in my lap. His normally bright gold eyes were dim in color. His father and mother cried out loudly when I ripped the clothing from his chest and saw the arrow wound.

"My love," he choked out.

"No, I'm not losing you," I sobbed. My hands frantically tried to rip the barbs from my wrists, but they wouldn't come off. Why wouldn't they come off? Blood poured from my wrists as I ripped my flesh to get them off. "Please, Cassius. I'll heal you once these come off."

"What did you do?" Haden's anger made me look up. He was yelling at Kace. Kace's face paled at Haden's confrontation.

"It's been you! You've been feeding Cerithia information about Crimson. You're the spy we've been searching for. You disappeared last night to warn them, and then you disappeared before they attacked today."

"You don't understand..." Kace started to speak, but Haden was too enraged to listen.

Without hesitation, he grabbed his dagger and impaled Kace. I didn't have time to process Kace's betrayal. I looked down at Cassius when his hand gripped my hands, stopping me from tearing at my skin.

"It's alright, Thea." His eyes focused on me as tears poured out of me. I shook my head violently because I didn't want to accept this fate. How sick and cruel were the gods? He wouldn't come back, and I would never know about my life with him. I would die too. My heart could not live without him. His eyes shifted over my shoulder, and I glanced to see Wisp floating close by, her color a dark gray.

"She's here to take me, little viper."

Shock ricocheted through me. Tears fell down my face as I shook my head violently.

"No!" I yelled at her so loudly that the ground shook. Her color turned white at my anger and pain. "You can't have him."

"I'm sorry we didn't have more time," he whispered as his hand rubbed my face, his pretty eyes tracing over every part of me. "Maybe the next life will be kinder for us."

"I can't live without you," I stuttered frantically as I felt death creeping closer to him.

He frowned before saying, "You're a lot stronger than you think, my love."

"I don't want to be strong. I want you not to die. Stay with me," I begged.

"Maybe not having memories will make living without me easier."

I pulled his chest into my face as sobs fell from me. Nothing would make this easier. Everyone watched us as Cassius tried comforting me, and I fell completely apart. My eyes flickered over everyone sobbing, and my mind raced as I tried to rip the magic barbs from my wrists again.

"Thea, my love, it's alright."

I leaned forward and kissed him. The smell of rain and forest surrounded me. I would not let this happen. It was my stupid plan that got him hurt and killed. My mind raced with anything I could do to save him.

Then it hit me. I pulled away from him and met his eyes with my own.

"Forgive me," I whispered.

"W-what..."

I turned to Wisp, her flames still burning with white-hot sadness. Cassius grabbed my hand as if to stop me.

"Della!" I called into the sky in anguish. As if sensing my panic, Della appeared within a moment. Her star-colored eyes looked at Cassius dying on my lap and frowned.

"Take me instead. Take me and spare him," I pleaded. Wisp's color turned an odd shade of purple before turning back to white. Then there were more wisps surrounding us, all smaller than the one that followed me constantly, my soul.

"Thea," Cassius pleaded. "Don't."

"I will bear his wounds and die for him; just do not take him from me!" I could feel the darkness swarming frantically inside of me, trying to break free. "I will burn the whole realm down if you take him from me. Even the gods will not be safe from my wrath," I warned her. "I will destroy everything if you take him."

A sense of pride filled the space between us. No one else could see her as I argued with her. I'm sure they all thought I had lost my damn mind. Maybe I had, but if it saved him, then it was worth it. My breath held as I waited.

"You'd give your life for his?" Della's voice rang out like a song I had forgotten long ago. My heart hammered in my chest at the sound—so perfect and peaceful. Her dark dress complimented her bronze skin as she watched me cradle Cassius in my lap. Her star-like eyes showed the sadness she was feeling at the sight of us.

"Yes," I cried.

She came and stood next to me. At first, I thought she was going to deny me. I thought she was going to take his soul right in front of me, so I shielded Cassius from her. If gods could die, I would kill her right here if she even tried to take him.

"Well, Thea Valeska, if you wish to take his place, then we will accept that trade."

Cassius was looking at me when I turned back to his face. His tanned skin was pale. He was so close to death. He opened his mouth to stop me, but I cut him off.

"Did you hear that? I will take your place. I'll come back again; you won't." He frowned and opened his mouth like he would argue. "Please don't argue with me. I would destroy the whole realm without you. We will have another chance, but only if I take your place."

"Della," Haden breathed out. My focus shifted to Haden and Della staring at one another for only a moment. My hands ran through Cassius' hair before I leaned in and kissed him softly.

Tears gathered in my eyes as I pulled back.

Then suddenly, pain was spreading like wildfire through me. My body collapsed to the hard ground next to Cassius, shaking as the magic burned through me.

"My love?" Cassius whispered as he sat up, his wound healing as his death was passed on to me. He wrapped his arms around me and cradled me. Something like white-hot fire raced through my veins, and the pain caused me to cry out as I took a shaky breath.

I looked down to see blood seeping through my shirt from an arrow wound.

His hands gripped me tightly against him. My head was swarming with blackness. I hardly felt the pain anymore.

"Thea, please," he cried out as he rubbed my curls from my face. His eyes glanced over my face and widened when he saw my wound. Fear laced his features. His hands worked quickly to get the barbs off me, trying to not hurt me with the frantic movements he was using.

"Maybe you can heal yourself, my love." But the barbs wouldn't come off.

Nothing was stirring in my chest. Neither magic nor darkness. The wisps floated near us, their color almost white. A color that I now knew meant hurt, anguish, and sadness.

"I can't feel my magic," I choked out as blood filled my lungs. "F-for you." I tried to hand him the bloodstone, but it made Cassius sob loudly.

"You did so good, little viper," he whispered. "But I can't take it right now."

Confusion spread through me. It would break my curse, and I would finally be able to remember us, remember him. Confusion closed in on me. It was difficult to remember what was going on or what had happened in the last few minutes. My eyes shifted to the faces surrounding us. Haden, Leer, and Zade all watched with silent tears streaming down their faces. Understanding washed over me as I met Cassius' golden eyes.

"I'm going to die again." Flashes of my pleading with Della only moments ago reminded me of what I begged for. Death was coming for me, and I was oddly at peace with the thought. If Cassius was spared, then all was right in the realm.

A painful sob escaped him. If I gave it to him, I wouldn't come back. Tears gathered in my eyes as understanding settled into me. Death was looming close by. Wisp watched me closely, but so did Della. I could feel her waiting to take me back into Exile with no memories of Cassius. But I was stubborn, so I ignored the pull and focused on Cassius, gripping him tightly.

"I love you so much," I whispered.

"I love you too, my love." He rested his forehead against mine. "I don't want you to go. I'm so lonely without you, so lost. I thought this time was it."

I reached up and wrapped my arm around him.

"We are two halves of the same soul, Cassius. I will always come back to find you."

His body shook with silent sobs.

His hands gripped me to him tightly.

"I love you beyond the moon and the stars, Thea Valeska, my wife, the future mother of my children, the future Queen of Crimson." He pulled back and pressed his strong lips to mine. The warmth spread through my body, coating over the coldness of death.

"I'm sorry," I wheezed out as blackness closed in more. "I'll do better next time."

"Please don't leave me, Thea." Cassius' frantic voice pierced straight into my heart. His pain laced every word he muttered as he prayed to the heavens and stars to let me live, but it was for nothing. "Don't take her from me!" he yelled at Wisp and Della, but they had no choice. His hands squeezed my face and moved it so I could see him. "Stay, my love." His hauntingly beautiful gold eyes made my chest tight with love.

"D-don't hide our marriage bonds next time."

"Please, stay," he begged me with everything he had.

Before I could say anything in return, though, it all went silent and black.

□□□□□

My eyes flickered through the darkness that now surrounded me as I was met with myself in my wisp form, her color still a bright white. Then, there were dozens of them surrounding me, and I finally understood why the wisps were always lurking; it was like my own army of the dead, here to protect me.

"You love him so much." Della frowned next to me. "I'm sorry, I couldn't just let you stay. I've tried to stop the rules my brother put in place, but I can't."

"He's going to be so alone," I cried. "What if I remember nothing about him next time, no memories?"

"I always get some memories through... I'll make sure to send you some without my brother knowing."

"Haden." I glanced at her. "He's the other death-marked soul. He could see you."

It was her turn to blink away tears.

"Yes."

Della. My mind flashed to the trials when the sirens had been in front of us, showing us our biggest desire. Haden had said her name. That was why it sounded familiar.

"He will always be my biggest regret. He will hate me as long as I exist, and it is the worst form of torture."

Tears filled her pretty eyes as she looked over at me. I went to ask her what she meant, but my wisp form reached out and touched me.

The touch ignited a cascade of falling stars to take over my vision. It was so beautiful. Then I saw flashes of mine and Cassius' time in this last failed attempt to free myself. Grief struck me before everything faded to nothing.

□□□□□

I jolted up in bed, waking from a terrible dream I couldn't remember. Fogginess swarmed my mind as I stood up and headed to the kitchen. When I stepped from my room, Sybil's bedroom door opened violently. Her blue eyes were frantic until they met mine. Her confused face fell when she looked at me.

"Good morning, Sybil." I smiled.

Then Sybil burst into tears. I went to comfort her, but our front door burst open, making me stop. The force of it shaking our small home. The twins stared at me like they were seeing a ghost. My eyes shifted to Sybil when she muttered something about being trapped in Exile again.

CHAPTER 37

Cassius

"Son." My father's voice was laced with concern. It had been since Thea died nearly a year ago. It physically hurt to breathe when she wasn't here. How did they expect me to answer them?

"Do you want me to bring you food?" my mother tried.

I just shook my head and pulled the covers up over my head. They didn't leave. They hadn't left me alone for longer than a few hours. I think I've left mine and Thea's room less than five times in the past year. This has been the worst time of my life.

Flashes of Thea's beautiful face plagued me. I squeezed my eyes tightly, trying to hold in the pain. I knew I would be seeing her again soon, but the pain at this moment was all-consuming. My body craved her touch, her laugh, her smile, and there was nothing I could do about it. I felt so tired all the time, which seemed ridiculous because I didn't do anything but sleep. Every time I opened my eyes, I saw memories of Thea. She haunted me, no matter where I was. It was too much to bear. I just wanted my wife back.

I heard my parents get up and leave, murmuring something about checking on me later. They hated seeing me like this, but nothing made me want to do anything. Unless Thea magically appeared in my room, I planned to stay in bed until she left Exile for the trials.

Someone shuffled into my room, but I didn't bother seeing who it was. A moment later, they lay in bed beside me, and my heart pumped with anticipation. No one ever came and lay in bed with me. Thea?

I ripped the blanket off my head and groaned when I saw Haden smiling. He shoved food into his mouth as he sat up against the headboard. I threw the blankets back over my head. Haden was a pain in my ass. He lingered more than anyone else. I rubbed my marriage bond on my arm for comfort. I didn't feel Thea through it often, and when I did, she was always confused and sad.

"Cassius, talk to me." Haden pleaded, but I didn't respond. The blanket was yanked off my head, and I glared at Haden, ready to punch my friend in the face.

"What the fuck?" I hissed.

"Do you think Thea wants you moping around? Get your ass up," he demanded like he was the Prince of Crimson.

"I can't." I fell back onto the bed and stared at Haden's concerned face. "I cannot stop thinking of her dying in my arms," I confessed.

Haden frowned as he moved to sit on the edge of the bed. "I think about it too," he said. "But she wouldn't want us torturing ourselves."

I knew he was right, but I still felt angry and wanted everyone to be angry like I was, so I lashed out at him.

"You don't understand. You didn't lose the woman you love!" I yelled so loudly that the walls seemed to shake with my wrath.

Haden looked at me. Something passed over his features that I couldn't decipher. "Maybe the woman I love isn't dead, but I still lost her." Haden glanced away from me. Gods, I was a fucking prick. "But I know what it's like to long for someone you can't have, to miss someone so desperately that you find it impossible to breathe."

"I didn't know you loved anyone," I muttered, feeling like a complete asshole.

"I loved Della with everything I had, and she betrayed me." Haden glanced at me with a sad smile.

"Della?" I sat up a little more. "As in Ardella, the God-dess of Life?"

"Yes," Haden sighed. "Even though she isn't dead, she might as well be because I can never have her. I can never forgive her, but this longing for her will not go away." I stared at Haden as he seemed lost in a bad memory. How the fuck did Haden fall in love with a goddess? I rubbed my eyes as I shifted to sit next to him on the edge of the bed.

"One day, I expect you to tell me how you and Della came to know each other."

Haden nodded as both of us stared at the wall, thinking about the women we loved, aware that we couldn't do anything to bring them back at the moment. But Thea would be coming for the trials soon if all went according to plan. That was enough to motivate me to get up and put on my uniform. Haden smiled brightly as he followed me out of the room.

"Thea will be breaking her curse this time. I need to be ready to help her in any way I can, and I can't do that by rotting away in bed," I said to Haden.

"Let's get ready to break this curse." He smiled as he patted my shoulder. "I know it's hard, but you've got me. I'll do anything for you. You gave me a reason to live when you approached me during the trials. You could have killed me, but for one, I can't die, and for two, you took a chance on me. I'm grateful for you and Thea."

I stopped mid-stride and glanced at Haden. "What do you mean you can't die?" I asked.

"Della cursed my soul, too. I can't die." He shrugged as if it weren't a big deal. "It's a long story."

"You know that I'll always be here to listen if you need it," I said.

"I know, man, but first, let's save our girl." Haden mocked me with the taunt he used during the trials to piss me off. "Just kidding." He smiled brightly.

□□□□□

I lay in bed, staring at the ceiling, wishing Thea was next to me. I thought of all the things we would do once she broke the curse. I looked forward to simply sleeping beside her, rubbing my hands along her soft skin, and hearing her voice. She always used to tell me stories as we lay awake at night. I could listen to her talk forever and never tire of the sound.

Cassius? Cassius, my love? Her voice called into my mind, and I instantly closed my eyes, going to her in her dream.

My heart ached as I watched her wander the woods of Exile, as if she were searching for something or... someone. Nearly every dream she had was of her wandering, looking completely lost. Her pretty, moss-colored eyes stared directly into the shadows where I hid. I smiled softly.

My wife could sense me nearby but didn't know who I was. Her head tilted to the side, causing her dark hair to tumble over her shoulder. Gods, she was breathtaking.

"I can see you," she muttered.

I froze. She didn't often see me in her dreams, and when she did, she never seemed to remember me.

"Come out, coward."

A soft chuckle escaped me, and she stilled at the sound. I stepped out of the shadows and watched her eyes trace over me, as they always did when she saw me. I could see her pupils dilate, her breathing becoming shallow. I never tired of seeing her reaction to me for the first time. I smiled at her, and she smiled back as if she couldn't help it. A moment later, she took a hesitant step toward me.

"Are you what I've been looking for?" she whispered.

Her words made my throat tighten with emotion. Yes. I'm what you're missing. She slowly raised her hand to my face, tracing over my jaw and lips. She had done this each time I saw her in her dreams. She never remembered me. This had never happened before, and it terrified the hell out of me. What if she remembered nothing about me when she left Exile this time?

I gripped her hand and kissed her palm, just as I had done all those years ago on the blood moon.

"Your eyes..." She stared into them intensely. "They're so familiar."

Her hand rubbed against my cheek, and I closed my eyes, leaning into her touch like a man starved. I couldn't stand it. My hand wrapped around her wrist, and I yanked her so she was flush against me. She didn't resist. I swept her wild curls over her shoulder before grabbing her face and pulling her in for a kiss. Thea melted against me, kissing me back. She moaned softly as I deepened the kiss. Giving her one last lingering kiss, I pulled back.

"Yes, little viper, I'm what you've been searching for," I whispered. "I've missed you."

It didn't matter if I told her; she wouldn't remember when she woke up. Dread filled me because she was so different this time in her dreams. It felt as if she had forgotten me completely.

"Little viper," she repeated the nickname as if it were familiar.

I smiled as I wrapped my arms around her, holding her close. Thea frowned deeply as she looked at me.

"What's wrong?"

"I wish you were real," she confessed, breaking my heart.

I felt our connection fading, meaning she was waking up.

"I love you," I whispered as she slipped away. Her mouth fell open in surprise.

I squeezed my eyes shut, trying to hold on to the moment she was in my arms. But as soon as I opened them, tears stung as I realized I was alone in our room, haunted by the memory of my wife.

SHAY TAYLOR

Subscribe to my newsletter for updates on projects, giveaways, and exclusive content!
www.shaytaylorauthor.com

Follow me on TikTok and Instagram
@shaytaylorauthor

I am thrilled to welcome you into my world of fantasy romance. I live near Glacier National Park, in northwest Montana, where I find myself constantly inspired by the beauty that surrounds me.

I am happily married and am a proud mother to a wonderful son. My day job is spent as a mental health therapist.

Reading has always been a passion for me, and there's nothing I love more than losing myself in a world of magic and romance, especially with a hot cup of coffee in hand.